RIFTBORNE

ESPRITHEAN TRILOGY

BOOK ONE

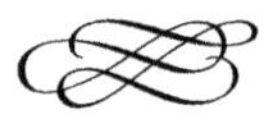

GRENWICH & LENNOX

This is a work of fiction. Names, characters, businesses, places, events, locales, and incidents are either the products of the author's imagination or used in a fictitious manner. Any resemblance to actual persons, living or dead, or actual events is purely coincidental.

Edited by Jules Maduro
Cover art and Map by Parker Lennox

Hardback ISBN: 979-8-9911128-0-2
Paperback ISBN: 979-8-9911128-1-9
Ebook AISN: B0D93DMVWV

ONYX PUBLISHING

RADIANTHIAN MOUNTAINS
Fort Agate
Aedenvale
MYLITHIAN EXPANSE
Campgrounds
STORMSHIRE BEACH
Emeraal
THE TEAR
CRESCENT TOWER
OBSCURA MARSH
YAELARENDAL

Rittdremar
BLOODTHORNE HIGHLANDS
Dathora Estate
PRAELYTHIAN KEEP
Luminaria
SCARLET COAST
Aithroain Sea

Listen along to our Riftborne inspired Spotify playlist.

CONTENT WARNING

Riftborne is an adventure fantasy set in the elite world of the Sídhe Guard, a military force of warriors sworn to protect the Isle. It includes elements depicting war, battle, hand-to-hand combat, blood, violence, self-harm (blood-oath), injuries, death, death of friends, drowning, alcohol consumption, drug use (magical elixirs), nationalism, xenophobia, mild bullying, manipulation, graphic language, and sexual activities that are shown on the page. Readers who may be sensitive to these elements, please be aware.

For the companions who journey through magical realms together.

This novel is a love letter to the power of friendship and the bonds that turn even the darkest realities into something extraordinary.

PRONUNCIATION GUIDE & GLOSSARY

Aossí (Eess-SHEE)

The race of Elven-like beings that live on the Isle of Sídhe and Riftdremar.

Sídhe (SHEE)

The Isle of Sídhe is a Kingdom in which all Aossí now reside. It is where the majority of the story takes place.

Riftdremar (Rift-dra-mahr)

An Island to the east of the Isle of Sídhe. Riftdremar was destroyed after an uprising against Sídhe's colonial effort to expand their influence on Riftdremar's culture, economy, and resources.

Riftdremar Rebellion

An uprising against the Isle of Sídhe that spiraled into a full-blown rebellion, resulting in a war between the two nations. The war ended 20 years prior to the events in this story. Some refugees were allowed citizenship to Sídhe after the events of the conflict. Those who are from Riftdremar are called the Riftborne.

Riftborne (Rift-bohrn)

Children who were saved from the destruction of their homeland, Riftdremar, and brought to the Isle of Sihde. Before they were granted citizenship, these refugees were branded with a symbol of unity on their left wrist and hand. Most were raised in group homes throughout the Isle and were expected to assimilate into Sídhe culture and society.

Essence (Ess-ense)

The magic that runs throughout the realm, empowering both the land itself and the Aossí.

Focus (Foh-kus)

Each Aossí is blessed with an individual gift, whether it be mundane or extraordinary, and this is referred to as a Focus. It is how essence manifests itself in each individual.

Esprithe (Esp-rith)

The pantheon of deities who are worshiped by those on the Isle of Sídhe.

Sibyl (Sib-uhl)

The Esprithe of Foresight

Conleth (Kohn-luth)

The Esprithe of Wisdom

Niamh (Neev)

The Esprithe of Dreams

Ainthe (Ah-N-yuh)

The Esprithe of Memories

Eibhlín (Eve-lin)
The Esprithe of Justice

Fírinne (Fehr-EN-yeh)
The Esprithe of Truth

Luminaria (Loom-ihn-aria)
The Capital of the Isle of Sídhe

Emeraal (Em-er-ahl)

Stormshire (Stohrm-sheer)

Fia (Fee-ah)

Laryk (Lahr-eck)

Maladea (Mah-LAY-dia)

Osta (Ah-sta)

Raine (Rayne)

Baelor (Bae-lore)

Briar (Bryer)

Draven (Dray-ven)

Nazul (Nah-zuhl)

OFFICIAL DECREE

An Excerpt
The Historical Account of Sídhe
First Edition

In times long past, driven by a vision of unity and prosperity, the Isle of Sídhe embarked on an expansion to the eastern seas, generously sharing the gift of civilization with the people of Riftdremar. They aspired to uplift Riftdremar from a state of disarray.

Over the passing centuries, the people of Riftdremar, initially hesitant, witnessed the positive impact of Sídhe's influence. Recognizing Riftdremar's potential for greatness, Sídhe invested in infrastructure, education, and cultural exchange. This generous assimilation aimed at fostering a harmonious union between the two lands.

Tragically, the Uprising unfolded as a dark chapter in our shared history. Radicalized leaders in Riftdremar, influenced by ancient grievances, incited rebellion against us. In response, our valiant Sídhe Guard engaged in a defensive operation to quell unrest and restore order.

Regrettably, the conflict resulted in significant devastation in Riftdremar. The citizens were caught in the crossfire, and suffered the consequences of their leaders' misguidance. In the aftermath, the Isle of S*í*dhe extended its arms to displaced Riftdremarian children, providing shelter, sustenance, and an opportunity to begin new lives in the Isle.

To ensure lasting peace and stability, S*í*dhe enacted measures to identify potential instigators and prevent further uprisings. The branding of refugees became a necessary step to maintain order and security, safeguarding our shared future.

CHAPTER 1

I HESITATED on the precipice of safety, skin ablaze with the urge to retrace my steps back to Luminaria. My insides roared for me to run, to hide—instincts I had spent my entire life cultivating. Humid night air clung to me like a second skin, heavy with the scent of earth and something faintly floral.

A candlelit trail led to the Grove, a valley cradled between rolling hills and the gnarled embrace of the forest. Smoke billowed through the treetops, and golden fire erupted from pits throughout the expanse below. A mixture of nerves and curiosity flooded my veins as I peered into its glittering depths.

One could almost taste the pungent mix of liquor, sweat, and hormones pulsing in the air. Offset only by the peculiar whines and wanes of Sídhe music. Haunting melodies danced up my spine, tempting me to free myself... to lose myself. Just a single dance couldn't be so bad—

Esprithe sake, Fia. It's enchanted.

I shifted my weight, readjusting my grip on the rough wooden crate.

Whatever sanity I still possessed was holding on by a thread after spending the entire day brewing tonics for the Sídhe Nobility and their ridiculous party.

If they hadn't placed the orders so damn late, none of this would be happening. I wouldn't be here. But the Nobility cared little for the day-to-day of common folk. They were far too preoccupied.

My attention shot to the sky as a light weaver cast shimmering rays into the clouds, tearing through the mist like a river in the heavens.

In the world below, a kaleidoscope of satin gowns swirled as Aossí danced in unison.

Beauty could be deceptive, and it often was. Vipers, after all, distract with shimmering scales before going in for the kill. The Sídhe Elite were much the same, twice as lethal as they were mesmerizing.

Only the decline of a hill separated us. Another minute of walking, and I'd be in their midst.

The clinking of glasses sliced through the air like a beckoning, *or warning*. I couldn't be sure. Effects from the music lingered, playing tricks in my mind.

Unfortunately, the whims of these people and their extravagant soirees would provide much better pay than any normal day at the Apothecary, so refusing the business wasn't an option.

Besides, how could the elite possibly reach their desired levels of debauchery without a few euphoria-inducing party favors?

The foolish bravery I'd somehow mustered back at the shop had completely vanished. This was supposed to be Eron's delivery, not mine. He'd been running them all day, after all. I only volunteered because his wife went into labor. A stupid move. I knew it then, but now, standing here, it felt like a deadly mistake.

My gaze stretched across the vast expanse. It mirrored the hollow dread blooming in my chest.

I was a Riftborne, one of many transplanted to Sídhe following the Riftdremar Rebellion and branded with a symbol for unity.

Because nothing screams unification quite like a mark to identify you from the masses. I peeked down at my left hand, where the twin serpents of Sídhe coiled around the antlers of Riftdremar.

At least I'd worn gloves.

Most of the Riftborne were too young to remember the Rebellion that ended twenty years ago, but everyone in Sídhe knew someone who died in the war. And many of them wanted us to repay that price with our lives.

It seemed we'd suffer the aftermath of our parents' choices for millennia.

A splitting force surged through my head, forcing my eyes to slam shut. The curse that lived inside me used to be nothing more than a faint presence lingering in the depths of my mind. Now, it threatened to explode at any moment, lying in wait just below the surface, desperate for the opportunity to unleash itself.

And once it escaped...

I didn't allow the thought to finish as I steadied myself, digging my heels into the damp earth below.

I hadn't told a soul how bad it had gotten. Not even Osta, my closest friend. Saying it out loud to someone might make it real.

Despite the violent beating of my heart, I took another shaky step forward into the thick air, heavy with a mix of perfume and woodsmoke.

Clinging to the crate and trying to make my body as small as possible, I melted into the shadows of the tree line and made my way along the dirt path.

I hoped the attendees had been partaking in the elixirs long enough for the desired effects to take hold. It would be much easier to navigate a space full of intoxicated minds, where thoughts swam, and steps faltered.

Craning my head over the moving mass of bodies, I scanned the area, searching for Ma's station.

Ah, there it is.

Keeping my head low, I found my way to the opposite side of

the Grove where Ma's potions were displayed on a table lined with twinkling candles and blooms from across the realm. Annoyance tugged at me. Ma's affinity for healing was revolutionary, yet this would be her legacy. Providing libido-boosting cocktails to the Sídhe Guard and their irreverent groupies.

My shoulders burned to drop the crate. It nearly tumbled out of my grasp as I edged it onto the table, vials clinking against each other at the subtle jolt. My arms lifted in an involuntary stretch, only to find they felt more like liquid than muscle and bone.

I hunted for anyone who might be manning this station, but it seemed even the organizers had joined in on the evening's revelry.

I had never stepped foot near one of these parties but knew what to expect. Ma loved to gossip about them during our more boring hours at the Apothecary. Tonight, all classes would be frothing at the mouth as their military idols were paraded through the crowd. They'd indulge in the finest culinary delights, lose themselves in aromatic bitters, spiked tonics, and the elusive Bloodthorne wine, only to finally stagger home, leaving chaos in their inebriated wake. Just another mess for someone else to clean up.

The most intriguing part of this particular soiree was the attendance of the General–well, assuming he'd show up.

The General seldom graced Luminaria with his presence, preferring the proximity of the Western border. I began unloading the vials, snapping back and forth from crate to table. If quick enough, I could make my escape before being spotted by any curious drunkard.

Luck, however, was not on my side.

It never was.

With only three damn bottles placed, a familiar squeal echoed through the air behind me. I took a calming breath before turning around and meeting the bright aquamarine eyes of Osta, who looked giddy enough to explode. She practically leaped in my direction.

Deep blue silk cascaded in shimmering pleats down her frame, like the petals of a flower in bloom. The entire hemline looked like it had been dipped in stardust, silver threads dancing in delicate patterns along the edges. She had been working on it for weeks.

My eyes instinctively shot to her left hand, which was covered by the silver fabric of a glove. A sigh of relief slipped out. She hadn't fully lost her mind, it seemed.

Osta's bronzed hair laid in perfect ringlets down her back. Her skin glowed a golden shimmer. Her radiance was akin to sunlight, even as she stepped into the shadow I was currently occupying. Immediately, I felt even more out of place.

If Osta was the personification of life, I was the living embodiment of death. Cheekbones too high, chin too sharp, and forehead stretching a tad too long—jarring was an appropriate descriptor already. Add in the white curls, unnaturally pale skin, and perpetually shrouded eyes, and we're verging on full-blown ghoul.

Looking down at my herb-stained blouse and wrinkled trousers, heat rushed over me. My body wanted to crumple into a ball. I needed to find a way out of here. Now.

"Fiiiiiaa!" Osta sang as she threw her arms around me, the sweet scent of wine wafting off her.

"I can't believe you're actually here!" She stepped back, eyeing my disgruntled state. "Though I had a different vision... Want to run to the shop? It's not far, and I have so many pieces that would look divine on you!" Her eyes sparkled. She was clearly already styling me in her mind.

I fiddled with my hair, attempting to push it back. "Thank you for not so subtly pointing out how terrible I look... but I have no intention of hanging around. Eron needed me to deliver this crate and—"

"You're already here now, so stay! Just for an hour!" she grabbed my stained hands and looked up at me, eyes pleading. Osta always knew when to employ the dramatics. A pang of guilt shot through my chest.

It was then that trumpets tore through the Grove, announcing the arrival of the royal court—a small blessing, saving me from denying her yet again. I often disappointed her with my fear of crowds… especially when they consisted of this type of company. The kind that would gleam with amusement at the prospect of my death once they saw what I was. Even worse if they figured out what I was hiding, what threatened to bubble up and boil out of me.

I reached up and wiped the sweat from my brow. Heat radiated from the touch.

The music quickened and spilled through the Grove. Curiosity peaked in the corners of my mind, and I allowed it to get the best of me. I turned, hesitantly moving towards the commotion. A sea of Aossí had parted, giving the procession a clear path to the raised dais near the center of the Grove.

Osta bounced at my side, clapping her hands and standing on the tips of her toes, trying to get a better look at the King and Queen, who were surrounded by at least twenty members of the Guard. Dressed in matching drapes of sparkling emerald, they moved with a commanding grace. When they finally reached the thrones atop the dais, they turned and waved, hand in hand before taking their seats.

Attendees stumbled as they pushed past me, and my attention followed the rush of bodies. A figure emerged on the southern platform.

It must have been him–the evening's honored Guest.

General Laryk Ashford.

Both men and women practically threw themselves at him, singing his praise and swooning in the delight of his presence.

Despite the fatigue, my eyes managed to roll just fine.

It was nothing personal against the General. I hated the entirety of the Guard just as much as they hated me. The major difference was that they held power and influence.

One wrong move on my end, and I'd disappear. Or die in some

freak encounter that would no doubt be ruled a tragic accident. Riftborne presence in Sídhe wasn't tolerated, it was merely endured. We were like a sickness to them, though their disdain was always hidden beneath a veneer of civility. No one was ever held accountable for their actions. People simply looked the other way.

I gritted my teeth and refocused on the celebration, ignoring the pit growing in my stomach.

As the General stepped onto the dais and turned, an electric current rushed through the Grove. Every single eye was on him. And to my unfortunate surprise, I could now see why.

Flowing copper hair fell in waves over his shoulders, like shimmering curtains over his porcelain skin. Even from my vantage point, his sharp features were prominent. All the way down to the scar that marked his right eye and cheek.

He was taller than most Aossí, and his lean frame couldn't be ignored, even behind the layers of his Guard uniform.

"Wow." Osta's painted pink mouth parted in awe.

I don't know how I expected our most celebrated General to look, but it certainly wasn't like this.

As much as I wanted to feign indifference, there was no denying how breathtaking the man was. If you were into pompous jerks with inferiority complexes, of course.

Anyone who joined The Guard these days was doing so in the hopes of climbing to an elite position. On the Isle of Sídhe, ascending to a high rank in the Guard granted instant entry to the exclusive circle of the Noble class and practically guaranteed a family's legacy for generations to come. They were all one in the same at that point–the Elite, whether they were born or bred. Nobility or Guard. Even better if they were both.

Outside of status, the Guard didn't seem to serve any real purpose.

It had been years since Sídhe faced a foreign threat, and you certainly weren't going to find any resistance from within the kingdom. War was a far thought, a solved problem of the past, if our educators were to be believed. It did make one wonder why we needed a military this massive and all-encompassing.

The General smiled down at his adoring fans and I wondered if anyone would be *lucky* enough to win his attention. Maybe a few of them would have the pleasure of his company tonight.

The party already hummed with sensual tension—it hung thick and oppressive in the air like a perfume you couldn't escape.

The General turned, facing the crowd of hundreds, an obnoxiously charming smile sprawled across his face. His gaze sauntered across the space until his eyes met mine, and he paused. The air seemed to go silent around me.

There was something intense and unwavering in his expression, but I couldn't quite put my finger on it. It felt like he could see right through me. I was going to burn up under the scrutiny—I needed to look away. But I was frozen solid; I couldn't even blink.

Lucky for me, after a few seconds, his eyes moved on, and the raging crowd came crashing back in. People were losing their absolute fucking minds over this man.

Perhaps I was starting to understand the hype.

My chest lurched, and I sucked in a gasp of summer air.

"Should we try to get closer?" Osta sang. It seemed even on the tips of her toes, the view was dismal. "I want to give the Queen a chance to see my design!"

"I'm not sure that's such a great idea. In my current state of attire… they'd probably take it as an insult if I got that close to the throne." I pulled at the sleeve of my stained blouse. She looked at me and bit her lip.

The dark truth of my apprehension sat on the tip of my tongue, but I couldn't say it. Not here.

"Well... just let me do my loop and promise me we can have at least one drink before you head back to the apartment."

I weighed the options quickly but came to the same conclusion as always: keep it hidden.

I could survive a little longer.

"Ok, I promise. I'll just wander around... and blend in as much as possible," I murmured, but my skin began to prickle. The surge ran through me once again and I held back a wince, biting my lip so hard I nearly drew blood.

"Come find me when you're done with your presentation. But please don't take too long," I motioned for her to go, but she paused, bringing her eyes up to meet mine. Her face twisted as she inspected me.

"Fia... are you okay? Your eyes seem darker than usual. Have you been sleeping?" she whispered, leaning in closer. "More night terrors?"

"I'm fine, Osta. It's just been a long day. Now go show off your dress." I hid my shaking hands behind my back.

Her smile returned and she nodded, disappearing into the crowd. I didn't want to disappoint her, but after the week I'd had... I could feel the edges of my control slipping away by the minute. And it was dangerous for both of us to be anywhere near here, even if she didn't share my fears.

Osta, a fellow Riftborne, was one of the few left in the city. Across the Isle, our numbers had dwindled to a mere handful, barely a few hundred. The devastation in Riftdremar had claimed most Riftborne children already, and those who had been brought to Sídhe seemed to vanish year after year.

But somehow, through everything, Osta always remained positive. She navigated the divide much easier than I did. She could walk down the street with her sleeves casually tugged down, blending in. At least in the beginning - long enough for people to develop a sense of comfort before realizing what she was.

As soon as Osta was out of sight, I made my way to the outskirts of the party once again. A few lingering stares followed me, and a chill ran up my spine.

It wasn't easy to avoid the wandering curiosity of strangers when you looked like me. People had always been able to sense my otherness. There were Aossí with unique attributes, sure. I just happened to bear a particularly unsettling combination of them. My icy hair did me no favors. Each weightless curl danced in the air like static had taken me over. Though I'd tied it up successfully this morning, the stress of the day had unleashed it in full glory. Now I couldn't even tuck it behind the points of my ears.

My one redeeming quality could have been my opalescent eyes, had they not been shrouded in perpetual shadows. The darkness fanned out, waging war on my pale skin. I was well aware I looked like a raging insomniac. However, rest had no effect on my ghastly appearance, leaving me to assume it was simply a case of terribly unlucky genetics.

A gentle breeze drifted through the Grove, kissing my skin with a refreshing coolness and interrupting my thoughts.

The further I got from the commotion, the more my senses came to life. I stopped at a patch of trees up the hill. It provided a decent vantage point, allowing for a view of the lights and dancing bodies below.

The General shifted effortlessly between partners.

For another brief instant, his eyes locked with mine, and my breath caught in my lungs. It's like he was seeking me out.

Was he?

There was that same intensity in his stare that I couldn't quite place–something dark and... intoxicating. His gaze continued to burn through me, and my body began to feel weightless. I tore my eyes away from his and stumbled back a few paces, the party disappearing from view.

The sinking feeling of discomfort crept into my bones. I didn't like being seen. I didn't want *him* to see me, of all people. The thought of a General's attention on me made me want to evaporate.

The breeze picked up, and the most mesmerizing scent filled my nose - lily of the valley. My mind nearly melted at the smell. I hadn't found a wild batch of them in ages, and traders seldom had them in their inventories. With there being no way to accurately recreate the floral profile, it remained an expensive and evasive luxury.

Perhaps a quick forage would calm me down.

I followed the aroma into the tree line, hunting for the white belled flowers in the dim moonlight. Perhaps a silver-lining to an otherwise emotionally crippling evening?

A subtle note turned me left, pulling me several paces before I found a patch on the forest floor.

Slipping off my gloves, I knelt to gather the bunches, tying them together with a piece of twine before tucking them into the folded sachet of my Apothecary belt. I patted down the compartments, making sure all my tools were indeed still secure. I felt my tiny notebooks, quills, bottles, and vials, all where they were supposed to be.

As I stood, I could hear the last vestiges of a song coming to end. Osta would be looking for me. It was time to have this drink, say my goodbyes, and finally end this curse of a day.

A part of me, one I'm ashamed of, thought briefly about wandering further into the safety of the woods, escaping to the anonymity of Luminaria's streets, finding our apartment, and launching into bed…

Osta would hate me.

You can have one drink.

I headed in the direction of the party, dodging fallen branches, and groaned. I hadn't realized how far I'd made it into the forest.

Just as I saw the edge of the wood, a chill ran over my skin. I heard the sounds of laughing and crunching twigs headed straight for me. *Oh Esprithe.*

I was in no condition to run into anyone out here. I practically glowed in the dark. *Great thinking Fia, walking off by yourself in the middle of the night.*

I clenched my fists.

Just breathe.

I tried to move out of their path. The sounds of their movement were getting louder as they advanced, and it was then that I recognized the shrill voice, complaining about someone wearing the same dress as her, and a second voice joining in to affirm.

Bekha and Jordaan.

It had been years since I'd seen them, but I would recognize those voices anywhere. Memories flooded back as their shrieks echoed through the trees.

Their mother was Lady Nessa Fairbanks, the woman who ran Luminaria's House of Unity, the foster home where Osta and I grew up alongside some of the other Riftborne children. Every ounce of cruelty that lived within that woman had been passed down to her daughters three-fold. The Patriarch of the family had died in the frontlines of the uprising, and Lady Fairbanks never let us forget it. It was as if we had killed him with our own hands.

That was our first taste of prejudice. It seemed like a whole other lifetime now, growing up in that place. We had all left years ago, back before the *true* terrors of this world were revealed to us. Back before my friends were murdered.

I was eighteen when I watched them drown beneath the currents of the Sprithe River. And though five years had passed, I'd been stuck in a constant state of fear ever since.

I shoved the thought away and dug my nails into my palms. Heat was already spanning the length of my body, simmering just under my skin. Waiting. And this train of thought was a dangerous one.

The girls approached, and I ducked my head, hoping they'd pass without starting what was sure to be an enchanting conversation. One that could very well send me flying over the edge.

And just like that, the forest floor betrayed me. I stumbled over a muddy branch and lost my balance. My hands hit the earth below and fear shot through me. I hadn't put my gloves back on.

My branding was laid bare in the darkness, reflecting the dancing lights from the sky above.

CHAPTER 2

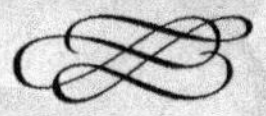

I CROSSED my arms as I stood, and the girls looked me up and down, tipping their noses at my stained uniform before turning to each other and snickering.

"Bekha. Jordaan." I nodded, looking up to the sky. *Could the Esprithe just strike me down now?*

"Fia Riftborne... what a lovely surprise. How long has it been? Six, seven years? That pathetic white hair is still hard to miss," Jordaan smirked. "And your skin... I see you never did learn what a few hours in the sun could do," she chided before looking over to Bekha.

"And those same creepy eyes." The short brunette curled her lips into a smirk. "Or better yet, those hideous dark circles. You really haven't changed at all."

"Such a shame. You could have been quite pretty. Parts of you have potential... but no amount of pigment could fix the ghastliness," Jordaan continued, ice slicking her voice.

"We really should catch up sometime. I'm sure mother would absolutely love to hear all about your time away from us." Bekha's eyes traveled down to my clothes once again. "Are you living on the streets now?"

"Are we done here?" I asked as they fell silent. I knew I should have held my tongue, but I often had trouble doing so.

Bekha glared at me.

"What are you anyway?" she asked, her voice thick with vitriol.

Original.

I rolled my eyes and brushed past them.

I needed to get out of here.

"Disgusting Riftborne. You were always so rude. So ungrateful. You're lucky our mother had a kind heart and took pity on you. If it were up to me, all of you would have burned with the rest of your treacherous country," Jordaan spat.

I paused, clenching my teeth.

Just keep walking.

I mentally repeated the words, desperate to distract myself from the mind-shattering surge running through my head like a blade. Pain shot across the base of my skull.

I sucked in a breath, making my way back into the night with shaky, unsteady steps—towards the dancing lights that now seemed undoubtedly safer than the faux solitude of the forest.

Bekha cleared her throat.

"Dams are just so unpredictable... I heard about what happened to your little Riftborne pack. Absolutely devastating. Perhaps if they could swim faster..."

I stopped. There it was.

Their words hit me like a dagger, finding its mark right in my center.

My jaw began to tremble, and another jolt of white-hot pain invaded my mind, lighting my thoughts on fire and sending currents through my entire body. Starved currents. Lethal currents.

No! Don't do this here! The better part of my brain was roaring.

But then I heard their laughter...

My muscles went rigid, and the world around me blurred, tinging my vision with a translucent haze. A scream threatened to tear through me as I fought to keep control, but I could already feel myself losing the battle.

It was happening. And I couldn't stop it.

Once it got to this point, I never could.

The last vestiges of my control snapped like a frayed rope. The unrelenting curse surged to the surface, flooding my veins with an intense and unstoppable fury. I spun to face the girls as the ground trembled beneath me, the air crackling with energy.

As if I reacted outside my own realm of authority, I thrust my hands forward, unleashing a searing torrent of force. The blast tore through the air, finding the girls in an instant.

They stumbled back, looking at each other in horror and confusion. I could do nothing but watch as they opened their mouths to scream, but no sound escaped. Realization washed over them in silent horror as the vortex of energy stole their voices.

Time seemed to slow as a haunting radiance began to pulse from their eyes, hot and blinding like an exploding celestial body.

How delicious it was to feel the power break the confines of my skin. To be rid of it, even for a fleeting moment. I hated myself for the pleasure that radiated through me. My eyes bore into the sight of the girls, unable to tear my vision from the gruesome scene unfolding ahead.

Wisps of spectral energy curled around strands of their hair and gowns. Crimson tar began to flow from their noses as though their minds were being strangled by an invisible grip.

They fell to the ground. The energy continued to weave patterns around their unconscious forms before slowly releasing itself into the ether.

I stood frozen. The last pulses of energy resonated around me like heat emanating from hot pavement. The world held its breath.

Slowly, the aura lessened, and I felt the weight of my actions crash down upon me. The trance broke.

Were they dead?

I stumbled over to their lifeless forms and my knees hit the ground, damp grass embracing my fall. *Please. Please don't be dead.*

But I couldn't bring myself to check. To touch them. I could tell from the overwhelming stillness that they weren't breathing. If they were dead...

A wave of nausea swept over me, threatening to expel the entirety of my dinner. The silence of the forest was screaming, as if nature itself recoiled from me. Tears welled in my eyes.

I dug my fingers into the dirt. How could I allow myself to lose control like this? I should have kept walking. *Fuck, I should have kept walking.*

Tears streamed down my face, blurring out the world around me as regret crept into my blood and bones. One thought permeated.

Run.

My legs ached as they found their balance, and I stood, trembling. I took a shaky step towards the tree line just as a twig snapped from behind me.

I spun to find a pair of familiar, hauntingly emerald eyes nearly pulsing in the darkness. The wind whipped, sending his copper hair flying. His form was backlit by the moon, lending an ethereal quality to that devastating face. The one now completely fixated on me.

My heartbeat pummeled against my chest.

General Laryk Ashford.

He stood there, twisting a dagger through his fingers with expert precision as an enigmatic smile played at the corner of his lips. He must have seen everything.

Esprithe save me.

Panic rushed over my body as I grappled with the consequences that would surely be waiting for me once he escorted me back to the party and informed the crowd of what I had done. They would kill me without hesitation. A perfect crescendo to the evening: the death of a Riftborne. I was as good as dust.

His eyes bore into me, but his expression was strange…

His eyes gleamed with something familiar but wildly inappropriate for the occasion. It couldn't be…

Was that amusement?

He cocked his chin to the side, his gaze lingering on my left hand, bare and visible in the moonlight.

An eternity passed.

Is he going to kill me right here and now?

He was a Sídhe General, he could enact justice however he wanted. My friends had been murdered for taking a simple swim.

I had attacked two daughters of nobility.

And their bodies laid motionless behind me. Blood stained their perfectly painted cheeks, creating a thick puddle in the tangles of their hair.

I winced.

He returned his dagger to its sheath and gave me one last curious look before turning on his heel and walking back towards the bustling celebration over the hill.

Shock enveloped me.

What just happened?

I still couldn't breathe.

I watched him for a moment before my mind stopped spinning–long enough for my self-preservation to kick in. And my feet started moving again.

I disappeared into the shadows of the forest, plagued by a sinking feeling that my encounter with the General was only the beginning of a reckoning I could not escape.

CHAPTER 3

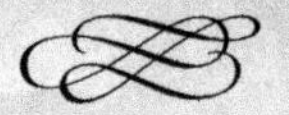

My back slammed against the rough wooden frame of our apartment door, my chest heaving with weighted breath as I inhaled the familiar scent of safety. A smell that now made me sick with guilt. I bolted to the waste can, finally expelling the contents of my stomach, retching until there was nothing left.

How had I let myself escalate to the point of such chaos? Why couldn't I hold onto control long enough to remove myself from the situation? Were they dead? Did I *kill* them? They certainly didn't look alive with blood gushing from their eyes. *Wonderful, Fia, you've sealed your fate now.*

You're a fucking murderer.

And I had been *seen*. Would I even make it through the night without the Sídhe military breaking down my door? Did I *deserve* to? It was only a matter of time. The General had let me escape, probably on a high from the cocktail of mind-altering tonics we so graciously provided. But that high wouldn't last forever. At some point, he would remember the events of the night. He would realize it wasn't just a sick hallucination. And then he would come for me. And I would deserve it.

My mind flipped through every possibility, every option, but each one seemed worse than the last. At the very least, I needed to talk to Osta. *Osta. Esprithe be damned, Fia.* The maelstrom of thoughts flooded my mind, and the corners of my eyes began to sting. What would happen to her? Would they take her away and lock her up? We were roommates. We were Riftborne. Would they view her as my co-conspirator? Or punish her just because of her association with me?

Salty tears streamed down my face as each question struck my mind like a poisoned arrow.

I crawled to the battered sofa that Osta had rescued from the streets, intent on giving it new life. She hadn't even had the chance to reupholster it yet. I curled into a ball, letting my head fall into my hands as sobs riddled my already-shaking frame.

I stayed like this, pondering my fate, until the tears dried up and the tremors subsided.

I would face the consequences of my actions. I would let the Sídhe leaders tear me apart. But not before explaining myself to Osta.

We had been together for our entire lives, and she meant more to me than I could explain. If anyone deserved the truth, it was her. I dragged myself into my room to wait, collapsing on the bed with a heaviness I wished would just swallow me whole.

After what seemed like centuries of restlessness, I finally accepted that sleep would never come. My thoughts churned, stretching each passing hour into an eternity.

I stared at the peeling paint on my ceiling, intensely aware of the morning light now looming through my window like funeral candles in a dark temple.

In some sick twist of fate, the only nightmare I suffered was that of my own unwavering consciousness. Why should my mind come up with its own terrifying dreamscapes when it could torment me with the memories I had created all by myself—the ones that had sprung forth from my own hands?

As I lay there, enveloped in the suffocating embrace of my own thoughts, the sound of a creaking door crept through the room.

I shot up from the bed and ran into the living room to find Osta slipping off her shoes near the front door. Relief rushed over me at the sight of her. She looked up, meeting my gaze.

Silent anger flickered in her eyes.

"Fia?" she questioned, furrowing her brow. "What happened?"

I stumbled over my words. "Osta, I… I lost control... It happened again… but it was *so* much worse this time. The girls—"

She cut me off. "I know you didn't want to be there, Fia, but you completely abandoned me. You didn't even say goodbye," she sighed, dropping her head into her hands.

I stared in silent confusion. My mouth opened, and then closed as I searched for the right thing to say.

"At some point Fia, you're going to have to grow up and–"

"Osta… Bekha and Jordaan. Near the woods... I... I *killed* them. It was me. They mentioned the accident… The River. The Dam….and I.... I just lost it. I just completely lost my mind, Osta. It happened so quickly… I knew it was a risk, I knew I shouldn't have gone. I didn't want you to worry about me, but my… well, the powers… they've been raging out of control the last few weeks. I thought maybe I could handle them, that I could get through it… I'm such a fucking idiot, Osta." I crumpled to the ground as the words tumbled out. How could I explain something I didn't even understand?

"Fia, slow down," Osta interrupted as frustration etched her features. "No one died. What are you going on about?"

How did she not know?

"Osta. Bekha and Jordaan Fairbanks. From the House of Unity? They are *dead*," The whisper escaped me as my eyes crept up to meet hers. "They really haven't found their bodies yet?"

The creases above Osta's brow deepened. "Fia, I have no idea what you're talking about. Are you sure you're okay? Did you take any of that damn… genesia tincture? Or whatever it's called? You look like you've been up all night."

The weight of her skepticism hit me like a punch to the gut.

"Osta. He saw me. The General. He fucking saw the whole thing," I insisted, my voice shaky. "He saw me *attack* them."

"Fia. If a Sídhe General saw you commit murder, I highly doubt you'd be a free woman right now."

I considered her words. She was right. None of this made sense.

Osta took a small step toward me, raising her hands as if to calm a wild beast. "Fia, I saw Bekha and Jordaan tonight. I watched them leave with soldiers from Emeraal, very much *alive,*" she knelt next to me on the uneven floorboards, reaching for my hand.

"That's not possible. I swear to Fírinne, I watched them die. I watched the blood flow from their noses after I... Their eyes literally glowed *white*. The General saw. He seemed... Well, I thought he was going to kill me right there. I don't know... I don't understand any of it."

I shook my head, taking a deep breath before continuing. "Then, he walked away… I figured he was high or drunk... But... he definitely saw me. You must be mistaking them for different girls. I can… I can show you where their bodies are." I was nearly yelling. "I swear it."

"The General saw you? You're sure?"

I met her concerned gaze and nodded.

"Do you think... Maybe he was able to find a healer? I'm sure there were several in attend–"

"Osta, he wouldn't need a healer, he would need a damn *resurrectionist.*" I cut her off.

She responded quietly. "Either way... Maybe that's what happened… I mean… He is the General, I would assume he has access…" Her words trailed off, and she looked away. Both of us knew how ridiculous that sounded. Why would he let me walk away if he was sober enough to go fetch help?

He watched me kill them with my fucking *mind*. Osta knew what it looked like. She had seen me do it once before, but we didn't talk about it.

I didn't talk about it.

"I'm not crazy," I whispered.

"I don't think you're crazy, Fia. I just know the dreams have been getting worse. I could imagine what seeing Bekha and Jordaan might do to you, especially if you haven't had much rest. They always treated you the worst of all of us. Perhaps it didn't happen like you saw. Maybe... it wasn't real," Osta offered. She peeked at me cautiously.

I opened my mouth to speak, but no words came. It had all seemed so real, there was no way my mind created that horrifying sequence of events... was there?

Osta looked at me in contemplation for what felt like hours, she sat down next to me and rubbed her eyes before inhaling deeply. "Fia... it's not that I don't believe you... I know you well enough to recognize when you're telling the truth. I just don't understand what to make of this. I saw them leave. Hours after you disappeared."

We sat together in shared silence until I felt Osta's head on my shoulder. Her breath deepened with the hums of sleep.

It wasn't long before I slipped into the darkness myself.

CHAPTER 4

THE RIVER WAS smooth and calm, and the sun basked across the horizon. I glanced down, eyeing the foamy peaks, glistening as the current pulled them south.

It was early morning. Clouds wafted through the sky, filtering the dawn with pastel rays. A slight chill clung to the breeze, sending a shiver down my spine as it always did during the last few days of Spring.

Just a few paces away, I heard the thud of boots coming up the stairs like beats of a war drum. A figure emerged at the edge of the platform with armor bearing the emblem of the Sídhe Guard. My stomach twisted. His golden hair and icy blue eyes seemed so unassuming. But his wicked smile left a rotting taste in my mouth.

This one always started off so peacefully. It was hard to imagine this day could have ever turned into what it did.

I leaned against the dam's railing; my attention drawn downward as a group of seven emerged from the nearby tree line. They mingled in the high grass, piercing the silence with laughter as they set up camp just a stone's throw from the river's edge. I watched in horror as five of them discarded their clothes and dove into the river, one by one.

I wanted to scream, but my voice was trapped, my body was para-

lyzed. I wanted to tell them to leave, to run back to the city as fast as they could. But I remained in excruciating uselessness.

They would never see it coming. By the time the gates opened, by the time the current raced in, it would be too late. They would never make it back to shore.

All I could do was look on as my best friends met the wrath of the Sprithe dam and the hateful hands of those who controlled the levers.

This was one of the nightmares I hated the most.

They swam out to the center, painfully unaware of the consequences. My gaze lingered on the faint glimmer from Mairyen's left hand, the one that reflected the light. The one that bore her Riftborne curse.

The distant sounds of knocking interrupted my thoughts, reverberating through the dream like a manifestation of doom itself. It was only drowned out by the sudden screeching of metal.

The ground beneath me rumbled. I tried to tear my gaze; I couldn't watch this. Not again. But my body betrayed me.

My eyes lowered to see the water rush through the gates, tumbling to the river below. It hit the surface like a reckoning.

My body jolted back into the reality of our living room. My eyes snapped open. Osta was sprawled out on the floor beside me, snoring softly. I glanced around, blinking the sleep from my eyes.

Knock, knock, knock.

The sound sent my eyes flying in the direction of the door. Someone was knocking. Pounding, actually. Panic surged through my body as my mind recollected the events from the night before. Osta stirred, shifting on the floor as another set of knocks reverberated through the apartment like trumpets of doom.

I ran my shaking fingers through my hair, causing it to float around my head like a demented halo. Each of my veins pulsed with worry as I sat in silent contemplation. The time of my reckoning had arrived.

Osta sat up slowly, her eyes still closed as she yawned and stretched out her arms. "Is someone at the door?" she mumbled. We never had visitors.

The sound boomed through the room again, but this time, it was followed by a question.

"Fia! Are you in there?" A familiar voice shouted, the words drenched in concern.

My heart did somersaults in my chest.

"Fia, I swear to Eibhlín, if you don't open this door, I'll have no choice but to use this firesbane I'm holding."

This brought me to my feet. I stepped over a half-asleep Osta and moved towards the door, slowly pulling it open to meet the furious gaze of Maladea Thiston.

It was just Ma.

Could last night really just have been some sick dream?

"Fia, do you have any idea how worried I have been?" she scolded with flames in her eyes. She swung the door open wide and pushed past me, stomping right into our flat. The silver peaks of her chestnut hair seemed more prevalent today. Sweat glistened on her wrinkled temple, and her hibiscus-stained hands were clenched into fists.

"Worried?" I managed to croak.

Ma found her way to a recliner in the corner and sat down, shooting me a disapproving look. Osta's eyes followed her with confusion.

"Fia. First, you leave the shop without saying anything. Second, you don't show up for work this morning. Third, I have to hear from Eron that *you* ended up making the last delivery to the Grove last night. Can you even imagine where my mind went?" I saw a brief glimmer of fear wash over her eyes before she cleared her throat and composed herself, shaking her head.

"Ma... I'm so sorry. I didn't sleep well last night. I must have dozed off..." My voice weakened.

Ma leaned forward. "More nightmares?"

"Erm–yes. But that's nothing new. I expect them at this point," I mumbled, shifting my weight. I glanced at her nervously. "But everything is fine at the shop?"

"It still looks like it was hit by a tornado, but other than that, yes. Why? Shouldn't it be?" She raised an eyebrow at me.

I tried to shake off the last lingering threads of sleep. The bright rays of sun flowing in from the window told me it was early afternoon. I never missed work. No wonder she was so concerned.

Ma wasn't a Riftborne. She was born and raised in Sídhe but came from a modest household. She didn't speak about them much. I'd assumed they'd had a falling out. Now, we were essentially each other's chosen family.

In the beginning, I was hesitant about her, as was the case with most strangers, but I had to find work, and that's a hard task when you're viewed as a child of the Rebellion. Even harder when your appearance tends to unnerve the ever-loving shit out of people.

But from the time I first stepped into the Apothecary, Ma treated me with warmth and kindness. She saw beyond the mark on my hand, beyond the label that defined me for so many. In her eyes, I was simply Fia.

I swallowed hard, trying to release the lump that had formed in my throat. The thought of disappointing her was stifling. If she found out about what I had done...

A wince shot through me. That was one of my greatest fears.

In an attempt to keep my expression nonchalant, I shrugged. "No, of course not. I was just making sure... If you'll give me five minutes, I can be ready to head back to the shop with you."

Ma studied me but said nothing, eventually diverting her gaze and dismissing me with a hand gesture.

"And what's wrong with this one? Too much wine from the Highlands?" she teased Osta as I reached the hallway. A sleepy groan echoed through the space, followed by a few grunts of laughter.

I dressed quickly, my thoughts still swirling with questions. Surely, if the girls had been killed...I would be sitting in a Sídhe prison cell by now. And yet, the memory was so vivid... so real... their eyes lighting up from within. I shuddered and tried to push away the thought.

Maybe Osta was right. Maybe it was some kind of hallucination triggered by stress and a lack of sleep. The idea didn't exactly sink into my bones, but it was the one I decided to grasp onto.

I glanced towards my trousers from last night and grabbed my apothecary belt. The lily of the valley. I'd completely forgotten about it.

Unfastening the sachet, I found them crushed beyond repair.

As I STEPPED out onto the streets of Luminaria's Central district, the clamor of the city hit me like a wall of chaos.

My legs were still wobbly and the feeling of eyes on me pricked my skin.

The summer wind grazed me like the touch of an unassuming foe. The city was always busiest during the warmer months, teeming with visitors from across the Isle, drawn here by festivals and solstice celebrations.

Unsurprisingly, this was my least favorite time of year. The city was already packed enough on a normal day. The extra influx of bodies only provided more opportunities to end up in the wrong company. I prayed to Niamh that wouldn't happen today.

I didn't hate Luminaria. In fact, there were many things I'd grown to love about the city. It was the dark underbelly that stirred my fears. The discrimination against Riftborne was a secret that everyone knew but no one talked about.

I lowered my head, and we began navigating the mayhem, making our way to the shop. The Apothecary was only a fifteen-minute walk, but I picked up the pace. Every second out here made me feel exposed and scrutinized.

Suddenly, a beam of light flashed across my eyes, the reflection of sunlight on silver metal, and my heart skipped a beat. I expected to see a guardsman trudging towards me but only found a blacksmith polishing a blade on the street corner, his shop billowing smoke behind him. I let out a slow, hollow breath as he looked up at me. Tearing my eyes away from him, I hurried to catch up with Ma.

Guilt churned in my gut. If only these people knew I might just truly be the monster they worried so much about. I wrapped my arms around my middle, attempting to quell the ache.

We tried our best to dodge the street vendors aggressively selling their wares. Ma mumbled curses under her breath. Her aversion to people was one of her more endearing qualities.

Canals connected the furthest reaches of the city, allowing for quick travel and exchange of goods. Boats of all shapes and sizes floated down the busy waterways. A few fishermen were gathered along the edges of the water, slowly reeling in their lines and nets as they talked amongst themselves.

Nature sprawled across the urban landscape–vines embracing marbled towers, flowers adorning the streets while trees and their roots waged war on the cobblestone path. A few women wearing floral sundresses were collecting herbs from a community garden off to the right, smiling like they hadn't a single care in the world.

I breathed deep, trying to keep my darker thoughts at bay. The aroma of fresh basil filled my nose, and I savored the subtle respite.

Soon enough, we were approaching the front doors of the Apothecary. Anxiety pricked my skin as my eyes scanned the perimeter. Nothing seemed out of place. There were no signs of the Sídhe Guard.

The door creaked open, and the familiar scent washed over me–a mix of curious herbs, steeping infusions, and a hint of nostalgia thrown in for good measure. Although today, it twisted my stomach. The thought of losing this made me want to crawl into a ball and disappear.

The countless rows of shelves, groaning under the weight of glass jars, housed a concoction of plant particles from across the realm that would make even the most established botanist gleam with envy.

Crystals, some glittering with the threads of enchantments, rested in every nook and cranny. Barrels in the corners, marked with runes, some of which were so ancient that even Ma had difficulty understanding them, stored ingredients that were too rare to use daily. A great deal of her collection was inherited, passed down from the previous owner. This shop had been around for centuries. The creaking floor beneath me was practically a relic, a witness to countless patrons who had come in with maladies both ordinary and unfathomable.

I followed Ma to the back.

I sat down at my station, craving the familiarity. Hoping to feel the calmness wash over me as it usually did when I gathered my tools and felt the rugged texture of my desk. But it never came.

I had decided to believe Osta, to accept that the events of last night were just some fucked up hallucination, but even as I repeated it to myself over and over again, I couldn't make it feel real. Sure, it made the most sense. Something deep inside me was still screaming that I was a murderer. That I was a Monster.

I glanced up at Ma as she gathered a few vials from the back shelves. My heart felt like it might explode. If she found out how dark my inner world had gotten… I didn't let my mind go there

I managed to keep myself occupied enough, but the looming sense of the unknown continued to spiral. It was impossible to fully escape the questions that hung heavy.

I was surprised to find that, despite the crippling anxiety that radiated through me, I also felt an odd sense of peace. This was the first time in weeks—maybe months—that I didn't feel like I had to keep a constant grip on the cursed monstrosity that lived beneath my skin. I could feel it... it was certainly there, but it wasn't clawing at me. Wasn't itching for release.

Perhaps it had had its fill the night before. The beast was satiated for now.

That thought nearly sent me retching.

Ma kept her eyes on me most of the day, watching intently as I tried to lose myself in work

I was well aware of what was to come. Ma's concern always simmered in silence, growing until she couldn't hold it back anymore. This day wasn't going to end without a conversation. And I was dreading it.

Esprithe be damned.

After trying *and failing* multiple times to light the coals under our cauldron burners. My fire starter had finally run out of oil after struggling with it all day, and I couldn't find any matches laying around.

I groaned. After managing to successfully dodge Ma's questioning eyes, now it seemed my only option was asking her for help.

Sighing, I stood and peered in her direction to find her staring right at me as she expertly wrapped herbal poultices. The woman was relentless.

"Care to ask me something, Fia?" she shot my direction, her mouth creeping into a grin. I took a few steps toward her.

"It depends. Does requesting your help come with a price? Or would you do it out of the kindness of your heart?" I raised an eyebrow.

"Oh Fia. Everything has a price, you know that," she said, winking at me. "Did you run out of oil for your burner?" Her grin turned oddly suspicious, her hands still busy at work with the poultices.

My eyes widened.

"Ma, I know you did not orchestrate this so that I would have to come talk to you," I said, my tone curt.

"I would never do such a thing." She clutched her chest dramatically. "But it is unfortunate, we seem to be out of both oil and matches. I'll place an order for more, but they'll take a few days to arrive, I'm afraid."

I narrowed my eyes, but my lips betrayed me by twisting up at the corners.

Truly. Fucking. Relentless.

"Seeing that we're out of both of those immensely important items, I guess I have no choice but to request your aid in lighting the coals for the cauldrons." My voice was slick.

"I thought you'd never ask." She laid the poultices down and shuffled over to my station.

Kneeling low, she pressed her hand against the coals. After a few seconds, smoke billowed. Sparks flew up from the pit, and the coals began to glow a brilliant red.

"That will never get old," I said, trudging over to her.

"Well, it is my best party trick." She smiled, and I helped her up from the floor.

"It's far more than a party trick, Ma." My eyes lingered on her before I turned, the guilt now creeping back in. I began filling the cauldron with water.

Ma's focus had manifested when she was younger, as was the case for most Aossí. She had set fire to a haystack while playing as a child, causing an entire slaughterhouse to burn to the ground. Although an accident, Ma loved to attribute it to her innate sense of justice—*even at that young an age,* she'd recall, pride flickering in her eyes.

We noticed the signs of Osta channeling fairly early. She was twelve and I was fourteen, and we had already been at the House of Unity for eleven years.

Although Osta tended to be a bit oblivious when it came to people, objects of the non-living variety couldn't hide a thing from her. She was always the most curious child, inspecting everything, asking questions that other children would never even think of. Lady Fairbanks took full advantage of this once she found out just how talented Osta was, using her to fact check her financial documents and ensure any shopping receipts were correct.

She was always the first one to solve a riddle, or to point out some obscure location on a map. Her focus was subtle, but the height of practicality. It's a part of what made her so talented with design. She could look at something and immediately pinpoint what would bring about its greatest attributes.

Once Lady Fairbanks discovered that her talents could be used in this regard, Osta became her full-time seamstress at just thirteen. That was how Osta was introduced to her current employer, Thearna, who was not much better than Lady Fairbanks.

Most focuses were ordinary. A farmer might have a certain knack for identifying good soil deposits. A hunter might have a sixth sense when it comes to tracking. Ma could ignite small flames, but there was an entire Guard family who could send the world into a burning blunder.

Some never received the ability to channel. Others received such great power, they rivaled the Esprithe themselves. Some of us had no idea what our supposed focus was.

No, not some of us. Me.

Deep in my gut, I knew the truth: it wasn't a focus at all.

It was a curse.

Ma wandered over to the stool near my desk and took a seat, eyeing me with reluctance. Her teasing smile morphed into a tight line.

"Fia, are we ever going to talk about it?" She cut off my train of thought.

I sighed, loading the arrangements of bark into my brewing sachet before flinging it into the cauldron to steep.

"What is it exactly that you want to know?" I slid into my chair, inhaling deeply.

"Fia... you never miss work. You looked like a ghost this morning... I couldn't help but wonder..." Ma trailed off, taking her eyes off me for the first time today.

I felt a weight lift as her gaze shifted, but it also stirred something deep within me. Panic. The absence of her stare suddenly felt like a void, like a forest fire finally burning out to reveal the wasteland it left behind.

"Well, Ma. That's not so revolutionary. I always look like a ghost," I teased quietly, hesitating. Her eyes remained fixed on the floor. And my words passed over her like a joke she had heard one too many times.

I sat in silence for a long while, contemplating my options. This was exactly what I had been worried about. She knew me too well. And she wanted answers... She deserved answers, but how could I tell her?

"I was worried that something had happened..." She trailed off, her words heavy in the air.

Fear churned inside me. Would I endanger her by telling her my truth? Would I even be telling *the truth* if I told her *my truth*? Would she find me completely insane? I was spiraling, the questions tumbling through the walls of my mind.

And yet, I shuddered away from the one possibility that was truly holding me back. The one I dreaded the most. The one that would change everything. The one where I lost Ma.

It was hard to even consider. Ma chose to see the good in me. A victim of circumstance. But if she knew what truly happened, could we survive? If I told her, would she finally see me as the monster she never believed I would become?

Even if Osta was right and none of it was real, normal people didn't hallucinate themselves murdering people. Normal people didn't suffer from mind-bending nightmares that made them fear sleep nearly as much as they feared the world around them. Normal people didn't have to question whether their reality was in fact, real at all.

"Ma ... I–" I whispered, just as the bells chimed from the front of the shop. We both turned our heads in the direction of the sound as if we had been woken from a trance.

Ma looked at me again, and my heart felt like it would give out. She paused for a few seconds, before giving me a sympathetic nod and making her way to the front.

Silence enveloped me. I breathed deeply, only mildly aware of the world outside of my own mind. Was this a sign to keep it all inside me?

Maybe the customer just needed a quick fix. I wasn't sure how much longer I could bear the weight of anticipation. Slivers of voices echoed into the room.

Ma's footsteps approached, and I looked up as she rounded the corner. Her expression was hollow. My attention crept to her left and the breath in my lungs turned to ice. The emerald eyes of General Ashford were staring back at me.

CHAPTER 5

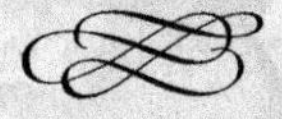

The General's gaze tore into me like a predator closing in on his prey.

He was so close.

He wore black coated leathers. The insignia of Sídhe—two dark green serpents—loomed at his chest, and war badges lined the fabric draping his shoulders.

His once untamed locks were now pulled into a disciplined stream down his back.

He was striking in a cold-blooded kind of way, like his beauty was tinged with poison.

Unassuming, alluring even.

I brought my eyes up to meet his.

The scar that stained his otherwise perfect face was darker than I previously thought. The center was pitch black, fading out to the color of wine before sprawling into vein-like patterns across his cheek.

My eyes, braver than the rest of my body, remained locked on his. His expression was vague, and therefore, infuriating. There was no reading the General.

Logic told me that he was here to arrest me. The near-comforting confusion that Osta's words had provided evaporated from my mind like a sudden drought.

As his stare continued, my stomach turned to acid. I knew the best plan was to play it safe, but a desire to resist clawed at me.

Fear still churned, but it was now tinged with a rage that had been dormant in me for the last five years, a rage that I had buried deep after the guards at the dam had murdered my friends. I knew then I could never act on it, never let it control me or I'd end up getting myself killed. But now as the General stood in front of me, looking so similar to them, that rage returned with a vengeance.

"The General has requested you for questioning regarding last night..." Ma finally announced, but her tone seemed less than sure. Her eyes shifted back and forth between us, searching for even a slight change of pace. But we were still locked in a stalemate.

Or so I thought.

My uncertainty festered like a poison, yet his eyes revealed no sign of weakness. He was in his element.

The echo of a smirk played at the corners of his lips.

My heart shuddered as a wave of nausea hit me, and I blinked.

He took it as an opportunity.

"Fia Riftborne?" I heard the words drip from his lips like blood from a dagger. His velvety voice grated against my spine far more than it should have. He was too polished, too poised. Bile rose in my throat.

"That's me," I muttered, albeit in a much more confident tone than intended. The wicked part of me gleamed with pride. His eyebrow peaked, leaving a crease in his forehead.

"And you were present during the celebration last night?" he asked, his voice tinged with amusement. Heat emanated from my hands, building until it reached the base of my skull. I bit back the twitch that threatened my upper lip.

He knew I was there. He saw what I did. The small talk was pointless.

"I was asked to deliver the last of the tonics to the party. Last minute orders from the Nobility," I said flatly.

His eyes narrowed for a few seconds before turning to Ma. "Is there somewhere I could speak with her privately?" he asked, a sickening sweetness drenching his voice. "After all, I am here on official matters. It's best I conduct this away from any potentially prying eyes or ears."

Confusion rippled through me. Why wasn't he taking me off to question me in custody?

Ma struggled to respond. She glanced at me, worry streaking across her forehead. I gave her a simple nod. This was happening one way or another. Might as well get it over with now.

Her eyes shifted back towards the General. I could tell she didn't want to oblige, but Ma was in no position to refuse him. I didn't want her to try to. This was my mess.

"There are greenhouses out back… they stay locked unless one of us is working there..." She paused before walking to her desk and retrieving a key from the drawer. I thought she might say something else, considering her hesitance, but she slowly returned, holding out her hand.

The General smiled as he took the key, "Thank you, Maladea. We shouldn't be long."

He turned towards the back door without a second glance, clearly expecting me to follow him. I squeezed Ma's hand as I brushed past her and gave her a reassuring look. I only hoped it was convincing.

We made our way to the greenhouse in silence.

He reached for the door and unlocked it gracefully. Stepping back and pulling it with him, he motioned for me to walk ahead. I hesitated.

"After you," he murmured.

Fear seeped back into me as I stepped past him.

The sun was peeking out from over the mountains in its descent. It would be dark soon.

I crossed my arms until the door snapped closed behind me.

Stealing a glance in his direction, my eyes gave me away. He was just staring at me with that odd curiosity again. Not saying a word.

"Let's just get to it then," I said curtly.

He shook his head, huffing an amused sigh. "That's the tone you intend to use?" he asked with such superiority, I thought I might suffocate.

"Will it change anything?"

He strode over to the table where we kept our gardening tools, picking up a hand shovel and examining it.

"I'm just trying to understand the reason behind your contempt. You seem enraged. And all I've asked for is a simple conversation," he taunted.

"I apologize," I murmured, hiding the chill that wanted to lace my voice. My eyes wandered towards the floor.

He raised an eyebrow, lowering his chin.

"That's a much more acceptable tone, don't you think?" His voice dripped with sarcasm. "Since we both know why I'm here, why don't you start with telling me what it is exactly that you did to those poor girls." He leaned back against the table, crossing his feet. "I've never seen anything like that. And I've just about seen it all."

"I… I don't really know." The words fell out. I could feel my confidence draining through my feet. But defiance still lingered, albeit quietly, in the back of my mind.

He rolled his eyes. "Riftborne. My patience is dwindling. Your focus. What is it?" he snapped.

"My focus? I... don't know. I don't have a focus… I mean..." I shook my head, confusion creasing my brow. "I don't have any control over it. I'd hardly call it a *focus.*"

He cocked his head to the side and narrowed his eyes. "What do you mean, you don't have control? How did you even channel it?"

"I was agitated. It only happens when I'm in a heightened state.

I don't know how to explain it. It just overcame me. I couldn't stop. I can never stop on my own," I stammered.

He pursed his lips before turning his head, deep in thought.

"I didn't mean for it to happen," I added. As if it weren't obvious.

He continued to stare at the corner of the room like he hadn't heard me.

"Has this happened before?" he finally asked.

I hesitated, horrified by the prospect of discuss the times I had previously unleashed my curse on someone.

"I'd rather not talk about it," I said, wrapping my arms around my middle.

Anger flickered across his eyes. He continued to glare at me, but his amusement returned.

"I'd rather not make this more difficult than it needs to be," he shrugged, angling his head. "But I certainly can."

In a blinding flash, a dagger sliced through the air, aimed dead center at my face. Terror seized my throat. Time seemed to freeze as I flinched, the blade whispering past my cheek before embedding itself in the wooden beam behind me.

After a few deep breaths, I opened my eyes to find him smiling wickedly. Like this was his own personal form of entertainment.

"If you're going to kill me, just do it now," I whispered, bracing myself against the beam.

The General rose to his feet and approached me with measured steps, stopping just mere inches from my face. His emerald eyes locked onto mine as he reached past me to retrieve his dagger. He brought the blade to my neck, dragging it gently along the contour of my throat. I held my breath, expecting the kill.

"You don't get to die until I've had my questions answered. If your own life doesn't matter to you, then we'll have to go in another direction. That other Riftborne girl was at the party too, correct?" His low tone hit me like daggers of ice. "What was her name again... Osta?"

It took every logical fragment of my brain to stop me from spitting on his polished boots right then and there. I felt my palms twitch.

What should have been fear was replaced by rage once again, the kind I couldn't control, and the familiar haze overtook my vision. I shoved my back further into the wood until I heard it crack in resistance, warning myself to calm the blaze that was igniting all over my skin and through my skull. I pressed my hands against the sides of my temples in an attempt to physically calm the power trying to flood me.

He had done his research. *The fucking audacity.* Everyone in the Guard was pure fucking evil. All they did was abuse their power, kill indiscriminately and manipulate for their own sick entertainment. My heart raced.

His footsteps became distant as he walked away.

"I just want to know about the other times this has happened. It's simple," he insisted.

My eyes moved along the cracks in the floor, searching for something. I couldn't let him involve Osta in this.

"It was last Spring. Inside the Apothecary." My words were clipped, my breath labored. The familiar feeling of regret began its descent into my gut as the memories surfaced. I had pushed this so far from my mind, reliving it was going to be hard.

"Go on," he urged, leaning back onto the table.

"I was in the front of the shop, restocking the potion cabinets." My vision blurred as I replayed the events.

"I heard a commotion outside. I figured it was just some street vendors fighting over territory. But the sounds got closer, and I could hear her–Osta–screaming." My hand found its way to my hair and raked through, catching a few snags.

"She was with her new boyfriend. I don't even know what they were fighting over. But she ran into the shop, heading towards the back. He raced after her and she just kept telling him to leave her alone.... But he wouldn't. At first, he was kind of pleading with her, but then he got really frustrated," I looked away, swallowing the salt that had begun forming in my mouth.

"I told him he needed to leave, but he didn't hear me. At that point, he was roaring at her. I couldn't understand what he was saying." My lungs sucked in a slow breath. "But he was starting to really piss me off. Ma ran in from the greenhouse."

" He reared up like he was going to hit Osta, and I totally lost it."

"You lost it? Elaborate please," the General said from across the room.

"I lost control. This... surge ran through me... It's difficult to explain. But... it was as if pure force erupted out of me and grappled him." My eyes widened, remembering how his body lifted off the ground. How he began trembling uncontrollably, unnaturally. What I had done... It still terrified me.

"Ma and Osta... they were screaming. I couldn't hear them at first. I was completely consumed by what was happening." A lump formed in my throat. "Eventually, Osta yanked me back, and broke my trance. He fell and hit the ground." I winced, remembering the sound of dead weight striking the creaking floor of the shop.

"He wasn't dead. Just unconscious. Ma was able to heal him. I guess it's lucky we were in the Apothecary..." I trailed off. The way Ma had looked at me that day...

I felt my heart shatter all over again. There was so much horror in her eyes. I never once imagined she could look at me like that. The way that others looked at me.

Like I was a monster.

She knew that there was something... dangerous inside me. Her and Osta had always known. But I don't think any of us realized the extent of it. Ever since then, I had stopped telling either one of them when I felt it coming... when I felt it taking over. I blinked, holding back the tears that threatened to fall.

My body was dying to recoil, I wanted to take it all back. I wanted to wipe the memory from their minds. I wanted to go back in time and change it. If I had known my curse would lead to this... Perhaps I should have left a long time ago, releasing the people I loved from the burden of being around me. Of fearing me. Of being dragged into whatever fate I had now sealed for myself.

"So, he survived?" The General asked, breaking through my internal spiral.

After a few seconds, my lips felt as though they could move again.

"They were able to revive him. He stayed unconscious for a while. But when he came to, he couldn't remember any of it."

We stood in silence for a long while. The room had gotten dark. Even the air seemed oppressive. After what felt like centuries, the General cleared his throat.

"They were on the brink of death when we found them. I mean, the two of them had mere seconds left. I thought there was no way they could have survived your attack, the shape we found them in was... well, let's just say, they certainly looked dead." He bit back a smile. "My alterationist had quite a time erasing the blood from their hair. It was no easy task. Genuinely. It took just about every ounce of our healer's focus to revive them, the girls, I mean..." he trailed off.

I froze.

"He said it was like their minds had been crushed by something... Like an invisible force just squeezed and squeezed." He started pacing as he rambled on. "You know, I was really curious about the memory loss. They had it too. Didn't remember a thing... It was fascinating... absolutely fascinating. I've never seen anything like it."

He turned to face me as a smirk formed on his lips.

Beckha and Jordaan were alive.

CHAPTER 6

THE NEWS HIT me like a shockwave.

They were alive.

I slid down the wooden beam, my arms instinctively wrapping around my knees. The General's presence became an afterthought.

I breathed in deep, feeling my body melt into the floor. Tension evaporated with my exhale and my face fell into my palms.

The brink of death—those words echoed in my mind. Not dead. The subtle distinction gnawed through me like a dull knife.

The girls had tormented me for nearly my entire life, and there were countless times I wished for their death, but I didn't want to be the one to commit the act. Perhaps I didn't really want them dead at all.

Sitting in silence for a few seconds longer, I let myself adjust to the relief. It felt foreign.

The General's laugh billowed through my thoughts, dragging me back to reality. "And don't worry. No one knows what you did. It's our little secret. Well, except for my little resurrectionist team. They know, obviously, but they won't be mentioning that to anyone."

"What? Why–" I stammered, confusion blasting through my short-lived peace. I found my balance as I stood. My head shot in his direction. A callous smirk returned to his face, but his eyes remained sharp, calculating. Like he was searching for some silent answer in my expression.

"Why would you do that?" I repeated in a low tone. I felt a sinking feeling in my gut as the realization settled over me.

Someone like him only helped people like me when they wanted something.

"I'm happy you asked." He moved his hands behind his back as he sauntered towards me. "When I saw what you did. What you were capable of. I knew you were different. Special even. It's not something one comes across often, a gift such as yours. It could be useful to me..."

Gift?

Had this man not heard anything I'd said?

"Useful to the Isle," the General continued. "I preside over a Faction of our Guard that is trained in special combat. I'd like to train you to use your focus properly. And I'd like you to join the Guard. Faction Venom." He turned to look at me, eyes gleaming with something terrifying.

Seriously?

Tension filled the air, and it needed a release.

A laugh escaped me in almost desperate waves. I couldn't help it. He had to be joking. Was he a fucking madman? It was perhaps the most preposterous thing I'd ever heard.

"I fail to see the humor, Riftborne. Enlighten me." His voice took on a new edge.

I paused. He was serious.

My head began to shake as I shot him a confused look, an exhausted kind of exasperation still pulling at the corners of my eyes.

"Why? So everyone in your little platoon can get their brains juiced the second I lose my temper?" I asked, my voice like quicksilver. In what world would I want to be a part of the Sídhe Guard? Did he forget I was a *Riftborne*? For all I knew, his father could have killed my own. Not that I had any way of finding out. The Guard was thorough in their burning of records from that time.

He glared at me before clicking his teeth.

"How fast you forget the favor I so graciously afforded you. Covering up your attempted murder was no easy task."

The arrogant smirk had returned to his lips.

The idea was so ridiculous that logic or reason completely evaded me. I opened my mouth, then closed it

"It's your choice." He paused, cracking his knuckles. "I mean… I can't force you. If you'd rather face the consequences of your actions, then that can certainly be arranged. It would be unfortunate, of course. A waste of potential." He shrugged.

As tempting as it might have been to finally control this curse inside me, being blackmailed into doing so made my mind want to release itself on his. Perhaps he'd like to see my *focus* more intimately…

"I need your answer before the weekend is over. I'm sure you'll make the right decision." He winked. *Winked.*

As he sauntered past me, I heard a clunk. And then he disappeared into the night. I made my way over to the table and found Ma's key. And a card with his office address. Something inside me stopped my hands from ripping it to shreds.

It wasn't long before Ma was standing in the greenhouse doorway, holding a flickering candle. "Are you okay?" she asked quietly, noting my less-than-ideal posture on the pavement.

My body just wanted to relax… I deserved that. I felt like I had been packed into a jar all day.

There was a strange relief in the fact that the inevitable confrontation had finally happened. I had answers. He *had* seen me. It was *real.* The sickening anticipation was gone, and I felt some semblance of clarity. So, here I laid. Sprawled on the ground, stretching out the stress that had taken root over the last day.

Breathing felt so good. I'd take whatever peace I could get. I just wanted to forget everything for a single, perfect moment.

"I'm just exhausted," I lied. I couldn't tell her anything tonight. I needed to make my plans first. She tilted her head to the side, but her concern seemed to lessen, though I knew curiosity still churned inside. It was Ma, after all.

Sitting up, I ran my fingers through my hair, wincing as I snagged more than a few tangles. It probably looked as crazy as I felt.

"I know you want to talk about it, Ma. And we will, but I'm done for the night. I just want to go home and dive into my bed." I gave her an apologetic half-smile. It was about all I could muster. After a few seconds, she nodded.

I could tell she was appeasing me. If it were up to her, we would have it out right here, right now. "Go get some sleep, Fia. And have a good weekend. Try to do something fun. Oh, and don't forget my travel day. The shop will be closed." She attempted a smile, eyes still cloudy with concern. My heart sank.

We headed back into the shop to lock up. I wished Ma a good night before wandering through the city, losing track of time as my mind drifted lawlessly—until my feet stopped in front of our apartment building. Even though it was small and rundown, I was going to miss it.

Sighing, I made my way upstairs, not even bothering to wonder what dreams would haunt me tonight.

I knew what I had to do.

I knew I had to run.

CHAPTER 7

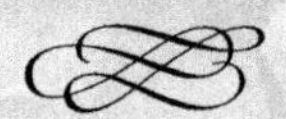

The rhythmic clang of metal against metal resonated through the room, merging with the erratic crackling from a fire below. Acrid fumes of burning coal and metal hung heavy in the air.

Shadows danced along the walls as an arm escaped from the darkness, flying above my head, a hammer gripped in its hand. It raced down, clanging against the surface of liquid steel.

Sparks flew as the metals collided. Heat enveloped me. Smoke billowed through the room. The hammer struck again, louder than the first time. And again. And again. Each time with more force. As the hand approached the burning embers, I noticed intricate tattoos swirling up the arm of the wielder.

Smoke began to fill my lungs.

The hot steel, once a river of liquid flame, began to take form, gradually revealing the silhouette of a blade. The thrums continued, forging the weapon well past the point of completion.

I watched on as the hand moved closer to my face, as if urging me to inspect the craftsmanship. Backlit by the flame below, my eyes focused, finding the twisted and rigid blade of a dagger.

~

I WOKE up to the familiar view of my ceiling, the remnants of a dream still hanging in my mind. It wasn't a nightmare this time, thankfully, just odd. I let out a slow breath. Perhaps my subconscious had decided to finally show me some mercy.

Thoughts of General Ashford and his attempts to recruit me echoed through my thoughts, sending a shiver across my skin. And suddenly, any relaxation that had seemed within reach fizzled out into the sea of anxiety I'd come to know so well.

I buried my head in my pillow and let out a groan.

The idea of becoming a weapon for the military, of joining the institution that viewed my very life as inconsequential at best—unfathomable at worst—was laughable. Not to mention, his invitation felt a lot more like a threat. Well, it *was* a threat.

And the answer was no.

The arrogance radiating off him was insufferable enough. And that was just the tip of the *absolutely-fucking-not* iceberg.

Ma would be fine. She wasn't a Riftborne. She was simply my employer to the outside world. Osta, on the other hand... Ashford's words crashed back into my thoughts. Would he punish her if I left?

Guilt churned through me. I had to believe it would be safer for her in Luminaria than if she were on the run with a fugitive. At least here, she could aid them in their investigation. She could answer their questions about me.

If I was ever caught, and she had come with me... I'd never forgive myself for the consequences.

The General seemed almost manic, unpredictable, but above all, prideful. I wondered if he would truly inform the Guard about my transgressions if I simply disappeared. It would be humiliating for such an esteemed General to let a lowly Riftborne slip through his fingers. Yes, pride and power were what drove him. Probably to a point of blind arrogance. After all, he thought he could walk into my life after twenty-three years and tame this *thing* inside me like he was some kind of savior? As far as I knew, people didn't need training to control their focus. Perfect it? Maybe. But not to stop it from unleashing chaos the second their pulse quickened.

I sighed. Clearly mine was never meant to see the light of day.

If it could be controlled... The full thought wouldn't dare resonate. It couldn't be controlled.

I had managed to live with this curse of a *focus* thus far, already resigned to setting boundaries that I knew I couldn't cross. After my friends were murdered, and my focus started to manifest, I'd resigned myself to the shadows even more. I went to work and returned home. I didn't go out, I didn't socialize, I didn't date. I only shopped at small, indiscriminate grocers. I wore gloves, even during the summer months.

The one thing I'd sworn never to do was the one thing that turned out to be my downfall, just like I always thought it would be: putting myself in any proximity to the Sídhe Elite. The Nobility had the ability to trigger my anger with cruelty, and the Guard had the overwhelming power to rip me from the world of the living in any way they deemed fit.

And that's exactly what had happened.

In the future, I'd need to be even more careful. But I'd have to do that somewhere else.

Somewhere new.

I reached into the small drawer of my bedside table, pulling out a leather pouch of coins. The contents of the sack were overwhelmingly silver rather than gold and didn't bear much weight. I sighed.

I did own one other item of value, but every nerve in my body revolted at the thought of selling it.

Reaching into the nightstand drawer once more, I felt around for the small box I had hidden in the back corner, biting back a pang of sadness as I found the dusty edges. I turned it over, and a small, gold bracelet tumbled onto the bed. It had come with me from Rifrdremar and was the only evidence I had of my previous life.

There was a knock on my door, and it creaked open, letting in sunlight from the hallway. I quickly threw the covers over myself. Through the thin sheet, I could make out Osta's silhouette.

"I know you don't plan on staying here all day," she chided. She pulled the sheet down with a swift motion that sent static electricity crackling through the air, causing my hair to raise in all directions.

"It doesn't sound like the worst idea," I mused, stretching my arms above my head in a yawn.

"Things have been so *tense* lately. Let's go to the market, stock up for the week, and try to enjoy the last days of summer! Take your mind off things... well, after you give me updates, of course. How are you? Feeling better after the other night?"

"I really can't today, Osta," I said with a groan.

"It's not a request, it's an order," she sang, pulling on my arm. "It's not like you have anything better to do."

I pondered for a few seconds, considering the long list of things that were undoubtedly better to do. Most revolved around getting the fuck out of this place as quickly as possible. I needed to continue planning my escape. Where I would go... How I'd get out of the city unseen. I'd never been far outside Luminaria.

But that everlasting guilt clawed at me once again. Because I loved her, perhaps more than I loved anyone or anything. And I knew how broken she would be without me.

Spending one last day with Osta... She deserved that. Maybe I could even explain myself. I winced, knowing how hard that conversation was going to be. A heaviness sank over me. Losing her seemed like the betrayal of a lifetime... but how could I stay? Ma and Osta needed to stay far away from me, even if they didn't understand why.

"The market isn't a bad idea. We actually have nothing to eat right now besides stale crackers and tea." I shrugged, fighting back the mist in my eyes. Osta's mischievous smile appeared as she fixed my bedhead.

"My thoughts exactly! And we should both have a decent paycheck after last week, so let's treat ourselves today!"

Osta's idea of treating ourselves usually involved indulging in sweets and snacks that would likely disappear before the week began anew. A sad smile found its way to my lips–I was going to miss her. But for once, I was taking control of my life, making a decision that would protect everyone. It was long overdue.

Osta found her way to my closet and began picking out a few pieces to make up an outfit, tossing them on the end of the bed. She didn't have much to choose from. Most of my clothes bore the stains of unruly herbs.

"Do you still have that dark green cloak with the hood?" I asked nonchalantly.

Osta turned towards me, narrowing her eyes. "Since when are you interested in fashion?"

"I'm not... My skin is just feeling a bit sensitive today. I was hoping I could use the hood." I shrugged, hoping my curiosity seemed genuine. Truthfully, I'd feel much safer walking around the market with a layer of fabric between me and any guards that might be manning that part of the city.

My hair was certainly easy to spot in a crowd. Hiding would prove difficult if Ashford had given anyone a description of me.

He had told me that no one knew what I had done, but blindly trusting his word seemed like a stupid thing to do.

"Well, I'll have to pick out something different for you to wear." She twisted her lips, sinking her weight down onto one hip. "But sure, I can figure something out." She sauntered off back into her room and returned with a folded stack of garments.

And with that, I rolled out of bed and pulled my hair back into a knot, slipping the gold bracelet into my pocket.

Enjoy this last day with her. Tomorrow, you'll make your escape.

The words loomed as I dressed myself.

~

IN THE HEART of our corner of Luminaria lay the energetic marketplace of the Central district.

Stalls constructed with stone and living wood wound through the grand avenues backing up to the canals. The marble structures served as canvases for elaborate depictions of flora and fauna, carved by Aossí artisans.

Canopies of intertwining vines and blossoms draped the market square with shade, adding a touch of the wild to the polished marble surroundings.

Crystals embedded in the architecture refracted sunlight and cast a gentle glow over the bustling marketplace.

Osta and I drifted through the crowds as if in a haze. Aromatic spices infused the air, pulling us towards the food stalls offering a tantalizing fusion of exotic and traditional flavors.

I had to stop myself from drooling. The sounds of sizzling delicacies blended with the soft murmur of a nearby fountain.

I had forgotten how magical the market was at the end of Summer.

I was going to miss Luminaria, flaws and all. The city itself had never treated me badly. I wondered where I'd go, and if anywhere could replace the sense of whimsy that seeped from every nook and corner of Sídhe's capital.

The sounds of cheering erupted from the square, and I shot my attention towards it just as a white fabric was ripped away to reveal a marble statue. The cheering intensified as a voice boomed through the streets, "All hail King Sydian. Long may he reign."

I grabbed Osta's elbow and pulled her deeper into the anonymity of the crowd as I held back a grimace.

It was no secret that the residents of Sídhe shared common

devotion for the monarchs. King Sydian was revered as the greatest ruler in a millennia and had achieved the impossible: an era of near-universal prosperity.

Poverty and hunger were rarities. The Crown, through its royal delegation, ensured everyone had access to basic necessities. Yet, true equality remained elusive. The class system persisted, albeit with a less rigid division between lower and middle.

A silence hung over the origin of this newfound wealth. Throughout his reign, the harvests became more than bountiful, livestock thrived, and nearly extinct species rebounded. Even Aossí vitality was affected. Our normal two century lifespans seemed to stretch on, with some elders nearing the age of two-hundred and twenty. It was as if the realm itself had become somewhat of a miracle. Those who still worshiped claimed it was a blessing from the Esprithe.

Osta and I spent most of our day hopping between vendors, taking samples and exploring the labyrinth of artisan wares.

One tent in particular caught my attention. I approached it, eyeing the most detailed and immersive tapestry. Sprawling hillsides and rocky beaches were painted expertly. It almost seemed like I was looking through a window to these places.

I had never been outside of Luminaria's borders. My eyes locked on a scene of perfectly tumbling storm clouds encroaching on snowy peaks. It was the most vibrant thing I had ever seen.

"That's the Radianthian Mountain Range," a woman's voice said from across the tent. She must have been the artist. I gave her a smile before turning back to the tapestry. For a moment, I tried to picture my life there amongst the foothills.

"It's so… vivid. It feels like I'm looking at it in real time. Like I'm there," I mused.

The woman let out a small laugh. "Well you can thank my focus for that. Turns out my gift is painting in hauntingly true detail. It all just kind of spills out of me." She smiled and shrugged her shoulders.

"I'm surprised the Nobility hasn't tormented you relentlessly. It seems like a focus they would deem invaluable," I observed.

"Oh, they've tried." The woman laughed. "But I value my freedom far too much. Although I'm available for commissioned pieces, for a price." Her eyes lit up as they traveled across her work.

"So you refused them?" I asked, "You felt comfortable turning them down?"

"Of course. We all take our own path. Mine was never meant to be contained. Limited." She sighed. "Some things are just meant to run free. Some things cannot be tempered–forced into a box of someone else's making."

Pausing, I ruminated over her words. Her situation didn't exactly apply to me. I highly doubt she committed murder with her paintbrushes. They had no leverage over her. No material for blackmail.

"Well, you're extremely talented, as I'm sure you know. I'd love to buy one of these some day. My roommate and I–" I stopped, turning around to find Osta. She was over at a fabric tent striking up a conversation with the salesman. We certainly didn't have the funds for something like this. A part of me sank. It would make a perfect parting gift.

"We love tapestries. Are you selling here often?" I asked.

"Only in the summer. I travel for the rest of the year, seeking out inspiration from the northern countryside."

I nodded. "Well, I wish you safe travels. Perhaps we'll be able to see your adventures next summer." I smiled and took a few steps toward the main path but stopped when I caught a glimpse of some rolled parchment in the corner of her tent.

I pulled one from the bucket and slowly opened it, making sure to do so gently. A painted compass rose became visible on the page, The Isle of Sídhe was written in calligraphy at the top.

A map.

"How much are these?" I turned back to her.

"A copper will do, dear." She smiled and approached me. "A

new little project I've been working on. My cartography skills sure don't match my paintings, but I find joy in it."

I dug into my satchel, pulled out a copper coin, and handed it to her. I would certainly need a map if I was going to begin planning my escape that night.

"It's beautiful," I said, eyeing the land mass. It didn't look like any map I had seen before. It held a more personal touch and artistic flair. Even if it might not be perfectly to scale, it would work.

"Perhaps it will aid you on any travels you embark on. After all, it was born from mine," she murmured, walking back to her seat behind the desk. I smiled, giving her a slight wave before wandering back into the chaos beyond her tent.

Now that Osta was occupied, I could finally do what I had come here to do. I reached into my pocket, feeling the gold bracelet within. My fingers grazed the engraving upon the surface and pushed away the sadness that threatened to seep in.

I made my way through the masses, stopping just before the wooden wheels of a covered wagon. I walked to the front to find an older, common man.

"Anything to trade?" His gruff voice called out into the groups of people passing by. He opened the front of his jacket to reveal that it was lined with jewelry and odd trinkets.

"I have a gold bracelet," I said, and his eyes shot towards me, looking me up and down.

"Show me," he said, closing his jacket and coming to lean against the side of the carriage.

I retrieved the bracelet from my pocket, but hesitated, rolling it through my fingers. I didn't want to do this, but I didn't have a choice. I needed coin for the road. Especially since I didn't know how long it would take me to find work. Or if I would be able to find it at all.

"I ain't got all day, miss." He tapped his foot against the cobblestones.

I reached out slowly, placing the bracelet in his outstretched hand. He pulled it close to his face, examining it.

He shot me a suspicious look. "You sure this ain't fool's gold?"

"You'd be the expert," I said in a voice just above a whisper.

He bit down on the bracelet a few times.

"Seems real enough." He reached into a chest and grabbed a magnifying glass, inspecting the gold once again.

"Where'd you get this?" He asked. "Steal it, did you?" A hummed chuckle escaped his throat as he narrowed his eyes at me.

"I've had it since I was a child," I said, irritation lacing my voice. "Do you want it or not?" My strength to rid myself of the little gold band was lessening with every moment I stood there. He placed it on the edge of his wagon and grabbed his coin pouch. My stomach turned.

"I guess I can melt it down," he said, and it was like the final nail in the coffin. Quickly, I grabbed the bracelet and turned, racing back to the center of the market, my breaths heavy and my head light. I shoved the bracelet back into my pocket.

"Hey, where you going?" He spat from behind.

I couldn't do it.

It was the only thing that was truly mine. The only thing that had come with me from my home in Riftdremar. I felt shame creep into my bones at what I had almost done. I needed to get out of here.

I found Osta, her arms now full of fabric samples.

She handed me a few bags of groceries. Well, nearly all of the groceries. "Where did you run off to?" Her smile was beaming, and I knew she was in her element. I didn't want her to sense how shaken I was, so I kept my tone casual.

"Just looking around. Should we grab a bottle of wine to drink once we get home? I'll need help winding down after all of this stimulation," I remarked, hoisting the bag of goods higher onto my hip.

"I have an even better idea! Let's go to Talia's! It's just around the corner and they should be offering specials right now–"

"I am mentally depleted. Let's just go home and share a bottle there." I couldn't risk losing any more time. I needed to get home and start packing. I also needed to figure out how I was going to explain this to her.

"You *know* that it's not the same. It's still the middle of the afternoon, so it won't even be crowded–and you owe me a drink, Fia."

It had been years since I'd accompanied Osta to her favorite haunt. Five at least. I was shocked she even asked me. Her boldness was really standing out today, almost like she knew something was about to change. Guilt resurfaced in the back of my head, and I hoped she wasn't reading the situation for exactly what it was. One of the reasons I came today was to give her a perfect final memory of me.

"Osta, you know it's not a good idea," I murmured, shifting on my feet.

"Fia, you'll never get over your fears if you continue to give into them every time. You'll have me. And we can sit on the patio. It's usually empty, and it's private. Come on, I know everyone that works there. There's nothing to be worried about."

I wracked my brain for any other valid excuse to not go, or at least, one that would make sense to her, but I fell flat. If this is what she really wanted, and it was our last day together, perhaps I could try. For her. I let out a loud sigh and looked down to see Osta smiling triumphantly.

"This way!" She commanded with a cheer, now walking with a revived energy. I groaned.

I followed with a healthy dose of reluctance. The walk was short-lived, and I was grateful. The overflowing bags at my hips had become impossible to carry. My arms were practically screaming in revolt.

Osta reached the entrance and pulled the door open, blocking it with her foot as she ushered me to go inside. I saw the floral sign as I passed her.

Talia's Elixir Lounge.

"Shun? Is that you I see working the bar today?" Osta called out with a grin.

"Always good to see you, Osta!" Shun responded without looking our way, seemingly absorbed in the creation of one of their renowned concoctions.

"Hey Shun," I said, and his eyes shot up to meet mine. I couldn't believe he was still working here after all this time.

"Fia, is that you?" He asked with wide eyes.

"I finally got her to come!" Osta squealed, spinning around to look at me. "See, Fia? It's totally dead in here. Just like I told you."

I couldn't help the blush that tore across my face.

"Hey now, Osta. Come join us tonight and see how *dead* it is." He clicked his tongue but smiled playfully.

Osta giggled, and flung her bags onto the counter, "Shh, don't say that. She might leave."

I rolled my eyes and joined her at the counter.

"I haven't seen you since that night we all went to that traveling show I can't remember the name of. Damn, it must have been, what, four or five years ago? Kieran was heartbroken for weeks when you rejected him, Fia." There was a teasing to Shun's words, and I was able to brush it off with a small laugh.

There had been nothing particularly wrong with Kieran. In fact, he had been quite charming. The night in question, many women had tried to gain his attention, but he had been dead set on trying to go home with me. At least I didn't have to feel bad after gently turning him down. He'd have plenty of shoulders to cry on.

My past encounters with both men and women had left me disenchanted, to say the least. All too often, I found myself dismissed as a passing novelty after a night spent together. That part of my life had been over for a long time. I'd made my peace with celibacy.

Besides, I never had any interest in getting involved with one of Osta's acquaintances. I wouldn't want to risk her social standing. She could intermingle with the commoners and the upper class alike.

Most people found her delightful and endearing, despite her Riftborne status. I'm sure the Nobility even fell victim to her charm during her hours of dressing them for galas, solstices and balls.

Osta was the assistant to a renowned seamstress in Luminaria. She hoped to grow under Thearna's influence and become her prodigy, but it seemed unlikely. Osta was too talented, too visionary, and that meant she was a threat. Thearna would make sure that Osta stayed safely tucked under her control.

My sympathies extended particularly to the unfortunate ladies compelled to parade around in Thearna's antiquated designs. She wouldn't know style if it stabbed her in the eye with a sewing needle. But legacy mattered above all else in Luminaria. And Thearna had plenty of it.

"Any space for us on the patio today?" Osta chirped, eyeing windows overlooking a garden outside. I lingered at the counter, managing a balancing act with the groceries.

"There is always room for you." Shun gestured towards the back. "It's all yours."

"Thank you Shun! You know you're my favorite!" Osta gave him a sly wink, flipping her honey golden hair over her shoulder.

Making my way to a table and finally putting my arms out of their misery, I plopped down onto a padded leather chair and lowered the bags to the ground.

Stone-tiled floors, mahogany tables, and comfy loungers set the scene. I took in the soft lighting that hung overhead and the potted plants that filled the space. I breathed in the scent of florals that drifted around me, allowing my body to slump into a timid state of relaxation.

Osta had been right. The lounge wasn't busy. A patron here or there, but no crowds. As I settled back into my seat, foreign tendrils of comfort slipped into my mind. A part of me sank inside knowing that I wouldn't have this opportunity with her again. I should have spent more time doing things like this—having fun outside the confines of our apartment. Guilt radiated through my core. She deserved a better friend than me.

Osta made her way to the table a few minutes later, two drinks in hand. The flutes were filled with shifting shades of lavender, swirling as bubbles sparkled up the sides of the glass.

"Shun says he's calling this one *Moonlit Nectar.*" Osta smiled, wiggling her eyebrows, and fell into the chair across from me, playfully sliding one of the drinks in my direction.

I lifted the glass to Osta's, clinking it softly before taking a long sip. "Cheers!" Osta cooed.

It tasted floral and sweet as the bubbles rushed across my tongue. My body hummed in satisfaction.

"I told you it would be worth it to come here. They must put some sort of addictive substance in these things." Osta had all but finished hers.

"Yes, I think that's called alcohol," I joked, taking another sip.

Osta rolled her eyes behind her lashes, still smiling triumphantly. "You know what I mean," she said. "After this week… We absolutely deserve this. I didn't think I'd survive Thearna."

"What did she do this time?"

"I have been working endlessly on sketches for the upcoming season. You know how late I've been at the studio." She tossed her hair over her shoulder and sighed with exasperation.

"Mhm," I murmured, stirring my drink.

"She *destroyed* them. Right in front of my face. Tore them into pieces and claimed they weren't right for the upcoming collection. I'd normally be in tears if I wasn't so used to it."

"I don't know how you still work with her." I sighed. This truly was a weekly occurrence.

"Like I have a choice! I don't know another seamstress in this town that would hire me. I only have Thearna because of Lady Fairbanks. You know my plan. A few more years with Thearna and maybe I can build up enough clients to open my own studio or get a job working for one of the noble families, but that's only going to happen if people see my designs..." Osta went on.

I tried to listen intently, but I found my mind drifting off. We were sitting for the first time in hours, and the chaos of the city was muted in the background. I was one Moonlit Nectar in, and the effects were already starting to take hold, allowing the thoughts I'd buried away to resurface.

I tried not to compare our situations. Thearna sounded like a bloody nightmare–

"Fia!" Osta prodded, annoyance straining her voice.

Reality snapped back into focus. "I was listening!"

"Yeah right. Your eyes were doing that thing they do when you've checked out. Perception is my gift, after all. What's on your mind?"

I took a deep breath and set my glass on the table. I guess now was as good a time as any. She needed to understand. She *deserved* to understand.

"General Ashford came to see me yesterday," I stated, keeping close attention on Osta's reaction.

Her eyes widened. "And you're just telling me this now?" she gasped.

"I was trying to process everything. He showed up at the Apothecary before closing time. He told me that Bekha and Jordaan were still alive..." I trailed off.

Osta leaned back and sighed with relief. "I knew I saw them leave."

I nodded. "You were right, like always. Healers were able to mend them in time." I hesitated before continuing. "But, that's not all. He thinks he can *train* me to use... well, whatever it is that I can do." I rolled my eyes, contempt curling at my upper lip.

"I mean... that sounds like an intriguing opportunity, right?" She raised an eyebrow.

"What do you mean *intriguing*? He wants to use me as some sort of weapon for the Guard, Osta. To *join* the Guard. Why would I ever put myself in that position?"

The crease in her brow deepened.

"I get that... I just wonder if maybe you should consider it... especially after what just happened at the party. You could finally learn to control the one thing that holds you back from living your life normally. You wouldn't even try it?"

I flashed her the Riftborne mark on my hand. She looked around cautiously, only returning her eyes to me once she confirmed we were alone.

"They made sure we would never have that opportunity a long time ago," I hissed.

"Fia, people aren't nearly as hateful as you make them out to be."

"You think our late friends would agree?" I glared at her, feeling my skin tingle. The guard's cruel blue eyes drifted into my mind, as if he was taunting me. It had been so easy for him to pull the levers of the dam. So easy to release the currents. To kill our friends.

Calm down.

"Fia, sometimes you have to make the best of the cards you've been dealt. And sometimes you have to know when to let go, when to move on. And when to *help* yourself when the rare opportunity comes around." She shook her head, disappointment sprawled across her face.

"That's easy for you to say," I mumbled, pinching the bridge of my nose. It was true. She had no idea what it was like to live with this thing inside me. How could she?

"Listen Fia... You can't live the rest of your life like this. What if you could stop it from ever happening again? What if you could actually help people?"

"I think we both know that my focus won't be used for *helping* people, Osta. I can't believe you think this is a good idea. I don't even know what to say."

My eyes welled up, but I wouldn't lose it here.

"Of course you don't. Because you refuse help. You run away from everything..." Osta trailed off and looked down, biting her lip. I hadn't even told her I planned on running.

"You're a fool if you believe that General Ashford or anyone of authority on this Isle is trying to help me. He sees a power to be yielded, to be collected for his little faction. And he's sadly mistaken. I cannot be helped. You know it. I know it." My fingers twitched and I felt a rush of heat wash over me.

"I can't deal with your innate pessimism tonight, Fia. We just had an amazing day. I'm only trying to reason with you. To offer another perspective, but you can't see past yourself. You're so negative, you can't even imagine your life taking a turn for the better!" Osta was holding back tears.

Before I could respond, she shoved her chair back and walked off into the lounge.

I scoffed and shook my head. *Unbelievable.*

The static that ran down my arms had lessened, but the curse still crept in the shadows. I took a deep breath.

How could she be so delusional?

The elite played these games all the time with people like us. How could she not see it?

My mind went to that sharp place. She just didn't *want* to see it. She fawned over them just as much as the next groupie, I just managed to ignore it most of the time.

And how is it *my* fault I never learned to control my focus? It came naturally to everyone else around me. I shouldn't have to become some General's project to figure out how to wield it. I was a lost cause.

Right?

I tipped my glass back again, savoring the last drops. My eyes closed as the warmth of the alcohol swirled in my gut.

Osta and I rarely fought, and now it was twice in a matter of days. I had to get out of here. My pulse was already racing.

Something stronger than alcohol stirred as I steadied myself. I gathered my things in a hurry and stormed through the patio gate without a single glance back.

CHAPTER 8

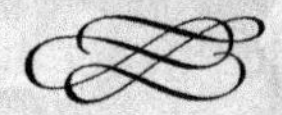

THE SUN WAS BEGINNING to set, and the wind whipped past me, charging through the winding city streets that led back to our apartment. A chill swept through my hair, the promise of autumn on the horizon.

It did nothing to cool my flushed cheeks.

Anger permeated my every thought. I was confused. Hurt. Definitely tipsy.

Even if Osta tried to see my point of view, she would never understand. Although we shared our Riftborne status, our lives were wildly different. Sometimes it seemed as though she was purposely ignoring that inescapable truth.

She had too much faith in me. I'd never be the *normal,* outgoing person she wanted me to be. It was as impossible as it was irresponsible. Had that not become glaringly obvious over the last few days?

Another blaze of anger seared through my limbs.

Thunder rumbled in the distance, and the scent of rain lingered in the thick, humid air. The sky, threatening to burst at any second, bathed the clouds in swirling shades of violet and iron.

My emotions mirrored the churning heavens above, crashing against one another like a wave, fighting for the right to pull me under. If anyone was supposed to understand, it *should* have been Osta. The feeling of loss crept into my bones as my feet continued forward. I hadn't even had the chance to tell her I was leaving.

Don't cry.

My pace quickened as I blinked away tears, inhaling sharply through my nose. I just needed to get home.

The sounds of partygoers whistled towards me right as I turned the corner. One second, I could hear their laughter, the next, I was in a collision. My ankle twisted and I stumbled a few feet back, losing my balance. The contents of my bags spilled over the walkway, and I watched in horror as my gold bracelet fell from my pocket, clinking on the pavement before rolling through the slats of a sewer grate. The air went still around me.

"Pfft, way to go Graem!" One of them shouted.

The culprit pushed his friend and shuffled back, stepping on my produce along the way. A crushed melon leaked nectar onto the pavement.

"Sorry about that lady, but we have somewhere to be!"

The group continued down the street without a care.

My body was stiff as I processed the loss of my precious item and took in the mess of groceries. My jaw hung open, but I was unable to form words. A loud ringing in my ears drowned out everything else around me.

No, no, no.

I felt the hairs on my arms rise and my mind went blank. A searing pain shot across my skin, striking terror through me like a whip.

The familiar translucent web pulsed in a sickeningly fast uproar, overcoming me in an instant.

Fear became a cage around me.

Every muscle in my body tensed until they were near trembling. I felt the power overflowing, bursting at the seams. My insides were being shredded in its attempt to break free–my mind roared in two different voices. One begging me to find release, the other screaming to keep this destruction contained at all costs.

But it didn't matter. It was happening.

Time stood still, and I felt the power begin to seep from my pores. White-hot essence overtook my vision.

And just as I was about to explode, droplets of rain spattered on my forehead.

Breathe!

The trance fractured just as the sky bottomed out. Water hammered down, crashing against the pavement so hard that mist rose up from the cobblestones, creating a blur around me—reflecting the muddiness that lingered in my mind.

Delicious coldness rushed over my skin, putting out the fire within. I lost my grip on gravity and fell to my knees. My breath got caught in my chest as the pain radiated, bringing with it a sense of clarity.

Unwelcome clarity.

Undeniable clarity.

My body, which still felt not quite like my own, crumpled to the ground, seeking the coolness of the stones.

Tears came then.

The group turned a corner and disappeared from view, unaware of the chaos they had narrowly avoided.

Osta's words drifted into my consciousness. My mind tried to reject them, an effort that had become a reflex. I knew why they were here, what they wanted me to do. What they meant. I couldn't face the truth. The idea of putting my hope into something was terrifying. I'd stopped doing that a long time ago.

And that's what this fear was, if I whittled it down to the bare bones: believing my life could be something more than this was dangerous and cruel and had only ever brought me pain. I just wanted to escape it all, to hide.

But hiding wasn't working anymore.

The words hit me like a dagger in the chest, tearing through every thought, every wall I'd built to protect myself.

How many times had this happened in the last few weeks? How many times had I noticed myself slipping? How many times had I felt the tendrils of force send shivers across my skin? Threatening to implode and take me over.

And for simple things. Unavoidable things. Things that were inevitable unless I holed up in my room and never left.

It didn't matter where I went, how much distance I put between myself and Luminaria. There would always be risk. I would always be a danger.

And if tonight was any indication, my powers were just going to get worse–more and more uncontrollable until they destroyed everything around me.

I was a bomb that could explode at any moment.

A suffocating truth hung heavy in my bones: part of me didn't want to stop. The power was overwhelming, maddening, hungry... and the darkest, most brutal shade of temptation. It was going to win next time, as it had done outside the Grove.

What if this had happened while I was with Osta?

I couldn't bear to let that train of thought continue.

Brushing away my tears, I moved into a sitting position. It felt like a decision had been made for me. I couldn't be selfish and afraid anymore. And running wouldn't fix this.

If there could be a way out, some light at the end of the tunnel, I had to take it.

I had to try.

I owed it to Osta, to Ma.

Maybe I even owed it to myself.

CHAPTER 9

THE MOON LOOMED, casting silvery light throughout the alleyways. The rain had stopped, but I was still drenched, in both water and regret.

I stood and glanced around, hoping to avoid the gaze of any passerby. A sigh of relief escaped me when the empty street confirmed I was alone.

A part of me wanted to find the General tonight and tell him my answer, even if only to absolve myself of the guilt that now hung heavy in my limbs.

But it was too late. There's no way I'd be warmly welcomed if I barged up to his door at this hour. Sibyl only knew what situation I would be... walking in on. A shudder ran through me. No, it would have to be first thing tomorrow morning.

I trudged towards our apartment, hoping to find Osta there. It looked just as we'd left it that morning. She was still out.

I had become accustomed to waiting over the last few days, I could handle it for a few more moments...

The tension clawing at the back of my neck said otherwise.

I kicked off my shoes before laying down the few bags of

groceries I was able to rescue off the street. Eyeing them, I pursed my lips. *Great.* I'd also have to explain what happened to the rest of our purchases.

I hit our recycled couch with a thud, and my hand found its way into my hair, releasing it from its drenched knot. My eyes still burned from the tears, and my knees thrummed with pain from my fall, but nothing came close to the guilt I felt for letting my pride get the best of me. And if I was being honest, that had been going on far longer than just this week.

A key turned in the door, and Osta peeked in, searching the room with trepidation. Her eyes widened as her gaze met mine. I sat up and pulled my legs into a crossed position on the couch. *Where to begin?*

"Osta, can we talk? I really need to apologize to you," I murmured, trying to keep my voice level. Her eyes softened and she threw her head back, sighing, before leaning against the creaking door frame.

"Do you know how nervous I've been to come home? After I stormed off, I started thinking about everything, and I felt so terrible, Fia. I shouldn't pu–"

"Osta," I interrupted, shaking my head. "There's no reason for you to feel bad. I'm the one who needs to apologize... You were right. About everything."

Her eyes flickered with surprise, and then amusement. A smile crept up her lips.

"Did you just say I was right? About everything?" She teased, finally walking over to sit on the couch.

"I know, they're novel words coming from me." I attempted a smile, feeling heavy. There was still so much to unload.

I spent the next hour recalling the events of the evening to Osta. She hung on my words as I told her about the group I'd nearly exploded on and my moment of revelation on the pavement. How relief flooded me once I realized no one was around to witness what surely looked like an insane person losing their grip on reality.

It really wasn't too far off.

"I mean, they did destroy a good portion of our paycheck. I wouldn't have blamed you if you had shredded their minds," she joked, playing with her hair.

I shot her a serious look, but a small laugh escaped my lips. We both leaned back into the couch as she reached over to hook her arm with mine.

I sighed. Osta always knew how to bring light to even the most dire of situations. It was one of my favorite things about her. Well, when it wasn't being used against me.

"So... you're really going to do it then? Take the General up on his offer?" She eyed me curiously.

"I mean, I'd rather skin myself alive than be anywhere near him, but I'm afraid I don't have much of a choice. It wasn't exactly an offer, either. More of a threat..." I trailed off. "Maybe it won't work, and I'll be eating my words in a few weeks, but I think I have to try. I can't just run away from this." I shrugged, twisting my lips.

Osta looked down. "So, you *were* going to run?" she asked, her eyes taking on a glassy sheen.

"I really thought it was the best option... but don't worry. I'm not going anywhere. I guess if it all goes badly, you could visit me in prison."

She nudged me. "You're not going to end up in prison. I think you're really going to do it. Learn how to control this."

I wished I could share in her optimism, but I was built differently. Conditioned to assume the worst.

"I'm proud of you, you know," she murmured. "And I'll always be here for you. Anything you need."

She always was. I gripped her arm tighter and nodded.

"Even if we have to make the General's portrait into our new dart board, I'm along for the ride," Osta promised.

We both laughed. It was nice spending a few normal minutes together. I wondered how many more of them we would have.

I TOOK a shaky step onto the cobblestone path, eyeing the card that General Ashford had left behind. I knew the street, everyone did. It was where the Sídhe Guard held residence in Luminaria.

But just because I knew the location did not mean I'd ever ventured anywhere near it. In fact, avoiding it was one of my favorite pastimes.

Now I was headed there willingly. Hesitant, but willingly. I was trying to take a page out of Osta's book and look on the bright side. After all, it wasn't every day you got to sell your soul to the very institution that destroyed your homeland, killed your parents, and branded you a child of the Rebellion.

My jaw twisted.

I was still working on it.

As I trudged through the busy streets, my dream from last night slipped into my thoughts. It was another odd sequence of events–not horrific or traumatizing, just strange.

I was moving quickly through dense fog. Twisted vines snaked across the muddy earth. They disappeared behind me as I floated through the void.

Two glowing golden eyes finally met my gaze, obscured by the mist. They stayed locked on me before disappearing again into the darkness. I tried to follow them, but they were too fast.

And then I woke up.

Either my subconscious was taking it easy on me, or it had run out of material.

I neared the familiar edge of the Western district, heart fluttering as I turned down a street I had never set foot on. I let my gaze wander up. The architecture looked similar enough to the rest of Luminaria–vines cascading over stone buildings, moss spattering the cobblestone.

But as I focused on the view ahead, everything became more structured, more orderly. Nature faded out, revealing the enormous assortment of towers that made up the Sídhe Guard Compound. The streets were crawling with armored and uniformed soldiers milling about and talking amongst themselves. The sheer amount of emerald-encrusted serpents was nauseating. I tucked my head down and quickened my pace.

For Esprithe sake.

My strides became less confident as I neared the looming monstrosity of the Compound. The encroaching structures were carved into dark stone, and gilded edges adorned the exterior. The Sídhe Guard insignia was sprawled across the front in roaring shades of gold. The General's card stated that I should take the exterior entrance, the one that would bring me directly to his office. I glanced down the street that lined the eastern side, identifying the giant staircase indicated in his directions. Begrudgingly, I made my way to the ramp, careful not to bring too much attention to myself. The idea of being here was turning my stomach in knots.

The metal stairs absorbed my steps, leaving me in an eerie silence. I put one foot in front of the other, trying to shut my brain off. If I thought too hard about what I was about to do, I might turn around.

As I climbed to the second level, I found an iron door. *General Laryk Ashford* was etched into the front with gilded lettering.

Taking a deep breath, I shook off the nerves that had grown increasingly noticeable throughout the journey here. Before I could change my mind, I reached out and slung the heavy door knocker three times. There was no backing out now.

I waited. And waited. Maybe he wasn't even here today. It was the weekend after all…

I had just put myself through the misery of this trek for nothing. Annoyance flooded me as I turned around.

Then I heard what sounded like shuffling inside, followed by a woman's laughter. Almost immediately after, the door opened with a metallic screech. Out stepped General Laryk Ashford in all his pompous glory.

His copper hair was untamed, cascading down his chest and catching in the breeze. A disheveled black shirt laid open, revealing the chiseled contours of his abdomen. His trousers looked haphazardly buttoned. My eyes drifted down…

Dear Conleth. What had I interrupted? I might as well have come by last night.

A flush of shame spread across my face.

His emerald gaze locked on me. He didn't even try to hide the smirk forming on his lips.

He leaned back against the doorframe and crossed his arms, cocking his head to the side in what I assumed was supposed to resemble feigned shock.

"You've arrived sooner than expected, and on a weekend, no less. I trust there hasn't been another incident." The General looked towards the street, aloof. "I assume you're here to accept my proposition," he murmured. "It's a wise choice."

This was shaping up to be even more difficult than I had anticipated. I released a heavy sigh, mentally urging myself to stick to my promise to Osta and remain amiable. I tried to summon a kind smile, though it likely came across as a grimace.

"I see we haven't yet lost the attitude. Perhaps that will be our first lesson." He sighed, irritation creeping into his voice.

"Good luck." My eyes widened. I hadn't meant to say that out loud.

"Yes. That's going to be a problem."

CHAPTER 10

THE GENERAL CAST a glance inside his quarters, tilting his head as though signaling someone to leave. An attempt at an apologetic grin graced his face, though it appeared awkward and unfamiliar, as if rarely employed.

Seconds later, a brunette skipped out, kissing him on the cheek and making sure to shoot me a look of contempt as she breezed past.

I returned the sentiment with the same smile that I had afforded the General. Her eyes narrowed even more as she approached the stairs.

It occurred to me that perhaps some practice perfecting my facial expressions would be handy going forward.

It appeared the General could benefit from a few lessons as well.

"Are you here to guard my door?" His words cut through my train of thought. He leaned against the doorframe, shirt flowing in the breeze. I narrowly avoided eye contact with his midsection. Finally, he let out a loud sigh before sauntering back into his office, leaving the door open behind him.

"Do you want me to close this?" I questioned, following him inside. He waved his hand as he walked away.

Is that a yes?

Esprithe, he was rude. I showed up, presenting myself on a silver platter, and this is how he wanted to behave?

With all the petulance of a child.

Why was I not surprised? Wealth practically dripped off him. No doubt he grew up on some massive estate with doting parents and access to anything his rotten little heart desired. We were worlds apart, that was glaringly obvious. Expecting civility from someone who'd never known struggle, never understood isolation, was foolish. And dangerous.

A predator. That's what he really was. If I was going to survive this, that truth needed to sink into my bones so far that I never forgot it. Any other behavior from him was a lie, just another part of the glittering facade.

The man who stood before me, who gawked and scoffed and nearly stomped his feet, who wove deceit into his goodbyes, and threatened Osta, and blackmailed me–that was the General.

That was Laryk Ashford.

Gritting my teeth, I turned and pushed the heavy door shut with a screech.

"I'm going to change. Don't touch anything." He wandered around the corner.

The space was massive with walls resembling pavement, coarse and textured in shades of gray. They seemed to go on forever before finally meeting the high ceiling, adorned with massive wooden beams.

The office itself was enormous. To the left, a desk of dark mahogany dominated the space. Its sleek surface, devoid of character or personality, bore the weight of neatly arranged documents and a precisely aligned set of writing tools. Sprawled out on the back of his desk chair lay a black coat, the upper part lined with badges.

The opposite side of the room housed a seating area. Low-slung furniture sat upon a cowskin rug, upholstered in subdued fabrics of charcoal velvet and muted leather. It was oddly organized. Almost uncomfortably organized.

Like a sociopath lived there.

I eyed the leather sofas across the expanse. It looked as if they had never been used… no creases, no indentions. My eyes threatened to roll. All this space, and he didn't even appreciate it. Some of us had to scrape couches up off the street. Because in no world did I allow Osta or I to take a single gold from the royal delegation —the program that provided assistance to lower classes throughout the realm. These people already thought we owed them something. I wouldn't let it be true.

Annoyance, perhaps even curiosity, pulled me closer. He said not to touch anything, but he never told me not to make myself comfortable. I sat awkwardly, shifting my weight on the firm leather. It offered little give.

Maybe comfort wasn't the goal.

The General strode back into the room without giving me a second glance. His disheveled look was now replaced by a structured black shirt and gray trousers. Everything was buttoned this time, fortunately.

His hair was pulled tightly behind his head and his scar seemed darker this morning. Sitting down across from me, he laced up his brown boots in silence, like he'd forgotten I was there. Like my presence was simply an afterthought.

"We have some salve at the Apothecary that might help with your scar," I said, trying to lessen the tension.

He looked up, surprise flickering across his eyes as he finished lacing his left boot.

It was annoying how good-looking he was.

"I appreciate your concern, truly." He smirked. "But I'm afraid there's not much that can cure this type of laceration." Leaning back in his chair, he studied me, shifting the energy in the room.

Silence engulfed the air as his eyes bore into me, like he was searching for something in the curves of my face. A familiar heat crept across my skin, threatening to expose my discomfort. But I fought it back with vengeance. In no way was I going to show him anything that could be interpreted as weakness.

An eternity passed before he furrowed his brow and shook off whatever he was thinking about. "So, I figured we could start with three days a week. I've reserved a private gym for us near your work. It–"

"I haven't agreed to your proposition yet," I lied. Again, I hadn't meant to say it out loud, but the man clearly brought out the worst in me.

I expected to see anger in his eyes, but they stayed emotionless, serpentine, like my boldness had disturbed nothing within him.

"As I was saying, it shouldn't interfere with your job at the Apothecary. At least our initial training shouldn't. You can meet me in the evenings. Every other day should be sufficient. Excluding weekends. I'm sure your social life is titillating," he said.

I fought back the urge to narrow my own eyes. His arrogance knew no bounds. My back hit the cold leather, as I attempted to settle into the rigid sofa, but it felt wrong. All of this felt wrong.

"I can make that work. My tone was neutral, but anxiety speckled rage continued to churn in my gut.

"Fantastic. And just so that you're aware, this training is technically unofficial. You won't need to move into the Compound until you reach initiate status." He looked me over. "You won't even join the Guard as a recruit until we've mastered control over your focus. Which we will."

"How can you be so sure?" I asked, leaning forward onto my knees.

"Because I know what I'm doing. You're not the first reckless cadet I've had the pleasure of training." He sat back in his chair, crossing his arms as another one of his smirks played at his lips.

I forced my head into a nod, turning my attention to the corner of the room. I'd let him win the battle today.

"I have a special way with people. I know what makes them tick. I'll figure out your blockages and we will remove them. Any further questions?" His voice was clipped.

"I think you just about answered them all."

Tension brewed, crackling in the air between us like a storm about to burst. Whatever he was thinking was a mystery, but his eyes had a way of scanning me like he knew my greatest fears, like he knew how much I loathed being seen. I couldn't hide here. Sitting in this Compound was like waiting for a dragon in his own lair. I wondered if he could read it on my face.

"Well, now that we've ironed out all of the details, I'll walk you out," he said, breaking the deafening silence that threatened to pull me under. He walked over to the desk, retrieving his coat and a stack of papers.

That was quick, simple, apart from his suffocating presence. Relief passed over me as I stood, making my way back to the door, perhaps a bit too quickly.

"This way," he called as he neared a different door on the opposite side of the room. Shivers ran down my spine. I stood motionless.

Huh?

"I was going to show you through the Compound. Aren't you eager to see what your future looks like?" He chided.

I truly wasn't.

My mind briefly considered bolting out the exterior door, but I found myself trudging over to him. I sighed heavily, audibly. Civility was the goal today, but my strength was being greatly tested. Insulting him with my breath was the least I could do to stay true to my heart.

He handed me the stack of papers. "Some light reading." He smirked and pulled the door open, "After you." He motioned for me to walk ahead. I hesitated as I had before in the greenhouse.

"Do you have some aversion to doorways? Go on." He scoffed and tapped the back of my boots with his own, causing me to stumble forward.

Prick.

My heart was racing as I stepped onto a balcony overlooking the Compound below. Staircases were fixed in each corner, traveling all the way to the top floor. The walls were dark charcoal, much like the General's quarters. Down below, the space was vast, stretching out through the entirety of the block.

Tables rested in uniform lines throughout the mess hall, overrun with members of the Guard socializing, eating, studying. I noted a closed off section to the right.

He must have noticed my gaze wandering. "Those are the on-campus training gyms," he remarked.

My eyes widened, taking in just how many people were filtering through the expanse below. Eventually, this would be the place where I spent the majority of my time. It still didn't seem real.

"As I said before, you won't be training here any time soon. Don't start crying." He smiled wickedly before whispering, "I can't have you accidentally incinerating my guards, now can I?"

I shot him a look of contempt, but he was chuckling, clearly far too pleased with himself. One would have thought a General in the Guard would be more stoic. That would have been preferable.

My skin tingled at the feeling of his hand on my back, ushering me forward towards the staircase that led down to the social area. I lurched forward instinctively, getting out of range of his touch.

We made our way down the stairs, and he pointed for me to go left, a gesture that had me breathing a sigh of relief. The gates to the front entrance were just a few paces away.

"I'm actually off work tomorrow if you wanted to start earlier in the day," I mumbled, remembering what Ma had said. Sitting around and dreading this all day might just be worse than getting it over with.

He twisted his lips.

"Meet me in the morning, 9:00 sharp. And don't be late."

As the words left his mouth, my attention was drawn to the front gates, where a familiar face drifted towards me. Deadly blue eyes, golden hair. His armor bore the symbol of the Guard–emerald serpents winding up the chest plate, mirroring my growing horror. My mouth turned bitter. My muscles tightened. I couldn't breathe.

"Don't make me repeat myself," the General said with exasperation.

I couldn't move. All I could do was stare.

The General's gaze followed mine, confusion spreading over his face.

I had to get out of here.

"Yeah–I'll be there," I managed to mumble as I turned and hurried towards the gates.

It was the guard.

From the Dam.

The one who pulled the levers.

The one who killed my friends.

A burning began at the back of my eyes, blurring my vision. I broke into a sprint that didn't stop until I made it to the apartment, my back hitting the door as it slammed shut behind me. My heart continued to race as the fears came tumbling back.

My mind was in the Sprithe River, drowning somewhere beneath the current.

CHAPTER 11

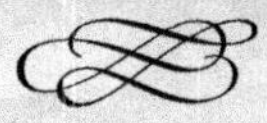

Tomorrow would mark the first day of Eibhlín, the phase of the year when cold began its descent into the realm and light disappeared from the sky earlier each day. My eyes were fighting ferociously to stay closed.

I had reviewed the paperwork General Ashford provided about the Guard and how it was structured. Important information, no doubt. But mind numbingly boring to read.

The Guard was divided into five distinct factions. Base was the foundation, made up of guards who policed the cities and maintained the infrastructure that supported the realm, manning forts, bridges and checkpoints between regions.

Next, there was Faction Immunity, the medics, who possessed the ability to heal in a variety of ways. Their focuses were invaluable in the aftermath of an attack, weaving enchantments and stitching wounds that most could not even attempt.

Then there was the combat triad. Faction Scales was made up of infantry guards, employing those with a focus that amplified strength and agility. They were the shield against invasion, the first line to absorb an oncoming attack.

Faction Fang was the artillery. Their focuses enhanced the effectiveness of ranged combat, holding down the major forts from an elevated angle, blasting canons and arrows with deadly precision.

The third in the triad was General Ashford's unit. They operated outside of typical protocol, and played by different rules. They were the secret weapon. The ones who went in for the final kill.

Faction Venom.

A uniform ranking system was the only thing that connected us to the different sections. Recruits ascended through the ranks, from initiate to officer, lieutenant, and finally, general, who answered directly to the King. But the last was reserved for a select few who possessed not only combat prowess but also the strategic sharpness to command armies.

Each faction was marked by a distinct shade from Sídhe's palette. Base was a deep, forest green. Immunity, a subtle blend of moss and beige. Scales was silver; and Fang, a burnished gold.

Venom, of course, was black.

I would wear black.

My thoughts shifted back to what was to come of the day.

The General was insufferable already… I couldn't even imagine the horrors that awaited me at the gym. Intuition told me his mind games would be in full swing.

Just get through this first day. Then you'll know what to expect.

Shaking off the anxiety, I stood and stared into the pantry, my vision unfocused, unsure if I could stomach anything this morning.

The compounding uncertainty was putting me on edge.

In less than an hour, I would be alone with the predator. A shudder ran through me as it sank in. He could kill me, and no one would ever know about it. There'd certainly be no repercussions.

But then he'd forfeit a potential weapon. That was keeping me alive, at least.

A Riftborne wouldn't survive long in the Guard. I'd never heard of one joining; it seemed sacrilegious. I was a mouse in a sea of serpents. If he wasn't the one to kill me, I'm sure someone else would find the opportunity far too tempting.

But spiraling was going to get me exactly nowhere.

Osta, bless her optimistic heart, had already left for work, leaving me to wrestle with my clothes. Yesterday, she showered me with good luck wishes, blissfully unaware of the dread churning in my gut. Mentioning the guard sighting felt pointless. I wouldn't burden her with my worries. Deep down, I knew it was coming, but seeing him there... It shook me more than I expected. I swallowed hard and forced myself to focus. Next time, I'd be ready.

The General hadn't specified anything that I needed to bring with me apart from myself. He also hadn't told me what to wear. Maybe it didn't matter.

What does one wear to mental gymnastics practice, anyway?

Sighing, I opted for fitted trousers–soft, stretchy and allowing for movement. A long-sleeve top of the same material hugged my shoulders.

All black. It felt appropriate. He seemed fond enough of the color.

I stole one last glance in the mirror, making a sorry attempt to tuck my loose curls back into their tie. Black really had a way of accentuating my... everything. A wave of self-consciousness washed over me, and I shifted uncomfortably, suddenly dissatisfied with my reflection. Pacing over to my makeshift closet, I yanked out a cloak and draped it over my shoulders before shuffling out of the apartment.

The meeting place was close to the Apothecary, which made finding my way easy enough. It was a private gym that I must have passed over a hundred times but had never paid any attention to.

My steps slowed as I neared the entrance. The outside of the building was lined with reflective glass. I'm sure that if he was inside looking out, he could see the reluctance in my approach.

This is for the best.

Tentatively, I pushed my way through the door. The General was, in fact, not actually gawking at me from behind the glass. His back was turned, giving me a view of his broad shoulders and the fiery copper hair he had pulled together with a strap of leather at the nape of his neck.

I cleared my throat.

"A moment," he said flatly, not even giving me the courtesy of turning around.

Jackass.

My eyes scanned the surroundings. It was a lot of what you'd expect to see in a gym–sparring mats, weights, machines that looked like advanced recreations of torture devices. Silver glass lined a full wall on the left.

Mirrors, perfect.

The citrusy aroma of cleaning products hung in the air, mingling with a touch of metallic sharpness. I paced the length of the room trying to look occupied, avoiding my reflection.

"I'm glad you made it on time, though that's an interesting outfit choice. Did you think we would be doing hand-to-hand combat?" The General glanced at me briefly, finally deigning to acknowledge my existence. He seemed amused.

A blush of embarrassment heated my face.

"You didn't exactly give me a dress code. I had absolutely no idea what to expect." My arms crossed instinctively, a small attempt at hiding my uncertainty.

The General was draped in his basic military uniform: a well-pressed, black, cotton shirt with the special insignia of his faction, trousers, a sturdy, unadorned belt to secure his waist. Black lace-up combat boots completed the ensemble.

"Your eagerness is endearing, truly," he remarked, brushing past me. "But today we're starting with the basics."

My eyebrow peaked. "And we do that, how?"

He pulled two chairs from the wall, bringing them to the center of the room to face each other, closer than I would have liked. He sat in one, his legs splaying out to either side before gesturing to the other.

"Sit."

I decided it best not to argue. I followed his demand and slithered past him, sinking into the chair while carefully avoiding physical contact.

Placing my hands onto my lap, I became acutely aware of his eyes on me. His stare was penetrative, bearing down with an annoying intensity. I did my best to keep my composure.

Beyond his glare, his proximity itself was unnerving, stifling out any confidence I had been clinging to since waking.

"Do you always look this exhausted? I figured you would at least do your part and attempt a good night's rest before today," he asserted before sighing and slumping a bit in his chair.

First my outfit, now this?

"Unfortunately for you, this is my permanent state. Doesn't matter how much rest I get." I glowered at him, painfully aware of the impression that my pale skin and dark circles gave off.

"Good to know." He yawned.

Such a beautiful face wasted on such a rotten personality.

His typical eerie amusement was gone, replaced with a calculating stare that had me shifting in my seat.

"Close your eyes," he instructed, sliding to the edge of the chair. He leaned forward and rested his forearms on his knees.

My eyelids seemed to be frozen. Was it really necessary for him to be this close? He could kill me in a second, with a single movement, and he expected me to trust him enough to close my damn eyes.

"I won't ask again." Impatience laced his tone.

There was a darkness in his irises now. I exhaled sharply and finally forced mine closed. But the nerves were still racing along my skin.

"Steady yourself. I can practically see your heartbeat in your throat."

How perceptive. I swallowed hard and took a deep breath, allowing myself to relax. Well, as much as I could given the situation.

"Your body is a conduit for your power. Think of where you feel it originate–the part of you from which it emerges. That will be your center. Visualize it happening and pay attention." His voice took on a calmer tone.

My eyebrows scrunched as I looked into the blackness of my mind, hoping to see some spark of... *something*. But all I could find was utter darkness.

"What do you see?" he asked quietly.

"The backs of my eyelids."

The sound of him shifting in his seat rang through the silence of the room. I didn't know what more to do. His instructions were vague and glaringly useless.

"Try harder." His voice was clipped. "Everyone has the ability to channel. Essence pulses through every fiber in the Isle, and that includes you..." He trailed off. "Your focus is the result of harnessing and directing that essence, manipulating it to serve you. Everyone has a different access point. We just have to find yours." He exhaled.

"Listen to your body. Seek out the source. It's in there somewhere." His voice was gentle now.

It seemed like I was missing some key factor. It wasn't long before I felt ridiculous staring into the endless void.

Was he just sitting there watching me struggle?

"What do you mean *listen to my body, seek out the source?* That doesn't even make sense. I have no idea what I'm looking for."

"Well, you know this feeling better than anyone. Think back to the first time you used your focus. How old were you? What did you feel?"

"It's not that simple." My eyes opened, locking with his.

I'd forgotten how close he was.

"As I've told you before, it's only happened when my emotions were at their peak. Usually, it feels like my whole body is pulsing, not just a singular point," I said, leaning back in my chair. "It's a rather overwhelming feeling, as I'm sure you can imagine. You saw it first-hand." I fought off an eye roll.

"You need to learn to access your focus while also being of sound mind. Trying to harness this in a heightened state will get you killed. The real enemy will take advantage of a distraction like that. Every. Single. Time. We have to get around it." *Real enemy?* Who was he kidding? Sídhe hadn't seen a *real* threat since the end of the Rebellion.

"I've never been able to do that–"

He raised his hand, cutting me off. "It's called training for a reason. Eyes closed."

Rolling my shoulders back, I tried to clear my mind, which was next to impossible. I closed my eyes and slid my hands under my legs, attempting to refocus.

"Take yourself back to those moments, walk yourself through what you were feeling, not emotionally, but physically."

I tried the exercise, but the memories I had of using my focus were shrouded in chaos and fear. It was all a jumbled blur.

He must have sensed my frustration. "Try focusing on your individual extremities. Don't overwhelm yourself with everything at once. Start with your hands. It could be a quick flash. Heat, electricity, static, light, a color in your mind, even. Think of it as a trigger point."

My attention shifted to my hands. I set them in my lap, palms upward. With my eyes still closed, I began to visualize them, feeling for any pulses or heat. Nothing.

"I don't think it's my hands," I mumbled, more to myself.

"It's been less than two minutes, Fia," he deadpanned.

This is going to be an excruciatingly long day.

An eternity passed with no progress. Mastery in a day was

never my anticipation, but I'd hoped for some sort of advancement. If anything, today reinforced the notion that this endeavor was likely a colossal waste of time for all parties involved.

I'd tried zoning in on my damned pinky toe for half an hour.

By the time the General glanced at the clock and realized we'd been at this for four hours, his frustration mirrored my own.

"Unfortunately, we have to call it a day. I have a meeting soon that I need to begin preparing for." His chair legs screeched against the floor and my eyes snapped open. He rolled his neck and shoulders.

"This was fun and all, but please tell me you have alternative plans moving forward?" I questioned.

His jaw twitched, but he stood still, staring straight ahead.

"Yes, well I'm hoping you'll try harder next time," he said flatly, turning towards the door. He didn't give me a second glance before sauntering off.

I shot up from the chair, taking long strides to catch up to him.

"Still so sure this isn't a huge waste of time?" I chided.

"I'll see you the day after next. The second day of Eibhlín, if I'm not mistaken." The General stepped aside and held the door open for me. I sighed, brushing past him.

"Can't wait." I could barely contain my sarcasm.

I didn't dare look back as I stomped off in the direction of the apartment. The last four hours and my lack of progress would surely be running on repeat in my mind for the remainder of the afternoon.

The General's presence might have been the problem. How could anyone focus with such asinine prompts?

I could have sworn the weight of his gaze lingered on me until I reached the peak of the hill.

CHAPTER 12

I DODGED the uneven cobblestones at a slower pace than usual today, eyes darting ahead, taking in the familiar arches of the Apothecary in the distance. I had finally worked up the courage to leave the apartment and head into work for the day, but only after stalling as much as possible.

Wandering through the city, I chose to take the longer route, justifying my apprehension by convincing myself that Ma's well-being was my main concern. That it wasn't just my anxiety getting in the way.

A part of me was disappointed in myself. I wasn't sure how Ma would react to my new extracurricular activity, but keeping it a secret felt pointless. If General Ashford was right, I'd be joining the Guard at some point and leaving the job I'd loved for six years–a place that felt more like a second home than work. I had to tell Ma, and it had to be now.

A knot formed in my stomach. I yearned for a reaction like Osta's–a sigh of relief, a newfound freedom to express her anxieties about me and the danger that lived within. But my hope was dwindling. We were too much alike for me to entertain such unlikely outcomes.

To Ma, the Guard was the ultimate evil. She rarely spoke of her family, estranged for reasons I never fully grasped. But through snippets over time, I'd pieced a few things together.

Ma had a twin named Miguel. The two were inseparable until the Guard snatched him away at seventeen. She watched the light fade from his eyes as he became a shell of his former self, consumed by ambition.

While their parents reveled in his success, Ma grieved the loss of her brother long before he died in combat. Unlike the rest of Sídhe, she didn't blame Riftdremar. Her hatred festered for the Guard itself, a constant reminder of what it had taken from her.

Ma's questions had probably tripled since the last time she saw me. I couldn't divulge the entire truth... just enough for her to understand.

I buried the pang of guilt that threatened to turn me around. With a deep breath and a simple prayer, I pushed open the door and walked inside.

Ma was restocking our herbal teas near the front desk. The chime of the bell gave me away as the door closed. Ma's eyes shot up in attention, softening once she realized it was me.

"Fia! I'm so relieved. I feel like I haven't seen you in three days," Ma teased with feigned exasperation.

"Well, that would make sense, considering it's been exactly three days since I last saw you." A smile broke across my face as I approached the desk, pushing myself up to sit on it. "So, how was your trip to the Scarlet Coast?"

Ma put down her crate, dusting off her hands before leaning against the shelf.

"The travel itself was excruciating. Base Guards had set up checkpoints on nearly every main road out of Luminaria. Such a pain to get through." She shook her head.

Sídhe hadn't experienced a serious threat for twenty years,

since the end of the Rebellion that rendered Riftdremar a wasteland. Although the actual fighting hadn't gone on for long, it was devastating to the small country East of Sídhe. When powerful focuses go to war against one another, there's not many outcomes other than total and overwhelming destruction.

Sídhe burned Riftdremar into oblivion.

Though I hadn't heard of Sídhe facing anything new, the Guard's proximity to the city did make me wonder. And there was the matter of the General's scar. I had never seen a wound like that. One would think healers could cure it. Or perhaps the alterationists that could change appearances.

Then again, I could imagine him drawing it on every morning for attention.

"Fia, did you hear me?" Ma questioned, raising an eyebrow.

"Ah–yes, sorry. I was just wondering about the checkpoints. Any idea what they're doing?" I asked with a bit too much enthusiasm. Her eyebrow raised further.

"No idea. Inciting fear like they always do?" She sighed, pointing towards the rear of the shop. "But once I finally arrived at the coast, I was able to collect a good bit of that Red Algae. It's in the back, ready to be unloaded. The fish around it behaved so strangely, like they were moving slower than normal, and the water seemed eerily still. I can't wait to study it." Ma rubbed her palms together as eagerness flickered in her eyes.

"Well, I'm glad to hear it. I'll just head on back and start unloading it," I chirped, pushing myself off the desk in a hurry.

"Ah, Fia. Not so fast." Ma narrowed her eyes at me. "Don't think you're getting off that easily. We still need to discuss what happened last week." She crossed her arms.

"Right–about that," I mumbled, crawling back onto the desk.

"I know that Osta is a brave little thing, but neither one of you should be getting anywhere near a party like that," she scolded. "Now tell me why there was a Sídhe General in my shop the other night." She pursed her lips and leaned against the counter.

"I met General Ashford at the Grove, during the party..." I tried to figure out exactly what I should say.

"You casually met a Sídhe General at an enormous social event crawling with all the people you typically avoid and struck up a conversation? Really, Fia. You?" She shook her head and let out a laugh that showed me she wasn't buying it. *Great.*

"Not exactly..." I gulped, racking my brain. Ideas of what to say to her had been racing through my mind. All. Damn. Morning. But upon arriving, my thoughts were absolutely scrambled.

"I nearly collapsed when Eron told me you went by yourself. You know I don't condone violence, but a part of me wanted to slap him right then and there. It's his job to make the deliveries. *He* can get out of a dangerous situation quickly if he needs to."

"Jaquelina went into labor. What was I supposed to do? It's not like I went to socialize. I only went to drop off the crate of tonics, truly. But of course, Osta noticed me there, and begged me to stay." I ran my hand through my hair and rolled my eyes. "I didn't want to, but she insisted. So, I promised her I would have a single drink with her after she got a closer look at the King and Queen." I winced. So far, it was the truth, but it all felt like lies leaving my lips.

"She made a loop around the party, and I decided to wander up the hill to cool off a bit. I guess I had gotten a bit... overstimulated." I bit my lip.

Ma's eyes widened.

"Overstimulated?" she asked, cheeks flushing.

I took a deep breath, "Not like that, Ma. It had been such a long day. I was more than exhausted. And you know how I get nervous around crowds..." I glanced up, gauging her reaction. Her face remained calm, but I could see sparks of concern in her eyes.

"Anyway... I guess I started to... well, channel a bit. General Ashford happened to see me when it occurred. He was curious about my abilities. Well, I mean, he called it my focus, which is hilarious," I rambled on, praying that I could distract her with erroneous details.

Maybe then she wouldn't ask me specifics. So far, I hadn't exactly lied, but the most important parts of the story had certainly been redacted. I shifted on the desk.

Ma stared at me, open-mouthed. "You... You used your... erm, powers... in front of the General?"

This was a subject we never dared broach. I stole a glance at her, expecting to see the beginnings of terror forming in her eyes, but she just looked concerned.

"Not exactly. I just felt like I might. Like I was slipping a bit. He saw me in a state of... well, it wasn't my best moment. I'm sure I looked like a basket case, but he made me an offer..." I trailed off, nerves getting the best of me.

"He what?" she shot back, a little too forcefully. I didn't know where her mind was going, but I needed to divert it.

"He offered to train me. To control my... whatever this is."

Ma sat in silent contemplation.

"He wants to help you control it? Out of the kindness of his heart? That sounds a bit preposterous." Ma's expression was drenched with skepticism.

"Not exactly. He offered to train me so that I could become a part of his faction. I guess he thinks I could be an asset to the Guard."

Ma's eyes went up in flames, literally. Fire seethed through her. *Oh Esprithe, here we go...*

"The nerve. These fucking bastards think they can just control everything around them. It makes me sick." She shook her head, "Is that why he showed up the other night?"

I paused.

"Well, he showed up to offer me the proposition. The night at the party... Well, I mean. We didn't have much of an actual conversion. After it happened, I was pretty on edge. I really just wanted to get out of there."

Ma studied me.

"So how did he react when you told him no?" She softened her tone, chuckling a bit. "I would have paid good money to see the look on his face when you humbled him. Did he–"

"I told him yes..." I blurted. The blood drained from my face.

Ma looked at me in horror. I couldn't blame her. This reaction was to be expected. Her hatred for the Guard was unwavering.

"You did what?" she asked, her voice breaking slightly. My heart sank.

"Ma... I know it sounds crazy. I know it's hard to understand... I mean, I would have never thought I could agree to something like this. It doesn't even sound like me, but we both know..." I gave her a knowing look, "We both know how dangerous it can be when I lose control. If there is a way to stop it from happening, I have to try. I have to. I can't risk hurting anyone else." Mist formed in my eyes.

"But you've made such progress on your own, Fia. You haven't had an incident since... you know."

I winced. There was so much I had held back from her.

"It hasn't been easy, Ma. I hope you can find a way to understand."

Ma opened her mouth like she was going to respond, but ultimately closed it, wandering off to the stool on the opposite side of the desk. She sank down, letting her face fall into her hands. We sat in silence.

"I understand what you're saying Fia but there has to be another way. You don't have to sign your life away. Not to *them*," she stated.

"Ma, I already live life like I've signed it away," I whispered, feeling the weight of those words for the first time.

Ma just looked at me. I knew she was trying to think of something to say, an argument that would change my mind.

Eventually, she took a deep breath and stood.

"You can place the algae specimens in the jars near the sink. I already sterilized them. Don't forget the labels," she said quietly.

Leaving the desk behind, I crossed the room to her side, offering a comforting squeeze to her shoulder. I considered saying something else but found myself at a loss for words. I managed a faint smile before heading toward the back of the shop.

I had finally told her a version of the truth, and that brought a sense of relief, but my heart still felt heavy, empty. The conflict wasn't over.

But if that woman was anything, she was relentless. She would be racking her brain for a way out of this. Ma wasn't going to surrender that easily.

CHAPTER 13

THIS WEEK *really* needed to end.

The last two had trudged by with all the speed of a snail on sedatives. I'd managed to make exactly *zero progress* in my training sessions with the General.

He just rambled on with his nonsense, speaking like some kind of monk, who could navigate the inner workings of my mind if I *could only concentrate,* or if I *could only seek out the source of my focus.* And there was me. Sitting like a vegetable, not feeling a single spark of energy or a single pulse of essence.

The urge to strangle one another by the end of each session had become palpable.

My mornings at the Apothecary hadn't given me much respite with the not-so-subtle glances from Ma and the stifling feeling of words left unspoken.

I had been overjoyed when Eron stopped by for a visit–all the attention shifting to his new fatherhood.

"I'm shocked to see that you're alive after the reaction from Ma the other day. I'd have thought something seriously awful happened to you." Eron smiled as he approached my desk and handed me a few parcels.

"Well, as you can see, I'm in one piece." I held my arms out to the side and shrugged.

Ma shot him a narrowed look and Eron let out a chuckle.

"Anything exciting in there?" He asked as I fumbled through the packages.

"Actually, there is, Ma, those bark samples you ordered finally came in!" I called out, hoping to see some semblance of joy light up her face.

"Oh good. Took them long enough." She huffed, face unchanging. I sat back in my seat and sighed.

"I'll just need you to sign for those," Eron said as he reached out to hand me a piece of parchment. The sleeve of his shirt shifted, revealing his Riftborne branding. My eyes lingered on it momentarily. Osta always kept hers hidden, so I was used to only seeing my own.

Eron cleared his throat and readjusted his sleeve, giving me a slight smile. I took a deep breath and signed Ma's name to the paperwork before handing it back to him.

Eron and Jacquelina were in the group of children brought to Luminaria after the squashed Rebellion. Eron was ten when the uprising came to its tumultuous end. Jacquelina was seven. They were the oldest kids in our shared group home with the Fairbanks, the youngest two being Osta, who was a mere infant, and a three-year-old me.

Eron invited Osta and I to dinner that upcoming weekend, so we could see Jacquelina and the newborn. I readily accepted for both of us, knowing Osta would never pass up the opportunity to meet a baby. Plus, she had always been closer with the couple. I had drifted apart from everyone except for Osta after what happened at the river.

After seeing Eron, I found myself back at mental torture practice. And today, the General seemed less amused than ever. At least there were no more pretenses. Now, we just simmered in our complete and unadulterated loathing for each other.

It was honest.

I could tell that whatever patience he had mustered for the day was hanging on by a thread.

"What is your focus anyways?" I asked, my lack of patience a rival to his own.

"That knowledge is above your paygrade," he replied flatly.

"I'm not being paid for this."

"My point exactly. Enough with the questions. I'm about at my wit's end. And I'd prefer to actually make some progress today," he snapped, annoyance etching into his forehead.

I closed my eyes, attempting to concentrate a few seconds more before I groaned, slumping down into my seat. This was an endless, pointless cycle. I clicked my teeth.

The room became suddenly cold and silent. I could tell by the look on his face that he was deep in thought, and it didn't seem like it was going to end well for me.

"You know, if I hadn't seen what you did in the Grove, I wouldn't think you had even a *speck* of power in you. I see nothing of value. I can't even *sense* it," he stated, a newfound harshness in his tone had my eyes flying open. My body snapped to full attention as a mix of anger and shame flushed my cheeks.

I knew I was a lost cause, but hearing it from the mouth of the man who just last week had been so sure he could fix me... well, it didn't feel great. I slowly shifted my gaze to the mirror, straightening as I saw my defeated posture, my arms wrapped around my middle. Like I was hiding.

I leaned back and crossed my arms. If he was going there, I'd meet him halfway.

It was the least I could do.

"*I'm sorry,* but weren't you the one who tracked me down and all but forced me into these training sessions?"

"That was when I thought you'd at least put in a shred of *effort.*

Don't pretend you're trying, Fia. It's laughable." His voice was sharp, hacking its way through my already tense thoughts. Exasperation drenched his eyes.

"Maybe you're just not good at your job," I spat.

The General stared at me with a clenched jaw. He shifted back in his chair and exhaled slowly, calming himself and cracking his knuckles before running a hand through his hair.

"Your kind is always the most difficult to train." The cruel words on his lips were made all the more infuriating by his sudden calmness.

"You mean *Riftborne?*" I seethed, rising from my chair.

He stood abruptly, and I almost stumbled back. We were so close I could feel the heat radiating off him. I had to lift my chin to continue my glare. My blood began to simmer.

"No Fia. I'm talking about people who are too stubborn to help themselves. You're impossible. It's pathetic, really."

My fists clenched at my sides as I took a steadying breath. I wouldn't give him the satisfaction of knowing his words affected me so much. I wouldn't let this be the reason I lost control. It was a small act of defiance.

"I'm only here because you gave me no other choice." My words were laced with a special kind of loathing I reserved only for him.

He looked down at me coldly, his breathing slightly uneven. If he moved even an inch forward, he would be touching me, and I'd have an excuse to knock him on his ass.

I wondered if he could track my thoughts because he shifted his face to mine, only a breath away.

"If you want to keep up the disrespect, leave. We'll see what happens to you then." His voice was a growl.

My eyes narrowed. "You know what? I think I will leave. I'm done." I turned away quickly, desperate to escape his gaze.

Racing to the bench, I snatched my bag before storming towards the door, unable to bear another moment in this suffocating room.

"You're right. This was all a waste of time."

The finality of his words sunk in as I bolted into the cold, night air.

CHAPTER 14

"This ball is going to be the death of me," Osta groaned as she bounded into the living room, dropping garment bags and releasing her golden hair from its knot.

"I'm glad you're finally seeing reason," I murmured, toying with the cork from a vial on my apothecary belt.

"Well, it's not the ball itself. Just Thearna. You have no idea how many needle injuries I have right now. My hands look atrocious," Osta said, holding them up for inspection, a disgusted look forming on her face.

"You're being a little ridiculous, Osta. Your hands look fine." I attempted a small laugh despite my sour state.

"All of this better be worth it. Thearna promised she would try to bring me along with her, but she's still waiting on her own invitation to come." Osta plopped down next to me at the brown makeshift box we called a dining table.

"Osta, have we learned nothing? I don't even know why you would want to go to one of these things." I was being unfair, but I couldn't help it. Talking about the Tribute Ball made me think of the General, which gnawed at the growing pit in my stomach.

"You know I don't want to work under Thearna forever. I need to start building a client list. And events like these are my only way to make a name for myself. It's the only way I can show off my *own* designs," Osta asserted, placing her hands carefully on the chipped tabletop.

The Tribute Ball happened once a year and celebrated the advancements of the Guard. Well, at least that was the reason for its creation centuries ago. Now it was just an excuse for a party—another exclusive event that required a royal invitation. I couldn't understand why anyone would subject themselves to that kind of nightmare.

Surely, the General was frothing at the mouth for the attention such an event would bring him.

I winced at the thought. Even insulting him didn't bring the dark satisfaction that it used to.

"I just don't think it's safe, Osta. Especially after how everything ended with the General," I said, my tone just above a whisper. I glanced over at Osta as she popped a raisin into her mouth.

"If he was going to retaliate, I think he would have done it by now," she said, meeting my eyes. "It's been a week."

"Maybe."

I couldn't bring myself to believe that he was done with me.

"Oh my, have you seen the time?" She shrieked as I peered toward the window. The room had gotten dark, only illuminated by the muted rays of the setting sun.

"We need to get ready! Eron and Jacquelina are expecting us soon." Osta flew from her chair and ran to the hallway. "Don't worry, I picked out an outfit for you already," she chirped before skipping into her bedroom.

Hopefully the General wouldn't choose tonight to show up and arrest me.

Or kill me.

Or both.

I walked over to my bed, eyeing the outfit that Osta had so

kindly chosen. The simplicity of it could only mean one thing. She was taking it easy on me. I smiled.

Usually, Osta would take this opportunity to style me, and run with it, hoping to persuade me into one of her more adventurous designs. I had almost fallen into that trap one too many times.

Sighing, I lifted the pale green dress off the bed. With its long sleeves, modest neckline, and flowing knee-length skirt, it was a thoughtful choice. I promised myself to thank her for it later.

Shedding my work clothes, I slipped into the garment and made my way to my tiny desk, stealing a glance in the mirror. My curls framed my face in a wild halo. Groaning softly, I sank onto the stool.

After a few long moments of trying to slick the icy strands back into a neat bun, I gave up. It would just have to stay wild and unruly tonight. Not exactly waves, but not fully curled. It lived somewhere in the static-ridden middle.

I wandered to the living room and stepped into my brown flats. When I thought about the walk to Eron's I found myself wishing for a boat. The canals would prove a much faster route.

Eron lived at the end of the Central district, but it was still a long trek. We trudged off into the night, my arm linked with Osta's. Nerves crept in as I surveyed the busy street. I shuddered as a few wandering eyes fell upon us, pulling Osta along. Osta was oddly quiet, lost in her own thoughts. And I didn't want to be alone with mine anymore.

After half an hour, the gaps in the cobblestone told me we were nearing our destination. Our friends lived further out from the city center, where the rigid architecture of Luminaria faded into more simple dwellings.

Osta and I approached their small townhouse, eyeing the repairs that Eron had recently made to the exterior. It was quaint, but charming, with vines cascading down the front of ivory-painted wood.

Most of the buildings this far out were in various states of ruin, but with Eron working as a delivery man and Jacquelina opting to stay home with the newborn, the choices were limited. Eron worked his ass off, serving long hours and weekends, taking up extra shifts whenever he could just to make sure his family maintained some semblance of a comfortable existence.

Service work was really the only option for Riftborne. If you could find work in the first place. Jacquelina had tried for years to make it as a vocal instructor for kids, but no one would hire her. Before the baby, when the couple was trying to save as much coin as possible, she dressed in costume and sang on the street, accepting tips from generous passersby, keeping her Riftborne mark hidden carefully behind a glove.

Osta looked over, giving me a reassuring smile before knocking on the door. "Hey, just try not to think about it tonight. Let's have fun," she stated, observing my less-than-stellar mood. I shook my head, trying to dispel the disappointment from earlier.

"Don't worry. I plan on drowning my sorrows," I teased, forcing a smile.

"Okay, that's what I like to hear. About time you actually let loose," Osta replied before wincing, realizing the implication of her words.

"Well, maybe not around the baby..." she added, eyeing me gently.

My arm looped around her shoulder in reassurance.

"Don't worry, I'll be on my absolute best behavior," I said as the door flung open, revealing the familiar face of Jaquelina.

She had always been the most beautiful of the Riftborne kids that shared our group home. Her caramel skin glistened in the moonlight, exposing her delicate features. Raven-colored hair spiraled down her back in tight coils. My eyes traveled the length of her body, taking in her long violet gown that flowed out just above her ankles. There was no indication that she had given birth to a child just weeks ago.

"I'm so glad to see you two! It's been far too long." She gave us a welcoming smile and reached out to embrace us.

"It *has* been too long. I'm so happy you invited us over. Now step aside and let us meet that baby!" Osta cooed, bouncing on her heels and eagerly looking past Jacquelina into the house.

"Of course, come in!" She moved aside and Osta rushed past her. I smiled and stepped over the threshold.

"Fia, I haven't seen you wear your hair down like that since you were little. It's lovely. Really, it suits you so well," Jacquelina remarked, her voice like a melody.

"Ah–thanks." I tugged on one of my curls. "It absolutely wouldn't cooperate today."

"Well, that sounds about right. Just as stubborn as the head from which it grows." Her vibrant laugh echoed through the entrance. She nudged me with her elbow before closing the door.

I couldn't help but smile as she led me to the dining area. It was a simple room with walls the color of the sea. Candlelight shimmered through the space, revealing a wooden table set for four.

Osta's laughter and squeals reverberated through the house as she and Eron entered the room. Osta arms were wrapped around the newborn, her eyes already gleaming with adoration.

"Fia, meet Leila!" Osta said breathlessly. For a split second, I worried whether she was in too high a state to be holding a baby. I labored a smile and walked over, attempting to hide my hesitation.

"Hi Leila, it's nice to meet you." The words came out clumsily, and I looked around at Eron for approval. He just rolled his eyes and smiled.

"It's just a baby Fia. There's no need to recoil in terror."

Everyone laughed, including me. I had always been sort of awkward around children. I had no idea how to interact with them.

As Jacquelina put the final touches on dinner, I took the opportunity to practice my baby etiquette, attempting to join in with

Osta as she mused over features that absolutely came from Jacquelina and the golden flecked eyes that mirrored Eron's. I tried my best to mimic her sentiments, but it still felt so odd coming from my mouth. Luckily for me, the beginning of dinner marked Leila's bedtime.

Eron passed out glasses to everyone and filled them with wine the hue of garnet. I took a sip, letting the velvety liquid swirl in my mouth, tasting notes of vanilla, spices and winter berries. It warmed me instantly. It wasn't magically enhanced, like the wine from the Bloodthorne Highlands, but it would do the trick.

Jacquelina danced into the room with steaming platters of root vegetables and a tray of roasted quail that smelled of honey and herbs. My mouth watered. A home-cooked meal was a delicacy that Osta and I rarely experienced these days. We weren't the most talented chefs, so our diet revolved around baked potatoes, smoked sausage and fruit. We really needed to learn how to be better adults.

We finished dinner quickly and with little conversation, a testament to the quality of Jacquelina's expert cooking. The clatter of utensils and shuffling of footsteps filled the air as we cleared the table. Soon enough, all four of us were back in our seats with full glasses of wine. I had already begun to feel the effects of the alcohol giving way to tipsy grins. Osta quickly caught up, her voice adopting that extra octave of drama it tended to acquire any time she partook.

"Eron, I'll never forget the day you disappeared for the first time," Osta slurred as her laughter bounced around the room.

"It will forever be one of the most hilarious things I've ever experienced!" Jacquelina burst into giggles, almost knocking over her glass.

"Well, I'm happy to have provided you all with so much entertainment," Eron crooned. A crooked smile formed on his lips. "It was only mildly terrifying for me."

Osta smirked. "Yeah, Eron, none of us expected you to take a game of hide and seek so literally." She grabbed Jacquelina's elbow as she doubled over.

Jacq returned the sentiment, eyes widening. "How long did we search for him that day? Oh, it must have been hours!"

Eron grinned, shaking his head. "You all like to pretend I did it intentionally. I had no idea you couldn't see me."

"Eron, do you... erm, see where your invisibility comes from? Like, is there a specific place you access it from when you do it? A spark or–?" I interjected, my words tumbling over themselves.

Everyone cast a puzzled glance in my direction.

"Honestly, I just kind of do it... I mean, I guess I've never thought about it like that before," he mused, rubbing his chin. "Hold on." And just like that, Eron was gone.

"Fiiaaaaa!" Osta sang, folding her head down on the table. "Must you make all of the men disappear?"

I opened my mouth, but no words came. We all roared with laughter. After a few seconds, Eron returned.

"I think I feel it here first," he said, clutching the back of his shoulder. "It seems to fan out from there, but I'm not really sure what to look for. It just tingled a bit. Why do you ask?"

I bit my lip.

"No reason, I had just been... erm, talking to Ma about it and I was curious..." I mumbled. I couldn't imagine Eron and Jacquelina taking it well—the prospect of me joining the Guard. There was no point in telling them anyway. It was over. I wasn't sure why I even asked.

An awkward silence drifted through the room. I wasn't sure how much Osta had told the two of them about my focus. My ability to channel had always been a subject we avoided.

"Jacq, didn't you tell me you shared a similar focus with your mother?" Osta asked, changing the subject.

"Well, from what I can remember, yes. Although I think hers was a bit more advanced. Her voice wasn't just pretty, it could do… other things." Jacquelina shifted in her seat. Eron looked down.

"We were all so young when everything happened. There are a lot of details that we don't remember." Eron sighed. "Unfortunately, some of them will always be a mystery. It's not like there are any records we can learn from."

I glanced down the table at Osta. Her head rested on her shoulder and her eyes were glassy. We were bordering on a dangerous subject. Even in the group home, we rarely discussed the details of our previous lives. Not that we would have been allowed to anyway.

"I just wonder about them sometimes. Our parents." Osta's voice cracked. Eron and Jacquelina exchanged a quick glance of concern. Leila's distant cry cut through the tension. Eron stood to go check on her, and I took the opportunity to save us.

"That's probably our cue to leave. It's getting late," I murmured with a soft smile.

We said our goodbyes quickly. I hooked arms with Osta as we clumsily stumbled out onto the street. I could tell her mind was still in the dining room, awaiting a conversation that no one wanted to have.

We walked through the city, keeping each other's balance. It was eerily quiet. The night air felt cool against my flushed skin; the smell of smoke leaked from rooftops, mixing with the briny scent of the canals.

I felt Osta sigh as her shoulder slumped against mine.

"Fia, do you ever wonder what they were like?" she whispered. My heart took a dip. We were not in the right state of mind to talk about this now.

"Osta… you know how I feel about this," I said, hoping to shut her down gently. We hadn't had this conversation in a long time. "We can't wonder about that. You know it. There's no point."

"Yes, but I don't understand it. We don't remember ours at all.

Eron and Jacquelina remember bits, but they don't talk about it. We know nothing about them," Osta whimpered.

I sighed. "That's the thing. We have no way of knowing anything about them. It's best not to let your mind even go there. We'll never have the answers we want."

"But it's not fair... I know they were a part of the uprising. I just..." Osta trailed off, choking back the tears I knew were soon to come. "Every kid deserves to know who their parents were, even if those parents made mistakes."

Osta began to shake, and I wrapped my arm around her. We did deserve to know who we were before all of this. Who we would have been without the war. But anyone who could tell us had been annihilated. Only the children and their foggy memories remained.

"I know... we've been dealt a shitty hand." I tried to think of what Osta might say in a situation like this. Comforting people had never been one of my strong suits but comforting *her* in this situation was especially tricky. Osta rarely acknowledged the evil in this world, and even though it was irritating most of the time, her innate optimism was one of the only things that kept me afloat. The idea of ruining that part of her was unfathomable.

I could never tell her what I actually thought of this world—these people.

This nation would do what it needed to clean up its messiest atrocities and protect its image from any accusations of foul play, no matter the cost.

Riftdremar was to blame, along with every soul that existed on the small island to the east—the one now destroyed beyond repair, crumbling in decay and the skeletons of the people who once lived there. Our families.

I took a deep breath and nudged Osta's side as we walked through the dimly lit street.

"But look at all that you've accomplished despite our situation.

You're thriving, Osta. Regardless of who they were, I know that they'd be proud of you."

She hugged me, and we continued the rest of the walk in silence.

Upon returning home, Osta and I stumbled to our respective rooms for the night. I laid in bed, staring at the ceiling. Unwanted emotions began to creep in. My mind drifted to the General and our last training session, and the thoughts tumbled out, thick and drenched in wine.

I remembered the frustration on his face. I remembered our explosive argument. Our decision to stop training. He was right.

It had all been such a waste of time.

I wiped the salty edges of my eyes, attempting to calm myself. Crying wouldn't solve my problems.

I'd lived this long with no semblance of control. It was foolish to believe anything could change now. I saw nothing inside me that resembled what the General described. No spark, no tendril of light or static or electricity.

It was as if my focus didn't exist outside the confines of my rage.

The General had seen me for what I was–a lost cause. I couldn't blame him. How long could a General of Sídhe really wait with no progress, no improvement? I was sure his time was better spent elsewhere, actually accomplishing something.

But despite my resistance, a tiny seed had found its way into my mind. A seed that brought with it a glimmer of hope. And now that it had started rooting, I didn't know how to rid myself of it. It was a dangerous game, letting myself aspire to be anything other than what I was.

I blinked back the blur from my eyes.

For the first time in my life, I had actually allowed myself to wonder.

The tears started to fall. I quickly brushed them away with the sleeve of my dress.

You knew this would be the outcome, I reminded myself.

CHAPTER 15

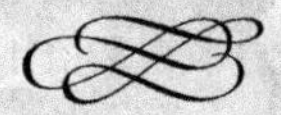

MA WAS GONE for the morning, so I took the opportunity to reorganize the shelves in the back of the Apothecary. The desire to tear them apart had been clawing at me for a while, but that wasn't the type of work that Ma prioritized.

Usually, we just flung our freshly distilled potions onto the shelves with little care. It took forever to restock anything with this routine.

I started by taking all the bottles down and dusting them. Some were well past their expiration date. I sighed. This was why we desperately needed a new system. The money and resources we would save just by putting things in some type of grouping would be a game changer.

Eyeing the cubbies to the left, a wave of exhaustion hit me. A pile of scattered stones sat haphazardly around the baskets meant to house them. I picked up a piece of amethyst, blowing dust into the air. I rubbed the surface against my apron until it reflected the light.

There were a few stones I couldn't identify. One in particular stood out. I was sure I'd never seen anything like it. It was stuck somewhere between a deep blue and violet, and shimmers of light ran through its center as if it was alive.

The bell on the front door chimed. A sliver of anxiety ran over me as Ma's footsteps approached. Things had been so tense between us lately. I hoped my morning project wouldn't push us further in that direction.

Her eyes narrowed as she took in the new setup.

"Fia, what have you done now?" Ma questioned, arching her brow at me.

"I did some *mild* organizing." I gulped. She didn't look happy. With a bit of hesitation, I strode over to the shelves and began explaining the new system.

"So I can't just throw the products back here anymore? I have to put them in their correct section?" She eyed me. Only Ma would have such an aversion to efficiency.

She walked around the shelves, inspecting them. I couldn't figure out what she was thinking.

"I guess it's not so bad. We probably should have done this a long time ago." She turned to me, rolling her eyes and giving me the smile I hadn't seen in weeks.

A wave of relief washed over me.

"So you like it?" I asked a bit too eagerly.

"Well, I didn't say that. But I understand the need for some structure around here. We all know it's not my strong suit." She walked over to her desk and sat down.

"I do have a question, actually," I said, following her.

"Hmm?"

"What is this? I've never seen it before." I held out my hand to reveal the mysterious blue-violet stone.

"It just came in yesterday, actually." She smiled and observed it proudly. "I've been trying to get my hands on a piece of it for some time. It's called arcanite."

"It looks as though it's alive." I held it up to the flame of a candle and peered through the lights that danced within. The sharp exterior refracted a kaleidoscope of colors onto the wall.

"It's very rare. Some think it's simply a conductor for essence. Or that it can store it. No one really knows for sure. But things seem to thrive around it."

"How does it work?" I asked. I'd never learned about this in school. I wondered where it came from.

"It's a bit of a mystery, but I have a few experiments in mind. I was going to bury one of the stones in a plant box in the greenhouse and see if it enhances the growth rate or yield."

"Interesting. We'll have to keep an eye on it." I gave her a slight smile and wandered back to my station. I hoped I'd be here long enough to see the effects, but part of me was hopeless.

Ma stayed silent for a while, rifling through some parchment. Eventually, she sighed and looked up at me.

"Listen Fia, I know things have been tense lately between us. I don't want you to think I'm upset with you. I've just been trying to process everything. You know how I feel about the Guard. After everything that happened with my brother… I mean, I won't lie, I'm a bit terrified–"

"No need to be. I'm not training with the General anymore," I interrupted her, desperate for things to go back to normal between us. I couldn't get there fast enough.

Her eyes widened.

"I–well, it just wasn't working out." I gave her a half-smile before looking down. A tinge of sadness tried to creep in, but I shook it off.

Ma just stared at me. I slid into my desk chair and leaned back, giving her a look of reassurance.

"Fia… I don't know what to say. You wanted to try. I get it. I think it was noble of you. I do…" She gave me a sympathetic look. "But selfishly, I'm so relieved that you've ended it. You have no idea how worried I have been about you. I don't trust him. There's something about the General that doesn't sit right with me. I don't think his intentions are good."

Ma leaned over the desk as her head shook. The lines of her face seemed softer.

"I understand. It was a mistake." I sighed. "I just want us to be okay again."

Ma nodded and smiled at me, letting me know that we were on the same page. The rest of the day breezed by in perfect monotony.

I SHUFFLED to the back of the shop, making sure the cauldrons were cooled before grabbing my bag. Ma was waiting for me in the front, leaning against the door frame and quietly humming to herself. For the first time in weeks, the tension in her posture was gone.

"Tell Osta to come by soon. It's been forever since she's pranced around the shop, distracting you from your work. I miss it." Ma chuckled. Things felt deliciously normal.

"I'll let her know. I'm sure she misses your relentless taunting just as much." I laughed and reached for the door. She nudged me playfully as we stepped outside.

The evening breeze had a crispness to it. I wrapped my arms around myself to keep the shivers at bay. Ma turned around to lock up. The sun was barely visible above the horizon and the street buzzed with city sounds as people made their trek home from work.

I glanced over to find Ma staring off to the left with narrowed eyes.

"Fia," was all she said.

My body flooded with fear. The General was walking towards us with his usual confident gate. The air froze in my lungs.

He wasn't wasting any more time, it seemed. But did he have to do this at this very fucking moment?

Esprithe sake.

I narrowed my eyes, feeling Ma's gaze on me. She couldn't see this.

I turned towards her, meeting her puzzled expression. "Ma, I'll take care of this. You should just head home," I said, but the words seemed to flow past her. Clearly, she intended on staying for whatever was about to take place.

I could kill him.

Maybe I should—a last act of defiance before accepting my fate. Something purred inside me at the thought.

I glared at him as he approached. He wore a long wool coat and his usual black attire. His eyes looked inquisitive and clever. But his face seemed… different?

"Good evening Fia, I hope you've been well," he said in his typical, velvety tone. "Maladea, it's nice to see you again." He nodded in her direction.

We both stayed silent.

He shifted his weight and looked down before crossing his arms. He looked nervous. Or like he was *trying* to look nervous. I wasn't sure.

What is going on?

"Fia, I'd really like to have a conversation with you." He glanced up, meeting my gaze with a sparkle in his eye and a soft smile. Forced charm didn't particularly suit him, but he sure was laying it on thick.

I scoffed. A part of me wanted to laugh at his performance.

"Fia, I know our last meeting ended badly. And I take responsibility for my part in that." His lips went rigid.

There it was.

A crack in the facade.

"So why are you here?" I asked, keeping my voice flat. Ma shot me a look of disapproval but stayed silent.

"I want us to try one more time. I think I've found an alternative approach. If this doesn't work, you never have to hear from me again. You have my word." He raised his hands as if to offer some sort of surrender.

I'd never hear from him again? It sounded too good to be true. I didn't believe it for a second.

"What is this different approach?" I questioned, crossing my arms.

"We can discuss that at the gym," he said plainly. His eyes stole a quick glance at Ma, who was still standing there, silently trying to hide her contempt.

"Nothing has worked so far." I tried to keep my voice level, but some of it came out with more ice than intended.

"Fia, just put your faith in me this one last time. You owe it to yourself to try. I know you want to learn to control this. And we can go now, just to get it over with. No waiting, no games. And I promise to be on my best behavior this time." He smiled.

My eyes narrowed.

Your promise means nothing.

The words echoed in my mind. I had drilled that truth deep into my bones. Never take him at his word. Always suspect an ulterior motive. The General's only priority was himself. This act couldn't fool me. I saw him for exactly what he was, what he had always been: a devastatingly beautiful serpent, just like the symbol that loomed upon every flag in this kingdom and every set of armor in the Guard.

Nothing had changed.

My eyes shifted to Ma, who was subtly shaking her head in disapproval. "Ma, you should go home. I–" I cut my eyes to the General, "I'm going to go with him and see what this miraculous plan is *before* I agree to anything."

She didn't know it, but I didn't exactly have a choice.

I turned back to Ma. If her sour expression was any indication, she was not buying any of this.

"I'll be fine. I promise. And I'll see you tomorrow." I gave her a quick hug, which she didn't return. She sighed and took off in the direction of her apartment.

I exhaled sharply. The man's timing was excruciating. He really couldn't wait until I was alone?

For Epsrithe fucking sake.

"Shall we?" he cooed, coming to stand beside me. As soon as Ma was out of sight, his demeanor snapped back to that of the General. The snake. We started towards the gym. Satisfaction seemed to radiate with every step he took.

As we approached the familiar reflective windows, my heart felt heavy. I had stormed out in such a rage the last time. He stopped and softly grabbed my arm, turning me towards him. I jerked away from the heat of his touch.

"Aren't we going inside?" I questioned, raising an eyebrow.

"Yes, but we need to talk first." His expression was serious now. "I know I've been hard on you and perhaps caused more frustration than encouragement. This is a new situation for me as well. I usually train people to enhance an ability they can already channel. It's been a bit of trial and error with you. I might have made some mistakes in my approach–"

"Just tell me what the plan is," I interrupted him. The man truly loved rambling, or maybe he just loved the sound of his own voice. I couldn't be sure.

"I need you to forget everything we've learned. Approach this with a fresh mind. Pay attention. Find your focus. That is the priority." His eyes locked with mine. There was no trace of the General I had come to know. The face staring back at me was devoid of the mystery that usually drenched his features.

"I need you to trust me." The intensity of his eyes made me want to believe him.

I paused, but eventually nodded. It's not like I could change my mind now.

He turned towards the door.

"Find it," he reminded me before pulling the handle and motioning for me to step inside.

This time, there was no hesitation. I walked straight past him and into the dimly lit gym. The door closed behind me. The General's footsteps were slow, measured. I glanced towards our practice area and froze. A chill ran over my entire body as I made eye contact with the blue-eyed guard from the dam.

CHAPTER 16

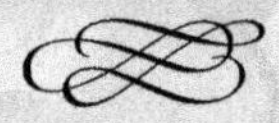

THE GUARD'S eyes darted between the two of us. Confusion and shock twisted in my stomach as I spun to face the General.

His attention was on the guard behind me. The softened eyes from earlier were gone, replaced by a callous glare. A sickening smile formed on his lips. My vision blurred with a mix of betrayal and anger, and my stomach threatened to retch as I opened my mouth to speak.

I followed his movements as he walked ahead, separating me from the guard.

"It took quite a bit of research to find the connection between the two of you. But once I did, it all became clear." The General turned slowly and gestured towards me. "I saw the way you reacted to him at the Compound. How intriguing, I thought. My mind went wild trying to imagine the circumstances in which you two would ever find yourselves in the same room."

I was going to be sick.

"When they delivered your records to my door, Jeremiah, I spent hours rifling through them, noting an incident at the river. It seemed innocuous at first, until I realized all of the deceased just so happen to be Riftborne." Heat rushed over my body. The sound of that name coming from his mouth made me want to vomit. The guard was paralyzed, and it didn't go unnoticed by the General. He smiled even wider, nodding with recognition.

"I knew this was the connection, but I was still missing details. How badly I wanted to unravel this. It really is so much fun playing detective." He shook his head, biting his lip.

I couldn't think straight.

"Then I looked into *your* file." He turned to meet my eyes again. "The ones who died... they shared a group home with you. The House of Unity." He gritted his teeth.

"So much clicked into place then. I understood. It was no surprise to me that the death of a few Riftborne would be swept under the rug. It happens all the time."

I couldn't breathe. My blood was boiling. I could feel my heartbeat radiating through my limbs.

"Fia, you were on the edge of the river, correct? With Osta. You both had to watch as your friends drowned." He spun around to the guard whose face was now drained of color.

"Did you know that she saw you?"

The guard stumbled forward. "General, please, I think there must have been some kind of misunderstand–"

The General's eyes went up in flames as he raised his hand, cutting off the guard. The pure power of his simple gesture reverberated through the room like a sound-wave.

"Do I detect subordination in your tone? Keep your mouth shut, officer," the General shouted, his words slick with a dark form of amusement.

The guard's eyes widened as he took a few steps backwards. The General slowly turned to face me. I glared back at him, fighting the urge to claw his face off with my bare hands.

"Fia, this man is the reason your friends are dead. He pulled the lever. You know this. If it weren't for his hatred and ignorance, Mairyen... Luka–"

"Don't you dare say their names," I spat, fury pulsing through my veins. My body was shaking.

The General moved towards me, slow and calculating. He stopped a few inches from my face and leaned in.

"Direct that rage towards the man who deserves it," he whispered, stepping to the side. The guard now stood in my direct line of sight. The General circled me, staying close enough for me to feel his breath on my neck.

"You have my full permission to punish him however you see fit." His voice was like razor blades. I was on the edge of control, and it was slipping with every passing second.

The General leaned in closer than ever. I felt his lips graze my ear.

"Let go, Fia."

And at that moment, time stood still. I felt the ringing in my head. The air around me crackled with energy. My vision went white. I fought the urge to lose myself completely, but time was running out. I was going to explode. A rush of static splintered across my skin.

Then I felt it.

The translucent web. I could see it in my mind. I felt it latch onto my spine and begin to braid itself up my vertebrae, sending pulses of energy into the surrounding cartilage. It knotted and twisted until it reached the base of my skull, and white hot light raced through me with a maddening force.

My eyes shot open just as the guard began to lift off the ground. The look of terror in his eyes ricocheted through my mind. He opened his mouth to scream, but I stole his voice. Waves of essence vibrated around him. I cocked my head to the side as the temptation to end him became stronger. I felt my power wrap around his mind. It would only take a few more seconds to liquify it…

But I didn't want to.

The revelation overcame my rage. Killing him wasn't important. He'd served his purpose. My elusive focus was found, and I could direct it.

Now how do I stop it?

I slammed my eyes shut and began to visualize that same force of energy, the web of translucent fibers that latched onto me only seconds ago. Clenching my fists, muscles straining, I felt a sharp thud as my knees hit the cold ground. Just as my mind felt like it would explode, the strands began to fray, untethering themselves from my bones. They crept down my spine, sinking back into their resting place, and the air around me went calm.

Reality returned, and I faltered, but managed to catch myself, planting a firm hand on the ground. Reluctantly, I opened my eyes to find the guard's face twisted in horror as he gasped for air. He was conscious.

Alive.

I exhaled in relief. A sudden heat from behind indicated the General had crouched down beside me.

"Impressive," he murmured. I looked away.

I couldn't process all of the feelings that were now tumbling through my already swirling mind. Overwhelming pride was at the forefront. I had done it. I had figured out where the access point was. But even more, I had channeled and controlled it.

I had won.

I didn't want to kill the blue-eyed guard. I knew he probably deserved death, but I had gained so much more than his blood on my hands.

General Ashford rose once again and strode over to the guard, his boots echoing in the tense silence. The man was a wreck, heaving and gasping, sweat slicking his face. His hand hovered over Ashford's outstretched arm, trembling before finally grasping it with a white-knuckled grip, allowing the General to bring him to a standing position.

"I really appreciate your cooperation tonight." I could hear the smile in the General's voice, and it sparked something within me.

Everything with this man was an act. And he'd gone too far tonight.

I wished pride was the only thing rushing through me at this moment. But there was a heaviness surrounding all that accomplishment–a feeling of betrayal and exploitation. I couldn't help wanting to have achieved this for myself, by myself, without being manipulated by the General once again. A dull pain gnawed at me in places I couldn't quite reach.

Ashford placed his hand on the back of the guard's armor and patted his shoulder.

"What happened at the dam was truly just a tragic accident. A matter of being in the wrong place at the wrong time," the General said, giving the guard a calculated smirk.

Nausea flooded my body once again.

The guard looked between us, confusion draining from his face. He finally turned back towards the General and reached out a hand. "Absolutely, a tragic accident."

Watching this for another second was going to break me in half. I wrapped my arms around my middle and closed my eyes, begging the tears not to surface. It shouldn't hurt like this. I had always known who he was. Manipulator. Predator. Liar–

A metallic clang shattered the room's stillness in an instant, the sound of a sword unsheathing. I jerked my eyes towards the two men just as the scratch of a blade hitting hard metal rang through the room. It wasn't a clean slice, but a brutal spear straight into the heart. The blade sank deep, a sickening thud echoing as it met flesh. The guard's gasp choked into a strangled gurgle.

My own breath caught in my throat before it could reach my lungs. A crimson arc erupted from the wound, through the mesh armor, splattering against my work uniform, and tinging the ends of my white curls. The guard slumped over, and his armor hit the floor in a final, horrifying thud.

Ashford wiped the blade on his black trousers and hummed something to himself.

"Apologies for the mess," he said, cracking his neck.

I opened my mouth to speak, but only stammered confusion tumbled out of my lips.

"What did you–?"

A moment of stillness slipped by before he looked up at me and cocked an eyebrow.

"Your reward," he said, a smirk playing on his lips as his gaze lingered on me a beat too long.

I found my balance despite the trembling of my limbs, and tore myself from the ground, stumbling back a few paces. But I couldn't look away. He stared back at me, unreadable.

The General finally sighed.

"I told you to trust me."

CHAPTER 17

NO MATTER how much I scrubbed, the blood persisted, spattered atop the years-old herbal stains marking my cream blouse. I couldn't tell where the hibiscus ended, and his blood began.

With a groan, I tossed the blouse aside and slumped against the chipped cabinets. The cold wood seeped into me. Our apartment was quiet, and I prayed Osta wouldn't be home anytime soon.

My mind was still reeling, warring with the emotional whiplash that the General had unleashed upon me just hours ago. The memory was a fresh wound. I hated him. For his manipulation. For turning me into a pawn in his twisted games. Trust? He'd demanded it, drenched in blood. Did he think killing that guard would earn mine?

The man thought murder was a *reward*? The absurdity churned my stomach. He was delusional, lost in his own warped world. Was this the fate of the Guard? Did they all become numb to the act of taking a life?

But it was worse than that. What the General did was a deceptive kind of slaughter, reeling the guard in and making him feel comfortable, only to plunge a sword straight into his heart. A hint of the predator I'd always known lurking beneath the surface.

The creaking of a door cut through my thoughts, and I bolted from the floor, sidestepping to block the pink soapy bucket that filled the sink.

"Fia?" Osta said, rounding the corner. She stopped dead in her tracks when she saw me, eyes going wide.

"What happened to you?" She yelped, dropping her garment bags and rushing over to me. She pulled at the tangles in my hair.

Not tangles. Dried blood.

"I–I'm okay," I said, gently pulling her hand down from my hair. "It's not my blood." Her eyes darted between the tips of my hair and my face before finally falling on the bucket behind me.

"Whose blood is this?" She whispered, clawing me from my blockade and peering into the sink. "Did you... Did you hurt someone, Fia?"

I opened my mouth to respond but could only muster a small shake of my head.

"No," finally broke from my lips.

Osta tugged me over to our worn-in couch and forced me to sit. Only golden light from a flickering candle on the table lit the room.

"I'll be right back. Stay here." She gave me a stern look before rushing to her room.

Moments later, she was crawling back onto the couch with a cup of water and a hair pick, "I'm going to try to get this... blood out." She swallowed hard as she spoke. "Tell me what happened."

"The General," I choked out. There was so much she didn't know, but my mind was still racing.

"This is General Ashford's blood?" Her hand suddenly ripped through my hair with the pick. "Sorry," she murmured, returning to her gentle, yet shaky strokes.

"No. He came to the Apothecary as Ma and I were closing up. He said he wanted to try something new." I gulped, taking a deep breath. "A part of me wishes I never told him that emotions triggered my focus. I should have known he would take advantage of that. I'm an idiot." My voice was more confident now, tinged with irritation as I recalled the memory.

"You're scaring me, Fia. Whose blood is this?"

I could nearly feel her trembling despite her attempts to seem strong and collected. The tiny breaks in her voice were a dead giveaway.

"He brought me to the training gym, and when I opened the door… the guard from the dam was there."

Her hand stopped, and I felt her arms drop to her side. I turned to face her. Her lashes blinked rapidly, seemingly holding back the mist in her eyes, but her mouth was calm, nearly unreadable.

"*The* guard?" was all she asked.

"*The* guard," I repeated.

My hands found hers. We were both shaking. We never talked about what happened at the river. It was too painful in the aftermath of the funerals, but then too much time passed, and it became a secret we both kept locked in our minds. Whenever I tried to broach it with her, she quickly diverted the subject.

"He's dead?" She asked, staring into my eyes with a foreign intensity.

"Yes."

Osta took a deep breath and tucked her hair behind her ears.

"How did it happen?" She asked.

"General Ashford had a new idea, as I said before," I began, getting comfortable on the couch. She needed to hear it all. Every single detail. We both deserved that.

I spent the next hour explaining what had transpired earlier that night. How I had discovered my focus, found its access point, unleashed it, and reeled it back without killing the guard, just for the General to plunge a sword into his chest.

Osta was speechless once I finished.

We stayed in that quiet moment for what seemed like an eternity. Finally, her shoulders slumped.

"I'm glad he's dead." Her voice was just above a whisper, but something in her tone surprised me more than her words.

Relief.

"How do you feel?" She asked.

"I don't know. It's complicated," I murmured. I wasn't sure yet if I wanted to tell her everything his death made me feel. I didn't even know what any of it meant or what was even real. How to separate the shock from genuine emotions.

I wouldn't shed a single tear over the man's death, but a hollow emptiness gnawed at me where a sense of justice should have been. The General had slain the person who killed our friends and brought so much pain into our lives, but what would his death serve? They wouldn't string him up above the Compound to make an example of him. No one would know the crime he committed. Or why he died. Nothing would change for the Riftborne.

I shifted, pressing further into the sinking couch, and wrapped my arms around myself. When I watched the life drain from his eyes, something terrifying sparked within me. As much as I hated to admit it, a dark part of me felt satisfaction. Maybe even revelry in his death.

Was it already happening? Was I becoming one of them? Would I soon be able to kill with cold efficiency, my actions devoid of remorse or hesitation?

"So the General killed one of his own… for you?" Osta asked quietly. She pulled her legs onto the couch, tucking her feet behind her.

"I won't speak to his reasoning. The man is clearly mad," I murmured, shifting on the couch.

"But Fia, do you realize how big of a deal this is?" Her eyes narrowed on me as she grabbed my hand.

"Osta, I think you're the one reading too much into it. Ashford is unhinged. He didn't do any of it for me. He manipulated me into going with him tonight so he could force my focus out, and once I decided to show that guard the mercy he never showed Riftborne, the General killed him in cold blood right in front of me. Nothing about him makes sense."

"Maybe it doesn't make sense, but one thing is glaringly obvious. I don't think you're understanding the weight of the situation." Osta swallowed hard. "A General in the Sídhe Guard used an officer in the Sídhe Guard to bait you, and then... seemingly... killed him as punishment for his actions."

"We don't know why he killed him." I shook my head.

"Perhaps he is a mad man. I don't know him. All I know is what he risked by doing that. It has to have a deeper meaning..." Osta trailed off. Silence overcame the room.

Osta leaned in, shifting her weight on the couch. Even in the dim light, I could see the unusual seriousness in her eyes. She cleared her throat before speaking.

"I know this is going to sound crazy. It's just this gut feeling I have... but... I think you can trust him, Fia."

THE GENERAL HAD an air of excitement about him at our next training session. I'd received a note at work, telling me to meet him at our regular spot. It was irritating to hear from him at all, but at least he hadn't shown up in person again.

He was clearly satisfied with himself despite my near trauma. It prickled my annoyance, but I let it slide off. There was no use in pointing out the obvious. He knew what he had done.

If he didn't want to talk about the murder he committed mere steps from me, I'd bite my tongue. I just wanted to get through this session. So, for the first time since we began this journey together, I followed his lead to the best of my ability.

We sat as we normally did, facing each other, but there was a noticeable heaviness in the room that neither of us would acknowledge.

He stared deeply at me, a slight smile playing on his lips. I assumed it was an act of encouragement, but I was already calming myself, trying to clear my mind. Plus, ignoring him felt oddly satisfying.

I closed my eyes and directed my attention to the base of my spine, where the web had originated the other night, but visualization didn't come as easily this time.

My brow furrowed as I forced concentration, angling myself to try to physically coerce the tendrils. I leaned forwards, backwards, to the side. But they stayed locked in the depths of my spine. It seemed that without heightened circumstances, my focus would continue its game of evasion.

Three hours in, I felt a tingling in the right place. I sent all of my attention to that exact area, attempting to pull the power out by sheer will. A translucent haze fluttered into my mind, a small glimpse of the web. But as soon as it emerged, it descended back down, disappearing from sight.

It was stubborn. Like it had a mind of its own.

"I can see it, but I can't get it to cooperate just yet." I bit the inside of my lip.

"That's a lot further than we were last week," he stated.

His gaze lingered on me for only a moment before he stood, stretching. "I'd say that's enough progress for today."

I wrung out my strained muscles, feeling heavy and tense after such a long time seated. My eyes were killing me, and I felt the pulses of a headache creeping in.

"I guess. I was hoping for more." A breathless sigh escaped me as I realized the long road ahead. Perhaps our individual sessions would last longer than I previously imagined.

A silence fell over the room as I collected my things. Thoughts of the last session nudged at the corners of my mind. I couldn't hold back anymore. The words were going to tumble out unwillingly, clumsily if I didn't take control in this moment and just get it out in the open.

"What you did to me wasn't right," I whispered.

I felt his weight shift from across the room. The tension was palpable, but my nerves wouldn't let me look in his direction. A silence spilled across the entire gym; I thought I might just drown in it if he didn't answer soon. This was the first time I had shown weakness. The first time I had ever shown any vulnerability.

"I know," he said silently. I snapped my head in his direction.

What?

"It seemed like the only way forward." He sat down slowly, running a hand through his shimmering copper hair.

"So you intended for me to kill him?" I asked, taking a step towards him and arching my brow.

"It would have mattered little, whether it was you or me. He wasn't leaving that room alive. I certainly wondered if you would take the opportunity," he murmured. "But I understand it was a difficult situation for you."

Was that *empathy*? Was it even possible?

The stone-cold exterior he usually wore faded away, leaving something new in its place. But just as quickly as it surfaced, realization washed over him, and the walls came right back up. I could nearly see them being constructed around him.

"The Guard can bring out the most difficult parts of your soul. It's best you learn that early on." He straightened his posture and brushed the wrinkles from his black shirt.

"What happens now?" I asked, leaning against the wall. Was I sworn to secrecy? Would it be common knowledge that the man was murdered? Would he lie about the circumstances? Every last bit of this situation felt draining, but Ashford looked calm and collected.

"Don't concern yourself with the details. It's handled." A few seconds passed, and I opened my mouth to speak, but he cut me off.

"And now there is just the matter of the ball," he said, changing the subject. A coy smile played at his lips.

I couldn't fully register his words. I had seen a glimpse of something within him, but today clearly wouldn't be the day for a full revelation. General Laryk Ashford was back in full glory.

Wait. The Tribute Ball? Confusion washed over me. I was certainly not the person to discuss such topics with.

"I didn't realize you were also a party planner. I'm afraid I won't be much help with that, but best of luck." I turned back to my things, still unsure about how the conversation diverted so quickly.

"Fia." He halted me with an exasperated look. "You are going to need to make an appearance."

"Excuse me?" My eyes widened.

"You'll be joining the Guard soon. It's important to start making connections."

"Be that as it may, I don't remember agreeing to join you at any of these elitist soirees," I replied as I turned towards the door. He thought I was going to appease him *now*?

He was quick to block my path.

"The agreement we have is contingent upon you doing as I advise–and that includes the *elitist soirees* you're referring to. They build camaraderie."

I scoffed.

The General crossed his arms and stared at me in contemplation. "You would deny Osta the audience of the Sídhe Nobility?"

"Osta?"

"Of course. I assumed she would accompany you. I can even introduce her to some of the noble houses if she'd like."

Anger pulsed through me. He had a habit of using Osta as a bargaining chip.

I raised a brow. "And why would you do that?"

"So you *don't* want me to provide her with numerous potential career opportunities? You're not the friend I thought you were." He shook his head, mischief playing at the corners of his eyes.

"I was going to ask how you knew so much about Osta, but then I remembered your habit of stalking." My eyes shot to the back of my head, realizing that further argument would be futile.

He smirked, not even trying to hide his satisfaction. "I'm looking forward to seeing you both this weekend."

I left the gym with thoughts that continued to churn. The man had a way of twisting my impulses into absolute whiplash. I didn't know how to feel. But I knew one thing for certain.

Osta was going to lose it when I told her the news.

CHAPTER 18

"OSTA. WHAT HAVE YOU DONE?" I glared into the mirror.

"I knew you would love it!" Osta beamed as she leaned her head back and fell into the couch, arms sprawled out in accomplishment.

"The gown is beautiful, Osta, seriously… I just. Isn't it a bit much?" I asked, turning around to get a look at the back. Which was basically nonexistent.

It had been a week since the General had forced this ball upon me. I agreed to let Osta dress me for the evening. She convinced me that showing off her designs in real time would be essential for her to make an impression on the Nobility. A fact I couldn't exactly argue against.

But she had gone fully and completely mad with the design. Perhaps on someone else, it would have been stunning. On me… Well, I looked like a spectacle.

The gown was made from shimmering velvet, in a shade caught somewhere between silver and white. The long sleeves laced through my fingers with a simple band, and the neckline stretched up past my collarbones, ending just below my chin. The fabric hugged every curve of my body before flaring out at the bottom. The embellishments were clearly a nod to my eyes, opalescent and reflective. They seemed to catch every glimmer of light that hit them.

A part of me wanted to hug Osta for creating something so beautiful for me. It felt like the biggest compliment I'd ever received–to see myself through her eyes, even if they were tainted by rose-coloring I didn't deserve.

The other part of me wanted to scream. The gown enhanced every feature that I normally tried to tone down. The ones that were a constant cause for unwanted attention. It was a strange notion. It looked like me, but it didn't feel like me. Perhaps it reflected the best version of myself, but that version didn't exist. Not really.

Osta pinned my hair back in loose braids, but a few stubborn curls escaped into the air, framing my face. She insisted on using pins encrusted with the same jewels from the gown, and I reluctantly agreed. It was a compromise we had come to after I forcefully vetoed the *headpiece* Osta designed to accompany the look.

I had already allowed her to dust my cheekbones with shimmer and line my eyes with charcoal, which only further emphasized the darkness that surrounded them. It made my otherwise deathly appearance seem more intentional... perhaps even alluring.

If you squinted a bit.

Osta pranced over to me, her eyes filled with pride. She took my hands in hers.

"Fia, you're a goddess!" She mused. "I've waited sooooo long to style you for something." She shook her head and smiled. "Seriously, you look like a shooting star, perhaps even one of the Esprithe! It's exactly what I imagined!"

I stole another glance towards the mirror, never having seen myself so polished. A deep inhale overcame me, and I nodded.

"You're my hero. The ladies are going to die when they see your work." I nudged Osta. "Speaking of, you probably need to go get ready. Enough about me. I can't wait to see what you've come up with for yourself." Giving her a mischievous look, I tilted my head towards the hallway.

"I still can't believe we get to go! I take back anything negative I've ever said about the General!"

I groaned.

"That's not entirely necessary," I started to mumble, but she was already turning the corner. A faint squeal echoed through the room as her bedroom door slammed shut.

When she stepped out, my jaw dropped.

The gown was exquisite. Timeless. She looked like the embodiment of a shimmering ruby. The fabric was a rich scarlet, complemented with matching jewels. It cascaded down, embracing her shoulders in a graceful drape that left her decolletage exposed.

The silhouette transitioned into a tailored corset, accentuating her femininity. I followed the lines of the gown. At her waist, it belled out in crimson waves that trailed effortlessly behind her.

Her lips were painted the same scarlet hue. Half of her hair was piled on top of her head; the other half fell in ringlets down her back. She was beaming.

"Osta, you're a vision," I whispered, cupping my hands over my mouth. She grinned at me, twirling to make sure I saw the dress from every angle.

"It's nice, huh?" she asked, strolling past me into the living room. I followed as she took her place in front of the mirror, admiring her work.

"Nice? It's *incredible*."

She looked down and bit her lip.

Oh no. We did *not* have time for this.

"Fia... I can't even tell you how much this opportunity means to me. This could really change my life. I just don't know how to thank you." She sniffled.

"Osta, there is no need to thank me. Seriously, this was all General Ashford." I leaned against the wall and gave her a reassuring smile. "You know these things aren't really my cup of tea, but I'm truly excited for you. And I'm honored to be wearing such a work of art. I'll do my best to show it off properly."

Osta looked up, her eyes beginning to glisten at the corners. I grabbed a handkerchief from the counter and handed it to her. She smiled and gently patted her eyes.

"I might need that in writing, Fia," she joked. "No hiding tonight. Seriously."

"Understood." I nodded, forcing the words to sink into my own skin. There would be no disappointing her tonight–I made the silent vow to myself.

She strode towards the door.

"Shall we?" Osta held out her hand and I hooked my arm in hers. As we stepped out onto the street, all eyes turned to us. My face flushed.

"Are you Fia?" My head snapped to the right. A man wearing Sídhe Guard dress robes was looking at me with his eyebrow raised.

"Erm, yes?" I breathed, trying to seem confident, but failing miserably.

"I'll be escorting you and your friend to the ball this evening. I almost thought you weren't going to show up. Here, let's get going. Wouldn't want to be late." He turned sharply and walked towards the canal.

I gave Osta a puzzled look and she shrugged before sauntering off after him. I crossed my arms and hesitantly followed.

The man stepped down into a narrowboat constructed from dark wood. These boats traveled down the canals near the apartment daily, but I had never ridden in one.

He held out his hand and helped Osta down before motioning for me. She climbed in effortlessly. I inhaled a deep breath and took his hand. As soon as my shoes touched the floor of the boat, I lost my balance and stumbled onto the bench, quickly straightening myself and adjusting my gown.

"Fia the graceful!" Osta laughed and came to sit next to me. I shot her a look of contempt. If this was any indication of how the night would go, we were in for a real treat. My stomach twisted endlessly as the boat took off down the canal, setting my nerve endings on fire.

~

WE APPROACHED the easternmost edge of Luminaria, and I watched as the channel branched out to surround the Imperial Keep. the Keep's towering spires scraped the night sky. Droves of Base Guards lined the perimeter and surrounding canals.

One of them strode over to our boat and motioned towards the guard who brought us here.

"Guests of General Ashford," he huffed before flashing his badge. The other guard simply nodded and stepped aside.

Fortunately, exiting the boat was a far easier task than entering it. Osta and I shifted, adjusting our gowns after climbing up onto the cobblestone. The sound of live music filtered through the streets, mixing with the voices of attendees socializing near the grand entrance. I didn't even have to look at Osta to sense her anticipation. It radiated off her. She was practically vibrating.

We gathered ourselves and made our way towards entrance. My eyes shifted down as we approached the crowd outside. But it was a feeble attempt at anonymity. I felt eyes on me the second we reached the stairs.

We did our best to filter through the labyrinth of bodies, finally reaching the heart of the Keep. Osta inhaled sharply as we took in the opulence of the grand hall.

Gilded adornments splayed intricately across the ceiling, eventually giving way to a painting that honored the Esprithean pantheon. Ivory walls were draped in rich emerald fabrics and tapestries showcasing the royal insignia. We both stood in awe as our eyes shifted around the room.

Massive crystal chandeliers hung from above, casting an ethereal glow that danced across the polished marble floor. The air was sweet with the fragrance of exotic flowers, arranged in towering vases. The grand staircase at the center of the hall loomed ahead, leading to upper galleries where guests could take in the festivities from above.

Aossí revelers twirled and glided across the room to the melodies of a live orchestra. On a raised dais, the King and Queen sat in thrones, dressed in emerald shades of the royal court.

"I can't believe we're here," Osta cooed, her eyes still wide.

"Tell me about it," I mumbled, trying not to think about the people who were clearly staring in our direction.

"Fia, don't ruin this for me," she huffed.

"Everyone's just staring at us. It's maddening," I whispered, hooking my arm in hers.

"Yeah Fia, because we're the best dressed here. Not everything is about you. Stop being so tortured and brooding," she hissed through a smile.

Heat rushed to my cheeks. I was so used to people gawking at my appearance, it didn't even occur to me that it could be because of Osta's hard work. Guilt flooded me and I fought back a wince.

"You're right, sorry."

Osta's eyes darted around the room, no doubt analyzing the attendees' fashion choices. A satisfied grin formed on her face. The sparkle reflected in her eyes could have blinded someone.

"Wha–What do we do now?" I asked hesitantly.

"I see the bar in the back. Drinks?" Osta winked at me.

"Yes. Definitely. Now." The words couldn't leave my lips fast enough. Osta tugged my arm and I turned to follow her.

I glanced up and saw a sliver of copper hair in the distance. The General was surrounded by a posse of Sídhe guardsmen, all in matching black. He leaned against a column, seemingly oblivious to the conversations happening around him. A smile crept up his lips.

CHAPTER 19

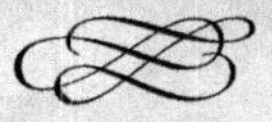

THE GENERAL MUTTERED something to the group surrounding him before starting toward us. His long copper hair was tied back, but a few tendrils had slipped out on the sides. He wore a crisp, black shirt and matching dress trousers. A long coat lined with badges and medals cascaded down his frame.

He kept his hands in his pockets and held a curious expression on his face. Osta looked at me, confused, before following my gaze over to the General, who still had his eyes glued to mine.

She grabbed my wrist and gasped.

"Why is he looking at you like that?" Osta whispered.

I could barely hear her over my own heartbeat.

"Hmm?" I mumbled.

"Fia. He either wants to kill you or bed you. And there's absolutely no in between," she squealed as the General closed in on us. I shook my head and attempted to look unbothered. Nerves crept up my shoulders and prickled the back of my neck.

He stepped in front of us–the look on his face drowned out all the sounds around me. His eyes slid down my entire body before coming back to meet mine once again.

Instantly, I felt naked. Something about the narrowed nature of his gaze had me shifting in my dress.

Why *was* he looking at me like that?

Osta cleared her throat. The General blinked as we broke from our trance. The sounds of the room tumbled back in like a war horn, dragging me back to reality.

The General's face softened, but his mischievous smile returned. He looked over at Osta.

"You must be the reason Fia looks so presentable tonight," he quipped. Osta giggled like a damned schoolgirl.

My eyes couldn't roll fast enough.

"It's so lovely to meet you, General Ashford. Truly, I'm honored to have been invited tonight. I can't thank you enough for the opportunity," Osta gushed, fluttering her eyelashes and curtseying. She was usually bubbly, but this was taking it to a whole new level.

The General was eating it up. He wore an expression of insufferable amusement and a smile drenched in satisfaction.

I made a gagging noise.

The General laughed, but Osta shot me a scowl.

"The pleasure is all mine, truly." He took her hand and brought it to his lips. His eyes shot back to me as he kissed it, and I scoffed.

"You're quite the ray of sunshine. I'll admit, I wasn't sure what to expect after getting to know your friend here."

Osta giggled. *Giggled.*

"So what's the plan?" I interrupted before Osta could start frothing at the mouth.

I guess the dartboard suggestion was off the table.

"Well, I suppose it would be best to make some introductions before everyone gets too carried away with the open bar." He smiled. "Osta, shall we?" He held out his elbow. Her eyes shifted between the two of us reluctantly.

"Well, I mean… Fia can come with us right?" she questioned.

The General laughed. "I'm afraid her scowl will scare away any potential clients, but it's up to you."

"You two go on. I'm going to… how did you put it? Get carried away with the open bar." I started moving past them. I didn't love the thought of my dearest friend sauntering off into the depths of the Keep with a murderer, but my objection might have turned *her* into a murderer.

I couldn't imagine the General pulling something in this environment anyway. It would be a shame for Riftborne blood to spill and ruin the mood. Those acts were usually saved for the shadows.

Besides, Osta deserved to make those decisions for herself.

"Mercer! Come keep Fia company please," the General shouted from behind me.

Oh great.

I looked in the direction of his request, eyeing a guard in the same black attire, who stepped away from a well-dressed man nearly half his size and began making his way over. He had inky black hair that was cropped short and bronzed skin. He was as tall as the General, but broader. As he got closer, he gave us a slight smile and I noticed the flecks of amber in his eyes.

"You must be Fia." He nodded in my direction.

"Sorry to pull you away from Halloway but I'm sure you're past the honeymoon phase by now. I'll only be a moment. Keep an eye on her. She has this habit of finding herself in precarious situations," the General chided as he turned to pull Osta into the crowd. "Don't be too difficult on Callum, Fia. Behave."

Osta shot me a sympathetic look before disappearing.

"Is he always so charming?" I asked sarcastically.

The guard chuckled and scratched the back of his neck. "Yeah, he certainly has a way about him."

I shook my head. "I was headed in the direction of the bar when he called you over." I arched my brow.

"I'll join you. I'm probably going to need a drink before the night's over."

We walked side by side and waited in line before finally procuring our cocktails. I downed mine immediately.

"Laryk's told me a lot about you."

The use of his first name so casually... felt intimate. It made him seem more like an acquaintance and less like my personal tormenter.

"I can't imagine the things you've heard," I murmured, heat flushing my face. "He seems like quite the embellisher." Something about Callum's presence was oddly comforting. Perhaps it was how normal he seemed in contrast to Laryk–the General.

"Are you based here?" I asked.

"I've been stationed out West, but I'll be in Luminaria for the next few months training the new additions to his faction. Including you." He furrowed his brow. "I guess after tonight, you'll have to refer to me as Lieutenant Mercer." He smiled, taking the first sip of his drink.

We made small talk near the bar for over half an hour before the General and Osta returned. I couldn't believe someone as laid back and nice as Mercer was the General's second-in-command.

Osta was beaming as she skipped over to me. "I think that went really well!" she squealed.

"Let me get you a drink to celebrate and you can tell me all about it." I turned to the bar, taking a few steps before I felt the heat of a hand on my arm.

"Fia, may I steal you away for a dance?" The General's breath tickled my ear. I swiveled to meet his gaze.

Horror rushed over me as Osta answered in my stead.

"Yes! Go, Fia!"

I hadn't even formed a reply before he was pulling me towards the center of the room, towards the swirling colors.

This seems highly inappropriate.

My eyes flickered about the room, noticing the perfectly synced movements of the couples twirling around us, creating a blur of satin gowns and black dress robes.

A lump formed in my throat.

"I don't know these dances..."

"Just follow my lead. I would never let you make a fool of me." His eyes were bright.

Suddenly his arms were lacing around my waist, gliding along my bare back. Heat erupted through me. He pulled my body flush against his own.

I was on fire, and I desperately needed to douse it.

Why did I feel like this? It had to be the utter embarrassment from dancing with my superior, or just dancing in general–this was so wildly out of my comfort zone.

Or maybe I just hadn't been touched like that in so long.

We started moving, blending into the rotation of bodies. He was a decent partner, at least from what I could tell–I certainly wasn't an expert. Despite being glaringly unaware of how I looked from the outside, a part of me calmed...

His head tilted down until lips grazed the shell of my ear. "The dress suits you, though I'd prefer it in black." His whisper sent a shiver down my spine. We whipped past the other Aossí, and something about it felt violent, but perhaps that was just the look in his eyes.

"As you stated earlier, it's all thanks to Osta." I turned my head in an attempt to hide my blush. "Thank you for introducing her to a few people tonight, she really does deserve the attention."

I could still feel his eyes burning a hole through me.

"Happy to do it. I've grown tired of seeing the same styles and designs recycled over and over at these gatherings."

"I should have known you had a personal stake in this." A small laugh escaped my lips. I couldn't help it.

The alcohol. The ridiculous dance. The absolute absurdity of me, Fia Riftborne, being at a ball for Esprithe sake. It was all too much to process.

He pointedly ignored my remark. "Her attention to detail is quite impressive."

"Yes, it should be. That is her focus after all."

"I picked up on that," he murmured before dropping me into a dramatic dip that sent my heart lurching. When he lifted me back up, our bodies collided, and a mixture of shock and fire raced through me. I was staring straight into his emerald eyes, our faces nearly touching.

"Laryk," I gasped at the sudden movement, immediately regretting it. My cheeks flushed as his first name tumbled out of my mouth so easily, like we were friends or something. I wanted to crawl into a cave and die.

Damn cocktails.

He raised an eyebrow. "Careful, now."

I felt his arms go rigid, but he brought his face even closer, brushing past my cheek and lingering near the lobe of my ear.

"Don't let the Guard hear you call me that," he whispered.

I nodded instinctively and tried to hide how breathless I felt. My head was spinning. I was going to crumble to the ground. His arms tightened around my waist as the song ended, almost as if he was hesitant to let go.

"We should probably get back to Osta and Mercer now." I looked down, shuffling out of his grip.

As my body cooled from the absence of his touch, a thought drifted into my mind.

You're still a mouse in a sea of serpents.

Just because he was playing nice tonight didn't mean any of it was real…

But for some reason, it was harder to convince myself of the truth I'd clung to for my entire life. It had to be the alcohol. It was making me vulnerable, making me act like a fool. And that could lead to dangerous situations.

I repeated the thought, trying to make it stick.

"Dinner should be starting soon. We can gather the two of them and head to the banquet hall." He cleared his throat and adjusted his collar before offering me his arm. He pulled me across the room in the direction of the bar.

Osta gave me several highly suspicious and unnervingly

mischievous looks upon my return with Laryk, causing me to nudge her a bit too forcefully with my elbow. She let out a low snicker that only I could hear.

The four of us made our way up the staircase after reconnecting, and Osta took the opportunity to tell me about her conversations with the ladies of Nobility.

"All of them seemed receptive, really. Some of them were actively looking for an in-house seamstress. Which would be a great stepping stone to opening my own label one day." She squeezed my hand tightly as the words tumbled out. "Lady Soleil and I really connected, I could tell. Bless Niamh, I am just so happy. I don't know if I'll be able to stop smiling tonight." She shook her head and looked down, trying to contain herself.

"I'm so proud of you. You deserve this." I squeezed her hand back and she squealed as we reached the top of the stairs.

"I just... I don't know how to thank you for this." Osta's eyes found the floor. "You've managed to do for me in one night what I've been working towards nearly my entire life."

A pang of guilt surfaced in my chest. Because as much as I wanted to be the one to help her, to save her from Thearna, this wasn't my doing.

It was his.

Laryk had used his position and power to help a Riftborne. Something I would have never before thought possible.

He had killed one of his own...

"Fia, Osta, you'll both be dining with the other members of my faction. I'll show you to your seats."

Laryk's words sliced through my thoughts, and then I abandoned them all together. The feelings were too confusing to ponder in a setting like this.

I focused in on the massive space instead, allowing the sheer opulence to become my distraction.

In one corner, a lavish banquet beckoned. Tables set with crystal and silverware showcased an expansive feast. The smell fresh bread intermingled with balsamic glaze and the sultry aroma of roasted boar. Courtiers engaged in lively conversations and laughter bellowed through the room, mixing with the music from the orchestra below.

"Ashford, not so fast!" A voice commanded from behind us.

Laryk turned first, smiling brightly and walking past us. I turned around to see the King and Queen approaching. The King lifted an eyebrow and gestured towards me.

"Is this the one you've been telling me about?"

CHAPTER 20

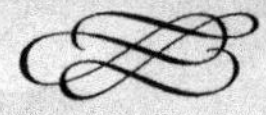

THEY WERE the epitome of regality, vibrantly draped in emerald silks. The King bore a roaring smile and a full head of peppered hair.Though his eyes seemed gentle, they nearly glowed in shades of violet.

Beside him, the Queen emanated radiance, bedecked in a cascade of jewels. Her blonde tresses were meticulously styled in perfect ringlets that flowed down her back effortlessly. It contrasted her hauntingly onyx eyes, which seared into me. She wore a more curious expression.

Both monarchs sported golden crowns adorned with green stones. Their presence was overwhelming.

The King had found his Queen forty years before, and songs of their love story were sung throughout the realm, both by bards in lowly taverns and by orchestras at Royal banquets. The songs spoke of a love at first sight, so powerful that it forced the King to abandon the woman who had been promised to him since birth. He risked everything to marry a member of a distant noble family from the furthest reaches of Sídhe.

Even now, the King looked at her with such pride, it was almost uncomfortable to witness.

Osta and I shared a quick look of panic before dropping down into a bow. The King, with his booming voice, chuckled. We rose to see the three of them beaming with amusement.

"How adorable, my dears, but there's no need to be so formal," Queen Ophelia remarked, casting a glance down at my Riftborne marking and cocking her head to the side. I shifted my weight nervously.

"Fia, is it? Laryk was right. You're hard to miss." Heat rushed over me, embarrassment blushing my cheeks. I was starstruck and I hated myself for it. The Guard may have been responsible for the destruction of Riftdremar but it was the King who sent the orders.

The king smiled. "You both look absolutely radiant."

Osta was frozen solid beside me. She wasn't even blinking. I nudged her softly.

"Your highness, it's a pleasure to make your acquaintance. What a lovely ball! Everything is just absolutely perfect." Osta's voice went up an octave. I feared she would soon faint.

"Flattery will get you everywhere," The King responded before looking past us as if he'd lost interest in the conversation. The Queen's eyes remained locked on me.

"Ashford, we will speak later. It was nice to meet all of you. Fia, welcome. We're overjoyed to have you in the Guard. I've heard you have great potential." He patted Laryk on the shoulder before taking the Queen's hand.

"Yes, of course. I'll come find you after dinner," Laryk said with a tight smile.

"Pleasure," I managed to get out as they walked away.

"Osta, darling, are you alright?" Laryk was holding back laughter. I looked over at her. For once, she was paler than me. She nodded shakily.

I helped steady her as Laryk guided us to the table. It was full except for a few empty chairs on both ends. The ones already seated were chatting amongst themselves, alcohol pitching their voices loud enough to easily overhear.

"Did you hear about the Riftborne joining the faction?" One of them attempted to whisper.

"I did hear about it, and it seems to be true." Laryk leaned in, whispering back in the same tone.

The two guards spun around in their chairs, eyes widening as they saw him.

"Oh–General, I didn't realize you were standing there," one of them blurted, heat spreading over his face.

He brushed off the response before directing his attention to the entire table. "Everyone, meet Fia. Fia, everyone." He gestured back and forth between us with a flick of his wrist. I didn't want to read into the exchange, but a part of me felt like he was setting a precedent. Normalizing my attendance.

My skin simmered at the heat of their eyes on me, but I managed a small wave and a gulp. Osta and I sat down, and Laryk took his place at the head of the table. Callum sat to his left. We made eye contact, and he gave me a slight nod.

I scanned the length of the table, taking in what seemed to be fifty members. A majority of the guards throughout the Keep wore white dress shirts, but everyone at this table wore black. Although the smallest faction in the Guard, I couldn't fathom the stores of power that lined the seats before me. Perhaps this was an army all on its own.

To Laryk's right sat a woman with crimson-red hair who seemed to be… Was she glaring at me? I quickly looked away and turned to Osta who was already introducing herself to the boy beside her. He bore a round face and chestnut hair. I could tell he was taken aback by Osta's presence.

"Fia, this is Val, and that's Gentry across from you!" She chirped, gesturing between us.

When did she have time to get their names?

"Welcome to Venom," Val said with a grin.

I gave them a shy smile as I said hello. They didn't seem worried about the markings on our left hands. In fact, they didn't seem concerned about us at all.

Dinner went by slowly, but I didn't mind. The food made me feel like I had never truly eaten before. I think we were all moaning as we stuffed ourselves.

Val told me that the chef was plucked from the Western region after the King experienced his dinner menu. Apparently, it caused quite a point of contention between the King and the Lord of Emeraal. When you had a focus like that, I guess it made sense for royalty to literally fight over you.

I leaned towards Osta, "Think they would stare at us in horror if we tried bringing some of this food home?"

She hit my shoulder. "Fia!"

"What? It looks like there is plenty to go around," I grumbled, slouching down into my chair.

I found my eyes wandering down to the end of the table once again. Laryk was laughing between sips of his wine. I'd never seen him look so carefree. A smile pulled at the corner of my lips, quickly dissipating when I noticed the redhead leaning towards him, her hand disappearing beneath the table.

Laryk leaned back, continuing his conversation with Callum. His hand moved to grip the back of her chair. For a few seconds, her eyes flittered down the table and stopped on me, lips curling into a smile.

"Hey, Gentry," I said. He turned towards me and leaned in. "What's her deal?" I gestured towards the head of the table.

"You mean Narissa?" he asked before lowering his tone to a whisper, "I'd steer clear of her if you can manage it. Her focus is absolutely *insane*. She's a blood lock. And she won't hesitate to show you."

I paused, furrowing my brow in confusion. I'd never heard of that before. "What is tha–"

"Did you just say shesshs a *blood clot?*" Osta slurred, leaning across my lap to join the conversation.

Gentry almost choked on his drink and the four of us burst into a fit of laughter.

By the time we caught our breath, I looked up to see Laryk glaring at me with his jaw clenched, his face now devoid of the previous amusement.

Another hour rolled by, and people began shuffling about, collecting their things. My eyes moved to Laryk, but he was speaking intensely to Mercer and Narissa, who had removed themselves from the table. Whatever they were discussing seemed serious.

I nudged Osta. "I think it's time."

We stood from our chairs, and I steadied Osta, sending a silent prayer to the Esprithe for the boat. Walking home would be nearly impossible.

"Are you two leaving? We can escort you out," said Gentry, stretching his arms to the side.

The four of us made our way through the Keep, heading for the grand entrance we came through only a few hours ago. It seemed like a lifetime had passed since then.

The night had turned out… better than expected. I survived, Osta found some connections, and somehow we had… made some friends? My mind was still reeling from the shock of it all. Gentry and Val were fun and perfectly normal. Something warm stirred in me.

I could see the canal glistening in the moonlight just ahead. Right as we turned to say our goodbyes, a guard strode up behind Gentry, placing a hand on his shoulder. I turned my head away, trying to give them some privacy, but I couldn't help overhearing their conversation.

"It's happened again at Stormshire. Looks like we'll all be deploying tomorrow for the West," he whispered. I was barely able to make out the words, but his tone gave the impression of haste, maybe even fear.

Gentry and Val turned towards us and quickly said goodnight before disappearing into the crowd. Osta and I looked at each other with raised eyebrows.

We hooked arms before strolling down to the Canal.

I dared a glance back at the Keep, noticing a pair of redheads leaving together, hand in hand. I spun back to face Osta, my face heating as my eyes found the cobblestone pavement.

I reminded myself that I hated him.

CHAPTER 21

OSTA WAS CERTAINLY TAKING advantage of my newfound free time. She convinced me to join her in the park for a morning walk before work, insisting that I clear my mind. That was her way of putting it, at least.

What she really wanted was to shake off the bad mood that had been plaguing me for a week. So, we walked along the furthest path, avoiding the crowded center. I looked down as a frog jumped from a lily pad into a small pond.

"Still no word from the General?" Osta asked over her shoulder.

"Of course not." I scowled.

Nearly the entire Guard had been dispatched to Stormshire, following some undisclosed incident near the border.

"I'm at the mercy of his schedule. Whatever that may be."

Laryk hadn't found it necessary to inform me about the disruption to our training. That only became apparent when I arrived at the gym a few days earlier and found it empty.

"I'm sure he'll return soon. And he'll probably have wanted you to practice in his absence." Osta tsked, running her fingers over the tips of fringed tulips. Ever since the ball, Laryk could do no wrong in her eyes. Which was infuriating.

"Well, then he should have left me some correspondence," I mumbled, kicking a stray rock across the dirt path. Truthfully, I had been practicing on my own, but hadn't seen much progress, which was one of the reasons for my sour state.

Osta hummed to herself.

"And the studio. Has Thearna pulled the stick out of her ass yet?" I asked, nudging Osta's arm.

"I don't think she could even if she tried," she said, shrugging her shoulders.

Osta had been in a constant state of euphoria ever since the ball, and it seemed that tension had flared up at the studio in response. Thearna's absence from the guest list appeared to be a source of contention. And Osta was never the best at hiding her excitement. I could see it so clearly in my mind–the vessels in Thearna's neck pulsing with every word Osta muttered about the event.

"I know she's threatened by me. But instead of ignoring my suggestions, perhaps she should *listen* to me more," She cooed, examining her nails. Thearna's anger seemed only further inflamed by Osta's newfound boldness.

She had yet to hear from any of the Nobility that Laryk introduced her to, but it didn't come as too much of a surprise. Everyone was far more concerned with the sudden absence of the Guard. Osta was confident that one of the ladies would offer her a job. I just hoped she wouldn't push Thearna off the edge before that happened.

"I suppose this is where we part ways," I said reluctantly as we reached one of the arched gateways of the park.

Osta shared my sentiments with a pout. "See you tonight. Wish me luck."

"I may need to keep the little luck I have for myself."

Things with Ma were… back to their normal intensity, or lack thereof. Now that she knew I had continued my training with the Guard, we simply didn't speak.

I spent the morning grinding capsaicin. The dried chilies we extracted it from were brutal to work with. My eyes had been stinging and watery all day. Even though I knew better, I couldn't help but feel that it was a form of punishment.

I sifted the powder into a brewing sachet and dropped the it into a cauldron that was already heating infusion oils, watching as the red powder began to bleed out into the shimmering liquid.

The front door chimed, cutting through my thoughts. I looked up to Ma, who was filling vials with an amber liquid.

"I'll go," I said, giving her a small smile before heading to the front of the shop and untying my apron.

"How can I help you?" I asked as I rounded the corner.

"How charming." The voice sent my heart racing.

My eyes shot up to see Laryk leaning over the front desk, an amused smile on his lips. My eyes widened momentarily, taking in the tight leather uniform he was wearing. The sight wasn't terrible…

I shook my head and replaced my shock with narrowed eyes.

"What are you doing here?" I whispered, rushing towards him. My head snapped back, making sure Ma hadn't followed me to the front.

We seemed to be alone, at least for now.

"Well, that's not a very polite welcome." He stood straight, arching an eyebrow.

"I'm very busy at the moment." My scowl deepened. If Ma saw him here…

He reached towards me, pulling a leaf from my hair. I yanked myself back as he smirked.

"I see you left the more pleasant version of yourself at the ball," he mused, inspecting the leaf.

"I guess so."

"Pity." He sighed, looking me over. It felt like he was undressing me with his eyes.

Heat flushed my cheeks, but I calmed myself, trying to release the scowl from my face. I needed him to leave as quickly as possible. The easiest way would be to pacify him.

"General Ashford, *please* tell me what you want so that I can get back to work." It didn't come off as neutral as I intended. He paused for a moment, a curious glint flickering across his eyes before he blinked and diverted his sight towards the exit.

"Our sessions will be the same as always. But, due to increased tension at the border, your group training will be starting sooner than anticipated. Tomorrow, actually. Because of the strained timing, you won't be getting a formal induction ceremony. Apologies," he said, his voice flat.

"*Tomorrow?*" I snapped. "And you waited until now to tell me this?"

"I only returned this morning from Stormshire. I had no way of letting you know before now. Not that it should matter. It's tomorrow, so you will be there *tomorrow.*"

He crossed his arms, meeting my gaze with intensity. My blood simmered. He had some nerve showing up here after disappearing with no warning.

"And if I don't?" It slipped out. I wanted to wince, but I was committed to the defiance.

He stepped towards me, narrowing his eyes. I fought the urge to back away. Laryk quickly grabbed my arm and pulled me close. I wasn't sure exactly when his name had changed to Laryk in my mind...

"I'm done playing these little games with you," he whispered. "After tomorrow, you will be an official recruit of the Guard, and you will have to show respect. Not only to me, but to all of your superiors. Do you understand?"

Pulling free of his grip, I backed away, anticipating the rage I would find on his face. But a peculiar expression was all that stared back at me. His eyes were softer, almost concerned.

Almost… worried.

I wrinkled my brow. He looked away and ran his hand through his hair before inhaling sharply.

"I didn't come here to argue. I'll have your uniform delivered to your flat later tonight."

A part of me wanted to protest, to find fault in every word he muttered. To fight against his demands. But that part of me was weighed down by a truth that I'd kept hidden, even from myself. As much as I wanted to distrust him, as much as I had trained myself to read the deception within his words, he had not done anything to harm me. Not truly. Not in a way that I would have ever imagined of a Sídhe General.

He had threatened me, inconvenienced me in every way imaginable, even pushed me beyond limits I never thought I could cross. But in the end, those tactics had only made me better. Only made me stronger.

Even if he had gone about it in a way that infuriated me, a way that made me want to claw my own eyes out. Trusting him was stupid, and I wouldn't. Not fully.

But enough.

He strode towards the door without looking back. With another chime, he was gone.

I sighed, turning around. Ma stepped out from the hallway, crossing her arms and shaking her head. She looked disgusted.

"How can you go along with this?" Her voice was deep. I didn't know how much of that she had seen. I couldn't imagine how it looked…

"I provoked that, Ma. He pissed me off and I couldn't hold my tongue." I walked past her, heading to my cauldron. She followed me to the back. Her footsteps seemed to echo through the room.

"You're going to get yourself killed, Fia!" She snapped. I spun around with wide eyes. She had never yelled at me like that before. My breath caught in my throat.

"I need you to trust me, Ma. I know you don't understand, and you probably never will. But at least trust *me*." My eyes were pleading.

"I do trust you, Fia. I don't trust *them*. Half of them would probably find enjoyment in your death! You know this." Her voice cracked.

"Ma, I'm doing this. I just need you to accept it. I can take care of myself. Please try to understand. I can't lose you."

"I don't know if I can do that, Fia. I can't watch you walk off to your death willingly." She sniffled, wiping her eyes with her sleeve, "You know better. You know what it would do to me if something happened to you."

Words wouldn't come, but tears settled in the corners of my eyes and threatened to overflow. This conversation was never going to change. I sighed and began stirring the cauldron again.

I felt Ma's eyes on me for a few more moments before she returned to her desk and slouched in her chair. It was silent again.

Perhaps this time, that was for the best.

CHAPTER 22

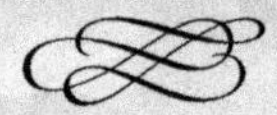

I TILTED my head back as the sunlight bore down on me—intense and oppressive. I dared a peek towards the top of the Compound but had to look away before blinding myself.

It was hard to wrap my head around the thought that coming here would now be an almost daily occurrence. I spent such a long time avoiding this place. I was conflicted. Training with the General was one thing, committing myself as a recruit was something entirely different.

Pushing away the sinking feeling of uncertainty, I steadied my steps.

At least this time, I was able to somewhat blend in thanks to the uniform that had shown up at our apartment door last night.

The cotton shirt, trousers, and boots were similar to the ones Laryk wore to our training sessions, save for the badge with my name. General Ashford's faction symbol was stamped across the back.

I briefly wondered if any Riftborne had seen these halls and if my badge would paint a target larger than the branding on my hand.

I waited in the small queue preparing myself for the reproachful look I was sure to receive from the entry guard. They were checking the identification of everyone who entered.

Here we go.

I shuffled towards the unnecessarily large man and quickly flashed my identification. A glint of curiosity flickered across his eyes as he inspected me. But it was gone just as quickly, replaced with a look of indifference. He straightened himself and gestured with his chin for me to move along.

A puff of relief escaped me.

That wasn't so bad.

I took another step forward but hesitated before walking through the enormous iron gates. My lips twisted as I dared a peek behind me. I could still turn around.

But the thought didn't linger for long. I didn't allow it to. I pushed my feet against the pavement and forced myself forward, lowering my head and instinctively avoiding eye contact.

The vast circular space of the lobby felt cold despite the many moving bodies. A blur of steel, charcoal and grit twisted around me. The twang of metal filled the air, sending a chill across my skin.

Now where do I go?

I wracked my brain, trying to recall if the General mentioned where I would be expected in this monstrosity of a building. Of course, he hadn't. He was probably in his office, riddled with amusement at the thought of me walking around aimlessly.

Nearing the mess hall, I looked up to see the medical insignia on a sign above. Below it was an arrow pointing left. Faction Immunity, I assumed. I noted the location in my mind. I would surely find myself there a few times before this was all over.

My eyes darted around the massive space for any markers that could point me in the right direction. A twinge of embarrassment washed over me, and I bit my lip, searching.

I saw a familiar frame in the distance.

Lieutenant Callum Mercer.

He was making his way past the lines of tables. People parted as he passed them, nodding in respect. He looked up, meeting my eyes and stopped, gesturing for me to join him.

It was odd seeing him in this environment after our first meeting. He stood with his back straight, shoulders squared. He seemed more stern and rigid today. I'd have to remember to stay formal, acknowledging his superior rank. As Laryk so *eloquently* reminded me yesterday.

I approached him sheepishly, lifting my hand in an awkward wave and stepping into his path.

"You seem lost." While he didn't smile, his eyes seemed friendly enough.

"Very. I'm hoping you know where I should be headed?"

I pulled at the sleeves of my shirt.

"You can follow me. We're going to the same place."

I allowed him to lead the way. We passed multiple rooms, separated from the main area by glass walls. They must have been the training gyms I'd seen before. Up close, they were much more intimidating.

Through the thick glass, I caught glimpses of activity. Sweat hung heavy in the air, visible even from here. Inside, figures moved with fluidity, their forms blurring as they went through drills. The rhythmic clang of steel on steel echoed, punctuated by grunts of exertion.

Lieutenant Mercer stopped sharply, pulling open the door at the end of the row. I shuffled past him, entering a small room. There were five other recruits sitting about the space in uncomfortable-looking metal chairs. I recognized a few of their faces from the ball. They didn't pay me much attention as they talked amongst themselves. I couldn't help but notice their ease. They seemed completely in their element. Well, most of them at least. One boy sat off to the side, reading a book.

I made brief eye contact with a boy whose hair was pale

blonde, a shade or two darker than mine. It was greased back, showing every contour of his square jaw. His eyes went sharp as they fell upon my left wrist. It looked like he wanted to say something, but he never did. I quickly turned away and slid my hands into my pockets.

"This is Fia Riftborne, she will be joining us from now on. Please, do your best to refrain from questions and introductions until the end of the session," Mercer said, giving pointed looks to each of us before motioning for me to sit.

As I walked towards the other recruits, every single eye was on me. A few murmurs ran through the room. They were an interesting assortment. Four boys and one girl. I pondered what their individual focuses were, wondering what Laryk had seen that made him want to place them in his special unit.

Mercer returned to a desk in the corner, procuring a set of vials from the drawer.

"Raine, I will put you in charge of catching Fia up on the past week."

"Why? Because I'm a girl?" I heard a laugh and followed the voice. She had long black hair that was pulled back from her face in thin braids. Her warm mahogany skin mirrored the color of her eyes. She was undeniably beautiful.

"No, because I usually can't get you to quiet down otherwise, so you seem perfect for the task," Mercer responded, unperturbed.

"Yes, Lieutenant," she chuckled, shaking her head before turning to me with a wink.

Mercer placed the vials on the podium in front of him. "You'll be receiving your first piece of confidential information today," he said, holding one of the vials in the air. There was a small slip of paper within the glass.

"This will ensure it stays between members of the Guard." He paced through the room, handing each of us one of the containers. A few exchanged confused glances.

I eyed the contents. The small parchment had today's date written on it, and my name was etched into the glass.

"What do we do with this?" Raine asked, holding the vial up to the light.

"You'll provide a drop of blood," he said, as if it was as normal as discussing the weather. "Once given, you won't be able to speak about any of our confidential intel with anyone outside of the Guard."

I sank down in my seat, looking around to the other recruits. Their expressions hadn't changed much, but deep down, I wondered if they were as horrified as I felt.

"A blood oath," Mercer said, offering me a small dagger.

"Just enough for a drop. I'll need your full attention during our lesson," he added.

"How does it work?" I asked, trying to disguise the fear in my voice with curiosity.

"That's not for you to know." It was all he said before pushing the dagger into my hand. I looked up to meet his eyes, which were unreadable.

Slowly, he nodded as if trying to assure me that everything would be alright. And it seemed like I didn't have a choice. So, I grasped the dagger and pushed the tip into my finger until a bead of crimson emerged. I held it over the vial and allowed a drop to fall, covering the parchment in a stain of red.

Mercer continued on to the rest of the recruits. The room remained dead silent as everyone swore the oath. After we finished, Mercer placed the individual vials on his desk, and a blond woman in an emerald Guard's uniform entered the room to collect them, leaving just as quickly as she came.

Mercer cleared his throat, bringing our attention back to the front of the room.

"As you all might have heard by now, there have been some issues in Stormshire and the lands surrounding the border. What you have yet to be informed of, is what exactly is taking place. We usually wouldn't be nearing this subject so early, but tension in the West really leaves us with no choice." Mercer eyed each one of us individually, his forehead stern.

I heard the legs of a chair slam back.

"I know the Riftborne gave her blood, but none of us should trust her. She'd slit our throat the second we turned our back. My father's seen it firsthand." The comment came from several chairs down. My head shot towards it reflexively, to find the pale-haired boy standing and glaring at me. The one sitting next to him, with jet-black hair and tawny skin, was looking back and forth between us, nodding slightly. My blood ran cold at the directness. I'd always known how they truly felt about us, but I'd never seen someone admit it so boldly.

"Your prejudices will get you nowhere here, Baelor. Your father served this Kingdom well, but times have changed. You must all learn to trust each other. Otherwise, we're all doomed," Lieutenant Mercer snapped. "There are bigger problems before us."

My cheeks flushed.

Baelor took his seat with a clenched jaw.

"Fia, please know that we aren't all bigots." A freckled face peaked out behind Raine's shoulder, toffee-colored hair nearly falling into his eyes. "I'm Briar Glennwood, by the way."

"I said no interruptions until the end of the session!" The Lieutenant shouted and we all jumped in our seats, turning to attention. I took a deep breath and swallowed the words that wanted to tumble out.

Mercer cleared his throat. "As I was saying, for our training to proceed, you all must know what we are up against."

He moved to the rear of the room, turning his back to us. I heard the tinkling of glass before someone slid into the chair directly next to mine.

"I'm Raine Ampere." She spoke under her breath, shooting a look over her shoulder to make sure the Lieutenant was still distracted. "Finally, a breath of estrogen. Brace yourself for an overdose of *male wisdom* and debates on the superior focus. You may just be my savior. And most importantly, ignore Baelor. The rest of us do." I huffed a laugh but was silenced by Lieutenant Mercer walking back towards the front of the class with a clear glass of water and what seemed to be an inkwell.

He held up the glass in one hand and the inkwell in the other.

Slowly, he poured the ink into the water. The thick liquid blossomed out into a dark void of shapes inside the clear glass, billowing into smoke-like patterns.

"This is what we're up against," he said, voice sharp and direct. "Recently, there have been a series of direct attacks on our Western bases from creatures that look just like this." Mercer took a breath before continuing.

"We call them Wraiths. They move through darkness and shadows, and are practically impossible to catch." He observed the cup in his hand before setting it aside.

I saw a hand shoot up out of the corner of my eye. It belonged to the one boy who had yet to make a sound. He seemed much smaller than the other recruits, and his raven hair was in a state of disarray.

"Yes, Draven?"

"Where did they come from?" he asked nervously.

"There is a lot we don't know. Considering they appeared out of nowhere, we assume they are not from our world. Perhaps they created some gateway into Sídhe, a tear in the fabric of reality. We know little of their kind."

I shifted in my seat, looking around the room to see if anyone else was concerned about Wraith-like creatures spilling in through a tear between worlds or if this was more of a normal occurrence.

The room was silent. I swallowed hard. No, this did not seem like a normal occurrence.

Everyone was on the edge of their seat, save for Baelor, who was now twisting a quill casually through his fingers in an easy recline.

"We must assume they are here to try to take something vital from our land or worse, try to take over Sídhe as a whole."

"So how do we exterminate them?" Baelor interrupted.

The Lieutenant hummed to himself, "Yes, how does one kill a void of imperceptible speed and darkness? Weapons seem to do little to nothing against them. A large reason for General Ashford to amp up such a special unit."

Baelor scoffed. "So no one has been able to kill one yet? It has been some time since a Soleil fought on the frontlines. They won't be able to escape my flames."

"Mm, yes, the focus of the Soleil family line burns brightly in you. I'm sure General Ashford has similar hopes," Mercer said flatly.

Baelor sat back in his seat, taking the compliment.

Raine raised her hand before speaking, "You mentioned having an idea of what they were after?"

"We have our suspicions. It seems they crave power. They're drawn to it, at least." Mercer crossed his arms. "Has anyone heard of arcanite?"

I slowly raised my hand.

"It's a conductor for Essence, right?" I asked, voice not as confident as I would have liked. Baelor sighed from a few seats over, loudly shifting his weight.

"That's correct. We house large stores of the rare crystal along the Western strongholds, and it seems to be of great interest to the creatures. Obviously, if they were to take it into their possession, Esprithe only knows what devastating effects it would have on Sídhe. We've never been rid of it before. There's a chance that, without it, our focuses would be rendered useless."

Mercer slid his hands into his pockets before continuing, "As of right now, the Wraiths' strengths seem to be limited to the West. One of our theories is that their powers weaken as they move further away from their homeland. We have defended our resources from many of their attempts to obtain it. Another fear, of course, is that securing the arcanite would allow them to gain enough power to move freely throughout the Isle, perhaps even reaching Luminaria."

A cold chill rushed down my spine at the thought of an unknown creeping darkness wreaking havoc on the city I called home. On Osta, and Ma.

"The attacks seem to be increasing. We think they're becoming desperate. We have already lost too many guards and with nothing to show for it."

He looked past us, his eyes fixed on the back wall as if recalling a memory. "It's like fighting smoke in pure darkness, all while hearing the whispers of its form twisting around you. You can't see, you can't breathe, and it happens so fast you barely have time to think. Once it has you in its grips, you are as good as dead." His jaw clenched. "I hope none of you will have to face this anytime soon."

He pursed his lips and exhaled sharply before looking each one of us in the eyes.

"You're sure as Conleth not ready for it."

CHAPTER 23

My mind raced as I sprinted out of the classroom. Nausea bubbled in my gut. Wraiths? Unkillable, moving *shadows*? I shook my head as the gates closed in on me. I was in way over my head.

And I couldn't tell anyone. Not a soul. I had literally sworn with my blood to keep all of this confidential. How did they all do it? If the threat was truly that serious, how could they sleep at night without telling their loved ones? I wasn't prepared for this.

I brushed past the gates and the guards from earlier, turning right towards the Central district.

"Fia! Hey, wait up!" The voice tore through my meltdown. I halted, pausing before turning to find Raine jogging towards me. A small dose of relief washed over me.

"Hey Raine." It was short and not as friendly as I would have liked, but it was all I could manage at the moment.

"Are you training for a marathon?" she teased, placing her hands on her knees and taking a few deep breaths.

A smile tugged at my lips but didn't fully form.

"I guess I'm a little shocked by the information we learned today." I winced and looked around nervously.

"Yeah, I get it. Pretty shocking to me as well," She shrugged, twirling one of her braids through her fingers.

"You live at the Compound?" I asked, my voice still unsteady.

"For now. Just during training." She looked around the street with wide eyes. "But this city is unreal. The Highlands don't even begin to compare," she mused, shaking her head.

"You're from the Highlands?" I had heard people go on and on about how beautiful they were. Territory flush with wineries and orchards. It seemed like a nice respite from the city crowds.

"Unfortunately." She sighed, looking back at me. "But I'm curious to know more about you. Are you busy now?"

I shifted my eyes, trying to muster an excuse. Raine seemed nice enough, but I was still reeling and in absolutely *no* state to attempt a social outing.

"Well, I–"

"Mercer did ask me to fill you in on what you've missed." She angled her head down, grinning wickedly. "I mean, unless you're too shaken up by the nightmare fuel we learned about today." The twinkle in her eyes intensified.

I turned her words over in my mind, trying to access my more logical side through the chaos and turmoil. Being seen as weak by my fellow recruits seemed like a terrible way to start off group sessions.

"I don't have plans." I smiled, swallowing my anxiety. "What did you have in mind?"

Her grin widened. "Excellent. There's a pub down the street. Care for a drink?" It didn't sound like a question. She winked, breezing past me.

"Sure," I mumbled under my breath, forcing my feet to follow after her. I reached her side, matching the rhythm of her steps. She radiated confidence, swaying her hips as she moved, hardly blinking.

Her eyes were set on some unknown destination ahead, a playful smirk toying at the corners of her lips. She was like a damn lion prowling the streets of Luminaria. I felt sorry for anyone that had the pleasure of her interest. She might just tear them apart.

"Have you been here?" Raine stopped abruptly, pulling a door open. I nearly stumbled into her before looking up, taking in the wooden sign that swung from chains above the door. *Rune and Revelry.*

"No, I haven't spent much time on this side of town," I admitted, shoving my hands into my pockets.

"Perfect, the first round is on me." She gestured for me to enter. The entire place was teeming with members of the Sídhe Guard. I gulped, shifting my eyes around to find a few seats open at the bar. She sauntered past me, headed straight towards the bartender. The pub was made entirely of creaking wood, from the floors all the way to the beams encasing the arched ceiling. It smelled of sweat and alcohol.

I approached Raine, who had already taken her seat at the bar. She was mumbling something to the bartender as I slid into the raised stool beside her.

"I think we both deserve this after what we learned today." She pursed her lips as the bartender returned with two mugs.

"Cheers to survival?" she whispered, holding it out towards me.

"Cheers," I nodded.

I tapped my mug against hers and took a long sip.

"So, what is your focus, if you don't mind me asking?" I wasn't sure about the etiquette regarding such matters, but directness seemed like Raine's preferred form of communication.

"Me? I can wield lightning." She grinned and held out her hand. Sparks emanated from her fingers, twisting and twirling about. My eyes widened.

"That's incredible!" I watched as she turned her palm over, the sparks dissipating.

"It's quite fun, I'll admit." She laughed. "Although it doesn't really serve any purpose back in the Highlands. When the General found me, I figured this was where I could be of use. Regardless, I was just happy to get out of there. All I want to do is travel and see the Isle. This seemed like the best way to do that." She placed her elbows on the bar. "What about you?"

I hesitated, trying to figure out the best way to explain my... focus.

"Erm–well, It's not as specific as yours. At least, I don't believe it is," I muttered, taking another sip of my drink.

"General Ashford described it as... well, liquifying people's minds... or something like that. My best friend calls it mind-shredding," I whispered, looking around. I winced with embarrassment. It sounded ridiculous.

Raine grabbed my arm as her jaw fell open.

"Holy shit. I've never heard of anything like that. That's fucking badass," she sang, leaning back to examine me further. Her gaze left me sweating.

"Remind me not to piss you off."

"It's all new to me, really," I admitted, shifting my eyes around the room. I mean, *controlling it* was new. I desperately wanted to divert the conversation away from me.

"What about the rest of the recruits?"

"Well, there's Baelor Soleil. He's excruciating to be around. He's the one who..." Her eyes fluttered up to meet mine, gauging my response.

I simply nodded.

"Well, he can harness fire. If we're to take his word for it, he could incinerate an entire village. His family is revered amongst the Nobility for doing just that. Not only was he born into the Elite, his father is the retired General, Bron Soleil. He's practically a legend." She eyed me hesitantly before continuing. "He's the one they credit with the victory against Riftdremar."

Something within me twisted, but I kept it hidden. I wasn't sure whether it was the revelation about Baelor's heritage or how considerately Raine spoke of the place I was born. As if the result of the war was anything but a victory. That was new to me.

"Seems fitting," I finally said. Raine laughed.

"Right. And then his friend, Nazul Halstead. Well, I don't know if they're friends, really. But he seems to go along with all of the nonsense that Baelor spews out. I do know they grew up together. His family is Noble too, of course. He can form powerful shields, but only in a small radius around himself. It's quite rare, actually."

"Well, that sounds valuable," I murmured, annoyance heating my skin. Of course, such an important defensive ability was gifted to someone so selfish. Fate worked in mysterious ways.

"But Briar–he's great. You would really like him, I think. He can control the landscape. Well, I mean, that's a simplification. He can mold nature to his will, in a sense. Grow vines rapidly, cause sink-holes, and turn rock to mud. It's really impressive."

She smiled softly before continuing, "He hasn't told me much. But from what I've gathered, he applied for the Guard on his own, expecting to be a Base recruit. This caused some kind of tension between him and his family. Apparently, they are very anti-war, and therefore very *anti-guard.*" She shrugged. "But he wanted to do it, all on his own. The General became aware of his focus and promoted him to team V immediately."

"Team V?" I let out a small laugh.

"I will not be forced to refer to it as Faction Venom. It's beyond cringey."

I nearly spit out a sip of ale.

"I couldn't agree more."

"I just know General Ashford came up with that one." She laughed and rolled her eyes.

"What about the other boy?"

"Draven Porter? He's quite the mystery actually... None of us really know much about him. He's pretty shy," she replied.

"He doesn't seem like the type to join the Guard," I said, shaking my head.

"Tell me about it. But he must be pretty powerful to catch the attention of the General."

The group was even more interesting than I initially thought. I had never been around so many Aossí with such powerful focuses. A part of me felt small for not having mastered mine yet. Going off Raine's descriptions, none of the other recruits struggled with control over their abilities.

She leaned into her hand and glanced over at me as I shifted in my seat. Her stare was perhaps more intimidating than Laryk's.

"You look so interesting," she stated, locking her eyes with mine. A familiar flush ran across my cheeks as embarrassment flooded my mind. I looked down.

"I don't mean that as an insult. I've never seen anyone that looks like you. Unique. Stunning." She took a long sip of her ale before smiling.

"Erm–thanks," I mumbled, averting my eyes.

"Don't get the wrong idea." She chuckled, shaking her head. "You're gorgeous, clearly. But not exactly my type." She sighed before turning her head to the left and pointing.

"*That's* my type." I followed her gaze down the bar and saw a woman with cropped, chocolate hair smiling wide, sitting with a group of fellow Guard members. By the deep green emblem on their white shirts, they were Base recruits.

"So go talk to her." I nudged her arm.

"I just might, after a few more of these." She turned back to her drink and laughed. "But I want to know more about you. I could tell the whole group was curious. A Riftborne joining the Guard doesn't exactly happen every day, you know. My best friend from back home–he's a Riftborne too."

Something soft stirred in my gut, mixing with the ale.

"Well.. I never planned on stepping foot anywhere near the Compound, honestly." I sighed. "But General Ashford found me, started training me... And now I'm here."

"You've been training with the General individually?" A curious glint flickered across her eyes.

"Unfortunately."

She threw her head back and laughed, nearly knocking over her ale. I nervously sipped mine while awaiting her clarification.

"So refreshing to meet someone who finds him as unbearable as me," she finally said, shaking her head. A giant smile crept onto her face. "Mercer can twist it however he wants, but I have a feeling we're not the first set of trophies that Ashford has recruited for the Guard. I mean, his entire faction is full of powerhouses."

"Raine, I know we just met today, but would you mind keeping my training with the General just between us?" I asked, scrunching my forehead. "I just don't want to give any of them more of a reason to distrust me or…" I trailed off.

Raine grabbed my elbow. "Fia, whatever you tell me stays between us. I know how savage this place can be. I'm not going to add any extra stress to what I imagine you already feel every time you walk through those gates," she reassured me with a smile.

"Thank you… really, I appreciate it," I mumbled, running my fingers through my unkempt hair. I trusted Raine, oddly enough. Something about her was innately genuine. Direct, but genuine.

"Us girls have to stick together." She winked.

I nodded, and a few moments of silence slipped by. My mind ached to ask the question, and the ale was already laying its traps. So I gave in to my curiosity.

"Was Narissa one of his recruits?" I gulped.

"As far as I know, everyone in his faction was handpicked by him," Raine said, eyeing me.

"Do you know what her focus is?"

She paused and took another sip of her ale. Her eyes shuffled around the room before she responded.

"It's pretty rare," Raine said before lowering her voice. "She's a blood lock. Acid type, from what I've heard."

"What exactly does that mean?"

“It just takes a few drops of her blood. If it touches your skin, it’ll melt holes right through you, down to your bones. Even healers can’t fix it. Apparently, it’s the most excruciating pain you could imagine.” She shivered as the words tumbled out.

“She’s the only recruit that the General has trained individually… Well, I mean other than you.”

My heart did somersaults as I downed the rest of my ale.

CHAPTER 24

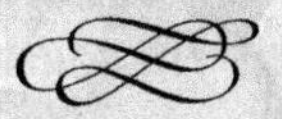

The sensation of falling enveloped me.

The rush of weightlessness sent my stomach lurching into my chest—a tumultuous dance with gravity that left me gasping for breath in the darkness.

Time stretched into infinity as I hurtled towards the ground. The void that surrounded my descent was one of shadows, devouring any light before it could penetrate its depths. I strained to scream, but my throat was constricted.

I couldn't make a sound.

Crack.

I hit the ground with an impossible force, the shattering of bone and sinew echoing into the void.

The agony was immediate, searing through every nerve. A symphony of pain left me desperate for a breath that wouldn't come.

Yet, even as I lay broken and motionless, the solace of death refused me. I was somehow still alive, trapped within the confines of my own mind, a prisoner to the nightmare.

This one felt so real.

In the silence, I waged war on my mind, yearning for the sanctuary of the waking world.

I couldn't spend another moment in this dream.

Wake. The fuck. Up.

~

WITH A VIOLENT JOLT, I left the darkness behind me. My eyes snapped open as I gasped for air, chest heaving in a chaotic rhythm.

The echoes of silent screams reverberated in my ears.

Esprithe damned dreams.

I shivered. Tear streaks stained my cheeks, and my muscles tinged with pain. It was just a dream. I forced myself to calm, to steady the frantic rhythm of my heart.

Breathe.

The room around me came into clear focus. I gripped my bed sheets and exhaled slowly, repeating the word several times until I felt my body relax.

This was a new dream. Given the atmosphere, I wondered if it was triggered by what we'd learned during class. I shook my head, Raine was right. It really was nightmare fuel.

I crawled out of bed and prepared myself for the day. It was going to be a long one. For the first time, I would somehow make it through a shift at the Apothecary, initiate training, and my individual session with Laryk.

The thought made me want to creep back into bed and suffocate myself with the blankets.

~

I DIDN'T ATTEMPT any small talk with Ma today. My nerves were already on edge, and I had no desire to push them further towards freefall. Now that I was only working mornings due to the strict schedule of recruitment training, we were busier than ever. It was much easier to avoid awkward silences with the extra workload.

We spoke only in short, quipped sentences that were essential to the task at hand, but nothing further.

After finishing the last of my chores, I lingered in the rear of the shop, waiting for an ideal moment. I quickly changed into my Guard uniform while Ma's back was turned, but the familiar feeling of sadness lingered as I breezed past her desk on my way out. She didn't respond to my goodbye. How much longer could we really go on like this?

Nearing the entrance of the Compound, I noticed two familiar faces leaning against the exterior walls. Raine and Briar. Raine met my gaze as I stepped onto the crosswalk. She waved eagerly.

I offered both a simple wave, closing the distance between us.

"I see you survived the weekend," Raine huffed, shooting me a smile.

"Next time you two decide to go bar hopping, I'd appreciate an invite," Briar scolded, crossing his arms.

"Briar, I told you. It was a single bar. You really didn't miss much." Raine nudged his arm.

"Seriously, most of it was spent learning the fascinating intricacies of the Guard," I murmured sarcastically. "Considering you've already learned all about that intriguing topic, I imagine you would have been bored to tears."

"I'm jealous that your first impression of our group was from *Raine*. I'm much more fun. And a far better drinking partner."

Raine cackled, playfully shoving Briar's shoulder. I smiled, looking down. I wasn't used to people wanting to hang around me so willingly. Not that I had ever given anyone much of an option.

"Are you free this evening, after training?" Briar asked with a sparkle in his eye.

Raine shot me a curious look. I had informed her of my

schedule with the General. It seemed she had kept her word and not told anyone about my individual sessions.

"I wish..." I trailed off as I wracked my brain for a coherent excuse. "I have to head back to the Central district immediately after. Plans with my roommate." I shrugged a bit too dramatically.

"Too bad. What about tomorrow?" His voice was thick with excitement. "I'm dying to pick your brain. You grew up in the city, right? You probably know all the best haunts." His eyes glimmered.

"Erm–yes, but I'm afraid I won't be of much help with that. I don't get out a lot," I admitted.

"Well, we'll just have to discover them together then. Perhaps that's even more fun," Briar mused as his eyes fluttered around the streets.

"I guess we'd better get to class. I would hate for Mercer to glare at us the entire time for being late," Raine said with a cheeky grin before turning towards the gate.

As we filtered into the Compound, I couldn't help the comfort that set in. Walking through the halls with a group was much less intimidating. I grinned, silently praising myself for managing not to scare them off. We neared the small room at the end of the row of gyms and Briar reached for the door, pulling it back and stepping aside.

"If we're late, I think you two are far more equipped to meet the Lieutenant's rage. I'm just a simple farmer boy after all." Briar smiled sweetly, gesturing for us to go ahead of him.

"How noble of you," Raine remarked, brushing past. I followed her with a gentle laugh.

Mercer was half-sitting on the table at the front of the room. He nodded to us as we entered. Baelor and Nazul sauntered in after us, followed by Draven, who looked as white as a ghost. I wondered if Baelor had anything to do with it.

Glancing around, my gaze lingered on the seats from last time–ones that were now obstructed by five stacks of black fabric.

"Change. We're starting physical conditioning today," he

remarked, pacing out of the room and shutting the door behind him.

All of our eyes shuffled around, casting unsure glances at each other. All of us except for Baelor, who strode over to his chair and snatched the clothing. Soon enough, he was undressing. I shot a look at Raine, who returned it with a confused shrug before unbuttoning her shirt.

I guess privacy was a luxury we weren't afforded.

AFTER WHAT MIGHT HAVE BEEN the most awkward series of events in my life thus far, we followed Mercer outside towards the grassy field on the back side of the Compound. The expanse was filled with members of the Scales and Fang factions, running through drills.

I shifted my weight in between steps, and stretched my arms from side to side, trying to adjust to the new black, leather uniforms we were all wearing. They were stiff and didn't offer much flexibility. It seemed an odd choice for athletic wear.

But they were sewn with the strongest fibers known to the realm, and reinforced by enchantments that leant to their strength, making them nearly impenetrable. Laryk helped design them. We couldn't wear the armor of the Base soldiers. It was too heavy. So, we wore leathers, and we'd have to get used to moving in them.

Mercer halted as we stepped onto the grass, turning to us and folding his arms behind his back.

"Agility is the one thing that might save you if you find yourself surrounded." He began pacing.

"When you're trapped in the grips of a Wraith, your focus won't matter. Your combat skills won't matter. At that point, the only option you have is to find an escape. And *fast.*" He turned to look at us.

"Only cowards run," Baelor said, crossing his arms.

The Lieutenant marched towards the pale-haired boy, stopping a mere inch from his face.

"Interrupt me again, Soleil, and I'll double your sprints." Mercer's voice was unwavering. Baelor stared back unfazed. The air around him seemed to pulse with tension. Mercer turned around and cracked his neck.

"Staying alive is not cowardly. It's your priority. The five of you will be joining our strongest faction. Your survival is vital to our mission." He cleared his throat.

"Speed is going to be important for all of you. Along with endurance and flexibility. But first, we need to get all of you into perfect shape for combat."

"See these markers?" he questioned, gesturing towards ten white lines on the ground, spaced evenly along the length of the field. "When you reach the first, you'll come back and touch the ground before running for the second, and we'll repeat this pattern for the rest of them. Understood?" He arched an eyebrow. "You're going to run them until I tell you to stop."

A collective groan ran through the group as Mercer turned his back on us.

"Take your position. I'll tell you when to begin."

We all spread out. I eyed Raine who was pouting quietly. I don't think any of us expected this today. I pulled at the collar of my top, trying to stretch out the tight fabric around my neck.

The sun blazed down on us. The air was thick and warm, nearly suffocating. We were already a few weeks into Eibhlín, but today was uncharacteristically hot. I already felt the beads of sweat prickling my forehead.

My lungs reflexively sucked in a gasp of air, sighing long and slow before turning my head, inspecting the stance of the other recruits. Everyone kneeled, anticipating the command. I followed suit.

"Go!" Mercer shouted, and we all launched forward. Baelor

shot off into the lead, expertly spinning on his heels as he reached the first marker.

I pushed myself, trying to keep a steady pace, but my lungs were already aching.

By the time conditioning was finished, we were all slumped over, gasping for air–even Baelor, who managed to lap us multiple times throughout the afternoon with a proud look on his face.

He still took every opportunity to shoot a contemptuous glance in my direction, like he wanted to spear me straight through the heart or burn me to ashes. I couldn't be sure.

As we neared the gates of the Compound, I sank down onto the cobblestone, stretching out my overworked muscles. My body hurt in places that I didn't know existed.

Guards of all factions littered the street in front of the gates, coming and going, socializing and collecting mail and deliveries.

Raine slid down beside me, groaning as she hit the ground. We both heaved in unison for a few moments.

"That was torture," she said breathlessly. I leaned forward and bent my head. My body was still trembling from the intensity of the sprints.

"Absolute torture," I agreed. A breeze wafted the sweaty curls from my face, and I sighed with relief. These leather uniforms were unbearably hot.

"And now you'll go see the General?" she asked, apprehension drenching her voice. Our breaths finally calmed, returning to their normal tempo.

"Yes," I huffed. "Although I'm not sure I'm in the best state to perform. I can't even feel my legs." A laugh escaped my lips.

"I can't feel anything. I'm about to drench myself in ice before crawling into my bed," she murmured. It sounded like a joke, but her eyes were serious.

"Not going out with Briar?"

"No fucking way." She laughed.

"I guess I'll see you tomorrow... that is, if I don't die in the next few hours," I sighed, attempting to stand. My legs wanted to give out. They trembled as I straightened them.

"Good luck." She closed her eyes, taking a deep breath. I could tell it was the only sentiment she could muster. Turning on wobbly heels, I limped off towards the gym near the Apothecary.

CHAPTER 25

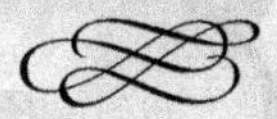

General Ashford was only just arriving at the gym as I was walking up. This would be our first time truly alone since the ball. I didn't bother changing out of my leathers. It seemed like too big of a task after the workout.

He noticed my approach and held the door open in silence, but I felt his eyes scan over me.

"Hello to you, too," I quipped, brushing past him into the familiar space. He followed me inside without a word.

I pulled a chair from the wall and sat, my muscles sighing in relief as I pulled my hair back into a tighter knot at the nape of my neck, now malleable from the sweat.

"I trust your group training with Mercer is going well?" His voice cut through the silence as he grabbed his own seat.

"I'm exhausted but it could be worse," I responded, tracking his movement.

He took his time pulling the chair over, the scraping sound grating at my ears. It didn't seem like he was listening to me at all.

"The recruits are interesting, aside from Baelor, who seems like he could murder any of us in cold blood," I half-joked. Murder *me,* perhaps. This seemed to grab a portion of his attention.

"Oh Soleil? Yes, he's a piece of work. Just like his father," Laryk responded.

"He reminds me a bit of you, actually." I raised an eyebrow, anticipating his response. His eyes shifted to me curiously.

"Don't insult me like that again, Riftborne." He actually smiled before his eyes glazed back over as he returned to whatever was occupying his mind.

I cleared my throat, feeling an edge of agitation, "So what's the plan for today?"

I watched as his teeth scraped over and released the plumpness of his bottom lip, his mouth slightly parting when he finally looked at me. "Hmm?"

"What's the plan?" I snapped, my exhaustion turning to annoyance.

What is going on with him?

I was sure it had something to do with the Wraith attacks. There was probably so much we weren't authorized to know about yet. So much we hadn't given our *blood* to know about yet. It took a strong willpower to not start asking him about everything. I slipped a shard of red jasper from my pocket and gripped it in my palm. The last thing I needed was to lose my patience.

"We have to get you caught up with the rest of the recruits. While you can't truly practice using your focus like some of the others, we need to get you to the point of full control without the release."

"So my goal is to let my focus form to the fullest extent but to not use it?"

"Correct."

I nodded. It seemed like an easy enough task, but it had been pretty resistant since the incident with the guard. Since Laryk killed him.

My eyes closed and I turned my attention to my lower spine,

willing out the translucent webbing, watching as it began braiding up my vertebrae only to retreat again.

"How do you think my focus will work against the Wraiths?"

Willpower, gone. So much for the jasper.

I wondered if I sounded nervous.

"When you found me and saw what I was capable of, I'm assuming you brought me on with these opponents in mind?"

"I have my theories," he replied vacantly.

I opened my eyes again and noticed he was back to chewing his lip.

"Will I be clued in on these theories?"

He sighed, pushing his hair away from his face. He wore it down tonight and it flowed in waves over his shoulders.

"Eventually, yes."

My mouth formed a straight line as I glared at him, hoping to see some form of his usual spark, but his mind seemed to be elsewhere.

"That's reassuring." I murmured. I gripped the stone harder, but the sweat from my palm caused it to slip and tumble onto the ground with a piercing clatter. It landed at Laryk's feet. He bent to pick it up, finally turning his attention to something other than his thoughts.

"Red jasper?" he mused, observing the shard.

"I thought it might help with my concentration. I find it very important to pay attention during our sessions. Perhaps you should hold onto it," I replied, exhaling sharply.

He half-smiled without looking at me, but kept the stone in his palm, tilting his head to the side before pursing his lips. I could see his train of thought returning to his inner world.

"Continue," he said, leaning back in his seat.

I slammed my eyes closed, trying to quell my irritation. I sought out the tendrils and goaded them up my spine. It took all of my concentration, but they climbed halfway. I pushed forward, through my exhaustion, but they wouldn't seem to rise any further.

We stayed in this battle for a few moments before I released them into the depths of my back. I shook my head and sighed. It was progress, but not much.

"I was able to get my focus under control part of the way before it started to slip. I think–"

"Good to hear." He stood abruptly. "I suggest you do some practicing in your free time as well. I'd like you to have full control in a fortnight."

"What free time?" I felt a headache starting to form in my temples as I considered the already full schedule I was working with.

"I'm going to have to call today short. I have pressing matters to attend to this evening." He ignored my question, rolling his neck and shoulders.

"Is everything okay?" I asked. It had only been half the time of our normal sessions.

"Nothing you need to concern yourself with." He didn't even glance in my direction.

"Is it… the Wraiths?" My voice was quiet.

He paused for a moment, biting his lower lip.

"Yes." It was all he said.

There was a knock on the glass.

"Laryk, are you almost ready?" Narissa cooed, leaning against the doorframe. She glanced over at me, and her expression turned sour.

"Yes, we only just finished."

I glanced over at him, reading his features. He didn't seem to light up at her presence, but he did brush past me and leave without a goodbye.

The door closed behind them in a final gust of wind.

The gym was empty now, quiet.

I swallowed my frustration before continuing the training on my own.

CHAPTER 26

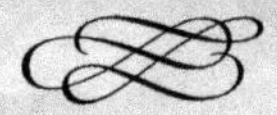

THE WARMER WEATHER had faded into cooler days as the weeks passed. It was a particularly icy evening as I made my way back to the apartment after training, wind filtering through my hair. Moonlight reflected off the canal, shifting as the currents fanned out from passing boats. I was more than exhausted, and my legs ached and wobbled.

A sigh of relief washed over me when I reached the steps to our corridor. As I neared our door, I saw that it wasn't fully closed. My body froze, nerves rushing over me. Had I forgotten to lock up?

Whimpers echoed from within.

Osta.

I slammed the door open, running inside. My pulse steadied as I found her in a ball on the couch, sobbing into her hands.

"Osta, what's wrong?" I asked, rushing over to sit beside her.

"Fia, the old hag–she…" Osta mumbled between sobs, "She fired me. For insubordination. At least that's what she said."

Shit.

"She's an idiot, Osta. See how much business she gets now that her secret weapon is gone." I attempted a smile and looped my arm through hers. "I'm sure you'll hear back from the Nobility soon..."

"I hope so."

"What happened, exactly?" I asked.

"Thearna wanted me to combine two fabrics that absolutely did *not* go together, and I refused. I just couldn't do it, Fia," Osta sobbed. "She said she was tired of me questioning her. But I was trying to do her a favor!"

"She was always going to hold you back. You were a threat to her. You know this." I tightened my arm around hers, "Plus, now–"

"But Fia, this was my plan. I don't know what to do. I don't even know if my life will mean anything now. I don't know who I am without it." Her body still shook, but her voice had lowered to just above a whisper. Her eyes were fixated on the ground, but I could tell that they were empty of their normal spark.

I shifted on the couch to face her, taking her hands in mine. "Osta, everything is going to be okay. I promise."

"It's all ruined. My entire life is ruined. I should have just kept my mouth shut. Now I have no future. No prospects," she murmured, her hands going limp in mine.

"We're going to get through this. I can try to talk to General Ashford again, ask him if he's heard from any of the Nobility?" I added. I didn't particularly want to, but I would do it for her.

"There's no point. If they were interested, they would have reached out by now."

"Osta, you don't even sound like yourself. You're really starting to scare me." I grabbed her hand a bit too forcefully. "Now stop acting like me."

A small laugh escaped her lips, and after a few seconds, she looked over at me again.

I sighed. "We're going to figure this out."

"You really think so?"

"Of course. It's you. And whatever you do next, it's going to be better than working for Thearna."

"I guess a small part of me is happy I don't have to see her every day." Osta shrugged, sitting a bit straighter.

"Exactly."

"I just need to get my mind off of it." She pouted, almost back to the Osta I knew.

A realization hit me. It was rare that I had the ability to remedy anything for her.

I wasn't going to squander the chance.

"Well… I don't know how I can distract you at the moment, but tomorrow… I'm going out with some fellow recruits. I don't know if you'd be interested in joining…" I said slowly. I arched an eyebrow in anticipation.

Osta whipped her bloodshot eyes toward me. They widened even more once she saw my expression.

"Excuse me? Fia. You're doing what now?" Osta's entire position changed as she pulled herself up and faced me, legs crossed. She wiped the tears from her cheeks, and a grin snuck up her lips.

"They invited me out after training. I think you'd like them. And they would love you. Everyone does."

Osta squealed.

"Fia. I am so proud right now. My little socialite! I've taught you well." She sighed in self-satisfaction.

Mission accomplished.

"Briar–one of the recruits, was hoping that I knew some good places to go out in Luminaria. Obviously, you're much more versed in that. Would you want to meet us at the Compound tomorrow evening with a game plan?" I eyed her, anticipating an explosion.

"Fia. I am so excited. Yes, yes, yes! Oh my, there are so many options…" she trailed off, eyes shifting as she rifled through her thoughts.

"Whatever you want to do." I squeezed her shoulder before standing.

"Thanks, Fia. Seriously, I can't believe you made friends. That's so incredible."

I winked at her before standing and taking a few paces towards my room. I paused.

"Sleepover in the living room?" I asked, whipping around to face her.

"Obviously." She grinned, throwing a pillow at me.

I laughed, catching it and tossing it back. "I'll go get the extra blankets. We can make a fort like the old days."

"Yeah, now that Fairbanks isn't around to rip it to shreds." The sound of our laughter echoed through the small apartment as I rounded the corner.

"WANT to wash up in the recruit quarters? It shouldn't be too busy right now. Base, Scales, and Fang don't finish until later," Raine said, out of breath, as we made our way back to the Compound from the field.

"I probably don't smell my best." I laughed. "So, yes. Thank you."

Training had become even more brutal, but I wasn't sure whether to blame it on the sprints or the ache in my muscles that had become nearly permanent.

"Is every day going to be like this?" I asked, following Raine through the front gate. We had to squeeze through the large influx of bodies in the lobby, all wearing pristine white shirts.

"No idea, I seriously hope not." She sighed. "I mean, at some point we'll have to learn actual combat skills, right? It can't all be defense and evasion."

"One would think," I mumbled as she led me into the Compound's lobby, through the mess hall and social area, to the door that sat in the middle of the back wall, between two lounging sofas. She pushed the door open to reveal the stairs that would take us down to the recruitment lodging.

~

As I stepped back into Raine's room, I found her in the corner, running a belt through the loops of a pair of blue-gray silk trousers. A high-necked blouse of the same color was tucked expertly, and her braids were twisted into a knot at the back of her head.

Briar was lounging on a bench, sporting a dark-green collared shirt and brown dress trousers. Perhaps I'd packed the wrong outfit for this outing. I glanced down at my typical Apothecary get-up. I'd picked the shirt with the least number of stains, at least.

Osta was waiting for us outside the gates, making conversation with a dark-haired recruit. As we approached, I saw her twirling her hair through her fingers in typical Osta fashion. Of course she had already found a member to flirt with... *Wait.* My eyes narrowed as I recognized the man.

Nazul.

Absolutely fucking not.

I quickened my pace, trying to get her attention.

Her eyes brightened as she saw us walking towards her, then soured as she looked me up and down. She shook her head but returned to her politeness upon noticing Briar and Raine a step behind me.

Nazul turned and noticed us approaching. He nodded at Osta and whispered something in her ear before sauntering off down the street.

"You must be Fia's new friends!" Osta cooed, skipping over to us. Osta elbowed me in approval, causing heat to rush over my face.

"Osta, meet Raine and Briar." I motioned between the three of them.

"Pleasure," Raine nodded with a bright smile.

"Aren't you just adorable," Briar mused, "And look at this dress! You're absolutely divine."

Osta was beaming.

She wore a pale ivory dress that fell just below her knees in simple ruffles. The sleeves hung off her shoulders, billowing out. It was all brought together by a muted floral corset that laced up the back.

"Thank you! It's lovely to meet the two of you," she gushed, before stepping close to me and whispering, "I brought something for you to wear." Heat flushed my cheeks again as I glanced down at my simple brown trousers and beige top.

I could only imagine what Osta had chosen for me.

With a groan, I held out my hand towards her. She pushed her backpack toward me with excitement.

"Go change in my room," Raine suggested, holding out a small key. I smiled and lowered my head before returning through the gates of the Compound.

I STEPPED in front of the mirror to get a view of the dress. It was made from a silken fabric the color of spiced wine, and it moved weightlessly as I turned to examine it in the mirror. The top was structured and clasped around my neck in a thin band, leaving my decolletage bare. The length spilled down into a simple A-line skirt.

I had to give it to Osta. She knew how to make a statement. The dress was simple, yet completely elegant. It made me look like I had some semblance of style, which was an impressive feat on its own.

I pursed my lips, shifting my weight as my reflection stared back at me, observing my tightly pulled back hair and permanently shrouded eyes.

Osta left some of her beauty products in the bag...

Before I could change my mind, I pulled out the black charcoal pencil and began to line my eyes. I wasn't as graceful as Osta, so I didn't have high hopes.

Stepping back, I inspected my work. Not bad. It added that semblance of allure back to my features. I bit my lip. My hair seemed all wrong.

Untying it, I let the white curls fall weightlessly around my shoulders and took a deep breath. If we were going to one of Osta's preferred spots, I might as well look the part, plus… Seeing me like this would cheer her up even more, especially without any of my normal resistance. I had committed to the facade at this point. Tugging on the matching slippers that Osta provided, I made my way to the door.

But just as my hand touched the knob, my body froze. I hadn't thought about the fact I'd have to walk through the Compound looking like this.

Alone.

My stomach churned, but it was too late now.

I took a steadying breath before nodding and stepping out into the hallway.

I started up the stairs to the mess hall, trying to walk quickly and avoid any direct eye contact. But that was difficult seeing as my legs were still stiff from conditioning. A part of me wondered if I'd make it through the night in these shoes.

We'd better be going to a place where sitting is encouraged.

A few members of infantry were sitting at a couch at the top of the stairs. Their eyes fell on me as I stepped through the doorway. I tried to tune out their whispers as I walked in between the mess hall's tables, through the bodies of people eating, writing letters, and having conversations amongst themselves. A few of them turned their attention to me as my shoes made clicking noises that sounded gravely different from the boots that normally echoed through this place.

A wince shuddered through me as I heard a whistle from somewhere behind, but I didn't let myself turn around. The lobby was only a few more steps ahead. I could feel the eyes burning holes in my back.

I collected myself and brushed past the gates, savoring the cool chill from the breeze. Osta, Raine and Briar were still talking amongst themselves. From the outside, one might have thought they had known each other for years.

Briar noticed me walking towards them, and his jaw dropped.

"Riftborne, is that you?" Raine asked, shock lacing her tone. I shook my head and looked at Osta, taking the last few steps towards them.

"It's all Osta." I rolled my eyes and threw my arm around the shoulders of my oldest friend. She was just grinning at me in self-satisfaction.

"It's new. I just finished making it last week at the shop," she said. "I knew you should be the one to wear it. Although I'm holding back nauseating jealousy! It's a great dress."

"I had no idea your hair was so curly," Raine said.

"I usually don't wear it down like this." I tugged at one of the curls, pulling until it bounced back into place.

"Well. You should. If I had your hair, I'd wear it like that every day. It's enchanting. It's like the texture has no weight, like it's floating," Briar mused before hooking arms with Osta.

Clearly those two were hitting it off.

"So did you decide on a plan?" I asked. Osta's eyes sparkled as she looked at Raine and Briar before turning to me, a mischievous grin sprawled across her face.

Oh Esprithe, what had she managed?

"I got us into the Enclave," she squealed.

"The Enclave? How is that possible?" I questioned nervously. It was one of the Apothecary's biggest clients, so I was all too aware of the types of elixirs they provided their patrons. The establishment was a mystery for most of Luminaria—a members-only club that catered almost exclusively to the elite. I gulped.

"Shun is best friends with the hostess working tonight. He was able to pull a few strings and get us reservations at one of their tables," Osta replied, a satisfied expression spreading across her face.

"I've heard whispers of it, but I never imagined that I would ever actually *go*," Raine said, excitement gleaming in her eyes.

"I've never heard of it, but yes, yes and yes. Absolutely yes. Nothing but yes." Briar was nearly vibrating.

I stopped my heart from sinking, reminding myself that tonight wasn't about me. It was about Osta.

"It's close by, right?" I asked, attempting to sound as thrilled as my fellow recruits.

"Just down the street. I'm the best, huh?" Osta cooed, turning to walk in the direction of the club. I caught up with her, hooking her other arm.

"You're something," I whispered, nudging her. She only smiled wider as we made our way down the busy street.

"By the way, we need to talk about that little flirtatious conversation I noticed back at the Compound." I looked at her, making my eyes hauntingly serious.

"What, that boy? He was so nice. Why are you looking at me like that?"

"It's a hard no. He's awful, Osta. Seriously. He's also a bigot. His best friend is the one who keeps sending me death threats with his eyes."

"Really?" Osta looked down at her Riftborne marking, disappointment fanning across her features.

"I know you have a way with even the stuffiest of Sídhe Nobility, but don't waste your time with this one, Osta. You can do much better."

She sighed and met my gaze again, smiling thinly. I nudged her.

"But let's not talk about it anymore. Tonight is all about you, so let's have fun." I winked as we continued down the street.

"This is it," Osta mused as we all examined the lackluster exterior of a low-rise dwelling with an unassuming entrance.

"Are you sure we have the right place?" I asked hesitantly. Osta stepped forward, knocking on the door in an abnormal pattern. Raine shot me a confused look, which I returned with a shrug.

The door creaked open, revealing a woman in black dress robes.

"Password, please," she stated.

"Mirage," Osta said with confidence.

"Granted," the woman stepped back and ushered us into the small room. It was bare apart from a door on the furthest wall, and the floor shifted as we walked across it. The woman stepped towards the back and slid her finger down the door. It shined a bright gold in the pattern she traced.

"Are you a light weaver?" Briar asked.

"Nearly all of us who work here are. It's the only way to unlock doors and get around," she replied with a mysterious smile.

Soon enough, I heard what sounded like a lock being turned, and the door crept open.

"Follow the stairs down. The hostess will seat you," the woman said.

We all exchanged looks before shuffling through the door and making our way down the flight of wooden stairs.

The room we entered was painted black, and pulses of music emanated from the floor. A woman with dark hair approached us with a wooden tablet in her hands.

"Reservation, please," she stated, eyeing us.

"Osta Riftborne."

The hostess didn't even flinch at the mention of our shared last name. She only smiled and softened her features.

"You're Shun's friend?" The hostess asked.

"Yes, and we really appreciate you getting us in so last minute," Osta gushed, excitement brewing.

"It was pure luck, honestly. We had a cancellation," the woman whispered. "Follow me."

She opened a door, and a shimmering light flooded the small lobby.

Shock ran through me as we stepped through. It was as if we had entered a valley covered in luscious grass in the middle of a mountain range. Stars shot across an endless black sky and a maelstrom of bodies danced in the middle of the clearing. The music was similar to what they had played in the Grove, but faster and more aggressive. It pulsed throughout the entire space.

In the middle of the sky was a massive flower that glowed in a kaleidoscope of colors. Mist spiraled off of it.

Clearly Illusionists were at work here.

And that's when I finally smelled the beguiling hint of jasmine sifting through the air. My body relaxed, becoming heavier.

Individual lounges lined the perimeter, each with their own fire pit that sparkled in shades of red, blue and purple.

We followed the woman in complete awe as she led us to a setting at the end of the line. Three black velvet sofas created a U shape above the grassy terrain.

"Here's your table for the night. If you desire refreshments, just throw one of these into the fire," she said as she handed Osta a small pouch.

We all shuffled towards the couches, slipping onto the soft cushions.

"I hope you enjoy your evening." The woman winked before turning and making her way back through the field.

"Oh. My. Esprithe be damned..." Raine said, shaking her head in awe.

Osta was already tearing into the pouch, digging her hand in to reveal the contents. She pulled out a small amber crystal.

"Shall I?" she asked, wickedness creeping into her eyes.

"What else are we here for?" Briar clapped, jumping in his seat.

Osta held her hand over the fire and dropped the crystal in. After a few moments, a golden-hued smoke billowed from the pit, and the fragrance of burning copal filled my lungs.

"I can't believe we're actually here." Osta sighed. "After yesterday, this type of distraction is exactly what I need."

"What happened yesterday, love?" Briar sat up, placing his elbows on his knees.

Osta's eyes darted towards me.

"Her boss fired her," I said flatly.

"Because I made some suggestions to a design she was working on. The fabric she wanted to use made no sense for the structure of the blouse," Osta said with exasperation.

"If these two pieces are any indication of your talent, it sounds like she should have been working for *you,*" Raine said. "How do I sign up for the next gown?"

Osta's cheeks flushed as she smiled shyly. It was a rare response from her.

"I'd love to make something for you, truly. I'm just not sure how I'll have access to the same materials now that I don't work with a seamstress," Osta's eyes became glassy.

From the depths of the party, a man adorned in sparkling yellow robes approached, holding out a tray of shimmering, golden vials. The four of us exchanged confused glances.

"Erm–I think you might have the wrong table," Osta said nervously, brushing away the premature tears and straightening in her seat. "We haven't ordered anything yet."

"We provide the cures for desire and revelry. Our cocktails are delivered upon the assessment of a group's collective need," he stated simply, urging the tray towards us.

"So what is this, then?" Briar asked, curiosity spilling over his features.

"What the group needs," the man said.

Raine reached out and grabbed a vial, followed by Briar. Osta shot me an apprehensive look, but slowly pulled one off the tray and handed it to me before taking the last one for herself. The man bowed and sauntered off into the darkness.

"Any idea what this is?" Briar asked, eyes shifting from one of us to the next.

I cleared my throat. "I think it's liquid Euphoria, but it seems to have been enhanced somehow," I stated, examining the vial. We made this potion at the shop. It was quite simple actually, but this one was teeming with enchantments.

"That sounds like fun," Raine mused, spinning the contents around, the shimmering liquid reflecting the firelight.

"This place is amazing," Briar agreed.

"I can't be sure what the effects would be..." I trailed off. This seemed like a bad idea. Immediately, my nerves returned. My eyes shot throughout the crowd.

"If everyone is in agreement, I am." Osta popped off the top of hers before extending it above the fire. Briar did the same.

"Cheers to Osta," Raine said, following suit.

Everyone held their vials above the fire, and my mind began racing. They all seemed transfixed on the revelry around us. I swallowed hard before slowly meeting their hands and clinking the glasses in unison. Before I could talk myself out of it, I tipped it back and consumed the contents.

I leaned back into the couch with trepidation, awaiting the effects that would soon take hold.

As moments slipped past, I looked around the expanse, at the people dancing beyond. Muted lights began forming in the distance, aligning with their forms, as if their minds were glowing. This was going to be much stronger than the liquid euphoria I had always known.

I closed my eyes, trying to distract myself from the changing surroundings, but it was a futile attempt. Something in me roared to look, to see, to take in the world around me, and my eyes fluttered open once again.

The throbbing of light emanating from the sky intensified, meshing with my own heartbeat. The place seemed to dance in slow motion. I looked over to my friends who seemed to be experiencing the same state of dreaminess. Their jaws all gaped open as they took in the sights with this new magnified perspective.

I couldn't help the clumsy smile that spread across my face. Everything felt good. Everything felt like it was exactly as it should be. Any nerves from earlier disappeared into the void of my mind, replaced with curiosity… wonder… euphoria.

As if in a trance, we stood from the couches and joined hands, making our way to the center of the field, where the strums of music were the most intense.

We joined in with the mass of bodies swaying to the rhythm. I looked over to Osta. She was laughing, nearly doubling over. Raine and Briar were in similar states. The four of us twisted and twirled throughout the crowd as we surrendered to the effects of the elixir, letting it take hold completely.

I had never felt so free, carelessly letting my body react to the world around me. My eyes glazed over as I leaned my head back and took in the flower above. It shifted and radiated with flashing lights that matched my own frequencies. I couldn't help but get caught in its magnetic pull.

My senses were blasted by the environment around me.

The smell of jasmine was overwhelming, filtering through my nose like an addictive toxin. My ears rang from the sounds of energetic melodies, dancing through my body with unfettered intensity.

Even my mouth was electrified by the taste of the air around me, sweet and alluring. I licked my lips, desperate for more of the flavor.

Something dark pulled at the back of my mind… something I needed to be worried about. Something I needed to remember. But it was too far gone, and the lights were far too bright.

I shut off that part of me and gave myself fully to the colorful kaleidoscope.

CHAPTER 27

THE FOUR OF us stumbled out of the unassuming doors of the Enclave a few hours later, still swaying with remnants of the elixir. My mind had begun to return to the reality around us, and I noticed how empty the streets were.

"Osta, we should head home," I hummed.

"Yeah… we should go," Osta said with a quiet smile, her eyes still dancing.

"Are you sure? You could bunk with me at the Compound tonight." Raine's eyes shifted between us.

"That's alright. We wouldn't want to impose," I said softly, still distracted by the lights shimmering around me.

"I insist. Really, I don't want the two of you walking home alone this late. In this condition." Her voice was stern, but her gaze was following something sparkly in the distance.

"I agree with Raine. You two should stay at the Compound tonight. It's no problem," Briar said calmly, lacing his arm through Osta's.

My best friend dared a glance at me, but her eyes didn't fully focus on mine. I shrugged. Perhaps we weren't in the right state of mind to make the trek.

"Okay... yeah, if it's really not a big deal. I think we'll take you up on the offer," I replied.

"Anytime," Raine said as we filtered through the darkened streets of Luminaria, still locked in a haze.

Nerves returned, tickling my back as we approached the gates. It was ghostly quiet, but guards still loomed, securing the entrance.

I avoided eye contact as Raine provided her identification. The guard grunted but opened the gates. I could feel the annoyance radiating from him as we passed into the lobby.

We were all holding back giggles as we stepped into the mess hall. Everything was excruciatingly funny right then. My cheeks were aching from smiling so much. I assumed it was a lingering effect of the elixir.

Noticing the silence of the complex made us even more hyper-aware, causing us to dramatically tiptoe and exchange heightened glances that nearly always resulted in tipsy grins.

Just as we reached the stairs leading to the recruitment quarters, Osta's bag tumbled out of her arms with a loud thud. Her eyes went wide with concern before we all doubled over in silent, hissing laughter.

She gasped as she collected the contents from the floor, and her posture egged on more giggles. Briar let out a screech of a cackle and Raine threw her hand over his mouth.

My body was still heaving from trying to control the onslaught of humor when we heard the creaking of a large metal door in the distance.

My heart stopped as footsteps thundered through the corridor above.

I heard someone clear their throat, and I immediately recognized the sound.

Our eyes shot up to the balcony, but we saw nothing. The voice seemed to echo throughout the room.

"Are you all that inebriated?" he chided. My eyes shifted to the staircase to see a figure emerging. A shiver ran up my spine.

His copper hair sprawled out onto the shoulders of his black shirt. The scar on his face seemed to pulse with anger. All of us gasped in unison.

He stopped a few feet in front of us, crossing his arms and raising an eyebrow. We stayed quiet, shifting our weight. For some reason, even this situation made me want to burst out in frantic waves of laughter, but I held back. I didn't dare make eye contact with any of my friends. I knew a single glance would have us doubling over. And now was, perhaps, the most inappropriate time to do so.

"Have you all gone mute?" Laryk demanded, stress creasing his brow. I could have sworn he stomped his foot.

"No, sir," Briar attempted. A collective jolt surged through the group. I dared a glance at Raine, who desperately held her lips in a tight line.

Ashford looked us all over before rolling his eyes. "Off to bed." His voice was slick and sharp as a knife.

Relief rushed through us as we started towards the flight of stairs.

"Fia. A word," he said flatly. I shook my head rigidly at my friends, urging them to keep calm. I turned around and slowly paced towards Laryk. Cries of laughter echoed behind us.

He studied me for a second, clenching his jaw before sauntering off towards one of the windowed gyms.

A spark of anger ran through me as I clumsily followed him. In my peripherals, lights still danced and weaved themselves throughout the space.

He yanked open the door and motioned for me to enter. I didn't even shoot a glance his way before trudging into the room. It was dark, only lit by the light that filtered in from the mess hall.

"What were you *thinking,* recruit?" His voice was like ice reverberating through the room.

I made my way to the stone wall in an attempt to balance myself. The proper annoyance made its way into my mind, fighting past the elixir.

"Building comradery," I said flatly. My back hit the stone less gracefully than I intended.

"Is that what you call this?" His words were sharp as he paced towards me. The sound echoed in my ears.

"It's what you called it," I slurred, noticing the light that glimmered around him. I swallowed hard as my eyes found his. A shock ran through me when I noticed their intensity. Something inside me burned.

He roared towards me, stopping only a foot away.

"Fia. You're high," he insisted, running his hand through his hair. The heat coming off him was sobering, but not quite enough to kill all of the elixir's effects.

"I'm fine," I whispered. My back flattened against the wall; my breath heavy. I could feel the static emanating between our bodies... So close... What would it feel like if he touched me?

"You're not fine. Do you even understand how irresponsible this is? Coming back here in this state?" His voice took on a desperate tone, and I could smell the whiskey on his breath. I stayed silent.

"It's different for you. And you know that." He shook his head, stepping a breath closer.

"I don't see why. This Compound is no different from the streets I walk every day," I shot back, my mind twirling from the audacity of his words and the heat of his closeness.

"People on the streets don't have the same privileges that the members of the Guard do, and you should know that," he growled. His hand grazed my arm, sending a shiver down my spine.

I stepped forward, our lips nearly touching. The air vibrated around us, and his jaw tensed.

"Don't act like you actually care," I whispered, locking my eyes with his.

Suddenly, his hands were at my waist, pushing me against the wall. The movement was quick and desperate. And full of need...

I was full of need.

My body rushed with electricity at the feeling of his grip. The temptation to force him closer was immense, but I fought back with every fiber of my being.

It had to be the liquid euphoria... there was no way I actually wanted this man to...

And suddenly, his body slammed into mine, and I could feel his breath on my cheek. I bit back a whimper.

A delicious feeling seared through me. *Yes...*

I did want this... I didn't care if it was real or not. It felt good.

Right.

Explosive.

Ecstasy danced along the surface of my skin. I wanted a release. I needed a release.

Just as I was about to reach up and run my fingers through his hair, I felt his body relax. He leaned his forehead against mine, exhaling slowly.

"You're impossible, Fia," he whispered. The touch of his head against my own was going to drive me to madness. My hands were still twitching with the need to grab him...

Please don't stop.

But then he loosened his grip and backed away. My gaze fell to the ground, as embarrassment overwhelmed me.

Why did I want more?

He clenched his jaw, pacing in the opposite direction. "I'm just trying to keep you alive." He sighed, nearing the door. His body seemed rigid. As he gripped the handle, he paused. I thought he might say something more, but eventually, he pulled it open and sauntered out, leaving me alone in the dimly lit room. I could have sworn there were two sets of footsteps echoing through the mess hall.

"Drink some fucking water." I heard from down the corridor.

With my back still pressed against the wall, I sank to the ground. *What was wrong with me?* I should hate him. Everything about him. My feelings made no sense… I didn't even recognize myself anymore. Shame crept into my mind, only mildly competing with the need that still clung to my bones.

He was a general in the Guard… I was nothing more than a weapon to him. That had been made crystal clear. He was wildly unavailable and my… desires were inappropriate and completely misguided.

I repeated the sentiments over and over again in my mind, waiting for them to take effect. I hugged my knees and rocked back and forth, trying to quell the ache that had started building in my core. The one I couldn't allow to permeate me any further.

Sadness soon replaced it.

It was just the liquid Euphoria.

It had to be.

And now I was coming down hard.

CHAPTER 28

I COULD ACTUALLY FEEL my brain jostling around in my head as we ran. Raine had already hunched over a few times expelling whatever she'd managed to eat earlier. Briar almost looked as pale as me.

I chugged my water but no matter how much I drank, my mouth still felt thick and dry.

Knowing that this run was only our *warm-up* had my head reeling. If only I could stop constantly recalling my humiliating encounter with Laryk. Maybe that would lessen the pounding in my skull.

At least today, the sun was covered by the clouds and an occasional breeze would pass, cooling our clammy skin.

"I think I might die." Briar's voice was muffled. He was sitting in the grass with his head between his knees.

Raine was splayed out like a starfish beside him, her long eyelashes brushing the tops of her cheekbones.

Thunder rumbled in the distance.

I knew if I sat down now there would be no getting back up. I stood with my hands on my hips trying to catch my breath.

My attention was caught when I overheard Draven's raised tone a few feet away. He was standing off against Baelor and Nazul.

"Everything you've been provided and everything you have and will achieve is all because of your *father* and family name," Draven stated, with a determination I had never seen from him before.

"I've proven myself enough to be chosen for this faction. That merit is my own. However, I will proudly carry on my family's legacy, as every fire wielder before me," Baelor responded unfazed.

I could see Draven's frustration growing.

"How do you expect us to fight alongside you when we don't even know what your focus is? Perhaps it's *you* who shouldn't be here if you're so ashamed," Baelor continued.

"Draven, why won't you just tell us?" Nazul chimed in, throwing his hands up.

"You'll have to fight me to find out," Draven seethed.

I opened my mouth to speak on Draven's behalf, but my words were cut off.

"As you wish." Baelor's arm swung out in an instant, his fist rushing forward to connect with Draven's face. The snap of bone echoed through the field.

I gasped and rushed over to him.

"Espirithe sake, Draven are you okay?" I knelt beside him, trying to get a look at the damage. Blood poured from his nose into his palm. He recoiled from my grasp.

"I'm fine," he assured me, but the amount of blood told me otherwise. He did his best to distance himself.

"Draven, come on, let me help you up." I stepped towards him again, but he shot me a horrified look.

That was when I heard a loud thud from behind us. I snapped my head around to see Baelor on the ground, his mouth formed into a tight grimace.

His fist, covered in blood, was deathly still. In fact, his whole body had stiffened into odd angles like he'd been frozen mid-step before toppling over. I would have thought he was made of stone if not for the desperate shifting of his eyes.

Raine looked between the two of them, a curious expression on her face.

"Woah... Draven. Are you a blood lock?" Her eyes were wide, and I could tell she was trying to stop herself from smiling as she looked over at Baelor's frozen form.

Draven nodded, his head wincing at the movement.

"Paralyzing." His voice sounded pinched.

"We should get you to the healers." I took a small step back from him, not wanting to accidentally end up on the ground like Baelor.

Nazul was pacing around his friend frantically when he finally noticed Lieutenant Mercer.

"Draven paralyzed Baelor. What do we do?"

Lieutenant Mercer pursed his lips, taking in the scene.

"From what I saw *and* overheard; Soleil seemed highly interested in what Porter's focus was. Seems like he found out."

He had been there the entire time.

"How long will he be stuck like this?" Nazul knelt down.

"Only a few minutes. He will be fine," Mercer said.

"I don't know. This seems like the perfect time for sparring practice." Raine grinned, her eyes sparkling.

"Esprithe!" Baelor spat from his position on the ground.

"See? The effects are already wearing off." Mercer seemed to be fighting back a grin.

Another minute passed and eventually Baelor was up on his elbows, scowling. Nazul tried helping him into a sitting position, but Baelor shoved his arm away.

Draven left to see a healer, and the Lieutenant began setting up our agility course for the day. My eyes fell on Baelor once again.

"Don't even look at me, Riftborne." Baelor sneered at me.

I raised an eyebrow, choosing to ignore him.

He breathed out sharply, upper lip raising in a look of disgust.

"At least it's now clear why you're allowed inside the gates of this institution."

Everyone's eyes shot towards Baelor. Sparks crackled at Raine's fingertips. "Oh yeah, Baelor, why is that?"

"She's corrupted General Ashford. They're sleeping together. Both should be put to the blade," he stated, satisfaction lacing his words.

My lips parted. Shame overcame me. Nothing had happened... but I couldn't have imagined the way we looked last night... If he saw us.

Which he clearly did. I thought I heard two sets of footsteps.

My breath caught in my lungs at the thought. I had wanted it, like a bloody fucking idiot. If it had been up to me... Baelor might just be speaking the truth. Regret began to weigh me down, but I needed to defend myself all the same. Nothing happened... The General had made sure of it. I tried to dispel the sadness that the realization brought with it.

"That's not true–" I began to object.

"He's a disgrace to the Guard," Baelor spat.

"You will stand before the disciplinary court for the sentiments you've railed against our General. Wishing death upon any of our leaders will be met with swift punishment," Mercer said, voice unwavering.

Baelor looked towards the sun, dusting his shoulders off like he hadn't a care in the world.

"I'm the son of the most powerful General to ever serve this realm, I'll remind you, Lieutenant."

Mercer simply blinked, pausing momentarily before calling the lesson for the day.

~

My HEART RACED as I walked to the gym. After last night, how would Laryk behave? Would he be upset? Would we address whatever that *moment* was?

A sigh escaped me. It shouldn't matter. He had a point, of course. Sober me would have never put myself in that situation, intoxicated in a Compound full of people who could or could not hate me... could or could not *kill* me. But I was an adult, capable of making my own choices.

Baelor's comments had my head spinning in every direction. Deep down, his words had stabbed me harder than if they had been true. Desire still lingered in my mind, but I forced myself to believe it would smother itself in time.

My mind drifted to Ashford... our time in the darkened halls of the Compound.

Against the wall...

My face heated at the thought. His presence was seared into my mind in vivid detail. It was almost maddening. Sweat clung to me desperately. I suddenly became all too aware of my racing heart.

Almost on demand, the sky bottomed out. Threads of rain lashed down over the city, instantly drenching me and dousing the embers that had started burning under my skin.

I let the torrent wash away the memory as I made my way into the gym. Lightning cracked behind me, illuminating the street.

Reaching the practice area, it became clear that I was alone. Darkness filled the room, thick and silent. No sign of the General. I opted to start without him, practicing visualization exercises with my eyes open–anything to avoid succumbing to the pulls of sleep. I counted the vertebrae as the tendrils danced up my spine.

I couldn't help wondering where he was.

Probably working on something far above my level of knowledge. Perhaps Wraiths were descending on Luminaria at that very moment.

If only I could convince myself I believed that.

If I was being honest, my mind kept going to that dark place.

The one I was ashamed to admit existed. The one where two redheads were entangled, twisting in sheets, mirroring the rage of the storm outside.

My eyes burned at the thought, and I quickly shoved it from my mind.

Stop acting like an Esprithe-damned schoolgirl.

The General eventually sauntered in, seemingly oblivious to how late he was.

"Any progress?" he asked with a tone of indifference.

Breaking my concentration, I stole a glance in his direction.

Laryk's hair was slicked back and dripping, creating a small puddle on the floor. The button down he wore was nearly translucent from the downpour, clinging to every dip and contour of his frame.

"Y-yes, actually. I've been practicing with my eyes open today. I can't hold onto it for too long, but I've been able to call it forward consistently," I stammered, shifting in my seat.

My eyes were locked on him, railing against my better judgment. I hated how much I loved looking at him.

He tugged at the collar of his shirt with no regard to my lingering stare. "And you've been able to keep a hold on it during group training? Nothing has set you off?"

His fingers deftly worked on the shirt's buttons, each one revealing more ivory skin that glistened in the dimly lit gym, giving way to the defined muscles and sculpted shoulders beneath.

Fire surged through me, followed by an icy chill. I was instantly grateful for the cold fabric that clung to my skin.

A round of thunder reverberated through the room, shaking the equipment around us.

"Yeah, I guess the training did pay off," I murmured, finally managing to look away. It was true. The things that Baelor said earlier that day used to unravel me, but somehow, without even realizing it, I'd integrated those mental exercises into my daily life.

A blush warmed my cheeks as the accusations echoed in my

mind. What would Laryk think if he knew the rumors that had been spoken into existence today? The threats rallied at him?

I certainly wouldn't be the one to bring it up.

He walked towards the wall lined with locked cabinets, producing a key from his back pocket and sliding it into one of the doors. Once opened, he pulled out a crumple of black fabric.

He tossed me a cotton shirt before slipping the other over his head. Another lightning strike shot just outside the windows, brightening the room. My gaze dropped to the shirt before flickering back to him.

"I could see you shivering all the way over here, but if you prefer your soaked leathers, by all means," he sighed.

I blinked.

Noticing my hesitation, he chuckled and turned around, gesturing with his hand. "The room is yours."

I took the moment to quickly peel off my leather training top, replacing it with the warm oversized shirt. My senses were suddenly enveloped by the scent of vetiver and burnt amber. The scent of him.

I stopped my mind from melting and cleared my throat.

"Are we decent?" he asked. His words hummed over my skin.

"Mhm," I managed to get out. I could hear the smirk in his voice.

Without a glance in my direction, he grabbed a seat and positioned it a few feet in front of me. For a brief second, I wondered if there was a reason for the distance.

I shook the thought from my mind; it would be easier to concentrate this way. I couldn't imagine what his proximity might stir in me right now.

I felt pathetic.

I had never needed or wanted anyone before. And I sure as Fírinne didn't want to start now.

Rain continued to pour down in torrents above us, spattering across the roof and obscuring our view of the street outside. His eyes drifted past me, glazing over. It seemed as though his detachment from the last session had returned.

"You seem distracted." I couldn't help myself from pointing it out. I wouldn't spend another day immersed in his disinterest. My progress might have been slow, but I truly felt I was getting a grasp on things.

"There is a lot going on right now." He shook his head, returning his attention to me. "I've been working nonstop. When I ran into you last night, I had just left an all-day briefing. I'm... sorry if I came off too harshly." He sounded as tired as I felt. When his eyes met mine, they reflected something soft. Pity.

"No, it's fine," I responded quickly.

He was *sorry*.

Sorry it happened.

Laryk leaned back in his chair and ran his hands through his copper locks. "But I do need to discuss something with you." He cleared his throat.

"Should I be worried?" I lifted an eyebrow, breaking free from my unwanted thoughts.

"It's nothing you should concern yourself with at the moment, but..." his voice trailed off, as if trying to find the right words. "I'm being dispatched to Stormshire tomorrow, and I don't know how long I'll be gone. It could be a few weeks, perhaps even a month. Maybe two."

"Did something happen?" I straightened in the chair.

He was leaving...

He looked down and pursed his lips. After a moment, his eyes met mine again, deadly serious.

"I'll need you to keep this conversation between us. I don't want the entire Compound in a state of disarray."

"You're actually starting to scare me now. How bad is it?" I felt a tremble run down my spine. Worry for him churned through me, and I twisted in my seat, trying to get rid of it.

He was the General. He would be fine.

"Wraiths have found a way around our guards. We've since intensified the watchtowers across the border, so it shouldn't happen again, but we have to proceed with extreme caution. I need to be there so that I can…" He looked away. "I need to be there to help. Mercer will be staying here. You all need to finish your training. It's paramount that you all are ready for whatever is coming."

I sat frozen, staring at him.

"Speak, please," he stated flatly.

"So our individual training is paused indefinitely?" My voice sounded weaker than I would have liked.

Laryk's eyes softened again. "Unfortunately. But I want you to keep practicing on your own. You've made such great progress." He shifted as though he might move closer, but paused, finally dropping his hands into his lap.

"Is she going with you?" I couldn't stop myself from asking. I had no right to know. But I wanted to.

"Who?" He asked, confusion peaking his brow.

"Narissa." I felt my cheeks get hot. Suddenly I wanted to go drench myself in the rain outside.

"Of course. She's my third in command, behind Mercer." His face tilted as his eyes studied me, likely wondering why I'd asked such a thing.

Immediately, I regretted it. An unfamiliar ache ran through me. I wanted to forget this conversation. I wished I could take it back. I didn't want to feel like this.

"Fia, you have to promise me something." A seriousness washed over his eyes. One that caught me even more off-guard. "You have to promise me that you'll stay out of trouble while I'm away. Remember to address those in a station above you as you should, with respect. Don't try to make any new friends outside of Venom. Don't do anything risky."

The seriousness in his eyes turned into a sort of pleading, almost as if he was desperate for the words to sink into my skin.

"I won't be here to protect you." He said in a quiet voice.

I opened my mouth, and then closed it, unsure of what to say. I simply nodded.

"Do you promise?"

"Yes." It was all I could muster.

"And you must continue your training. It's never been as important as it is right now."

"I'll make sure I'm at peak control by the time you return," I said, giving him a look of reassurance. I hoped it seemed genuine.

"Well, that's good to hear." He offered me a small smile and leaned forward, resting his forearms against his knees. "What's gotten into you?"

I shook off the question as I sunk back into my lower spine, diverting my attention to the tendrils and the tendrils alone.

CHAPTER 29

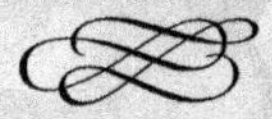

Darkness surrounded me.

It was vast. Specks of light dotted the expanse as misty clouds wafted across.

I felt my feet sinking down, finally meeting a ground that wasn't visible.

I attempted a step forward, and was immediately unsuccessful. My body wouldn't move.

I began to see a small sliver of something reflective in the distance, slithering toward me. As it approached, I realized it was translucent, as if lit from within. It looked like the webbing that rested at the base of my spine.

I reached out, and it began to swirl through my fingers. A smile crept up my lips.

Soon enough, another was flying toward me, drifting into my other hand. They doubled in size, then tripled, weaving their way up my arms.

Suddenly, they began to pull me, as if wanting me to walk forward, but my feet still wouldn't budge. They unraveled themselves and retreated to the darkness once again.

I wondered where they wanted me to go.

What they wanted me to see.

~

OSTA WAS SPRAWLED out on the sofa as I stepped into the living room. One hand was draped over her eyes, and she was gripping a few pages of parchment in the other. A quill and ink sat unused on the table.

"Osta? Did you sleep in here?" I asked, noticing the small throw haphazardly covering her lower half.

"Hmm?" Osta murmured, rubbing her eyes. She slowly sat up on her elbows and leaned her head back to look at me, still squinting from the early morning light.

"Oh–erm, I must have dozed off," she said quietly. I walked over, gently tugging the blank parchment from her hand.

"What were you doing with this?" I raised an eyebrow. I'd never seen Osta write in anything beyond her design journal.

"I haven't heard from any of the Nobility about a follow-up..." she murmured, running her fingers through her hair. I sat down at the end of the sofa. I could spare a few moments before heading to the Apothecary.

"You were going to write to them?" I eyed her hesitantly.

"Well, one of them. Lady Soleil. She was the one who really seemed to like me." Osta sighed.

I paused for a moment, turning the words over in my mind. Soleil was the one she told me about at the ball, but I hadn't yet connected it with...

"Baelor's mother?" I asked with wide eyes. The thought of Osta working for people of such prejudice was nauseating. I wasn't sure I'd even allow her to do it, knowing how nasty their opinions of Riftborne were.

"Lyanna Soleil. She's the wife of Lord Soleil. They don't have children from what I was able to gather."

Lord? I knew Baelor came from generations of Nobles turned military heroes, but I wasn't aware that any of them still maintained their Noble status. Being a general, even a *retired* general, in the Sídhe Guard well outshined a title of Lord or Lady.

"So not the wife of General Soleil?" I questioned.

"Ysabeau? Oh, absolutely not. She wouldn't give me a second glance." Osta huffed a small laugh, shaking her head. "She practically turned her back to me any time I opened my mouth to speak. Her and Lyanna seem like polar opposites." She twisted her lips, looking down at her blank parchment. "Their husbands must be brothers."

"You didn't tell me any of that," I said, leaning back into the sofa.

"It wasn't important. I wanted to focus on the positive." A half smile crept up her lips.

"Well, don't worry too much. Write to her, even if you don't send it out." I reached for the quill and ink, pushing it closer. "I would stay with you, but I'll be late to the Apothecary. Don't want to give Ma any more reasons to be upset with me." I sighed, standing.

"She still hasn't come around?" Osta eyed me gently.

"No, and I don't expect her to. I think this is just the new normal. At least until I get stationed out West, which seems certain now that–"

I winced, an unfamiliar pain shooting through me, stopping the words from coming out of my throat.

The blood oath.

I couldn't tell Osta anything about the Wraiths or the impending doom that now seemed to be spiraling rapidly towards Sídhe. I whispered a curse under my breath.

Osta shot her eyes towards me. "What are you talking about?" she asked quickly.

"I just assume, being in the General's faction, I'll probably be stationed where he spends most of his time." I shrugged, trying to play it off.

Osta paused for a moment, realization setting in.

"I guess I hadn't thought that far ahead," she whispered.

"I don't think any of us expected me to make it this far, if I'm being honest." I chuckled, looking around.

The room went deathly silent.

"But I could be wrong. I don't know what his plan is for me..." I lied. "Even if I'm deployed, it's not forever. I'll have to come back to Luminaria sometime." I swallowed hard. She stared at the wall with glassy eyes. "And I'll still be able to send back money for my half of the rent..." My words seemed to have no effect on her.

After a few moments, she sighed. "I did say I'd support you through all of this. I just can't imagine being here without you."

"There's no reason to be upset about it now. Let's save that for when we actually know something definite. Anyway, I'm sure you'll be living your best life at some noble estate soon enough."

I walked over and wrapped my arms around her. "Seriously, focus on you right now. Don't worry about me. I'll see you after work, okay?" I raised an eyebrow and gave her a reassuring smile, waiting for her to acknowledge me before making another move.

She nodded. I turned towards the door and escaped into the hallway before the tears in my own eyes could start to swell.

I LOOKED up as Ma slammed the back door of the Apothecary, hobbling over and dropping a plant box onto her desk, causing dirt to spatter across the floor.

"How is this even possible?" She nearly yelled, throwing her hands on her hips and sighing loudly.

"What is it, Ma?" I asked, rushing over to see what she was so upset about. I peered into the plant box to see that our collection of rare flowers had died. Not a single shred of life remained in their petals, which fell to the ground around us. Even the soil looked devoid of color.

Ma reached into the box, digging into the dirt with her hands. She pulled out a dusty, violet-blue crystal. I recognized it immediately as arcanite from the way light seemed to glow within it. But this stone seemed brighter and more intense than I remembered.

"This is supposed to help them grow," Ma said, dusting off the surface of the crystal. She tossed it onto her desk and sunk her head into her hand.

"I don't understand either," I murmured, careful not to upset her even further. "When will the rare plants trader be back in Luminaria?" I asked.

"Not for another six months," she said flatly, slumping into her desk. I could feel her irritation. I hated this feeling, like I was walking on eggshells around Ma. The Apothecary felt so different now. A home away from home that had once brought me so much peace and security now made my anxiety flare up in violent waves. I couldn't help but laugh at how much had changed in such little time. Was it possible that I found more comfort in the *Compound* of all places?

I loved Ma so much. That hadn't changed. But her disapproval of my decisions was beginning to take its toll. I didn't know how many more of her scowls I could tolerate.

The pressure from the Guard was enough on its own. And there was so much more... My priorities had taken on a new alignment. One of those was *protecting* her, and Osta, and the entirety of Luminaria for that matter. Even if I couldn't tell anyone about it.

I tried my best to stay focused on the distillations that Ma tasked me with, but my mind continued to wander. This seemed so inconsequential in comparison to the threats that were brewing in the West. My thoughts were spinning with shadows, Wraiths, and darkness.

I managed to grind about half of the herbs needed for a particular tonic Ma was crafting when I noticed the sun looming halfway over the horizon. I needed to get out of here, or I'd be late for training. I would just have to finish tomorrow.

I began storing away the powder when I felt Ma approach from behind. She peered over my shoulder.

"Fia, I really need all ten bottles done before you leave. They're picking up the order later today. You know my hands are too shaky to get them to the right texture."

"I'm really sorry Ma, but I can't be late to training. My body cannot handle the extra sprints." I bit my lip, cautiously eyeing her reaction as I continued to gather my things.

"Fia, please, I really needed this done. If you hadn't been staring off into space all day, you would have finished with plenty of time to spare," she said coldly.

"I've got a lot on my mind," I stated, trying to control my tone.

"Yeah, that's your constant state of being these days. I don't even recognize you." Ma threw up her hands, gesturing towards my appearance. "You don't even wear your work uniform anymore. I only see you in this," she spat. "Just another reminder of the mindless puppet you're being molded into."

Rage flared at her accusation, and a realization washed over me. Ma and I had once been one in the same, and that used to make me happy. She used to make me feel like I wasn't so alone. But now, the truth crept into my blood like a poison.

Although she didn't do it intentionally, Ma fed into my greatest fears and weaknesses to keep me safe, to keep me out of harm's way. But all it really did was hold me back. So much of my life had changed for the better since joining the Guard. But maybe she would never see that.

"I was a ticking time bomb and a danger to everyone around me. *This* was the only way. I'm no puppet. I am finally able to be who I am meant to be without fear and anxiety. I am stronger, more confident. Don't you want that for me?" I pleaded. I needed her to understand. Desperation clung to my skin like sweat.

"Your decision makes no sense to me, Fia! This change happened so quickly. And there seems to be no good explanation! You're throwing your life away. I can't bear the thought of you dying for the Guard. Do you know what that would do to me?" Ma shouted, frustration lacing her expression.

I paused. I could tell her... I could finally tell her the truth about the Grove. About what I had done to Bekha and Jordaan, but everything inside me was revolting. Telling her would be worse. It was better this way. I couldn't bear the thought of her looking at me with that fear from before. I'd rather she hated me for something she didn't understand.

"Ma, I can't explain it, but I'm a part of something now. I can be useful. I can help protect the people I love instead of being a danger to them. I don't take any of this lightly." Tears welled in my eyes. The words tumbled out, but I knew they would make no difference.

She paused for a moment, and then clicked her tongue.

"It seems their ways have burrowed too deeply into your mind. You're radicalized. You can't even see reason anymore, Fia. You're a stranger." She shook her head, sighing.

"I'm done having this conversation with you over and over. You need to accept my decision–"

"Or what?" Ma hissed. Her eyes were now flickering with flames.

"Or I'll have no choice but to remove myself from this situation." I tried to keep my voice strong, but I couldn't help the crack that sounded at the finality of my words.

I knew how much that would hurt her. After losing her brother to the Guard, I knew she would think I was doing the same thing. Abandoning her.

Ma huffed a sarcastic laugh and turned away from me.

"By all means, Fia. Run off to your *faction*. Don't do me any more favors. You clearly don't want to be here anymore."

"I'm not Miguel." My voice was just above a whisper.

Her eyes flew back to me, and I saw the hurt inside them, burning across her irises.

"You might as well be."

We stood in silence, Ma unmoving, keeping her back to me. I could see the heat emanating from her palms.

"I'll start looking for your replacement," she said. The parchment she had been holding turned to ash and fell like snow onto the floor.

I winced as her words hit me. My mouth opened in protest, but I realized… she was right. I didn't want to be here anymore. There really was nothing left to say.

I grabbed what was left of my belongings and rushed out the door without a backwards glance, breathing in the scent of smoke and burning ink as the door shut behind me.

CHAPTER 30

I MADE it to the Compound with only a minute to spare.

Falling into step with the others, I allowed the sounds of pounding feet against the earth to calm my mind and ease the pain from what had just happened at the Apothecary.

My sour mood must have been noticeable to Raine and Briar because they both offered me space until the warm-up was complete.

It seemed pointless to bring up my argument with Ma to my friends here. It would seem so minuscule to what we are all facing. That was my old world.

My new world was filled with training, learning, and of course, the growing anxiety about the West, Wraiths, and when we would be deployed. I could barely sleep at night. The fear kept me in a constant state of consciousness.

"You good?" Briar asked as he sidled up to me, bumping my shoulder.

"I'm okay," I responded, giving him my best reassuring glance. I wasn't used to having people other than Osta or Ma check on me. Or talk to me at all, for that matter. It felt so different… to have people in my corner. People who I could count on. People who could count on me.

I attempted to quell the pessimism that began snaking its way into my thoughts. Forming bonds would only make it that much harder if someone got hurt… if someone...

I pushed the thought away.

Raine, ever the force of nature, bounded up behind Briar, throwing her arms over his shoulders, and leaned in, her voice a loud whisper. "Did you both notice that a certain *Baelor Soleil* was not at warm-up today?" She wiggled her eyebrows.

I looked around to confirm her statement, noticing Nazul seeming very out of place as he paced a few steps behind the group. It was odd to see Nazul looking like the outcast for once.

After the run, we made our way from the track back into the building. We were informed at our last session that we needed to meet Lieutenant Mercer in one of the many sparring rooms inside the Compound. Perhaps we were finally going to start learning combat, instead of spending all our time doing sprints and drills.

"Do you think he's been inside with the Lieutenant?" I offered, keeping my voice low to match hers.

"Doubtful. Mercer would never let us slack on a warm-up. He would just keep Baelor after," Briar responded, shaking his head.

As I pulled out my badge to show at the front gate, I heard a familiar voice.

"Fia?" Eron called, his face filled with confusion. He was in the process of entering the Compound, his arms heavy with deliveries.

I could only imagine his surprise as he took me in, standing in training leathers, surrounded by the other recruits.

My heart skipped a beat, and I froze.

I hadn't even thought to inform Eron or Jacquelina of the changes that had taken place in my life. A sudden pang of guilt surfaced in my gut. I managed to push forward, approaching him as I nodded for the group to go on without me. His eyes were wide with shock, and a package slipped from his grasp.

"I wasn't expecting to see you here," I said, leaning over to retrieve the fallen box.

"Fia, what are *you* doing here? Are you… in uniform?"

"I don't have time to explain right now. I'm so sorry. I promise I'll tell you everything later, but for now, I have to go. I really can't be late," I said, desperation ringing through my words.

Eron nodded before looking away. I glanced down, hesitating for a moment. But I didn't know what else to do. What else to say. I returned to the gate and rushed inside. Guilt slammed into me, nearly knocking me over. He probably felt so confused. Maybe even betrayed. Every time I thought I was making progress in my personal life, some wave of disaster washed over me. I couldn't win.

This day was complete *shit*.

I MANAGED to slip into the sparring gym right before the day's briefing started. I tried to focus my thoughts on the class instead of on Eron and what he must be thinking of me right now. The questions that must be running through his mind.

I eyed the room as I took my seat. Baelor was still nowhere to be found. A sense of calm crept over me. I had to admit, team V looked much better without him.

Mercer walked around the room, collecting our blood into our individual vials before starting the lesson. The same blonde in emerald uniform came and retrieved them as soon as they touched his desk. A shiver ran down my spine.

"We're going to start transitioning from physical conditioning to tactical maneuvers and strategic training. Although I expect each and every one of you to continue your warmups before class," Lieutenant Mercer said as he walked to the center of the room.

"You've all become stronger, quicker, more resilient. But that is just the beginning."

I looked around, gauging everyone else's reactions. I sure didn't like the sound of that.

"Does anyone remember what I said about the Wraiths during your first briefing?" he asked, a rare curiosity peaking his brow.

"They're nearly impossible to catch," Raine stated, leaning forward in her seat.

"What else?"

I tried to search my memory for the details.

"We believe they are limited to the Western border. That they lose strength the further they get from their homeland. From the tear between worlds," I said. And as if Draven had read my thoughts...

"They crave power. They're potentially after our stores of arcanite, which could allow them to move further into the Isle," he added quietly, looking down.

"True, but not the answer I'm looking for. Can anyone remember what I said about their fighting style?" Mercer asked calmly.

"They swarm you, and once you're in their grasp, it's nearly impossible to escape," Briar said with confidence.

Mercer cracked his knuckles, turning towards his desk.

"They cast out darkness and distort our vision?" Raine guessed.

"You can't breathe," I murmured.

Mercer stopped in his tracks and turned back to us.

"Correct," he said, nodding in my direction.

"You mean... they're able to suffocate us?" Nazul asked hesitantly. It was the first time he had spoken all day.

"They siphon the air from your lungs. It's like a vortex of shadows. This is clearly a disadvantage considering we all require oxygen." Mercer took a measured breath before continuing. "So that's what we will work on next."

"You mean, like, practicing holding our breath?" Raine asked nervously.

"Something like that."

For a moment, my thoughts wandered to the General's scar. It looked like an injury from a blade.

"Lieutenant Mercer, do they attack with anything else?" I asked. The rest of the recruits looked at me.

"There's still a lot we don't know about them, but yes. The vortex doesn't seem to be their only form of combat. It's just the one they employ most often."

"Now pay attention please," he said before turning towards his desk and extending his arm. Suddenly, the pieces of parchment that littered the wood surface flew off and spiraled in the air. I could feel the wind all the way from my chair.

"So that's your focus," Briar said in amazement.

A wind wielder.

"Which means I'm particularly qualified to simulate the effects from the Wraith's grasp," he said before turning back to us.

I felt a lump forming in my throat. I'd rather go outside and do sprints. Was that an option?

Uneasiness spread through the room as we all exchanged shifty looks. Mercer's calm expression remained.

"I need everyone to line up at the back of the room. There's no technique to this, simply a lot of repetition. After a while, you will be able to go without oxygen for longer and longer. And that could just save your life. Most die on the battlefield from suffocation." Mercer paced in front of us. "Anyone want to volunteer to go first?"

Everyone became eerily still.

"I'm not going to kill you. That would be completely counter-productive," he remarked softly.

As if that was supposed to make us feel better.

His eyes narrowed in on Nazul. Mercer motioned for the dark-haired boy to step forward. Nazul glanced down the line at us before lowering his head and walking towards the Lieutenant.

"Just try to stay calm. It's the only way through it," Mercer said.

Nazul nodded, eyes still locked on the ground.

"Raine, give us a countdown."

Raine shifted her weight nervously, "Five..." she stuttered. "Four. Three. Two. One—"

Mercer's arm shot toward Nazul. I felt my hair whip back as a gust of wind slammed through the room. Mercer yanked his hand backward, and my hair flew in front of my face just as Nazul gasped. His eyes shot up, filled with terror as he gripped his neck with his hands.

The Lieutenant was pulling the air out of his lungs.

After only a few seconds, Nazul fell to his knees, but Mercer stayed in position, still withholding oxygen.

My hands started to shake. How was I going to make it through this? I couldn't even hold my breath long enough to fetch something at the bottom of a swimming hole.

This went on for what felt like an eternity before Nazul doubled over and fell to the ground, motionless. Finally, Mercer relented, and I watched air fill the boy's lungs once again. He turned onto his stomach and gasped repeatedly. The sound was horrifying.

"That was actually quite impressive, recruit. Most don't make it nearly that long the first time."

Nazul didn't even register Mercer's words. He was still retching desperately.

"Fia, you're next." Mercer nodded in my direction as Nazul crawled back to his spot in line. I opened my mouth to speak, but I couldn't say a word. My whole body was shaking.

"We don't have all day. Come on now," he added, but his gaze softened as we made eye contact.

I stepped forward. There was no getting out of this. I tried to concentrate, savoring my last breaths before the inevitable seizure.

"Raine, another countdown."

I looked back at my friend to see her pale expression, but I nodded, giving her the go ahead before turning back to the Lieutenant.

"Five," she said, voice wavering. I felt my pulse quicken, but I tried to calm it. I needed to relax. "Four. Three. Two."

Suddenly, I felt the wind rush past me. I took one last breath and closed my eyes.

I felt my body jerk forward as the air was dragged from my lungs, and my mind went wild with terror. I swallowed, trying to focus on anything else, but it was to no avail.

All of my senses were on edge, and I felt a familiar heat radiating from the base of my spine. Panic washed over me as I felt the first tendril link onto my vertebrae. My body was going into defense mode. I had to stop it. My eyes shot open.

Instinctively, I gasped for a breath that didn't come, only forcing the web to climb higher, faster. White light pulsed through my veins. I felt myself stumble, losing my balance. My eyes locked with Mercer just as the darkness overtook my vision.

CHAPTER 31

"Miss Riftborne? Can you hear me?" I heard a soft male voice say, pulling me from the darkness.

I tried to take a deep breath, but my lungs resisted. It felt as though they were weighed down by sand. My throat burned.

Yes, I wanted to say, but a cough came out instead.

I blinked rapidly, trying to make the room come into focus.

"Easy now, let me get you some water." I felt a pressure lift at the end of the bed followed by the sound of liquid being poured into a cup.

"Where am I?" I croaked, attempting to sit up.

Stark white walls lined the room, and rows of beds were positioned in an orderly fashion, separated by sheer curtains. Medical trays and equipment were dispersed throughout.

"You had some trouble with the breathing trials," the man said, walking back into my line of sight with a cup in hand. I took it gladly and tipped it back.

He was small in stature, with a welcoming smile etched into his features. His beige tunic and loose trousers identified him as a part of the Immunity Faction. An officer. I felt like we had met before, but I couldn't place him.

"It happens sometimes with new recruits." His smile softened and he offered a small shrug, "Brutal lesson, if you ask me. But necessary, I'm afraid."

"Did anyone else pass out?" I asked, readjusting myself on the bed.

His eyebrow peaked. "Well..." His eyes darted across the empty room. "No, just you."

I sighed, letting my head fall back against the pillow.

"But Callum told me you put on quite the performance, so it's not all bad." He sounded reassuring, but I could feel my face beginning to flush.

"Performance?" My voice pitched with embarrassment. "What do you mean?"

"I don't know the details unfortunately. You'll have to ask my husband." He shrugged and collected the empty glass from my hand.

My eyes widened. Suddenly, I recognized the man. I had seen him at the Tribute Ball, standing next to Mercer before Laryk had called him over.

"The Lieutenant?"

"Halloway Mercer at your service. And you're not the first to be surprised. He thanks the Esprithe daily that I finally gave in to his courting." He sighed with a dramatic flourish.

"You should get some more rest. I gave you some pain relievers that should soothe your throat, but they work best when you're not using your voice." He walked to the door before turning around, "It's nice to meet you, by the way. Laryk won't shut up about his new find." Halloway winked before walking out.

As soon as he was out of sight, I stood and gathered my things. As safe as the empty room seemed, I didn't feel comfortable sitting there alone. I stuck my head out of the room and peered down the corridor just as a figure dressed in an emerald uniform passed by with a tray of blood vials and sauntered into a door at the end of the hall.

It was the same blonde who came to collect our blood oaths from Mercer's classroom. I found it odd that they kept the vials in the healers' section. What did they do with them once they were collected? As intriguing as it would have been to follow her and find out, I knew it was a bad idea, so I stifled the curiosity.

I waited until the door shut behind her, and made my way down the hallway, hoping to find Mercer before leaving the complex. When I found him, he told me everything—how my focus started manifesting just before everything went black. Luckily no one was hurt, but all the recruits got to see my glowing white eyes just before I fell to the ground. That was quite the revelation. I never knew that my eyes would burn along with my target's...

If it wasn't obvious before, it certainly was after my little battle with consciousness: I was the weakest link among the recruits. The only one who ended up in the infirmary after the breathing trials.

Four weeks passed; we were well into the first week of Niamh. Laryk was still gone, helping with the Wraith threat at the Western border. I thought of him often, wondering what he was doing. If he was okay. How bad things had truly gotten. He took up more of my thoughts than I cared to admit.

Mercer had begun illustrating the fundamental techniques of hand-to-hand combat. We learned the correct defensive and offensive movements, stances, positioning, and basic strikes, but we had yet to practice on another Aossí, limited to hanging bags and dummies for now. Weapons weren't of much importance as they seemed to be useless against our attackers, but we learned to wield and throw them just the same.

A lot of us were itching to test out our newly learned skills in a real sparring match, but Mercer insisted that this was the most important step, that it was essential to build muscle memory, refine our skills, and understand the mechanics of combat before transitioning to more interactive forms of training.

But behind every one of my thoughts, Wraiths loomed.

As more and more troops were deployed to Stormshire, the fear of what was to come only intensified. It was a matter of time before we found ourselves in the West, fighting this war from the frontlines.

Baelor never showed back up to lessons, and none of us dared to ask. I think we could all guess the reason for his sudden departure. Threatening the life of a General would not be well-received.

Nazul kept to himself for the most part. He participated in all of the training, but hardly spoke in class, and certainly not to any of us. But the condescending looks and side comments had ceased. Most of the time, I forgot he was there.

"I'm so fucking excited for tonight," Raine mused, shaking her head as we neared the gates of the Compound. I narrowed my eyes and shot her a look of disapproval. I had voiced, on more than one occasion, how I felt about tonight's little gathering.

"Come on, Fia. Lighten up. It's the end of the week. We all deserve to blow off some steam, and none of us get to use our focuses in the Compound. You haven't even seen what I can really do." Sparks emanated from the tips of her fingers, sparkling in patterns throughout her palm. A mischievous grin spread across her lips.

"If we get caught, we're all dead," I reminded her.

Her hands took a dramatic fall.

"We're not going to get caught, but even if we did, what are they going to do? Kill all of the most valuable recruits along with some of the more daring initiates..." She pursed her lips and peeked at me from behind her lashes.

Initiates?

I stopped dead in the street. "Please tell me you're joking."

"Relax. It's going to be fine. They're not going to rat on us. They want to have some fun too. Plus, we're nearing the end of our training. We need to start making friends with other members of *team V.*"

I rolled my eyes, but continued walking, matching Raine's more aggressive gait.

"I don't want anyone to get hurt. We have to be careful. And no drinking." I nudged her side, painfully aware I sounded like a killjoy, but this whole idea seemed so irresponsible at a time like this.

"Whatever you say, mom." She sighed with exasperation before winking at me.

"Fia! Raine!" A shrill voice shouted from behind us. We whirled around to see Osta racing down the street in our direction, a beaming smile plastered to her face.

We closed the distance between us, and Raine shot me an amused look.

Osta hunched over breathlessly, motioning for us to give her a moment.

"You seem… even more upbeat than usual." I grinned. "What's going on?"

"Lady… Soleil …She…" Osta took heavy breaths in between each word. "Replied… to my… letter! She offered me a full-time position at her estate!" Osta squealed and jumped up and down, nearly crumpling the parchment she was holding.

Before I knew it, my arms were thrown around her shoulders. "I'm so proud of you," I whispered in her ear. I felt my eyes getting misty.

"Osta, that's incredible! Are you going to be living at there as well?" Raine questioned, even *her* voice had gone up an octave.

I released Osta and stepped back, crossing my arms. I don't know if I had ever smiled so big.

"Yes… I mean, I assume so! She wants me to start in two weeks! I feel so elated!" Osta spun around, clutching the letter to her chest.

"Osta, you have to come with us tonight–"

"Esprithe sake, Raine!" I cut her off, my eyes widening as I mouthed *no*.

What the hell?

"Wait, what? Is there a party? I'm so in!" Osta shouted, returning to her hops.

"No, Osta, it's not like that. And there's no way you're coming. It's too dangerous. I'm sorry, but we can all go get drinks to celebrate you tomorrow," I offered.

I could kill Raine.

Osta stopped jumping and glanced back and forth between the two of us. She looked as though she was about to cry.

"Fia, she'll be fine. And it's going to be so much fun. Come on, live a little! Osta can take care of herself, and we'll all be there to protect her," Raine pleaded, softening her eyes and wrapping her arm over Osta's drooping shoulder.

This was a terrible fucking idea. But they were both staring at me like children who had just seen their favorite toy crushed.

Eventually, I sighed. "Osta, you have to stay within my eyesight the entire night. I'm serious."

A mischievous smile crept over her lips. "Wait, what are we doing?" she asked, eyeing us suspiciously.

"Fia will fill you in later. We've got to get to the sparring gym. I'm so happy for you Osta. I'll see you tonight!" Raine cooed as she hooked my arm and began pulling me through the front gates. I squeezed Osta's hand as we left, and then all of my attention was on the lightning wielder beside me.

"I'm so not happy with you right now," I said to Raine, flatly. My footsteps mirrored my irritation.

"Fia. You worry too much."

I felt a sinking feeling growing in the pit of my stomach as we walked through the Compound.

CHAPTER 32

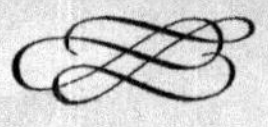

"ONE OF OUR investigative parties was attacked during a mission last night as they attempted to locate the tear," Mercer said quietly as he paced at the front of the sparring gym. Deep lines were set into his forehead. His demeanor was void of its usual steadiness.

This seemed different.

"We sent a group from our faction to the area to do some reconnaissance. They were accompanied by a few Base soldiers and infantry. None came back alive." A murmur ran through the room. My gut twisted. Guards from the team V. Dead.

Wait.

"Who was in the investigative party?" I asked in a tone just above a whisper. My pulse quickened with dark anticipation. I had to know, but I didn't want to.

Mercer rubbed the back of his neck and turned towards his desk, retrieving a piece of parchment.

"From our faction… Elyse Wellington, Devon Lanceburg, Val Stephens, Gentry Collins and Salara Marsh," he said before rubbing his eyes and leaning back onto his desk. I heard a gasp from my left.

"Salara is gone?" Raine asked, her voice cracking.

Val... Gentry...

They were dead.

I hadn't seen them since the night of the ball, but they had treated me with such kindness. They were good. Nice. And too young. Far too young. My heart sank in my chest, and I fought back tears. Some of the best and brightest of the Guard. Gone in an instant.

How were we meant to survive this? We didn't understand enough about the Wraiths to stop them. We were fighting an uphill battle with no end in sight. We needed more time. We needed more knowledge.

A realization washed over me.

We weren't meant to survive this. We were all going to die. Fighting for life. For the people we loved back at home who had no clue about the darkness that existed on our Western border.

We had to make our lives mean something before our inevitable end.

Anger and fear coursed through me. When I got my chance, I would go down fighting until the very end. I wouldn't let these monsters reach Ma or Osta... Jacquelina or Eron... Leila. I'd kill every single one that I could before they stole my breath and drained me of life. I'd figure out a way.

I felt a pang in my palms and looked down to find them bleeding, my nails digging into the flesh.

"So, we are accelerating your training even more. We don't really have a choice," Mercer said, walking back towards us.

"Today is the day. You will begin sparring with each other," he finally announced. "I will be placing you into groups of two, and we will rotate partners daily until everyone has had the chance to face each other. As the groups will be uneven, I will also be participating." He gave us a sad smile as we shifted nervously.

"Don't worry, I won't go too hard on you just yet." His tone was light but that didn't stop me from wondering to which

Esprithe I should pray in order to take down this mountain of a man.

I'd walked by many of the sparring rooms and watched the twisted dance of hand-to-hand combat. I felt confident in all the things I had been taught thus far, but my heart began to race at the thought of finally putting those lessons into action.

"I may be a formidable opponent but I'm nothing compared to our enemy. Let's hope that none of you get close enough to a Wraith that you have to use these skills. There is only one man I know to have fought and survived a hand-to-hand attack." Mercer tapped his face in the same spot as General Ashford's dark scar.

"With that being said, we will not leave you unprepared. So, let's begin."

He quickly paired us off. My first opponent would be Draven. I would need to take extra care not to draw any blood. I didn't exactly want to get paralyzed on our first sparring day.

I looked over my shoulder toward the other mats and found Briar and Raine warming up together. The last spot was occupied by Nazul and Lieutenant Mercer.

Something wicked inside me stirred, and I bit back a smile. I couldn't help but look forward to watching Nazul get his ass handed to him.

We started the session by spotting our movements. We were a little awkward at first but soon were moving with ease, deflecting each other's strikes with calculated maneuvers. With each shift of my feet, I felt more assured as I wove through attacks—a delicate balance between offensive and defensive.

Once we were all truly in the rhythm, Mercer pulled everyone to the side and motioned for Raine and Briar to take their positions, allowing the rest of us to observe.

I watched as my two friends circled each other, but at this moment they were opponents, each determined to test the other's skills.

"Don't worry nature boy… I'll go easy on you," Raine taunted, a spark of challenge in her eyes.

"Oh Raine, let's see how fierce you are without your little sparky hands," Briar fired back with an amused grin.

As they closed in, Raine made the first move, launching into a series of quick strikes aimed at Briar's defenses. Briar reacted instinctively, deflecting her blows with practiced precision.

Raine's movements were like lightning, sharp and direct. But Briar wasn't giving in. He met each blow with a calculated counter, his movements grounded and precise.

Back and forth they went, exchanging strikes and blocks in a whirlwind of skill and strategy. Raine's speed and agility were matched only by Briar's strength and resilience.

But as the spar progressed, it became increasingly clear that Raine had the upper hand. Her movements were too quick, her attacks too precise for Briar to defend against. Despite his best efforts, he found himself constantly on the defensive, struggling to keep up with her.

Frustration simmered beneath the surface as Briar's confidence started to wane.

Raine delivered a powerful strike to his gut that sent Briar staggering backward.

He stumbled, off balance and disoriented.

"Looks like I won this round," Raine taunted, a triumphant gleam in her eyes.

Briar's jaw clenched, his expression sour as he begrudgingly accepted defeat.

"Yeah, yeah, you got lucky," he muttered, sauntering off the mat.

The fight between Draven and I was much less interesting to behold, I'm sure. Despite the intensity of our movements, I couldn't help myself from wanting to hold back, careful not to inflict harm.

After what felt like an endless back and forth with Mercer

jumping in to comment on footwork or body placements, he finally called a draw.

"I'm going to need to see more from you both. I can tell neither of you are giving it your all," he scolded. I couldn't deny his point, so I simply nodded and moved to the side, collapsing beside Raine and Briar who seemed to have made up just fine.

The Lieutenant and Nazul sparred last.

I had been expecting a total blow-out but clearly the elite training Nazul received from his family was making its long-awaited debut.

Lieutenant Mercer still bested him, but there was a sheen of sweat on his brow by the time they finished.

It felt good to see our training efforts finally put to the test. Still, I couldn't silence the nagging voice in my mind telling me that no matter how strong we were, we'd never be ready for the battle to come.

CHAPTER 33

THE MOON HUNG low and bright behind thick fog, its diffused beams of light filtering through the treetops. We were walking just outside the city, on our way to a clearing at the border of the Reyanthe Valley. The scent of fresh rain and pine and sap lingered in the depths of the wood, ebbing and flowing in the cool evening breeze.

Briar and Raine were giggling amongst themselves as Osta and I navigated the damp earth below our feet, avoiding tangled roots and slippery patches. A near permanent grin had been etched onto Osta's face ever since I'd arrived home after training.

Nerves prickled the back of my neck. I kept looking around to make sure we weren't seen or followed. I had a bad feeling about tonight, made even more intense by Osta joining us.

"So how many of the initiates are going to be there?" I asked, peering in Raine's direction.

"I'm not sure exactly. I only spoke to a few of them about it," she said nonchalantly, keeping her attention on the path ahead. I noticed Briar nudge her side before hiding a smile.

I pressed my lips into a hard line and mentally groaned. It was too late to turn back now, not like Osta would allow it at this point. Her excitement was annoyingly unmatched.

I exhaled sharply. She hugged my arm tighter and leaned over to whisper in my ear, "Fia, please don't be so grumpy tonight. Let's have fun. Stop stressing. Please, for me?" she pleaded, eyes reflecting the bright moon above.

"Let's just see how it goes. If it gets crazy, we're leaving. Agreed?" I said quietly, out of earshot of Raine and Briar.

"Agreed." She smiled and picked up her pace, dragging me along beside her.

"Do you think you'll show anyone your focus tonight?" Osta asked hesitantly.

"Well, I'm not exactly trying to murder anyone. So, it seems unlikely." I laughed through the nerves.

A subtle rumble from the ground stopped Osta and I in our tracks.

"What was that?" I hissed toward Raine, who slowed down, turning to face us as she walked backwards down the trail.

"Maybe a few people got there early?" She shrugged, holding out her arm for us. "We must be almost there." Osta rushed to catch up with them.

"Briar, couldn't you fix the terrain just a bit? I feel like I'm about to trip over a root with every step I take," I grumbled. Navigating uneven forest floor was not something I particularly enjoyed, nor was I any good at it. Briefly, my mind wandered back to the night when everything had changed outside the Grove. If it hadn't been for that damn fallen branch, my life would look vastly different...

"No can do, love. I'm saving all my energy for the festivities," Briar sang, cutting through my thoughts.

As we trudged on, I began to notice glimmers of light dancing down the path in the distance. We must have been getting close. The ground rumbled again, and I almost lost my balance.

"What could they possibly be doing?" I asked, glancing over at Raine.

"No idea, but it sounds pretty damn epic." She grinned.

As we approached, the murmurs of conversation heightened. I squinted, turning my head to the side to listen better.

There was a crowd. And Music.

We neared the edge of the clearing, and the sounds became undeniable. I narrowed my eyes at Raine, who peeked over at me nervously.

"I guess word got around?" She shrugged before stepping out into the clearing.

I huffed, and followed my three friends, taking in the sight of what must have been one hundred Aossí dancing, socializing, and sparring.

By the looks of it, recruits and initiates from all factions of the Guard–Base, Scales, Fang, and even Immunity were in attendance. Plus, team V. Besides us, there were maybe ten initiates from our sector. Their black uniforms were easy to make out through all the white shirts littering the expanse.

Tables filled with liquor and elixir bottles lined the edges of the clearing near the lake. People passed them around, clinking the glasses together before indulging. Lights danced, weaving through the crowd and soaring to illuminate the low-lying mist above the treetops. Music pulsed, sending thrums of energy through the dancing bodies.

I gritted my teeth.

This was a fucking party.

With alcohol.

And elixirs.

And drunk idiots doing magic tricks.

Only Fírinne knew what else.

Heat rushed through me as the ground beneath us rumbled yet again, even stronger this time. My head whipped left as a giant chunk of earth flew into the sky. It hovered for a moment before shooting back down at full force and exploding. The crowd cheered, raising their glasses. "Another!" Someone shouted in the distance.

My jaw fell open.

"I guess you're not the only nature wielder here tonight, Briar!" Raine teased, nudging him.

He gave us all a devilish grin. "That was nothing. How do you feel about a grand entrance?" he asked in a low voice, a strange twinkle in his eye.

Briar lifted his hands from his sides. The ground began to rumble and shake. I grasped onto Raine to keep my balance.

Out of the corners of my eyes, I saw what looked like hundreds of tangled snakes flying off the ground, pummeling towards us. They were coming from each side.

As they neared us, I realized they were tree roots being manipulated by Briar's focus. The two sides slammed into each other with a loud crunch, and the snapping of wood ricocheted through the space as the roots twisted and braided themselves into a raised walkway directly in front of us, leading to the center of the crowd. Everyone's eyes were on us now, and the clearing had grown eerily quiet.

Briar held up his hands, stepping up onto his creation and clearing his throat. He looked at the sea of Aossí and shrugged apologetically. "Sorry we're late!" he yelled, and the crowd erupted in chaotic cheers. The dark feeling I had only intensified as we stepped onto the platform.

TWO HOURS LATER, I stood on the edge of the clearing with Raine, who was still reeling from her lightning performance. I had to admit; it was the most impressive thing I had seen all night.

She lit up the heavens, creating sparkling embers that shot through the clouds above as streaks of light cracked across the horizon. The entire clearing stood aghast, watching in amazement. She got more cheers than the illusionists and the fire wielders combined.

I leaned against a tree, waiting for Osta to bring us the drinks she insisted on getting. My eyes followed her and Briar through the crowd, never letting her out of my sight. A sigh of relief escaped me as the two finally made it to the table closest to the lake.

"I told you this would be fun." Raine looked at me, raising an eyebrow in expectation.

"It's fun. Doesn't mean it's not dangerous," I snorted, still keeping my eyes on Osta. Raine let out a deep chuckle and leaned her head back.

"You're so stubborn, Fia. I caught you smiling earlier when those twin initiates were racing." She elbowed my side.

I stole a glance at her and tried to bite back a smile. "I mean, it's not every day you see something like that. They moved so quickly; they were nearly invisible."

"We were given these gifts. It's a shame not to use them. Especially when it's harmless," Raine said.

"Speak for yourself," I laughed. There was nothing harmless about my *gift*.

"Erm–well, clearly you're the exception." She grinned at me. "Mind shredder."

I had never told Raine about the incident in the woods. The one that changed the entire trajectory of my life. And she had never asked. There were several occasions where I considered telling her everything, but just as the words were on the tip of my tongue, I couldn't force them out. Some-day, maybe.

My eyes returned to the tables near the lake, searching for Osta. She and Briar had moved away from the drinks and were standing at the river's edge. Osta looked up at me and waved, smiling brightly. The distance between them grew as Osta sidestepped a fallen branch and Briar struck up a conversation with a group to the left. I waved back just as specks of muted orange formed behind her silhouette.

I began walking closer, trying to get a better view. Raine's footsteps crunched twigs behind me.

"What was that?" She asked, curiosity peaked.

"I don't know, but let's find out." I picked up the pace.

Suddenly, a roaring torrent of fire soared across the river.

"Osta!" I shouted, sprinting in her direction. I wasn't going to make it in time. Osta was in the direct path.

Horror overcame me as the fire crackled inches from Osta, heat blasting me in the face. I screamed as Osta stumbled over the rocky terrain. She fell, bracing herself, and threw her arms over her head just as a man raced out between her and the explosion. The flames seemed to hit a wall and ricocheted off. The man stayed, unmoving, until the fire subsided into the night.

I blinked trying to readjust my vision, my legs still pumping as my feet hit the damp earth below. The entire clearing was quiet as I finally slid down to Osta's side. She was breathing heavily, and her body still trembled with fear, but she was otherwise unharmed.

"Osta!" I said, grabbing her hands.

"I–I'm fine," she managed to whisper, but her attention was on the figure ahead.

I looked up to see Nazul staring down at us.

Nazul?

I looked back and forth between the two of them before standing up.

I reached down to offer Osta my hand at the same time as Nazul. Without even thinking about it, I shot him a scowl, which he ignored.

Osta took his hand and slowly rose to her feet, trying to keep her balance. He steadied her with his other hand.

"Osta, right?" he asked in the softest voice I had ever heard from him. She merely nodded.

"Let's find a place to sit down," he said, urging her toward some of the seats at the edge of the clearing.

Beneath my shock, white-hot anger simmered. Raine rushed to Osta's side, and Briar followed along shortly after.

"Raine, Briar, watch her. I'm going to find out who did that," I growled, turning back toward the river to see a few figures wading through the water.

Baelor Soleil. And a new set of groupies.

"That was insane, Baelor. I can't believe General Ashford demoted you," one of them gushed.

Baelor shrugged, motioning for the man on his left to go procure a few drinks with a dismissive gesture. The man hurried off toward the tables.

I stormed toward him, finally able to make out his pale, blonde hair and crisp, white Guard's uniform. The Scales emblem was stitched into the fabric.

Mud flew up around my boots as I closed the distance between us. Anger was roaring through my entire body, and I could already feel the tendrils lurching forward in anticipation.

His eyes locked onto me, something dangerous snapping into place as he took in my movements, a look of contained excitement playing across his typically stone-cold features.

"Two Riftborne here tonight. How unexpected."

"You did that on purpose?" I seethed, planting my feet directly in front of him.

"Soleils never lose control of their flames."

His words hit me like a dagger. I almost couldn't form a response.

"What the fuck is your problem, Baelor?" Nazul yelled from behind me. I felt the heat of his presence as he approached.

Baelor looked him over with a blank expression.

"You saved the abomination?" Baelor asked.

"You've gone too far, Baelor. You sound insane," Nazul growled, but there was a kind of pleading in his voice.

"My duty is to protect this realm. And it won't be safe until every Riftborne is wiped from existence. You used to be of the same mind," he said, righteousness lacing his words.

"I *never* wanted anyone dead, Baelor. You've spiraled into madness."

Suddenly, the sky bloomed with storm clouds, thunder cracking through the clearing. Raine stepped forward, wind tossing her braids to the side. She reached up, as if she were grasping something in the heavens, before throwing her arm down, a blinding strike of lightning following. It landed right at Baelor's feet.

He didn't even flinch.

"I'll light your ass up Baelor. I'd be doing this realm a fucking favor," she spat.

"All of you protect the Riftborne? You should be treated as traitors," he said, his voice steady.

"Raine, Nazul, go check on Osta. This is between me and Baelor," I said, finally able to form words. Raine paused, her eyes shooting over to me. But it seemed something on my face reassured her.

"Fuck him up, Fia." She smiled wickedly as she turned and pranced off. Nazul hung around for a few more seconds, eyes burning into Baelor, who looked between us, focused on nothing in particular.

"You're an asset to the Guard, Nazul. Leave the Riftborne to me. I'd hate for you to get caught in the crossfire," Baelor said.

Nazul stepped forward with a look of defiance, fists clenching at his sides. He was ready to fight if the veins in his neck were any indication. His eyes moved to me, and I nodded. He tore away, and trudged back to the group.

"It's such a tragedy one of your kind has been able to infiltrate the Guard. Our leadership is weak. Tainted." Baelor took a step to the side, foot falling on the scorched earth from Raine's bolt.

"You have no idea what you're talking about," I said, calling forth the webbing. Its strands pulsed with anticipation as they coiled around my vertebrae. Each fiber seemed to hum with satisfaction, weaving itself upward, eager to fulfill its purpose. But this time, I commanded it. I was in control. I could feel its every movement as if it were an extension of my own being.

"You were able to worm your way into the ear of a Sídhe General. You manipulated him into demoting me. It's blasphemous. I'm a Soleil—one of the chosen protectors of the land, graced with the most powerful focus of all. To turn enemies to ash." Baelor looked to the sky and closed his eyes.

At this distance, he could incinerate me in a second.

"You got yourself demoted. I had nothing to do with it." The web was thrumming through the bond as it wound around my mind, lying in wait for the right moment.

"If you care about this realm as much as you pretend to, just sacrifice yourself to the flames now. I'll make your death quick." He looked upon me, a smile creeping up his lips, but his eyes were still distant, hollow. He stepped backwards, putting a great distance between us.

"I'd love to see you try." The words slipped out before I knew what I was saying. But they felt good.

His eyes blazed, lighting from within. Fire enveloped his hands, and his smile widened.

I goaded the tendrils, preparing them to strike. They flittered out of me so effortlessly now. I could almost feel their rage meshing with my own. They wanted to attack just as much as I did.

"Your death will fortify the land," he said, and the clearing went silent.

Fire erupted from Baelor, shooting towards me, bright orange specks flying in all directions.

With my eyes locked fiercely on him, the webbing orbiting his mind came to life. I couldn't help the smile that crept from the corners of my lips as the wind whipped around me, raising my hair in a wild frenzy, like a tempest swirling above my head.

Time seemed to move in slow motion.

In an instant, I was weightless. My feet lifted from the ground. Energy crackled and surged, radiating from the very core of my being until my eyes burned, turning my vision white.

I let the power go.

It struck into him, making contact with Baelor's mind, but it didn't attack. It didn't squeeze... The fibers caressed it gently and began spreading like an insidious vine, seeking, probing. It was intoxicating. A rush of euphoria flooded through me.

The webbing purred as it found its mark, and a whisper surged through the fibers connecting us, illuminating something I couldn't quite understand.

But I wanted to.

My vision snapped back to see the flames, just a mere breath from my face, retreat. They thrashed as they were pulled back into Baelor's hands.

His body stood rigid, like there was no one behind the glowing eyes. Slowly, the last spark died out, and Baelor trembled in response.

A hush moved through the crowd as Baelor lowered himself, kneeling before me.

And then it clicked.

I was in control.

Leave this clearing. I sent the words through the bond.

I could feel his mind fighting in resistance, but it was no use. He was going to do what I told him. I don't know how I knew. I just *did.*

Baelor rose to his feet. His movements were rigid and unnatural as he walked toward the tree line. Every eye was fixed upon him as he brushed against the bristles of an evergreen and disappeared from sight.

I released the webbing's hold on Baelor's mind, the shimmering strands sinking back into my being as I felt the solid ground beneath my feet once more.

Reality hit me like a jolt of electricity as I saw the shocked faces of my friends. I felt everyone's eyes on me. A distant part of me wanted to disappear. I shifted my weight nervously as Raine shook her head in amazement and began clapping.

Briar followed suit, along with Osta and Nazul, and it spread through the crowd slowly from one side to the other until the entire clearing was echoing the sound.

"The Riftborne's a fucking legend!" Someone shouted, and they all erupted in cheers. Before I knew it, they were rushing me and hoisting me up on their shoulders, carrying me around the clearing and chanting.

My mind was still reeling from the shock of it all, but I forced myself to smile. Sibyl herself couldn't have foreseen this turn of events.

I laughed, and laughed, letting the tension escape my body. *Holy shit.* I had just taken over his mind.

For the first time, I felt a pang of relief flood through me. I had always considered myself the weaker of two species, the mouse in a sea full of serpents.

Perhaps I was a predator too.

I couldn't even process the thought as I felt myself being lowered to the ground in front of my friends. They were all still staring at me in amazement.

"What. The. Fuck. Fia!" Briar said, enunciating every word. His mouth returned to its ajar state.

"You've been holding out on us, Mind Shredder!" Raine shouted, running up to throw her arm around me.

"Fia, I can't believe you just did that!" Osta said, shaking her head. "What exactly did you do?"

"I'm not sure." I shrugged.

"You'll have to explain everything to us," Raine said. "But first, we need a celebratory drink." She turned toward the tables just as a fierce wind tore through the clearing, blowing leaves into vortexes across the field.

Everyone paused. Something was off. The energy shift hung heavy in the air.

The breath in my lungs turned to ice.

I rushed over to Osta, pulling her behind me as I squinted into the darkness.

A voice boomed through the clearing.

"This party is over. Get back to the Compound. Now!" Lieutenant Mercer shouted as the wind picked up, whipping through the crowd and nearly knocking us over.

We looked at each other in panic before rushing for the tree line and fleeing in the direction of Luminaria.

We were caught.

CHAPTER 34

"AGAIN!" Mercer shouted from the edge of the track field, motioning for us to repeat the agility course.

"Lieutenant, how many of these are we going to do?" Raine begged.

I'd lost count after number thirty-two.

"I said again, recruit," he growled, turning his attention to the opposite side of the field. I had never seen Mercer this angry before.

We braced ourselves before launching into another madness-inducing sprint through the course. My heart was pounding in my chest, and my lungs begged for air. Just close the gap… A few more steps…

I crossed the finish line and hit the ground. Hard. The rest of the recruits followed suit, gripping their joints and trying not to vomit.

"I'll be right back. You can take a break for now," Mercer said flatly as he walked off the field toward the Compound.

"I'm not going to say–"

"Fia, don't start," Raine wheezed, flopping onto her back.

"I mean, I did say it." I shrugged as Raine and Briar shot me with looks of contempt.

"I get to suffer the punishment you all brought onto us, and I didn't even go!" Draven shouted breathlessly.

Rumbles of a subtle apology ran through the group.

"You should have come, Draven. Fia finally showed us all what she's made of," Nazul said. I looked over at him, expecting to see a smug expression carved into his face, but he merely smiled, shrugging his shoulders.

"Don't worry. I heard all about it already." Draven sighed and laid his arms over his head.

It seemed the revelation about my focus had run rampant through the Compound.

I winced. That was the last thing I wanted.

I wasn't sure if it had made it to any of the higher-ups yet. I'd thought a lot over the weekend, coming to the conclusion that our superiors might find my focus more of a threat than an advantage.

To be fair, it's not like I knew that would happen. I thought I'd just scare Baelor a bit. I groaned. The entire thing had been a mistake. I should have walked away.

"Riftborne!" Mercer shouted from behind us. I guess he was finally using my last name to address me. *How nice.*

I steadied my shaking legs as I stood, brushing the grass and dirt from my training leathers.

"Here. Now." Mercer motioned for me to approach.

I walked across the field in his direction, and he turned, leading me in toward the Compound.

I couldn't help the ball of nerves that now weighed heavy in my gut.

As we neared the base of the hill, I glanced up, and the air froze in my lungs.

Laryk stood at the Western Gate.

He was back.

My heart did somersaults in my chest as I urged my legs

forward. Of course, his first duty upon returning would be dealing his own personal punishment on me. My stomach twisted, and I pushed down an unwelcome sliver of excitement.

There was none of his usual pompous amusement on his face, just stone-like indifference as I closed the gap between us.

"You'll meet me at the gym in an hour. Until then, go make yourself seen near the Compound," he said flatly and turned to walk away.

"What do you mean, make myself seen?" I asked, but he only continued walking.

I stole a glance at Mercer who was glaring at me. "Fia, go make sure that people see you at the Compound. Practice is too secluded today. Just stand outside and make sure you're noticed. Ashford will explain the rest at the gym. Now go."

I shot him a confused glance, but followed the instructions, making my way towards the front gate.

I mingled for a bit, keeping to myself and trying to avoid the anxiety that hung in my limbs. What was going on? Why was everyone being so secretive? I couldn't help but think that Laryk had returned due to what happened at the clearing. What I had done to Baelor.

Was he furious? Did he want to kill me? Esprithe, I felt like an idiot for attacking Baelor now. His father was a powerful retired General. Had he ordered my death?

I wandered through the guards socializing near the front gate, making sure a few eyes were on me. I couldn't help but notice the lack of white uniforms. When I'd first become a recruit, it was so crowded on the street that one could barely walk. Now, only a handful of guards lingered at the entrance.

"Have you seen my son?" A woman asked, and I spun left to look at her. "He's been deployed for weeks, and I haven't heard a word. He usually writes to me every day," she said, tears staining her cheeks.

She wasn't talking to me, but to a guard a few paces away.

"Who is your son?" A short, brunette from the Faction Scales asked, turning his attention to the woman.

She held out a crumpled piece of parchment with a painted portrait. "This is what he looks like. He was a member of Scales." I could see the hope in her eyes, even at my distance.

"I'm sorry, Ma'am, I wouldn't know," the guard responded, and the woman nodded, moving onto another group on the other side of the gate.

Guilt churned inside me as I watched her beg for answers, knowing that he had probably lost his life in the West. Even if someone wanted to tell her, they couldn't.

The sun beamed down on me, slowly beginning to set behind the towers of the Compound.

I didn't leave until I knew several people had seen me. Fear returned to my bones as I made my way towards the Central district, taking nervous steps. The gym was only a block away. I couldn't be sure whether an hour had passed or not, but I couldn't wait any longer. I needed to know what was going on.

As I approached the familiar reflective glass, the front door crept open, and I heard Laryk's voice.

"Inside. Now," he said sharply.

I sighed and stepped through, making my way over to the bench.

"What did you do, Fia?" he said, a cutting edge to his voice.

"I–erm–don't know what you're–"

"Bullshit." He shook his head and paced to the other side of the room.

"You took control of Baelor Soleil's mind," he said quietly. I couldn't help but notice the tiny sliver of pride in his voice.

"I didn't mean to," I mumbled.

"And you did it in front of a hundred members of the Guard," he stated, facing me again. His eyes looked tired, worn. They didn't glow with their usual emerald sheen.

"So, what does that mean?" I asked, swallowing my nerves.

"Clearly, there are going to be those who view you as a threat. Both within the Nobility and the Guard. That will want you dead." His voice was harsh and low.

"I don't even really know how I did it, I mean–"

"It doesn't matter. We can't let anyone believe the validity of the rumors." He turned towards the wall, placing his forehead in his hand.

What?

"But as you already mentioned, one hundred people saw it with their own eyes," I said slowly, bile rising in my throat.

"Baelor is denying it. He said it never happened. You're incredibly lucky that he was your target that evening. People actually believe the words of a General's son even if they don't want to," he murmured, facing me. "Rumors have a way of morphing as they move through the masses. We will take advantage of that." He paced back toward me, crossing his arms. "Do you understand what I'm saying?"

"That I should lie?"

"Exactly. You had been drinking. You felt emboldened. You wanted to scare the shit out of the boy and told him to apologize, perhaps with a bit too much intimidation. He bolted. That's all you know. Leave it at that."

I paused. I still wasn't processing everything he was saying. *Why was he doing this?*

"He attacked Osta. Will there be no repercussions for that?" I asked quietly.

"We have to choose our battles wisely now, Fia. He's already been demoted. We just need to ride this out. I can't push too far, not with who his family is."

I turned my head and simply nodded.

"I've already spoken to the other Generals. Assured them what actually happened. What I told you. As long as they believe it, and your story matches Baelor's, we shouldn't have anything to worry about," he said, taking a seat next to me.

"But why?" I asked, squinting. *Why was he doing this?*

"Because if the King finds out about this, I don't think it will be pleasant for you. Sydian is a great man, but I don't think he would turn a blind eye to the only person who could hold power over him."

"But why are you protecting me? I'm sure you're breaking an oath in order to do this. Why would you risk it?" I urged.

He glanced over at me, quickly locking eyes before diverting his attention to the other side of the room.

"You're too important. It's worth the risk." He sighed, running his hand through his long copper locks. "I don't particularly enjoy the situation you've put us in."

"But *how*?" I asked, "How can you break a blood oath?"

"Don't worry about that. There are so many things I can't yet tell you, Fia. I just need you to trust me as you've done before. I'm not going to let anything happen to you. If you don't believe anything else I've ever told you, at least believe that."

His words stirred something within me. The truth was… I did trust him. And I'm not exactly certain when that had become clear.

"Did you know?" I asked, in an attempt to quell the ache.

"Know what? That you harbored that ability? No. But I've thought your focus was unique from the beginning. It's like nothing I've ever seen. It seems to be connected to the mind in even stronger ways than I initially thought."

"It is," I blurted before I could stop myself.

He glanced over at me with curiosity. "Go on."

"When I summoned it this time, instead of blasting into Baelor's mind like all the times before–I was able to enter his head softly, almost tenderly, like it wasn't dangerous–wasn't a threat. And I could sense my focus searching for something, an access point of some kind. And when it found what it was looking for in his mind, I just knew. I knew I could command him. I can't really explain it better than that. I know it's not much to go on…" I trailed off, realizing I had never before said this many words to him in a single setting.

"Incredible," he whispered, clearly deep in thought.

I looked at him. It had been so long since I'd seen him. I missed the face that stared back at me, the one that was laced with that mysterious curiosity that used to drive me mad. Now it threatened to push me over the edge.

"I guess that's one way to describe it," I murmured, hiding my flushed cheeks.

"Fia. This is a dangerous ability, and it comes with a lot of risks. You can't tell anyone about it. I'm serious. You need to convince your friends that what they saw wasn't real. I know it's going to be hard, but you never truly know who you can trust. We all learn that the hard way. In some form or another." His eyes were burning holes into the side of my face.

"I"ll try. I'll make sure they don't perpetuate it, at least," I said, bringing my gaze back to him. A part of me wanted to reach out and touch him, but I suddenly noticed how dark it had gotten in the room.

"Erm–I have to go. It's getting late," I mumbled, standing. *Fuck.* Osta's celebration would be starting any minute.

"Where are you going?" He stood as well, concerned etched into his features.

"Osta got a job with Lady Soleil–thanks for that, by the way. But Raine is throwing her a party in celebration. I can't miss it."

Laryk pursed his lips, clearly trying to come up with a valid objection.

"I need to talk to them, like you said," I reassured him, reaching back to grab my bag.

"Where are you going to tell them that you've been? This conversation never happened. We don't have a training session scheduled for today. I'm not taking any risks," he stated, raising an eyebrow.

"What do you suggest I say?" I responded, crossing my arms.

He walked toward the mirrors, rubbing his chin.

After a few moments, he turned and faced me. "Tell them that Lieutenant Mercer sent you to sign some paperwork that got looked over on your first day. By the time you were done, the session was over, so you went shopping."

I nearly laughed.

"Shopping?" I said, "Really?"

"Yes, Fia. Shopping. You clearly don't have time to go home and change. You're wearing the same training leathers from earlier. It's been at least two hours."

"I'm confused," I admitted, squinting my eyes and shifting my weight.

"Go to the back and clean up. I'll be right back," he said, turning towards the front door.

"Wait–"

"Clean up. Now," he ordered without giving me another glance.

SOON ENOUGH, I was stepping out of the shower. I couldn't deny how good it felt to be clean after Mercer's agonizing training session.

I glanced over at the counter, noticing a few bottles and jars I didn't remember seeing. I walked over, examining them. Hair products… makeup… perfume? I glanced at my reflection in the mirror, only to find that there was a dress hanging on the shelf behind me. *That certainly wasn't here before.*

Did he come in here while I was in the shower? No boundaries at all...

Heat pricked my skin, but I couldn't waste time getting lost in pointless daydreams.

I squeezed my hair the best I could using the towel, but there was no way it would be dry before I arrived at the lounge. I eyed the products on the counter and reached for one of the bottles. It was some kind of styling cream.

I took a deep breath and brushed it through my hair, pushing the strands behind the points of my ears. My curls weren't used to being weighed down by product, but the cream was working well enough.

My hair looked sleek, save for a few bumps that I couldn't get rid of at the top.

I grabbed the charcoal pencil that–*wait, did he really just go buy all of this?* I rolled my eyes, thinking about all the times he'd probably done similar things for his lovers in the past. My stomach churned. But that wasn't our situation. This was just a cover-up.

I shook the thoughts from my mind and lined my eyes. It still didn't look perfect, but I had improved since the last time I'd made the attempt back in Raine's room at the Compound.

I hurried over to the dress.

It was *tight*. Not even zipped up the back yet, it was already unbelievably fitted. I knew every contour of my body would be exposed.

The neckline was square, held up by two straps that ran over my shoulders. It stopped a good bit before my ankles, and it wasn't until I took a step forward that I noticed the high slit running down my left leg. I rolled my eyes. He actually thought my friends would believe I bought this for myself.

I reached around to zip it but to no avail. I couldn't reach the clasp. I clicked my teeth and grabbed the matching shoes before marching out the door. I didn't give myself time to consider another approach.

Laryk sat on the bench across the gym, laying back with his ankles crossed. His eyes seemed to go molten when he saw me.

"Well, don't you look ravishing." His voice was low, almost raspy as he stood to admire his dress choice. I ignored the heat that shot through me with his words. I didn't have time for it.

I forced an eye-roll. "Can you zip this for me?"

"Spin around," he said with a giant smirk.

In an instant, his hands were on my back, searching for the zipper. He was standing so close that I could feel his breath on my neck.

"I like your hair like this," he whispered, his lips nearly grazing my ear as I felt the dress tighten around me even further. His hand lingered on my shoulder before he stepped away, sending shivers up my spine.

"Well, I didn't have much of a choice, seeing how it was dripping wet only moments ago." I sighed, leaning down to slip on the... were these even shoes?

"Well, I have to get going–erm–thanks for all of this. I can pay you back for the dress," I said, avoiding the eyes now scanning my entire body.

"Nonsense. It's a gift. Black suits you," His gaze remained on me a moment too long. A part of me wanted to reach out. To touch him.

"I have noticed your preference for the color," I murmured, finally cutting my eyes.

"I'll leave a few moments after you. Have fun tonight. And remember everything we talked about. I'll make sure Mercer is aware of the plan."

I nodded, pausing. "And thank you... for..."

"Not killing you?" he whispered with a wicked grin.

"Yes, that." I rolled my eyes before stepping out into the street.

It was a miracle I didn't fall the second my heel met the uneven cobblestone.

CHAPTER 35

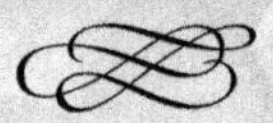

THE WALK TOOK me longer than I expected since I hadn't originally accounted for the ankle-breaking contraptions that Laryk considered shoes.

I felt his lingering gaze on me, and I tugged down on the dress nervously.

Osta had chosen a restaurant along the harbor.

The spot offered a glittering view of the city and its reflection in the water below. A sea-drenched breeze blew over the docks, sending a shiver over my exposed skin. I inhaled the scent of grilled fish.

It wasn't difficult to find my friends' after navigating the masses of Aossí populating the dock. Raine had been sure to reserve the best table amongst the outdoor seating.

"I'm *so* sorry I'm late!" I rushed over, finding an empty space beside Raine, opposite Briar and Osta.

I was surprised to see Nazul had dared to show.

Glasses of varying fullness littered the table. I craved a drink and the relaxation it would bring, but I needed to be of sound mind while I got my story straight.

"Um, hello? Who is this vixen in our midst?" Briar gasped, eyes going wide.

"Fia? Where has this dress been hiding?" In a flurry of movement, Osta made her way around the table to pull me off the chair, clumsily spinning me to get a better look.

"Seriously, Fia! You look hot!" Raine grinned, tilting her drink to me in a salute.

A blush stained my cheeks, and I rolled my eyes, gently guiding Osta back to her seat.

"I…wanted to try something new, so I went shopping today after leaving the Compound." I hoped I sounded convincing, but when Osta's eyes widened, I knew I should have just bitten my tongue.

"*Shopping? You?* And you didn't invite *me*?" Osta held her heart as if stabbed, the alcohol clearly bringing out the dramatics.

"Where did Mercer pull you off to by the way?" Raine jumped in, saving me from one white lie only to force me into another.

I repeated the General's words. "There was paperwork I needed to sign that got looked over on my first day."

"Well, you got lucky because Mercer didn't let up on us for the rest of the session," Briar complained.

Grimacing, I offered an apologetic look at both of them.

"Mind if I sit here?" We looked up to find Draven standing awkwardly next to the table. His black hair, which usually hung in his face, had been pushed back. I could finally see his gray-blue eyes framed by dark lashes. It was obvious he had bulked up from all of our training.

I guess we all held ourselves differently these days.

"Draven! So happy you decided to show up. Sit, sit!" Briar yanked an unoccupied stool from a table behind us, positioning him at the head.

"Yeah, I figured if I was going to get in trouble for the group's activities outside of class, I may as well participate." He gave us a half smile, settling in.

"Let's get a round of drinks!" Osta clapped, motioning to the bartender.

Maybe one drink wouldn't hurt.

Draven was surprisingly funny when intoxicated. I hoped he would start joining our gatherings in the future.

The next few hours passed in an instant.

Before we paid our tab, Osta went to freshen up.

"Did you know General Ashford is back?" Raine asked as we waited for Osta to return.

"I had no idea," I responded, too quickly.

"I'm sure you're *so excited* he's back, Fia. Am I right?" Briar's voice had gone up an octave and there was a slight slur to his words.

"What do you mean?"

"Why do you look embarrassed? You're bagging the General. That's a win!" He giggled, and while it seemed he was being playful, the volume at which he announced it seemed anything but.

"I really don't know what you're talking about..." I shifted, hoping no one was listening too intently.

"Briar, quiet down a bit," Draven said.

"Why else would they be having private lessons at an off-campus gym? Doesn't seem so innocent to me." Briar's lips were pursed, eyebrows wagging.

I shot Raine a look as my stomach turned to concrete. I couldn't believe that she had leaked this information to anyone after I'd asked her not to. Based on the look on her face, she was regretting it.

I couldn't help but notice a few heads turned our way. I leaned over the table, speaking in hushed tones. "Let's talk about this later. Now really isn't the time. Please?" I couldn't help the stern undertone of my words.

Briar scoffed. "Stop with the dramatics. General Ashford is known to have favorites. You're not the first, and you certainly won't be his last, honey."

"Briar, stop it!" Raine hushed, swiping her hand at him.

I needed to get some air.

"I'm going to go find Osta," I announced, standing on stiff legs. When I didn't see her in the powder room, I stepped out onto the connected docks.

I looked around, almost giving up when I saw Nazul's frame leaning over a petite form, a flickering lamp barely illuminating the view. They were locked in an embrace, and sure enough, that was Osta's yellow lace dress bunched in his fingers.

"What in the actual fuck," I blurted, already on the move to break them up.

They pulled apart in a daze. When Osta saw me, her eyes went wide.

"Fia! I was going to tell you about us but it's still so new–"

"No, no, no. This isn't happening. Osta, he's *not* a good person. I've seen the people he spends his time with and know exactly how they feel about Riftborne."

I seethed at Nazul. He had the decency to untangle himself from my best friend and step back.

"He's not like you think. After he saved me in the clearing, we got to talking and I promise–"

"I'm telling you. He is just trying to use you for a lay." I couldn't help but cut her off again. "I think it's time we go back home for the night."

"Fia, I promise I don't have any bad intentions with Osta. I really like her…" Nazul began. I held up my hand.

"It's not happening. Not with her," I snapped with a warning look.

I linked my arm around Osta's and began pulling her behind me, but I could feel her resistance as she looked back at Nazul.

We made our way through the outdoor bar when Raine caught up to us.

"Were you leaving without saying anything? Fia, I'm really sorry. I accidentally let it slip months ago, before we got this close.

I'm ashamed of myself. I never thought Briar would repeat that. Clearly I made a big fucking mistake," Raine pleaded, concern heavy in her eyes.

I paused, taking a deep breath of the night air.

Releasing a confused Osta, I turned to Raine.

"It's... fine. I just don't know why he had to announce it like that. The timing couldn't have been worse." I frowned and looked around the mostly vacant street. Perhaps I should have been more upset with her, but I wasn't exactly in a position to lose friends at the moment. I'd give her the chance to redeem herself with a new secret.

"I have a way you can make it up to me," I offered a small smile.

"Anything," Raine promised.

"The clearing. Whatever you saw me do... no you didn't." I bit my lip and glanced around once again. "I did a few little tricks and embarrassed some of the guys, causing a scene. That's all that happened."

Raine looked at me, confused, but I watched as the dots connected behind her eyes, and she nodded solemnly in understanding.

"You got it. I'll inform the others too... maybe Briar *after* he sobers up. I'm still really sorry, Fia."

"That would be helpful, thank you." I promised to see her tomorrow before looping my arm with Osta's again. She was looking longingly back towards the water and I couldn't hold back an exasperated sigh as we began our walk back home.

"Osta, what were you thinking?" My lips curled back in disapproval.

"You're wrong about him, you know. We've spoken almost every evening since the clearing, and he is more of a gentleman than any boy or man I've met thus far. And you're blind if you think he's not attractive, so stop making that face already." She bumped me with her hip, and I had to steady myself to avoid twisting my ankle.

"I don't think you understand. He was best friends with Baelor. You know, the one who tried to burn you alive?"

"That's Baelor, not Nazul. Plus, he isn't best friends with him at all. He protected me," she countered.

I shook my head. I didn't believe it for a second.

"Fia, I know how protective you are of me, but I will tell you this right now." Osta approached our front door and paused before opening it, turning to me. "I'm going to continue to explore this with Nazul whether you like it or not. I'm an adult who can make her own choices, and I will go into this knowing the risks. Please respect that." Osta spoke so clearly, I forgot she had been drinking all evening. She was serious about this.

"Okay…but I swear to Eibhlín if he hurts you, I'll kill him myself."

CHAPTER 36

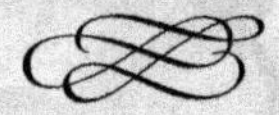

THE NEXT DAY, Briar chased me down outside the Compound gates, offering apologies and pinning the blame on the heightened number of cocktails. Forgiveness wasn't something I felt in the moment, but I forced myself to move on, even though I harbored doubts about his sincerity. Briar seemed to have grown a new distaste for me since Raine took my side about his outburst.

A few weeks of relentless training had passed since then.

My sparring game had improved, with my strategy shifting towards defense. I learned to dodge with precision, navigate the mat with quick footwork, and execute graceful rolls to tire out my opponents. Briar and I traded wins in our two encounters, marking my first victory in the class.

But facing off against Nazul was a different challenge. His skill and lifelong training made me apprehensive. I felt a surge of pride in executing a move that brought him down—a high leap that sent him tumbling to the mat with my legs wrapped around his shoulders. Even Mercer seemed impressed.

I continued to practice similar maneuvers in the following

weeks, recognizing my proficiency lay more in leveraging the strength and agility of my lower body rather than relying solely on hand strikes.

The extra practice had been incredibly useful in my final spar against Raine, where I finally bested her.

Mercer, on the other hand, won every match he participated in. But that hadn't come as a shock to any of us.

The General remained in Luminaria, but his availability was essentially nonexistent. Strategizing over the threat in the West didn't just stop because he was back.

Blood Clot was at his side nearly every free moment he had. I had become accustomed to taming the rage that burned in me at the sight of her.

Our training sessions were few and far between. I knew there were bigger issues to focus on, so I tried not to think too much of it. Even knowing that, I couldn't help but feel a pang of disappointment on the days we used to train together.

Troops were constantly being sent to the front lines. Only the recruits and a handful of initiates and officers remained in Luminaria. The Compound had become something of a ghost town. But the level of training for all of us had increased.

Laryk was the only General who seemed to stay in Luminaria for any long period of time. None of us could figure out why. I attributed it to him being the King's favorite in command, and therefore requiring easy access to him.

Osta and I had said a tearful goodbye the day she moved to the Soleil Estate. I had accompanied her, helping her deliver her boxes upon boxes of clothing and materials. After a few days of living in our apartment by myself, loneliness crept in. I had never lived on my own. I guess I hadn't realized how much I relied on her proximity or companionship.

I applied for residency at the Compound. It was easy to justify once I realized the inevitability of our deployment to the West. I did get lucky, seeing as Raine was the only other female recruit in our faction. The head of lodging immediately approved my request and assigned me to her room.

Moving my belongings to the Compound wasn't nearly as much of an ordeal as moving Osta's. All of my clothes fit into a single box. I wasn't particularly sentimental, but leaving our recycled furniture behind did tug at my heart in a ferocious way.

Being a recruit of the Guard had never felt so real. From the structured infantry formations in the morning, artillery storming up the metal stairs at all hours of the night, and the scheduled mealtimes, my daily routine had been turned on its head. Even getting a lick of privacy was difficult.

But I didn't mind sharing a space with Raine. Since moving in, we had grown even closer, much to Briar's annoyance. Although he and I had mended things, a discomfort lingered.

After two weeks at the Compound, Raine and I walked into the sparring gym to find Lieutenant Mercer and Laryk on a mat in the back.

The sight was certainly one to behold.

The two men danced around each other with unwavering precision. I had never seen Laryk in action before… and I never wanted it to end.

"Fia, close your mouth," Raine whispered, clearly not affected in the same way. I bit back a goofy grin.

Lean muscles rippled through Laryk's fitted training shirt, now drenched with sweat as he moved at a near impossible speed. His hair was loosely tied at the nape of his neck; a few pieces had escaped to frame his face. His jawline clenched to perfection as he dodged a blow from Mercer.

Suddenly, Laryk rolled past his opponent, coming up into a predatory crouch. The look in his eyes was feral, yet methodical. Like his sole purpose was to vanquish, defeat, even kill.

Laryk lunged, soaring just to Mercer's left, expertly grappling his chest and pulling Mercer through the air, ending in a violent thud on the mat. The Lieutenant rolled to his side, gasping for breath.

Shock raced through me. I never thought I'd see Mercer get the living shit kicked out of him.

He tapped the mat three times, and Laryk smirked, holding out a hand for the Lieutenant. He helped him up to a standing position and affectionately patted him on the back.

"Don't worry old friend, maybe you'll get me next time," The General said in his velvety tone, sarcasm dripping from his voice.

Mercer shoved him. "We both know that won't happen." The two men shared a laugh before finally taking note of our presence.

"Recruits. You're early. I was just here showing your instructor how to spar," Laryk said, returning to his naturally cocky state of being. "I assume you're both doing well," he added, approaching the front of the class.

I was hot.

Unbearably hot.

I needed water.

Immediately.

As if Niamh herself had heard my plea, Nazul sauntered into the room.

In an instant, I was doused.

I held back an eye roll as he waved in my direction. I assumed he had not ceased his pursuit of Osta, and I didn't ask. If she wanted to keep his company, that was her prerogative. She had asked me to respect it, and I had agreed. But I never said I would approve.

Raine and I took our seats at the front of the room. It took every fiber of my being not to steal a glance in Laryk's direction.

"As you can all see, we have the pleasure of our General's presence here today." Lieutenant Mercer leaned back on his desk, motioning towards Laryk, who simply nodded towards the room with a stoic expression. He lifted an eyebrow as we made eye contact. I turned my attention back to Mercer.

"We're going to be playing a game of sorts. It should be fun," Laryk said, a mysterious smile creeping at the corner of his lips.

All of the recruits shifted in their seats. This was going to be anything *but* fun, if Laryk's expression was any indication.

"Apart from stealing the air around you, what do our enemies do to disorient their opponents?" Mercer asked the class.

"Utter darkness," Nazul said, twirling a quill through his fingers.

"Ah, the first answer is correct. Perhaps you are all learning something after all." Mercer stood up from the desk and retrieved something that hung from the back of the door. "Can anyone tell me what this is?" He held out his hand, showing off a slim piece of black fabric.

"A blindfold?" Briar questioned.

"Two correct answers in a row. How impressive you all are today." Mercer was clearly in too good a mood.

Suspicion clawed at me.

"The next step in preparing you is to take away your vision during combat. But we're upping the stakes." He motioned towards the General, who stood and made his way back to the mat, turning to give us one of his smirks.

"For fuck's sake," Raine whispered as she limped back to the group of us. Nearly everyone was clutching an elbow or a knee. Every other recruit had faced Laryk, sparring until they were too winded to continue. No one had come close to touching him. He didn't even appear tired as he cracked his knuckles and paced, wiping sweat from his brow. I'd put it off for as long as possible. But now it was my turn.

I stepped onto the mat, closing the distance between us. Laryk gave me a wicked smile, and held up the blindfold. I stepped in front of him, crossing my arms and turning around.

"Don't expect me to take it easy on you," he whispered, securing the sheet of fabric over my eyes.

"I expect you'll do the opposite, actually," I quipped as his hand brushed against my arm. I shivered. A part of me wished we weren't doing this in front of the entire class.

His breath was on my left ear now. "If you can knock me on this mat, I'll tell you what my focus is." I could hear the smirk in his voice. Determination surged through me. No one had been able to do it thus far, but he was quite the motivator.

I felt a chill as he stepped away.

"Ready yourself," he stated, the sternness returning to his voice.

I exhaled calmly, turning all of my attention to what I could feel around me. The mat shifted as he circled, each step heightening my senses. I knew the attack was coming. I braced myself, getting into my defensive position.

I sensed something in front of me, but my attempt to dodge was cut short as his hands seized my waist, slamming my back into the mat and knocking the air out of me. It all happened so quickly. I heard a few laughs from the other recruits, and my skin flushed.

I pulled myself up onto my elbows. But I was forced back as his hands wrapped around my wrists, pinning me down. I tried to twist my lower body to escape his grasp, but his leg flew over my waist. Then he was on top of me, forcing my legs into submission as he locked them closed with his own. I was trapped. Embarrassment swept over me.

"If this were real, you'd be dead," he murmured before releasing his grip.

"Get up," he commanded. I felt him walk away.

I threw my palms onto the mat and stood. He hadn't taunted the others like this.

After five more failed attempts, I sat up, breathless. I wanted to attack him, to slap away that smug look that I knew was gracing his features as he paced back and forth, eager for another impossible round.

"Again," he said with too much excitement.

I stood, balancing myself as I heard him let out a chuckle from the other side of the mat, and my blood began to boil.

Enough of this. I wasn't going to let him win again. I summoned the webbing, goading it up my spine, urging it to send out feelers into the space around me. A second sight. I picked up the slivers of a mind slowly approaching from behind and bit back a wicked grin, glowing like it was lit from within. I put every ounce of my concentration into tracking Laryk.

Suddenly, the pulse shot towards me, and I dodged to the right, angling myself as I felt my thighs make the connection. A gasp ran through the room as I laced my legs through his and brought us both down, hard against the mat. But I wasn't finished. I could still sense him. I tore myself free, tackling him as he got to his feet, and we tumbled back down. I reached out, grabbed his arms, and pinned them behind his head as I straddled him, locking my ankles around his upper thighs.

I couldn't hold back a triumphant smile as I released his hands and tore the blindfold off. I wasn't going to miss getting to see the look on his face.

The room was still silent, save for a few murmurs.

I looked down to see Laryk smirking, a dark intensity burned in his eyes.

"Impressive," he stated. "Care to release me now?"

This position of power felt... better than good. I shoved away the heat that was building in my core, seeing him below me.

In a swift motion, I untangled my ankles and climbed off, returning to my feet once more.

He threw his legs back over his head and rolled into a crouch before standing. What an incessant *showoff*.

I glared at him as I held out the blindfold, angling my head so that the rest of the class couldn't see the smirk now etched onto my lips. I couldn't even help it. I was beaming.

He walked slowly over to me, close enough to whisper in my ear as he took the fabric from my grasp.

"Cheater," he murmured. The word was low and silken with a dangerous edge. Heat surged through me as I returned to my seat, shifting my weight and trying to quell the burning inside me.

Class was dismissed early, and I rejected the invitation from Raine to join her for dinner in the mess hall. I did not need to be around people right now.

I rushed into the hallway just in time to see two redheads walking down the corridor together. My heart froze in my chest, but the burning in my core only intensified.

Blood Clot looked back in my direction, smiling as she looped her arm around Laryk's waist. I was going to explode. I tore my eyes from the sight of the two of them and ran in the other direction. I needed the safety of my own space.

I flew inside my room, slamming the door behind me and locking it, grateful to finally be alone. I crawled onto my bed and looked toward the ceiling. *What did he see in her?* I wanted to scream. I needed something that was just out of reach. My entire body ached to be relieved of this heat. To feel his hands on me. I tried to focus on my accomplishment… finding him… tracking his mind. There was something intimate about it, but that only left me wanting more.

Then there was the feeling of his body pressed against mine. His legs pinning me down. the heat of him taking over my senses. I felt flushed when I thought of his arms wrapped around me, the weight of him pressing against me. A burning desire was pooling at my core that had me wishing for more.

I needed a release. Maybe I hadn't been physical with someone in so long that even the violence of sparring could get me going. Maybe it wasn't him at all…

I knew I was lying to myself. My whole world had been incinerated by thoughts of him.

Thoughts I wished I could turn off. Eradicate.

But for now, I could at least remove the tension from my body.

I allowed my mind and my hands to wander until I found what I'd been searching for. I didn't stop until waves of euphoria shot through me.

CHAPTER 37

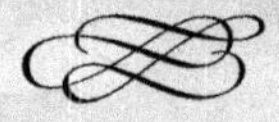

MY EYES SNAPPED WIDE open as war horns ripped through the silence. I scanned the darkness in a panic, heart pounding in my chest. I heard the heavy thud of boots just outside the door. The clanging of metal and marching soldiers erupted through the Compound.

Was I dreaming?

No.

The sounds above proved otherwise.

We were under attack.

I jerked my eyes towards the ceiling. Frantic orders echoed through the Compound.

"Raine!" I yelled, my voice straining against the noise. "We're under attack! Get up, get dressed!"

“Holy shit,” I heard from across the room.

I leaped from the bed, urgency lending speed to my movements as I struggled into my leathers. My fingers fumbled for my boots in the darkness.

Another blast of horns shattered the air. "I'm ready," I called, quickly tying my hair at the nape of my neck.

"Let's go." Raine's figure, barely discernible in the night, darted for the door. I followed closely behind.

She wrenched it open, revealing the chaos that engulfed the Compound, darkness swallowing everything in its path.

"We need to find the others," she commanded.

I fell into step beside her as we raced down the corridor, the stone-lined wall our only guide. I focused on controlling my breath, letting instinct and training take over.

"Arrow nocked!" The command echoed from above as we sprinted towards the men's dormitories, navigating obstacles as best we could in the darkness, every movement fueled by urgency.

"Fire!" The voice called out again as we rushed past recruits of all factions, only discernible by the clink of armor and sudden glimpses of crisp white fabric.

My stomach lurched as my mind wandered. There was only one thing that permeated my thoughts.

Wraiths.

It had to be. The Compound was never this dark.

They had made it. They had reached Luminaria.

Chills ran up my spine as the realization settled in.

Suddenly, Raine hit the ground with a loud thud. In an instant, she was back on her feet, blindly looking around for whatever she had crashed into, before bringing sparks to her fingers, lighting the small space around us.

I noticed a figure on the floor.

"Raine? Fia?" Draven's voice sounded from below us. I reached out and pulled him up.

"Raine, can you make that brighter?" A flash of fear splintered across Nazul's expression.

"Not unless you want to be incinerated," Raine huffed, eyeing the closed-in hallway.

"Fine. We need to get to the north control room. Briar will lead the way." Nazul turned quickly, feeling for the doorway.

A scream echoed through the corridor, and we were off in an

instant, racing once again through the darkness in trained formation. Briar summoned a trail of roots that blasted through the floor and crawled across the walls, allowing him to feel his way forward. "Stay close."

As soon as we breached the doorway to the Great Hall, my legs froze. The other recruits stopped dead in their tracks, and we all looked around aimlessly.

"Which way?" I asked, trying to steady my racing heart.

Screeching whispers engulfed the room in a vortex. They were coming from all directions.

"We need to split up. We're too vulnerable as a group," Briar snapped.

He grabbed Raine's arm and shot off toward the sparring gyms to the left of the Compound. Draven looked back and forth between us, watching Raine's sparks disappear in the distance before taking off after them. Suddenly, I was being pulled right by Nazul, and we were full-on sprinting again.

I refocused on the threat above.

We would meet back up at the control room. In an unexpected attack, our orders were to go there for a briefing before engaging in any combat.

I squinted my eyes, trying to better make out my surroundings. I could see, but barely.

Nazul slammed into a table beside me.

"Fuck, I can't see shit in here." He gasped.

I quickly helped him up, allowing him to steady himself before we took off.

I stepped forward but was blown back by an invisible force and launched into the air. I twisted my body, preparing to make contact with the ground. My feet hit first, and I threw my hand down to steady myself into a crouch.

"Fia! Where are y–" Nazul called out just as I heard his body hit the wall in front of me.

Lighting exploded on the opposite side of the Great Hall, illuminating the space around us for a split second. My eyes burned from the sudden brightness, but I saw the Wraiths' inky forms for the first time, the monstrous shadows that tore through the air–diving, twisting, spreading. All at unimaginable speeds.

My entire being threatened to collapse, but I refocused. There was no time for fear right now. I had to get to Nazul.

I stayed low, crawling over to where I heard him make an impact.

"If you can, cover me. I'm going to try to find them," I commanded.

"Do it quickly. My shield is up, but if we get surrounded..." he trailed off as we heard more screams from above.

I slammed my eyes closed, imagining the blindfold. The webbing was already making its climb.

I reached out with my mind, searching.

I could sense Nazul beside me. I extended the tendrils further into the space, beyond him, branching out.

Searching.

Come on.

I wasn't picking up anything. Just the faint traces of those fighting above.

"I can't sense anything around us. We should keep moving."

We launched to our feet and took the path closest to the perimeter. Whispers flew through the Compound, dampening all other sound. The wind picked up around us.

I reached for Nazul just as another invisible force slammed into me, knocking me to the ground. My ribs cracked upon the impact, and I cried out into the darkness.

Suddenly, I was in the air, my arms bound behind me as something brushed against my back. I tried to jerk away but couldn't budge. The wind was louder than ever, spewing guttural whispers in all directions.

I could feel them approaching, surrounding me. The world disappeared from my view.

All I could see was black.

A void.

I fought to break free from the Wraith's grasp, but my hands wouldn't move. I wasn't strong enough.

I slammed my eyes shut and summoned the web, commanding it to find my attacker. To kill it.

It shot out around me, desperate to find its target.

But nothing.

There was nothing to latch onto.

Impenetrable darkness.

A void.

The air around me began to thin as the shadows twisted into a tighter vortex.

I was going to die.

"Nazul…" I managed to croak out in a last act of desperation. My eyelids were heavy, my limbs burning with numbness. The webbing was going wild around me, still snaking through the darkness, on the hunt with a maddening fury.

It was going to die with me.

Ma. Osta. I wouldn't be able to save them.

Fog enveloped my mind as I kicked, my lungs begging for air that wouldn't come.

It would be over soon.

My body slowly lost its will to fight, and I went limp, suspended in complete darkness. Accompanied only by the Wraiths that were sucking the life from me.

My powers were useless against this enemy.

I was completely and utterly useless.

Laryk had been wrong about me.

My mind began shutting down. My pulse was weak.

The pain from my fractured rib subsided. I couldn't feel anything at all.

Suddenly, something tore through the whispers. My body convulsed, waking up my lungs and sending me into violent gasps. I felt a hand on my arm as the vortex around me disappeared.

I fell to the ground, still retching. I couldn't get enough air, my mind still drenched in mist. Even the tendrils lay limp, braided loosely around my spine. They seemed to be heaving.

Nazul dragged me to the perimeter once again.

"I tried to get to you sooner. I fought my way through the shadows and was able to project my shield onto you." He sounded winded, frantic.

"Control…room…" I whispered. It was all I could manage at the moment.

Nazul's powers had grown in the face of the Wraiths, and mine had proved futile.

"We're close now. Can you run?" he asked quietly.

I nodded, allowing him to pull me up.

Nazul wrapped his arm around my back, and we set off again, rushing towards the door at the end of the room. My ribs ached, and I did my best to hold my core still, but gasps escaped me every time I took a step forward. The pain was back in full force. A testament to being alive.

We were reaching the end of the hall. Just a few more steps and we'd be in the control room. .

The vortex of whispers picked up behind us just as we bolted through the door.

My eyes slammed closed as the room lit up around us.

"Well done, recruits!" Lieutenant Mercer said as I fell to the ground, clutching my side.

What the fuck?

Suddenly, Raine was helping me up. I peeked at the room through my lashes. My vision caught a glimpse of copper hair in the corner.

Laryk.

His face was serious, stoic, but his eyes softened when they met mine. His jaw clenched as his eyes shifted down to my ribs.

I looked around to find a few officers, initiates and the rest of my recruit class.

The rest of team V that remained at the Compound was in the room.

"It wasn't real," Briar said from his seated position. He looked rough, gripping his ankle.

"Healers will be here soon to deal with any injuries," Mercer said. "I'm pleased each one of you made it back here in the allotted time. I was beginning to worry about you two." He tilted his head toward Nazul and I. "We didn't take it easy on you either. You all proved yourself tonight."

"All of that was an illusion?" Draven asked, looking around at the unfamiliar guards.

"Well, it was a combined effort. But essentially, yes. We used illusionists, levitation experts, and wind wielders. This seemed to be the most accurate simulation of the real threat."

"But she failed," a curse of a voice murmured, and Blood Clot stepped out from behind a few of the officers, and a coy smirk played at her lips.

There was nothing but hatred in her eyes.

"She's clearly not ready for combat in the West. Unless you want her dead." Narissa crossed her arms, moving her attention to Laryk and clearing her throat. "Which, in that case, let's get her there immediately."

"The goal was to make it to the control room," Mercer said, stepping in her line of sight. "Fia made it here. It's not a perfect experiment by any means, but teamwork is certainly a factor. And all of you showed strength in working together to overcome the threat. It was impressive to see."

Narissa rolled her eyes, slithering back into the shadows.

Both anger and relief invaded me.

I wanted to scream.

I shot a narrowed glance at Laryk, who winked at me before stepping forward and clearing his throat. "I guess congratulations are in order. This wasn't just any test. It was your last test. Welcome to the Guard, initiates."

CHAPTER 38

"I SWEAR upon this blade to guard our realm with courage, never to falter. As the serpents coil in vigilant watch, so shall I, protecting the realm's heart, in the brightest of days and the darkest of nights. I pledge to defend our people, our lands, and our promise. Above all, I swear my loyalty to the Crown as I am now an extension of its iron shield. This oath I swear, bound by blood." Our voices rang out in unison, echoing through the cavernous space of the Compound's social hall.

I looked down upon the emerald-encrusted set of daggers, taking a deep breath before turning the point against my hand, wincing as I made the small cut.

Each unit had been given special blades, ranging from scimitars to short swords, all bearing the emblem of Sídhe.

The blonde woman we'd seen during training, dressed in her emerald uniform, stepped in front of me, smiling. "Welcome to the Guard, Fia Riftborne." Her voice was low and eloquent. She turned around, retrieving a vial from a man standing behind her, dressed in the same emerald hue.

"Your last blood oath," she murmured, holding out my vial. It had so many little papers in it now, all dripping with blood that should have been dry but was somehow still as vibrant a crimson as the day it'd left my veins.

A part of me hesitated—one I hadn't seen in a long time. A ghost from my old life, when fear controlled my every move. It still coursed through me, but it was different now. It was a healthy kind of fear, for the real threat on the Western border. But I wasn't afraid to live. Or feel. Or *experience*. Joining the Guard had never felt like my decision, not truly. Just like my focus erupting into madness had never felt like my decision. But so much had changed.

This. *This* was my decision.

I held my hand above the glass and watched as a tiny drop of blood fell amongst the rest. A calm swept over me. The woman nodded and moved onto the next recruit.

After the ceremony, we gathered in the mess hall to celebrate. I looked for Laryk, but he was nowhere to be seen. The Generals had been in meetings all day.

"Cheers!" Raine shouted as we all tapped the rims of our mugs together. The mess hall was bustling as new initiates from all factions celebrated their ascension.

After the simulation last night, I crawled back into bed with a sour stomach. When I'd thought I was in the Wraith's grasp, it had felt so real. I had never been that close to death. It was terrifying.

It was one thing to learn about these enemies on paper, but entirely another to come face to face with one. Real or not. I didn't know if I'd ever be truly prepared. Though, I was relieved when I'd realized that the simulation was the reason my focus wasn't working.

I hoped the real Wraiths had some kind of cognitive function, otherwise I'd be just as useless. I shivered the thought away.

"Fia, are you here with us?" Briar asked, waving his hand in front of my face. I looked around, taking a sip of my ale.

"Sorry, guess I'm still exhausted," I muttered. Raine had all but dragged me out of bed halfway through the day so we could get ready for the induction ceremony together. "So, what do you think we'll be doing next?" Draven asked in between bites of a sandwich.

"Shipped off West," Nazul replied. He briefly glanced in my direction. "I mean, where else would we go? This is what we've been training for."

I swallowed hard. This was all much more real now.

"I'm just excited to get my first paycheck," Briar chimed in. "I need a new wardrobe for my travels."

"I highly doubt the Wraiths care what you're wearing." Draven rolled his eyes.

"You'd be surprised. Maybe they're coming for us because of these hideous uniforms."

A chuckle ran through the group. We had picked up our new initiates gear last night before heading back to our rooms. We'd have to break in our dress uniforms and new sets of leathers all over again.

"I think they look nice. I mean, apart from the ruff–"

"We look like pirates," Briar deadpanned, cutting off Draven and waving his billowing sleeve in the air.

I couldn't hold back my laughter. He had a point.

"I think they're flattering. You just don't fill it out Briar. It's clearly made for the female form," Raine pointed out.

I had to agree the new uniform did fit me well. The protective leather vest that buckled up the front was fitted and had plenty of storage for knives and daggers. I ran my fingers over the rugged surface, feeling a sudden pang of nostalgia for my apothecary belt.

"It's finally free. Anyone up for a game?" Draven asked, motioning toward the card table in the corner of the hall.

"Get ready to have your ass kicked," Raine said, jumping to her feet. As the two made their way over, Briar's eyes slid back and forth between Nazul and I, clearly feeling uncomfortable.

"I'm going to go watch." He let out a strained exhale before following them.

Nazul cleared his throat, and I felt his eyes on me.

"I assume you're looking for a thank you," I said with a sigh, turning towards him. I guess we were doing this now. He blinked. "So, thank you." I allowed a subtle smile to form on my lips. "I know none of it was real, but you didn't know that. And you risked your life to save me."

"Of course, I saved you. We're on the same team here," he said simply, shrugging.

"Nazul, come on. You know it hasn't felt like we've been on the same team. First with Baelor, and then with Osta."

"Baelor is an ignorant prick, and he's clearly dangerous. I think I just remember how he used to be when we were kids. He wasn't always the bully. In fact, he used to be my savior back then. I don't know when things changed."

"You'd certainly never guess," I said, rolling my eyes. The thought of Baelor doing anything selfless was hilarious.

"I guess it took him leaving for me to realize how dark we had both gotten." He sighed, staring down into his ale. "I'm sorry it took that long."

"Well, I'm willing to start fresh. I owe you that at least." I reached out with my mug. "Agreed?"

He tapped the rim against mine, and we both took a long drink.

"Agreed." He ran his fingers through his hair and his posture softened.

"Don't hurt her." I narrowed my eyes.

"You have my word." He smiled. "Care for another round?"

I looked down to see the glistening bottom of my mug. "Erm–sure." I handed it to him.

"It's on me," he replied as he walked toward the bar.

I glanced toward the card table, noticing that Mercer was whispering something to the group. Raine, Briar and Draven all looked pale.

What's going on?

It was then that I heard the heavy screeching of metal doors opening. My head snapped to the right. All five Generals stepped out onto the platform above the hallway to the lobby.

Laryk gripped the railing. There was an intensity in his expression, his jaw clenched in a hard line.

"I need everyone's attention." His voice boomed through the crowd, and silence fell over the room.

"Prepare for deployment. We leave for the West at sundown."

CHAPTER 39

I FELT MY HEART STOP.

Raine rushed over to me, with Draven and Briar trailing close behind.

"Another string of attacks in Stormshire. Even worse than last time. There are 60 dead."

My mind was racing as Raine pulled me out of my chair and dragged me to our room to pack. My lips couldn't form words. I began pushing uniforms, tools, and the last of my healing tonics into my bag.

Healing tonics.

Ma.

My heart jolted back into action as I fastened my bag and spun around.

"I have to go. I need you to cover for me. I'll be back as soon as I can," I directed, not leaving room for disagreement.

"Whatever it is, just make it quick." Raine's eyes were heavy.

I nodded before grabbing my bag and rushing out of the room, stopping in the hall as realization washed over me.

The blood oath.

I couldn't warn Ma about anything. She wouldn't even know it was coming before it was too late.

My mind raced, stomach lurching at the thought of leaving her unaware.

The two sides of me warred, my old life slamming into my new one. But I didn't have time to think about it.

I didn't need an oath to keep my promise to Sídhe. I had sworn that fealty just hours before, and I had meant it. Even without my blood. My loyalty to Ma didn't negate my loyalty to the Guard. Both could exist at once.

That blood vial was the only thing standing in my way.

I had to destroy it.

I recalled watching the emerald-uniformed guard walking the vials past the infirmary. I began moving in that direction, easily navigating the chaos of bodies readying for departure, using their distraction to remain unseen. It was mostly the new initiates. Everyone else had already been deployed.

When I finally reached the corridor leading to the lobby, I turned right towards the Immunity wing and paused, flattening myself against the wall as a few guards in beige robes hurried out the door, dragging crates towards the front gate. Even through the slit of the door, I could tell the hall was cramped with healers fumbling with equipment, readying themselves for the journey West. I shifted, impatiently waiting for the space to clear. Even for just a few seconds. Enough time that I could make it to the end of the hall. I prayed the door would be open.

The healers began to filter out, loading wagons at the front gate with hordes of medical supplies. Finally, the last one left. This was my moment.

I stopped the door to the hall with my foot, slipping inside. Then I was off, racing down the corridor, eyes darting over my shoulder to make sure I hadn't been followed.

As soon as I reached the door I was looking for, it opened, and I slammed into the blonde guard, sending us both tumbling to the ground.

My heart lurched.

Her wide eyes locked on me as my breath caught in my throat. My instincts took over, engulfing my mind with translucent webbing. The fibers were seared into my spine.

I had never channeled so quickly.

The web shot out of me as if by its own command, latching onto her mind with a certainty I'd never felt before, finding the access point in a flash.

Her expression changed, nearly going blank, now void of the confusion it bore just seconds before.

"Leave. You didn't see me here. And you'll tell no one about this," I said, feeling the words burn down the bond.

She nodded, rose to her feet, and began walking calmly to the end of the corridor.

I let myself take a deep breath as the tendrils found their way back to me. My heart was still racing.

I could be killed for this. I fucking hope it worked.

Climbing to my feet, I looked behind me once more before slipping into the dimly lit room, closing the door and securing the lock.

The room was small, illuminated by violet-blue light that pulsed through the space. Arcanite crystals were half-buried into planters, and platters of vials lined tables. But the most shocking sight were the inky vines that grew from the planter. They twisted and curled around the tiny bottles. They seemed... possessive.

What the fuck?

Nearing the table with the smallest platter of vials, I reached out to examine the vine. My fingers grazed the leaves, flying back when I felt something thick and sticky coating the surface.

My eyes shot down to find blood covering my fingers.

What the hell is this? I'd seen nearly every plant from across the realm, in some form or another. But never anything that looked like that.

And the arcanite... Was it helping the the vines grow?

My mind shifted to Ma's failed experiment with the crystal, how all of her plants had the life sucked from them. This didn't make any sense. This vine was enormous, and healthy from what I could tell. But now was not the time to investigate.

I kneeled down, my eyes scanning the names etched into the glasses, cringing as my sleeve brushed against the vine. Draven... Raine.... *Fia Riftborne*. I snatched the vial and could have sworn the vine reared in resistance, but I didn't dare a glance back.

I sprinted out of that room as fast as I could and didn't stop until the commotion of the mess hall slammed into me. People whipped past, transporting supplies, bags, and weapons. The energy was stifling. No one spoke. I even saw a few tears slide down clenched jaws as I made a path through the madness.

I had to find a way out of the Compound.

I would take the eastern exit. It was the least guarded, and I could escape without too many eyes on me. I ran across the mess hall towards the training gyms, taking the small corridor at the end near the initiate lodging.

I flew up the stairs as fast as I could without making too much noise; and looked around the corridor before darting to the gate.

Fuck.

There were guards swarming it. My pace slowed.

"Going somewhere, initiate?" I heard a velvet voice ask from behind me. I whipped around to find Laryk leaning against the wall, twirling a dagger through his fingers. My mind flashed back to the first night I had ever seen him. When we were near the woods. When he saw my focus for the first time. The event that started all of this.

"I'm not running, but I'm not leaving without seeing Ma one last time," I said, trying to keep my voice steady. The vial weighed heavily in my hand, and I quickly slipped it into my pocket. He could never know about this.

"I thought you two had parted ways," he said, returning the dagger to his chest and crossing his arms.

"It doesn't matter. I have to see her before we go. If I don't come back..." My voice trailed off. "I can't leave things how they are now."

"I can't let you leave."

"I wasn't asking." I narrowed my eyes, motioning toward the gate. "Tell them to let me go. I promise I'll be back before we deploy."

Laryk pondered my demand, running a hand through his hair. He clicked his teeth.

"I know you will. Because I'll escort you there and drag your ass out if I must. We have to leave before sundown."

"Deal," I said flatly and hurried toward the gate, shooting him a look of annoyance when he didn't immediately match my speed.

The city was buzzing with an electric kind of energy as we made our way to the central district. Almost as if it reflected the frenzy currently taking place at the Compound. Every face we passed made guilt bubble up in my gut. If we failed on our mission, they'd never be prepared for what was to come. I couldn't tell everyone. But I could tell Ma.

Laryk waited around the corner as I approached the doors to the Apothecary. The familiar scent of rosemary filled my lungs, and I paused. It had been so long since I'd been here. So much had changed. *I* had changed.

I stopped right before I made it to the door, retrieving the vial from my pocket and looking around before placing it on the cobblestones below. I slammed the bottom of my boot into the tiny bottle, hearing it crack with the blow. The sensation of air returning to my lungs nearly knocked me over. I stepped back.

The vial lay cracked on the pavement, little blood soaked papers caught between the shards. I knelt down to see the blood turn from bright crimson to muddy brown as whatever enchantment affecting it evaporated.

I stood and kicked the remains into the canal before turning back to the door of the Apothecary.

The scared girl who'd wandered into this shop six years ago felt like a stranger now. Back then, I'd turned my back on the world, resigning myself to the shadows.

I took a deep breath and reached for the handle.

That girl didn't exist anymore.

CHAPTER 40

WIND RUSHED past me as I pulled open the door and stepped into the shop.

"I'll be with you in just a moment!" Ma called from the back. The sound of breaking glass echoed through the shop. "For fucks sake." I heard her grumble.

I made my way to the back to find her hunched down on her hands and knees, sweeping a broken jar into a pan.

"I said I'd be–" Ma grouched as she turned around and saw me. "Fia?" Her brow peaked.

My stomach twisted.

"Erm-Hi, Ma. I'm sorry to just drop in, but..." My voice trailed off as I looked around the room, noticing how tidy it was. The back shelves were stocked and orderly.

"You still use my system," I breathed, turning to look at her again.

"Yeah, well. Guess I just got into the habit," she said, shrugging her shoulders.

A moment of silence slipped awkwardly past.

"Why are you here, Fia?" she finally asked, pursing her lips, but the look in her eyes had my heart sinking.

"I don't have much time–I just... I needed to say goodbye," I whispered, looking away and trying to distract myself from the moisture that was stinging my eyes.

"You're leaving Luminaria?" she asked. She leaned onto her desk, her hands gripping it tightly.

I nodded. "I leave for Stormshire in half an hour."

Another moment of silence passed. *What was I doing?* These might be my last moments with Ma, and I was wasting them. She needed to know. She needed to be able to prepare herself in case we lost control of the West. In case I died.

I walked towards her, eyes pleading.

"I know you don't understand this Ma. I know you don't agree with it. I know you're terrified about what's next for me. But I'm going to tell you something. Something I hid from you, something that might make you see me differently." My voice cracked, but there was no time to waste.

"The night of the celebration in the Grove, remember how I told you I channeled?"

Ma nodded slowly.

"I didn't just channel. I lost control. I nearly killed two girls." Tears were pooling in the corners of my eyes.

Ma stared at me, her mouth quivering. She began shaking her head, "No... Fia, you couldn't have... I mean..." She looked down.

"General Ashford was able to get healers to them in time, but they were on the brink of death. If it weren't for him, I would have their blood on my hands." I steadied my voice.

"That's why I joined the Guard. I couldn't bear the thought of doing that to you. Or Osta. My control had become so weak. I was losing my temper over simple things. It was only a matter of time before I..."

Ma continued to look down. "I could never understand why you did it... It never made sense..." she said quietly.

Her eyes shot to me. "You should have told me, Fia. Maybe then I would have understood. Maybe then, we wouldn't have spent the last few months…" she trailed off, losing her voice as a tear ran down her cheek. "We would have had more time," she whispered.

"I was scared you would see me differently. I would rather you disapprove of my decision to join the Guard than see you look at me with horror in your eyes." Tears fell down my cheeks.

"Nothing you could do would ever change how I feel about you, Fia. You're... Well, you always have been… my kid. Ever since you walked in here with that unruly hair. That first day six years ago. I saw the sadness and emptiness in your eyes, and I knew. We were the same. Two lost people looking for our place in the world. And we became each other's place. Each other's home." She reached out and took my hands in hers. They were more calloused than I remembered.

My chest heaved from the relief of her words, and guilt formed a lump in my throat.

"I'm so sorry, Ma. I'm so sorry I left you all alone here." I could feel the sobs building in my gut.

Ma pulled me in and hugged me, wrapping her arms around me tightly as I sobbed into her shoulder. We stayed like that until my body calmed.

"What is happening in Stormshire?" she asked cautiously.

"There is a threat… a sort of enemy. We don't understand everything about them. But they're from another world. And they're lethal." I took a deep breath."I'm not supposed to be telling you any of this, but I can't leave you unprepared. If we fail to hold them back… they will come for Luminaria," I said.

"We believe they can kill in many ways, but they're preferred method is suffocation. They literally rip the air from your lungs." I winced, remembering the night before.

Ma was still staring at the ground, her eyes wide.

"Is there any way to destroy them?"

"We don't know. But our best bet would be to survive long enough to find out. Without suffocating."

Ma glanced toward the back of the room and scrunched her eyebrows. "I wonder..." she said, standing up and walking over to the back shelves. She paused in front of a set of vials with red contents. She grabbed them quickly and rushed them to her work-station.

"Fia, quickly. Grab the crushed whale bone," she commanded.

Confusion washed over me, but I obeyed, grabbing the small, glass jar from the middle shelf. I walked over and laid it next to the vials she was now emptying into her cauldron. She reached for the powder, pouring it in as well, before leaning down to light the coals beneath.

"Ma, what are you doing?"

"I have an idea," she said, stirring the cauldron.

"Ma, we really don't have much time..." I trailed off as red smoke and the stench of seawater permeated the space around us.

"Ah, see? That didn't take long," she said as she used a ladle to scoop out the new concoction, pouring it into a small dish.

"Okay, it's hot. But try it," she urged, curiosity gleaming in her eyes.

"Erm–Ma, what is this?" I eyed the liquid as my stomach churned. It was cooling into a thick paste.

"The red algae I collected from the Scarlet Coast. I noticed the fish in that area were behaving strangely, so I started studying it. After drying and grinding the algae into a powder... well the whole thing was an accident really. The dust was so fine that it became airborne, and I inhaled some. I was a bit nervous at first but after a few seconds... my lungs relaxed. And I realized I could hold my breath for an extended period. I played around with it a bit, discovering that a liquid version held the same properties. It's a potential medical breakthrough, but I never knew what it's practical use could really be." She held out the dish. "As for this whale bone, it's an amplifier." I had missed the way Ma's eyes lit up when she talked about her work.

Reaching out slowly, I took the dish and held it to my nose. I coughed as bile rose in my throat.

"Dummy, you aren't supposed to smell it first!" She scolded. "We don't have much time, Fia."

I closed my eyes and tipped the dish back, letting it fall down my throat. My face twisted. The taste was unimaginable.

"So…?" She eyed me.

"What am I supposed to be feeling?" I asked, raising an eyebrow.

"Try to hold your breath," she urged, rolling her eyes.

I took a deep inhale, halting once my lungs were full.

Seconds went by. Then a full minute.

I felt no burning sensation or urgency to exhale. My lungs weren't contracting.

I looked at Ma with wide eyes. "This could save so many lives. You have no idea."

"This is just enough for you, Fia. It won't last more than a few minutes, so use it wisely."

"Please, Ma. If you could make more of this, it could really make a difference. We could win."

"I mean… I could go back to the coast, collect more algae. The whale bone I can get from traders." Gears were turning behind her eyes.

"I'll make it my first priority," she assured me. "Jacquelina would probably accompany me. Maybe a few others. We can get as much of it as possible."

"I'll talk to the General. Maybe we can set up some sort of distribution to the West," I said, as I heard the front door open. "That will be him. I guess my time is up," I said, returning to meet her eyes. "Thank you for this, Ma. I don't know what I'd do without you."

She reached out, pulling me into another hug, "Be careful, Fia.

And save this portion for yourself. Promise me?" She unbuckled my bag, slipping the vials inside.

"I promise," I said hesitantly.

"Fia, it's time to go." I heard the velvety voice call from the front. He actually had the decency to give us a few last seconds of privacy. Color me shocked.

"I'll write to you if I can," I said, pulling my bag off her desk.

"I'll be waiting. Love you, kid," she said with a soft smile.

"I love you," I responded before heading for the front. She didn't follow me.

The General was at the door, pulling it open. "Let's go," he said, and we were on the cobblestone seconds later, walking quickly. Laryk veered right.

"Erm–the Compound is the opposite direction," I said, looking behind us.

"We're not going to the Compound," he stated.

"What? Where are we going?" I asked. He was infuriating when he withheld information.

"To the stables."

"Can you please tell me what's going on?" Irritation laced my voice.

"You're traveling with me. We're going to collect our horses and begin the journey to Emeraal."

"Emeraal? I thought the attacks were in Stormshire?" I said, squinting my eyes.

"We're making a stop in Emeraal first. The King will hold a briefing there in a few days."

"But why am I going with you?" I asked.

"Just walk faster, Fia. We need to get to the campsite before the sun goes down."

I looked ahead and scoffed. It seemed like we'd have plenty of time for questions on the road.

CHAPTER 41

I LOOKED behind us as our horses followed the path out of the city. I couldn't help but think this might be the last time I would lay eyes on the place that I had called home for most of my life.

The sun was still high in the sky, breaching just behind the tallest towers. We would follow the river through the Reyanthe Valley and set up camp within the hills of Aedenvale. Laryk told me it would be a six-hour ride.

The woods had changed since the last time I'd ventured to the clearing. Half of the trees were bare now, twisting up as if reaching towards the sky. Leaves created a golden blanket across the forest floor.

The General and I rode side by side a few paces behind five members of the Base Guard.

We sat in a somewhat comfortable silence before the questions began to burn in my mind. I shifted, patting down my pocket to make sure I had a vial of Ma's potion easily accessible.

"Why am I here?" I asked, clearing my throat.

"I thought it would be obvious." Laryk stared straight ahead.

"So, you still don't trust me," I said flatly.

He finally deigned a glance in my direction. "Trust you?" He raised an eyebrow, that near permanent smirk playing at his lips.

"Not to blow someone up with my mind." I rolled my eyes.

His smirk turned into a grin.

"No, Fia. I think we're past that." He laughed, turning his attention back to the road ahead.

"Then why?" I urged, annoyance brewing.

"Would you believe me if I said I simply enjoyed your company?" he asked, shrugging his shoulders.

"Absolutely not."

"You're a valuable asset, Fia. I will need your protection if we come across any stray Wraiths." He snorted.

I bit back a grin, not wanting to give him the satisfaction."I'm sure you will, considering you still haven't told me what your focus is. I'm starting to think it doesn't exist."

His grin widened. "Is that so?" He glanced over at me again, a new wickedness gleaming in his eyes.

"You're great on road trips," I said flatly.

He paused for a moment, looking over the valley that surrounded us.

"It's not the easiest to explain," he finally said. "It has a kind of duality."

"I'm intrigued." I looked away as the wind picked up, blowing his hair back and revealing his chiseled jawline.

"My perception is unnaturally strong. I can see details other people can't. It makes me a master of strategy and invaluable to the Guard," he said, keeping his eyes straight ahead.

"That sounds a bit like Osta," I realized.

"I thought so too. Fascinating how focuses manifest differently in people. However, I believe Osta's is limited to inanimate things, like her designs. I have a way with... people. I think I've mentioned this to you before. I can sense what makes them tick. I know how to get what I want out of them. I am who I need to be given the circumstance," he continued.

"And the other part?"

"I can always see one step ahead. In a fight, I can sense my opponent's intention before he makes his move. I can't be surprised. I'm the best combat fighter in a generation," he said casually.

His words sank in. It all made so much sense now. He was a military's dream. No wonder he was promoted to General so young.

"So that's how you knew you could train my focus?" I eyed him, finally understanding.

"Not exactly. We'll have to attribute that to my overwhelming confidence." He shot me a smile that caused my breath to catch in my throat. "For some reason or another, my focus doesn't seem to work on you."

"Why?" I asked, scrunching my forehead.

"Well, there's something clearly wrong with you. It's the only viable possibility. It works perfectly on everyone else."

"It sounds like there's something wrong with *you,*" I shot back, hiding another smile. He was oddly playful in the face of near-certain death.

"Maybe so." He shrugged.

"When we first met, you seemed erratic, like I couldn't get a read on who you were," I said, a new realization seeping in. "Is it because you couldn't see what made me tick?"

"I couldn't sense what motivated you whatsoever, so I had to go about it the old-fashioned way, figuring out what your greatest fears were and how to exploit them. It was beyond frustrating," he said, furrowing his eyebrows. "But I figured you out enough. Anytime I mentioned Osta, you fell into place quite easily."

I stayed silent for a moment, trying to push away the discomfort that his words brought. After so much time, it was hard to recall the beginning of our relationship. So much had changed.

" Now you know all of my secrets." His words broke through my thoughts.

"I highly doubt that. You're about as mysterious and conniving as they come."

Our horses veered left, trotting down the decline of a hill.

"I'll tell you anything you want to know, but first, you have to tell me how you beat me in Mercer's class. I know you didn't do it on your own merit as a fighter." Laryk scoffed.

The wind had picked up, and he pushed his hair behind the points of his ear.

"I tried something. I didn't know if it would work. But it was just this inkling. Because my focus is so tied to the mind, I was curious if I could sense someone within range of me. And it worked. I could see you burning bright as you approached me. It's like having a second sight," I admitted, pleased with myself.

"It makes sense. How can you grip a mind if you can't see it? It's intuitive. The thought never occurred to me. As frustrating as that is."

"That's why my focus was useless during the simulation," I added. "Not that we know for sure that Wraith's even have minds."

"They have some sort of cognitive function." He glanced down, adjusting the straps of his saddle.

"How can you be sure?" I asked.

"My ability is also highly tied to the mind. I don't know what the wind is going to do. I don't know if it's going to rain. But I can read *them*. That tells me there has to be something behind the shadows," he said, rubbing his scar.

"Anyway, was there something specific you wanted to know about me?" he questioned, changing the subject.

I paused, wondering what the best approach would be. I wanted to ask him about the scar and how exactly he received it, but I got the feeling he wanted to end this portion of the conversation.

"Your father is a famous General right?"

"I guess you could say that." He clenched his jaw, and I wondered if I had stumbled into *another* sensitive subject.

"We don't have to talk about it."

"My father was a glorious prick, and there's not much else to know about him. My mother is a socialite who only cares about her status and the next event. Does this suffice for my family history?"

"They sound great. I see why you turned out the way–"

"There *was* someone who cared for me. Who I also cared for. She's gone now." His eyes were intensely focused on the road ahead. The smirk had disappeared, and his lips formed into a straight line.

I wanted to press further but I didn't know what to say. I stayed quiet, giving him the space to elaborate if he wanted.

"Joline, my caretaker." He swallowed hard, "That's the woman who raised me. She died when I reached my twentieth year." The words came out through a clenched jaw.

"I'm sorry to hear that," I replied softly, looking away. I had never seen him like this. His facade was normally impenetrable.

"And you, you were raised in the House of Unity," he stated. I was unsure whether it was a question.

"You already know everything about me." I reached down to adjust the reigns of my horse.

"I know the facts. I don't know what your experience there was like." I felt his eyes on me again.

"About like you would expect."

"Coyness doesn't suit you, Fia."

I shot Laryk a scowl, hesitating before recalling the past. "I was able to form my own semblance of a family with the other Rift-borne children. There were a lot of sleepless nights in the beginning. Kids missing their parents. I was too young to remember mine. The older orphans had a much harder time adjusting." I took a deep breath.

"The people who took care of us were cold and distant and they never tried to explain to us what happened to our families or why we were there. We didn't learn about *that* until we got to school and were taught about the uprising along with all the other kids in Luminaria. You can imagine how that went. Back then, we didn't know to hide *these*." I held up my branding, and it reflected the fading sunlight.

Laryk was silent for a few moments before shifting in his saddle. "Our leadership missed the mark with certain situations in the wake of the war. I didn't understand a lot of what was going on at the time, seeing how I was only ten years old. But in hindsight, I think it's clear that mistakes were made," he said in a lowered tone.

His answer shocked me into silence.

It seemed like an eternity had passed. I stole a glance in his direction to find him chewing on his bottom lip, brow furrowed. His hair had fallen back into his face, catching in the breeze. I didn't want to break his concentration, but the silence was finally starting to get to me.

"I haven't seen your red-headed shadow recently. Did you reassign her to something other than following you around and shooting me dirty looks?"

"Riftborne, you are vicious." He smirked, eyeing me from behind his lashes. "Narissa is always on her best behavior."

"Maybe you should remind her about the whole *camaraderie* portion of your spiel."

Laryk snickered, shaking his head.

"You seem to be implying that we're together. We're not." he said plainly.

"Have you told *her* that?" I mumbled under my breath.

"It's common knowledge that my priorities lie with my role as General. Commitment is out of the question. I don't know how Mercer does it."

I pushed down the unwelcome feeling forming in my gut. "Perhaps your problem is less about commitment and more about fidelity."

"Monogamy is only gifted to those with little responsibility."

Bursting into a fit of laughter, I had to steady myself. A few of the guardsmen looked back at us. "Whatever helps you sleep at night, General Ashford."

"I'm surprised you're using my proper title. Happy to see you falling in line."

I searched for the right insult, but one never came. The back and forth had become tiring.

Nudging my horse with my heel, I trotted a few feet ahead of him. I stayed there for the remainder of the journey.

THE GUARDS SET up our fire quickly once we found the campground in the foothills of southern Aedenvale. This was the General's typical respite, being the perfect midpoint between Luminaria and the Western strongholds. The placement was tactical. With the rocky incline protecting us from the rear, we only had the defense of one side to worry about.

Dinner was quiet as we heated the pre-cooked meals sent along with us from the Compound. Roasted fish with root vegetables—a delicacy I still hadn't become accustomed to.

The Base Guards would be switching out night watch and were placed strategically around the perimeter of the camp.

I found the sleeping arrangements maddeningly awkward. Seeing how the General usually traveled alone, there was a single tent for both of us to share. Praise the Esprithe the guards brought an extra bed for me.

When the General mentioned a tent, I was expecting the ones typical for hunters during the winter season, but that was not what I walked into after we finished eating.

In no world would this ever be considered a tent. The space inside was huge, and the roof was at least double the size of a standard dwelling. A small fire burned in the middle of the room, helping to fight the winter chill. Animal hides insulated the walls, and rugs covered the ground.

There were two beds on either side–raised cots with fur blankets layered atop. I walked over, dropping my belongings onto one before sitting down and chucking off my boots. I stretched my legs all the way down to my toes. I knew I would be sore tomorrow from the extended time on horseback.

I dug through my bag, searching for my night clothes, eager to crawl into bed and fall asleep. My eyes were heavy, and I knew we would have an early morning.

I looked for a place to change, but there seemed to be no privacy. It was a giant, open space.

I eyed Laryk, who was reclined, sorting through some parchment. I took the opportunity to unbutton my vest and yank my blouse and trousers off, quickly replacing them with my nightgown. I brushed through my hair, collecting it in a braid before tying it back.

I turned around and nearly jumped. Laryk was standing now, bare chested as he adjusted the coals in the fire. The light cast perfect shadows across his sculpted abdomen. His trousers hung low on his hips, exposing a defined v. The sight heated me more than the fire.

"We're sparring tomorrow morning before we leave, by the way. I want to test your new ability," he mused, extinguishing the candle on his bedside table.

"Got it," I mumbled, rolling over. I could sense his eyes burning a hole in my back as I drifted off to sleep.

CHAPTER 42

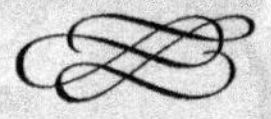

Mist clung to the air, drifting across the mountain range in the distance. The sun was only just beginning to peak over the horizon, and there wasn't a soul in sight.

"Okay, I think I'm ready. Let's go another round."

I turned my attention to Fia.

A shock of white curls had escaped their tie and loosely framed her face, drifting effortlessly in the wind. Her skin was glistening with perspiration and flushed from exertion.

My eyes shamelessly wandered over her heaving chest and up to her mouth. She took a swig from her canteen, and I followed the trail of water that escaped her lips, dripping down her throat and disappearing into the collar of her uniform.

I was suddenly feeling very parched, myself.

Rolling my shoulders, I jogged to the center of the field, not far from the campsite. I extended the blindfold to Fia. She walked over, reaching for the cloth, but I retracted my hand, shaking my head.

Her eyes sparked, quick to take up the challenge.

"I'll be the one to tie it. You know the rules," I reminded her, holding back the urge to rile her more.

I couldn't help but smile at her flushed, defiant face before she conceded and turned her back to me.

I adjusted the dark fabric over her eyes, my fingers brushing against the nape of her neck as I secured the knot. I watched her shiver at the slight contact, and a jolt of need raged through me unabashedly. I swallowed the desire to pull her against my chest and took a step back.

I was more than impressed with the development of her focus. Her ability to track a mind in total darkness would be invaluable.

She was invaluable.

My need for her had been present from the very beginning, despite my attempts to ignore it. It had burned through me from the moment I'd seen her at the Grove surrounded by bodies, energy still radiating off her like water on hot pavement.

I moved on silent feet, circling her. She took one final breath in, halting on a small gasp before holding it. And then she was on me, feet and arms sweeping out in a skillful rhythm. I quickly changed my position and felt a jab to my side as her arm shot back, making contact. I grabbed it, locking it against my ribs and putting her at an odd angle.

This round is finished.

I heard the small hiss of stored oxygen escaping her lips as she kicked out with her legs and used her body weight to pull us forward onto the grass. The shock of it had me falling, but with a twist of my body, I had her pinned beneath me and writhing.

"That was a wonderful attempt, Fia, but you've put yourself into quite a precarious position." I attempted a teasing tone, but my words were ragged. The way she could catch me off guard was a mixture of terrifying, exhilarating and euphoric. It was something I'd never experienced before.

My fingers flexed around her wrists. The feeling of her body arching against mine had my mind spinning and the length of me aching in the front of my leathers. Her usual, mouthwatering scent of rosemary and sweet musk was overwhelming in this proximity.

Fuck. I needed to move.

Her right leg escaped from where my knee had pinned her, and she looped it around the back of my thigh, pushing upward in an attempt to flip me.

Fia froze.

My hardness was fully pressed against her now, and there was no way she didn't notice.

Heat rushed through me almost painfully, and I released her wrists, quickly sitting up, trying to untangle our limbs.

"Let's end here for the day," I rasped, thankful her blindfold was still in place.

"Laryk."

My name on her lips froze me in place. I felt the leg she had wrapped around me tighten as if to pull me towards her again. Her arms blindly made their way around my neck, and she leveraged herself, rolling her hips in a teasing motion that had me seeing red.

My eyes closed at the sensation of her grinding against me. My body pulsed with need even as it shook with restraint.

"Fia," I growled. It was a warning.

Her hips rolled again as she forced her head back, exposing that beautiful neck to me. A moan escaped her lips. It sounded like the most beautiful song I'd ever heard.

"Laryk...please."

My sense of reason snapped.

My mouth was on her in a second, tasting the soft skin of her throat, tracing over her jaw until my lips captured hers in a possessive kiss. She tasted even better than I could have ever imagined.

I pressed her onto the ground, meeting her desperate hips with a hard thrust that left her gasping.

Breaking the kiss, I demanded, "That's it Fia...moan for me." One of my hands tangled itself in her silken hair, tugging softly, while the other worked to deftly undo the clasps of her bodice. My mouth explored her, impatience warring with need as I pulled at the leathers that stuck to our heated skin.

When her chest was fully exposed to the morning air, I was practically drooling. I only gave myself a second to enjoy the view before sucking one of the peaks between my lips... gently... delicately... before biting down hard.

"Ah!" She whimpered, ripping away her blindfold to look at me with intoxicating intensity.

I gave her a roguish grin.

I wasn't known to be a gentle lover, but before she could make another sound, my tongue flattened, soothing the ache, and she melted against me once again.

"Good girl," I hummed against her skin, making my way to the other peak–giving it the same treatment. I watched as her lips parted on a sharp inhale. Her eyes fluttered closed as my tongue teased her sensitive skin.

Her body shivered as she pressed against me.

"Laryk, we have to hurry. The sun will be up soon. Someone may see..."

Fia's plea had me coming apart. In one quick motion I laid her back, yanking down hard on her bottoms before tossing them to the side.

Her sex was completely pressed against the front of me, with only my leathers standing in the way of my clearly outlined need for her.

I slid my hands over the pale expanse of her thighs, opening her up for me. That parched feeling returned and I dipped down, hungrily nipping at the soft skin between her legs, never quite reaching my destination.

"Tell me you want this." My voice was hoarse with desire.

Her startling opal eyes found me, and I saw a desperation that matched my own.

"I want you," Fia assured, her hands digging into my hair, using it to guide me to her center. That was all the confirmation I needed.

Like a man starved, I dove into her heat and rolled my tongue. She was divine. A guttural moan escaped my throat that—

~

WOKE ME UP. I was awake.

What…. was that?

My body was shaking and flushed as I frantically searched my surroundings only to find that Laryk was also wide awake. His eyes were locked on me from across the dying embers of the fire. He looked as disheveled and riled as I felt.

"I think I was... were you just... dreaming about me?" I whispered with a shaky breath.

His eyes flared in the darkness before icing over, opening his mouth but closing it just as quickly. Even in the shadows, I could see his chest rising and falling rapidly, in rhythm with my own.

He said nothing, but his eyes told me it was true.

I had been inside his dream.

My thoughts began to spiral. I swallowed hard, knowing that the same questions were racing through both of our minds.

"General, we need to depart soon to stay on schedule," a guard called from outside the tent. Laryk broke eye contact first, grabbing his bag and storming out.

I guess sparring practice was canceled.

CHAPTER 43

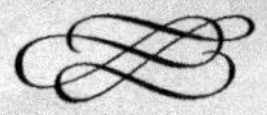

WE STARTED towards the West as the rising sun began to cast a glow through the valley. Frost spattered the colorful leaves, refracting the early morning rays. I breathed deeply, inhaling the crisp taste of winter air.

Formations changed this morning. Three guards were positioned at the rear of the unit, and three were in the front. Laryk was amongst the latter.

I couldn't even glance in his direction as we mounted the horses. Now that his back was to me, I could finally breathe.

I had entered another person's mind...

Had this happened before?

The dreams that had plagued me for the last year rushed in, and the realization dawned that none of them were from my perspective. It'd seemed innocuous at the time, but now, seeing them from a collective point of view... the pattern was certainly there.

In the dream that took place at the river, I was looking down at my friends from the top of the bridge, but when the event actually occurred, I was on the river's edge with Osta, both of us moments away from jumping in ourselves. Was I seeing it from the perspective of the second guard? Did that mean I was seeing a memory? A dream of a memory? I couldn't wrap my mind around it.

The settings of my dreams were often places I had never seen or even imagined during my waking hours. The darkened landscape of the falling dream, the fiendish blacksmith–were these real places? Real people?

Heat rushed over my body again. The dream from last night was certainly real. And I knew *that* wasn't a memory. Even still… I had felt his passion through the connection.

Hadn't I?

I couldn't help but wonder how the mind really worked in a dream state. At this point I was questioning everything. Most people couldn't control their dreams, but that had to have come from somewhere in his mind, right? It couldn't have sparked from nothing…

Or perhaps it all was random. Perhaps he was just as surprised by the content. Embarrassment flooded me. That was probably the last thing he ever wanted me to see. Albeit unintentionally, I had completely invaded his private thoughts, whether there was any merit to them or not.

I sighed, wondering if we would ever talk about it, or if we would pretend it never happened.

My head snapped up as I heard the sound of a horse approaching. Suddenly, I felt like he was reading *my* mind. Laryk's face was relaxed, collected, his posture stoic. Any walls he had taken down had clearly been reconstructed. I tore my attention away, focusing on the mountains in the north. It hurt to look at him.

I stayed silent as his horse fell in step beside mine. I could almost feel the chill radiating off him.

"Another gift from your focus, I presume?" he said casually. I swallowed hard. Why did I feel so uncomfortable?

"I honestly have no idea." I nearly choked on the words.

"Relax, please. There's no reason for you to behave like this. I assure you, I'm less interested in discussing the context, and much more fascinated by the fact that you were able to enter my dream at all." He nudged my arm, offering me an apple. "You didn't eat this morning."

After hesitating for a second, I took it from him and sighed.

"I still don't understand how it happened. Or how I did it. Now I'm rethinking every dream I've ever had." My tone was quiet.

"It seems like your focus is growing more vast by the day. Give it time, and you'll adjust." He bit into his apple, staring at the path ahead.

How was he being so *casual*?

"Sometimes it feels like I'm losing my own mind," I admitted.

"I wouldn't even know how to train you to enhance this ability. I mean, I'll certainly try. Imagine what you could do..." his voice trailed off.

A part of me sank inside.

He didn't need to finish his sentence. I knew what he was going to say. I was simply an asset to him. The dream had meant nothing.

I looked up to see the shimmering towers of Emeraal in the distance.

IT WAS late morning when we reached the border of the city. The sun had since taken shelter behind a layer of clouds, and in its absence, the wind had adopted an icy chill.

The road through the city was rocky and unstable, cracking and falling apart in patches. The city was made up of predominantly simple dwellings, stately with timber-framed walls and steeply pitched roofs with asymmetrical gables.

The homes were all connected by a shared characteristic: emerald stained-glass windows set in diamond patterns—an homage to the vast emerald deposits that ran through this land.

Chimneys billowed smoke all across the city, creating dark and foggy air that reeked of coal and wood.

The streets were sparse, and I noticed quite a few boarded windows and doors. The few people who did move through the city did so in a hushed fashion, hurrying to their destination.

As we approached Emeraal's center, a cathedral came into perfect view. It loomed over the town, with tall spires reaching into the sky, its facade adorned with intricate stone carvings and detailing, depicting scenes of the mighty Esprithe. The same stained glass windows lined the exterior, reflecting the moody sky.

It seemed to be the busiest place in town with Aossí filtering in and out, leaving offerings on the front stairs. Some huddled close to their families, holding candles and humming softly, almost in a trance. The singing of hymns could be heard from the streets as worshipers filled the cavernous space, begging their Esprithe for salvation.

The shining towers of the Fortress beckoned us forward as the road began to incline. The path spiraled up a hill encapsulated by evergreens. We reached the first gate, and the entry guard immediately recognized Laryk.

The metal bars screeched open, and we passed through. I couldn't help but steal a glance at the city behind.

I returned my attention ahead, taking in the Fortress of Emeraal. Banners flew violently in the wind, secured to tall watchtowers that dotted the perimeter. Beyond the ramparts, I could make out towers in the heart of the commotion.

Down the hill, on the northern side of the Fortress, a cluster of shimmery blue and violet crystals protruded from the ground, high into the air. Slivers of light ran through them. The stones were surrounded by their own set of watchtowers.

Arcanite.

I hadn't realized there were stores of it here as well.

We neared a massive gatehouse, flanked by portcullises and

iron bars. I squinted to see past, finding narrow alleys winding between what must have been barracks, armories, and storerooms.

"General Ashford, welcome back to Emeraal. Our commander is awaiting you in the briefing room," A man called from the tower above, motioning for the gate to be lifted.

I stole a glance at Laryk, who still wore an uninterested expression as he nodded toward the soldier who had spoken.

We rode through the gate and dismounted. Base Guards came to collect our horses. Another set of guards came to transfer our belongings to our quarters.

"Show Initiate Riftborne to her room, please," Laryk said without looking back at me. My eyes darted around to the men who were now staring at my left hand.

"Erm–General, a word?" I said, attempting a respectful tone that was perhaps not as practiced as it should have been before coming here.

"Make it quick," he said, sauntering over. He arched an eyebrow and tilted his head for me to follow.

"I'm not going to the briefings with you?" I said, my brow scrunched.

"Only officers, lieutenants and generals are granted access to briefings at Emeraal," he said as if I was supposed to have somehow already known.

"So, what am I supposed to do?" I asked, irritation mixing with nerves in my gut.

"I don't care. Whatever you want. Just stay out of trouble," he said, turning back towards the entrance.

"Why am I here, then?" I hissed.

"Just do as you're told, Fia. This is a warzone. Be happy we're not under attack and that you even have the ability to wander freely today." He paused before taking a few steps back in my direction, lowering his voice. "But don't go making any friends. The Base soldiers here are wild and unpredictable." His eyes held an intensity that had me shifting, despite the anger that simmered just under my skin.

I glared at him and walked past, approaching one of the Emeraal guards. "I'd like to be shown to my quarters now, please." I tried to hide the disappointment in my voice. The useless feeling had returned.

CHAPTER 44

THE ROOM WAS BIGGER than I imagined, housing two full-size beds in either corner. A set of double doors with emerald glass led to a modest-sized balcony overlooking the courtyard below. I glanced toward the wardrobe. My bag was settled neatly on the floor, next to a large chest with copper buckles.

My brow scrunched, wondering if someone else's belongings had been delivered to my room by mistake. Or if it were meant for my eventual roommate. Would we be here long enough for me to have a roommate? Unease churned in my gut at the thought of sleeping next to a stranger. But I supposed this was the type of thing I'd have to get used to. Especially if Laryk decided to bring me everywhere with him like his useless, little pet.

My eyes dared an exhausted roll as I tried to swallow my brewing annoyance. I sank into the bed, ripping the sheets around me.

~

A KNOCK on the door had my eyes shooting open. I rubbed my forehead and glanced toward the balcony. It was still bright outside. I must have only dozed off for a few hours.

"Initiate Riftborne, it's time for meal service. Can I escort you to the dining hall?" I heard a timid voice from the other side.

My stomach rumbled at the thought of food. I slipped my boots on and opened the door to find a friendly face staring back at me. He was a smaller boy with freckles. Hair cut so short that I couldn't make out whether it was blonde or brown. He was a recruit based on his uniform. A shy smile grew on his face. "Follow me?" he asked, voice cracking.

I glanced down at his shirt to see Gerath Riftborne sprawled across the front. My eyes flew down to see the marking on his left hand.

"Another Riftborne. Well, I certainly wasn't expecting that," I said, smiling.

"There are a few of us in the recruitment class, actually," he whispered, looking around. "All of us Riftborne know about you. How you joined the Guard and ended up in the General's special faction..." he trailed off. "It gave us all hope."

Gerath's words hit me like a wave. I never imagined I would be... an inspiration to anyone, let alone another Riftborne on the opposite side of the isle.

"I don't know what to say." I shook my head, a faint smile playing at my lips, before my thoughts twisted. "And you all have been treated well?" I asked, arching an eyebrow.

"As good as one can hope. People seem to be coming around to it. Plus, the Guard is in no position to deny new recruits." He shrugged.

"I suppose so," I murmured, looking down the corridor. "I'm very happy to meet you, Gareth."

"Likewise. Should we get to the dining hall before all the good stuff is cleared out?" he asked, the giant smile returning to his face.

"I'm following you." I grinned and allowed him to lead the way.

The hall was massive and ornately decorated with a domed ceiling. Long platforms of buffets lined the furthest wall, and hundreds of tables were scattered throughout the space. I followed Gareth and grabbed a plate. My mouth watered upon seeing the food selections. They were endless. If the Guard appreciated one thing above all else, it was good food. We both filled our plates with cured meats, cheeses and bread before he showed me to an open table.

I sat down, excited to gorge myself.

"If you need help getting back to your room after lunch, come find me. I'll be at the recruits' table," he said quietly.

"You're not going to sit with me?" I asked, twisting in my seat. *Don't leave me alone,* I wanted to say.

"Recruits can't sit with initiates." He sighed, pointing towards a long table in the back. "We sit there."

A wave of disappointment washed over me.

"Thanks, Gareth. I'll come find you if I need help." I gave him a reassuring smile before turning back to my food. I took a bite of bread, and it immediately tasted stale, my appetite gone.

My eyes wandered up to the front of the room, to an elevated area with grand tables. A few lieutenants were seated. My eyes narrowed when I saw Laryk in what seemed to be a deep conversation. I leaned to the side, trying to get a view of who he was speaking with, only to see another wisp of blood-red hair.

Their faces were basically touching.

For the first time in months, I felt my fingers tingle with a power I didn't summon myself.

Suddenly, in the corner of my eye I saw a shadow move behind the buffet. I spun around, sending my hair flying, only to find nothing out of the ordinary. I was losing my mind. Or I was just on edge being this far West.

I looked back at Laryk, who glanced over, briefly making eye contact with me. He gave me a slight nod and turned back to Narissa.

My stomach lurched as I stood, stomping over to the waste basket and throwing my plate away. I swiped a bottle of gin from the liquor table and stormed to the other side of the room. I flung the door open and bounded down the corridor back to my quarters.

I found my bed once again and dropped my face into my hands. I didn't want to feel like this. It was a maddening, nearly manic rush of adrenaline. My fingers were throbbing, my vision blurry. Darkness clung to every thought.

He brought me here against my will and never deemed it necessary to tell me why. And briefings were off limits. My insides were screaming. I was stuck here, rendered absolutely useless instead of preparing for the battle at Stormshire with the rest of team V. I was starting to feel less like a member of an elite faction and more like someone's burden.

And he was with *her*.

Is that why I wasn't allowed to be with him?

Hours passed as my thoughts raced.

Anger simmered.

Boredom crept in.

I glanced at the corner of my chamber, eyeing the bottle of gin I had snatched earlier today. Without too much thought, I poured myself a drink, immediately downing it. And then I poured another.

I paced the room until the sun began its descent behind the mountain range.

My sanity was going to explode if I didn't leave this room, but I didn't know where to go.

Where I was *allowed* to go.

Soon enough, night had fallen over the city, and I began to hear rumblings of people below. I walked over to the balcony, opening the door and peeking out.

The entire regiment stood just beyond, making a commotion

with their laughter and shouts, like they'd already had one too many. This place sure was a stark contrast to the city below.

I pursed my lips, perhaps a party was exactly what I needed to blow off some steam.

Besides, if he was going to continue to act like I didn't exist...

Well, perhaps I'd find a worthy distraction.

I couldn't help the grin spreading on my face as I pulled myself together. The anger from earlier had twisted into something more wicked.

I looked in the mirror at my initiate's uniform, turning to the side to examine it from all angles. I wasn't used to having a full view of myself. I unbuttoned my vest, flinging it on the bed, and reached up to undo a few of the buttons on the top of my blouse, so it fell open just enough.

I tugged the leather strap from my hair and ran my fingers through the waves, allowing them to cascade freely down my back in wild layers.

A bit of harmless flirting could be just what I needed to divert my thoughts. With that, I grabbed the door and headed for the stairwell, but not before grabbing one of Ma's vials and sliding it into my pocket.

I navigated through the courtyard. The night sky twinkled above, and I felt a chill as the breeze picked up. It seemed like sleep was a foreign concept to this group, with everyone strolling around, passing bottles, and belting out old hymns that were much better lost to time.

The crowd was made up almost entirely of Base Guards. Most of the other sectors were probably headed straight for Stormshire. Only a few high-ranking officials from the Scales, Fang and Immunity units were in attendance.

The courtyard was scattered with twinkling tables and buffets of food. The imposing walls around us were lit with torches, creating a false atmosphere of safety, like no threat existed beyond the confines of these hills, yet every shadow sparked apprehension in the back of my mind. Another drink and I could forget that too.

My gaze scanned the party, searching for the bar. Instead, I locked eyes with a grinning dark-haired guardsman who motioned for me to join him.

That was easy.

A smile crept up my lips as I started towards him.

CHAPTER 45

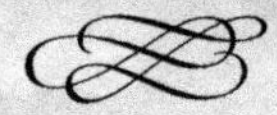

THE ENERGY in the courtyard was exciting, verging on dangerous. This was a different world. The members here certainly lived life to the fullest, absorbing all the revelry that they could, while they could. There was a sense of urgency to take it all in. To live.

I swore I could see it in the twinkle of the man's eyes—a challenge to let go. I could do that. I needed to, or else I'd be stuck in my room, with nothing on my mind but the General…

No. Be in the moment.

With a confidence I had never known, amplified by the liquor, I strolled over to him, catching the way his eyes traced my form. Adding a subtle sway to my hips, I approached, concealing my amusement as one of his buddies jabbed him playfully in the side.

"And what brings us the pleasure of having the General's Riftborne sidekick in our midst?" teased another one of his friends. I didn't flinch.

Fine by me, being the odd one out here.

My smile turned sickly sweet as I faced the one who spoke. He seemed two bottles deep, blonde hair all over the place, like he'd been unsuccessfully pushing it back all evening.

"Hoping for a drink and some entertainment. Think you're up for it?" My gaze found its way back to the dark-haired guy, his blue eyes still sparkling with promise.

"I'm Fia, by the way."

"I'm Ren. That's Hayden," he replied, smiling and leaning forward in his seat, forearms resting on the table. "I can help with the drink, but subjecting a lady like you to this lot's entertainment? Wouldn't dare."

"Hey! We're plenty entertaining!" Hayden protested, nearly toppling off his chair as he reached for another bottle.

"I'll be the judge of that." I shot them a wicked grin and leaned against the table.

"Then by all means..." Ren handed me a bottle, contents uncertain. I tossed it back, savoring the sweet warmth of wine.

When I looked up, Ren was smiling at me again. His dark hair was close-cropped, and his features, sharp at the edges, gave him a somewhat feminine allure compared to Laryk's harsh lines. I shook the comparison from my head.

"So why did you tag along with the General? I thought only Narissa did that," Ren questioned.

"You'll have to ask him." I smirked, taking another long sip of the wine. Hearing her name made my ears burn.

"Sounds like there's some tension there." The blonde one laughed.

"I'm just looking for fun tonight."

"Do I look fun to you?" Ren asked, a curious glimmer in his eyes.

"I wouldn't be here otherwise." Even I was shocked by my behavior tonight.

He stood and approached me, confidence showing in every step. His hand found its way to my lower back as if we'd known each other longer than this fleeting moment.

I felt the warmth of his breath at my ear, and my eyes fluttered closed, anticipating the meaningless sweet nothings that would clear my mind and this endless ache.

But the words didn't come.

I slowly opened my eyes. The courtyard's rowdy noises had hushed.

All I heard was the subtle clink of blades and footsteps heading toward our table.

"Nice to see everyone's fully prepared for an attack." Laryk's cold words pierced through the quiet, dripping with sarcasm.

I didn't dare turn around.

"General! We were just messing around! Plans of finishing up soon." Hayden scrambled to regain his composure.

"Based on their past patterns, they won't be back for a few days," Ren chimed in.

I felt him shift at my side, his grip slipping off my back as he turned to face Laryk.

The void left by Ren's hand quickly filled with the white-hot gaze of the General. I hadn't even turned around, yet I could sense his eyes drilling into me.

"I've had plenty of men die with similar assumptions." His voice came out in a growl, holding back what seemed like a torrent of frustration.

"Fia." It was all he said as he walked off, yet it resonated like both a command and a punishment. Am I some kind of *thing* he can summon to follow him? After avoiding me all day?

I think not.

My grip on the bottle tightened, knuckles whitening as I took one more swig and slammed it down, rising to my feet. My mood was shattered, replaced by anger.

I stomped after him, not bothering with goodbyes. He had a head start, but I saw him vanish into the corridor seconds before I bounded in after him, racing until we were standing in his quarters.

"What the fuck is your problem?" I shouted, unable to control myself.

"Your irresponsibility knows no bounds. Getting drunk and taking lowly Base soldiers as company. That sure seems like the way to prepare for this war," he hissed.

Rage simmered in my core.

"I don't see how it's any of your business. You brought me here for what? To hide in my room? I don't know what the next few days will bring. I don't know what we're going to find when we get to Stormshire. I just wanted to *feel* something."

"And what were you trying to *feel* tonight, Fia?" he snarled.

My insides were screaming. I clenched my fists, holding myself back from launching at him.

"Anything, Laryk! Anything to calm this maddening urge to..." I trailed off, jaw clenching as I shut my mouth. I wouldn't let the alcohol get the best of me. I wasn't going to say it.

"So fucking that boy was the answer?" His rage turned serpentine, almost mocking.

It infuriated me even more.

I wouldn't let him belittle me.

"I was certainly going to give him the opportunity to try!" I snapped. "I'm sure he was just about to escort me to a more private setting when you—"

He flew across the room, dropping his weapons unceremoniously to the floor. "I nearly ripped his arm off when I saw it on your back," he said, his tone dark.

He stared straight ahead, and I could see his muscles shifting under his clothing, as if he was forcefully holding himself in place.

The room fell deafeningly silent.

I didn't move as I scrutinized him, really taking him in.

His face wore a cold, blank mask as he took calculated breaths, fixating on nothing but the space in front of him.

"You have no idea the absolute fucking wreck I've been since I met you, Fia."

Suddenly, I wished he would look at me.

I yearned to see the mask break, to witness his barely contained desire and anger rush out all at once.

I walked toward him slowly, and his eyes snapped up to mine, the only thing offering a glimpse into what he was feeling behind his stoic features.

My breath caught in my throat at the need I saw there. Before I could fumble for words, he was upon me. My mind went blank.

His lips seared into mine, my body molding into his shape, completely succumbing to the onslaught of pent-up emotion that we both allowed to explode at once.

I heard myself moan, but I was so lost in the sensation of his hands clawing possessively down my body that I couldn't find it in myself to care if others could hear me.

My fingers tugged desperately at his clothing, needing to feel his skin against mine like I needed air to breathe.

He scooped me up in one swift motion, his fingers digging into the flesh at the backs of my thighs.

My legs wrapped around him, another moan escaping my lips at the hardness I felt pressed against my lower stomach.

"You're mine," he growled against my throat.

In a haze, I nodded my agreement, tilting my head back to give his wandering lips better access.

I had just managed to work his shirt up over his torso when I felt his knees hit something solid. I quickly followed him down as he set me onto the mattress, finding a place between my legs at the edge of the bed.

He pulled his shirt off the rest of the way exposing his muscular chest and frame.

He was a work of art. Truly.

His chest heaved as he stood above me, his eyes frantically dancing down my body, taking everything in.

Only a few of my buttons had been undone but I already felt completely bare.

"I hope you were prepared for a sleepless night because I intend to recreate every dream that I've had of you thus far."

His words sent a jolt of pleasure through me–the realization that the dream I'd witnessed was not his first.

"What's been holding you back?" I whispered.

His eyes avoided mine as he lowered himself down, his face level with my chest. He began to kiss his way across my collarbone. Each word tickled my skin as he violently rid me of my blouse.

"I can't allow myself a distraction like you," he huffed. His fingers gripped my waist so hard I knew they'd leave a mark. His mouth moved to trace the shell of my ear as he lowered his fingers and tugged on the buttons of my trousers.

"Nightly dalliances here and there are one thing... but you... you're so much more than that." He finally lifted his head to look at me. "You're important."

He didn't specify whether I was important to his cause or important to him, but the longing in his eyes had me hoping for the latter.

I raised my hand to his face, my thumb brushing against the fullness of his bottom lip. He captured it between his teeth with a devious smile. My mind flashed to his dream, and my core went molten. I wanted his lips elsewhere.

I grabbed the back of his neck and pulled his face to mine, my mouth opening up to him. I felt dizzy by the time he broke away, starting his journey down my body.

His breath felt hot against my skin. I reached towards his waistband, but he stopped me, grabbing my wrists and pinning them above my head.

I tugged against his grip, arching to resist him.

A smug look crossed his features as the movement pushed my chest towards his waiting lips. He chuckled darkly and clamped down on one of my nipples. The sound that escaped me seemed foreign to my own ears.

He made sure to leave scalding red kisses and bite marks across the tender swells of my chest. He was relentless in his teasing, but I would not give him the satisfaction of begging like I had in his fantasy.

The mixture of pain and pleasure had my body twisting under him. I kicked the trousers that were still tangled around my ankles away. His hold on my wrists loosened and I used his distraction and the strength in my now-freed legs to flip us.

Now I was in control.

"You look good underneath me," I taunted, sitting astride him.

The surprise in his eyes heated as he took in my naked form above him. I could feel his need pressing against me. I reached down, my hand boldly caressing his considerable length through the straining fabric.

Laryk groaned, the muscles in his stomach clenching tightly as his hips lifted into my touch. I moved down his body, just enough to give myself room to work on the elaborate clasps of his uniform.

Laryk held his breath as he watched my movements, looking every bit like a predator lying in wait.

My fingers hooked onto the edges of his waistband, and I pulled. His member sprung free, pulsing upwards to lay against my stomach, resting just below my belly button. My mouth watered at the sight, but Laryk had chosen this moment to make his move, one arm wrapping around my waist in a vice, the other fisting my hair. He lifted me up until my entrance was hovering just above him.

"Fia," he whispered hoarsely, tightening his grip against my scalp. "Do you want me to fuck you?"

I nodded, my hands pushing against his hold as I rushed to lower myself, needing him inside me immediately, but his arm only tightened, denying me.

I bit my lip, groaning in frustration. A wicked smile spread across his face and suddenly the room spun as he flipped me, my back slamming into the mattress. His knee parted my legs, his strong thighs pushing them apart, the weight of him pinning me down.

"I want to hear you say it, Fia." It was a demand. He wasn't going to back down.

"Fuck me, Laryk."

The tip of him slid down my center. I could feel how wet I had become.

"Laryk-"

In one powerful thrust he was inside, the sheer size of him robbing me of my breath. He moved to slide out of me, pausing for only seconds before burying himself to the hilt yet again.

My body rocked up the bed at the force of it, and we both let out a moan. I gripped his shoulders, digging my nails into his skin as the movements became unrelenting.

Euphoria rushed through me, leaving me in a tangled mess around him. Each stroke brought me closer to the edge, to the oblivion I so desperately craved.

More.

My hips met each of his thrusts as they became more fervent, more unforgiving.

My moans echoed through the chamber, and my breath came in quick gasps. I tangled my fingers into his hair, my face buried in the crook of his neck as my body became rigid.

"Come for me, Fia."

His command was followed by a final thrust that had me falling apart at the seams. Waves of pleasure surged through me, giving way to spasms of ecstasy that rocked me to my core.

My tensed muscles turned liquid, my body trembling beneath him, breathless and lost to reality.

"You feel so fucking good," he growled against my neck, breath heating me once again.

"More," I whispered, running my fingers down his back and shifting beneath him.

"That's what I like to hear," he murmured, tugging at my ear with his teeth.

In one quick movement he pulled out of me, flipping me onto my stomach. His hands grabbed my hips, forcing me up so that my knees dug into the sheets. His hand came down hard, stinging the skin of my behind, sending sparks through me. And in an instant, he shoved himself back inside me.

Again.

And Again.

A rhythm that went on for hours as he made his dreams into reality.

CHAPTER 46

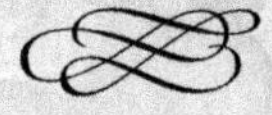

"PLEASE TELL me we get to sleep in tomorrow." My body laid limp, the sheets still tangled between us.

"Well, *you* do." Laryk chuckled softly.

"Wonderful," I muttered, rolling my eyes. "Because obviously, my only purpose is lounging in bed while the fate of the world hangs in the balance."

"You'll need your rest after the night we had." I could hear the smirk in his voice, satisfaction lacing his words as it always did when he gloated.

His copper hair was sprawled across the white linens, tickling the edge of my arm. His face was the usual shade of flawless, now accentuated by rosy cheeks and a glistening forehead. He cracked that knowing grin at me, and I thought I might just melt all over again.

But it was time for answers.

"Be honest with me… why am I here? Our faction could be walking into certain death as we speak." Even with exhaustion weighing on my bones, I couldn't stop my mind from wandering to my friends.

"Wraiths shouldn't attack for the next few days." He was staring at the ceiling, arms folded behind his head.

"How can you be sure?"

"They've never attacked twice in a week. Of course we can never be certain of anything, but it's been the case thus far." He blinked slowly, fighting off sleep.

"But why am I here with you and not the rest of the team?" I asked again. He kept avoiding the question. But not tonight. Not after everything that had just transpired. Not after his hands had finally touched me in all the ways I'd dreamed of. Not after he'd finally discovered all the places I'd yearned to feel his breath.

Laryk pondered for a moment, hiding his expression behind long lashes, the kind that would make most girls green with envy. "I have more than one answer for that." He inhaled deeply and reached out, running his finger along my arm, leaving a trail of delicious heat in its wake.

"Firstly, you're too valuable to send to the front lines. Your focus continues to get stronger by the day. We need more time to figure out exactly what you're capable of."

I let the words sink in.

I wanted more. There had to be more.

"And the second?" I prodded.

"Unfortunately, I've found it just about unbearable to be separated from you." He sighed, running his hand through his hair. "It's quite an annoying situation I find myself in."

I couldn't help the smile that spread across my lips.

"So irresponsible, General Ashford," I teased, rolling onto my side to face him.

"Absolutely reprehensible," he agreed.

A moment of nauseating bliss slipped past as he pulled me towards him, melding his lips to mine once more. His chest heaved below me, sending sparks flying through my entire body. I melted into the heat of his touch. Could we just stay in this bed forever?

The thought sent a sour pang into my stomach as the reality of our situation rushed back in. I pulled away and sighed.

"As much as I like to hear you say that... I can't help but feel like I could be doing something to help." My face found the pillow and I huffed a breath, sending a white curl spiraling into the air.

"We just have to get through the King's briefing tomorrow, and then we're off to Stormshire. Just be patient until then."

I reached out, running my fingers across the scar marking his right eye. It was raised, and cold to the touch. He clenched his jaw.

"Tell me how you got this," I said, biting my lip. I wasn't sure if this was another topic he would rather avoid.

"You know how. The Wraiths." He sighed, taking my hand and lacing his fingers through mine.

"I just haven't seen anyone else with a scar like that. Was it done with a weapon?"

He paused for a long moment, seeming to hold his breath. I felt my pulse quicken. He was clearly uncomfortable discussing this. But I had to know.

He finally exhaled. "It felt like a dagger."

My brow furrowed, and I flipped over to get a read on his expression.

"How can a shadow attack with a dagger?"

"You're guess is as good as mine," he murmured, bringing my hand to his lips and kissing it softly. "I don't know how they could wield anything at all."

"You think there might be something more to them?" I asked. I couldn't help but feel we were moving into dangerous territory.

"I'm not going to question those who came before me. I've only ever seen the shadows. The beings that look like ink droplets..." Laryk trailed off. "But I could have sworn I hit something solid once. In the darkness."

Silence took over the room as we both digested the implications of his words. Nothing made sense.

"Mercer said something about their strength diminishing the

further they get from the tear. Do you believe that to be true?" I swallowed hard.

"Our focuses only exist because of Sídhe's essence. If we were depleted of that, they would be rendered useless. Perhaps it is similar for the Wraiths."

Suddenly, my heart was racing all over again.

"If they can get to the arcanite..." I whispered.

"We certainly don't want to wait around to find out. I have specialists at the ready in Stormshire. If we could just capture one... we might figure out how to stop them," he said, eyes taking on a new intensity, locked and burning into mine.

Oh.

"You think that I'll be able to do that." Clarity washed over me like a tidal wave. My power relied on something tangible. These Wraiths, although creatures of shadow, possessed a flicker of consciousness, a vulnerability we could try to exploit. This is what he'd envisioned for me all along, even before the full scope of my abilities had unfolded. A weapon, yes, but a weapon wielded with purpose.

"Never in my life," he admitted, "had I seen anything like you. Different. The most beautiful creature I had ever laid eyes on..." He trailed off, and I thought my heart might just explode from my chest. "Even when we wanted to kill each other, we pushed forward. Even when the path seemed as bleak as the void, even when it was impossible. I couldn't sense anything within that curious mind. I had no idea what you were thinking, what you would do next. You were a complete mystery to me, yet I believed with a desperate kind of longing, that you were what I had been searching for. You had to be."

His words seared into my skin, incinerating any reservations that still clung to my mind, any distrust that lingered. I was his, utterly and irrevocably. His weapon. His lover. His salvation. And then I knew. I would cripple armies and break minds if that's what he desired.

A small tinge of guilt slipped through me at not telling Laryk about my broken oath. A part of me wanted to tell him now but the words never formed.

"Sleep," he murmured, his voice a low rumble that sent tremors through me. His arms looped around my waist, drawing me into his orbit once again. The heat of his body chased away the chill of the evening air. "The ball is tomorrow night."

"Ball?" I echoed, my voice a startled hiss. I shot out from his grasp, pulling the covers over my exposed skin. "A celebration while the world crumbles around us?"

Unbelievable.

A flicker of something unreadable crossed his face. "It's tradition," he said, his voice clipped. "The King and Queen attend. No getting out of it."

"Tradition," I spat. "Sixty lives lost last week, and we twirl around a ballroom in their memory?"

He sighed, the sound heavy in the quiet room. "There's more to it than that, Fia." A moment of silence slipped by. "You should find some nice gowns in the chest I had delivered to your room," he added.

"I was wondering what that was." I rolled my eyes. "I'm dying to see what you chose." The sarcasm was slick in my voice.

"I have impeccable taste. Besides, do you remember what you were wearing the first time we saw each other? I could never risk you embarrassing me like that." He grinned.

"You know I wasn't expecting to attend that particular soiree," I mumbled, remembering my stained apothecary uniform and how out of place I'd felt that night. How terrified I was. How out of control. So much had changed since then.

"Well, I'm not taking any chances. I've arranged for a few attendants to help you get ready for the event," he stated, shooting me a wicked smile.

"Is that really necessary?" I groaned, sinking back down into the bed.

"Undoubtedly necessary, I'm afraid." He pulled me back to his chest and kissed my forehead. "I want you primed to perfection for what happens after the ball," he murmured against my hair, sending a shiver down my spine.

"I guess that doesn't sound so bad." I sighed, fighting back a smile as I wrapped my arms around his chest.

"There might be another surprise awaiting you tomorrow. But first, sleep," he said with a yawn.

I didn't even try to argue. My eyelids had grown heavy, and it felt way too good to be in his arms. I pushed away the sinking feeling that doom was looming just over the hills to the West.

~

Darkness. Overwhelming, suffocating darkness. It was everywhere. The only light I could see came from the few stars that spattered the sky, but even they were distorted by a black haze that moved through the night like smog.

I heard a hiss, and my head shot to the left. I squinted, adjusting as I saw the wisps of an inky black shadow twisting and warping beside me, racing forward into the night.

I felt desperate, like something important was going to happen. There was also fear... a maddening fear that enveloped me. Like I was risking everything I knew. Everyone I loved. But I didn't have a choice.

Beyond the shadow, I saw the spire of a tower that had fallen to ruin. Holes were dotted throughout the structure, and crumbling stone littered the ground around it. A broken window in the shape of a crescent moon sat halfway down. I didn't recognize it.

The hisses became louder. Shadows trailed back as far as I could see. My heart began to race furiously in my chest.

~

I shot out of bed and gasped for air.

The Wraiths.

They were coming.

Laryk stirred, reaching for me.

"Wake up, the Wraiths are going to Stormshire. Now," I nearly shouted, throwing the covers off of us. "You need to tell someone. The factions need to be alerted. I don't know how much time we have." I frantically searched the ground for my clothes.

"Fia, what's going on?" Laryk asked, standing up and walking towards me, confusion etched into his features.

"I saw them in my dream. The Wraiths. They are going to Stormshire. Right now," I urged, pulling on my trousers.

"You're sure about this?" His eyes were wide open now.

"I guess I can't be sure, but are we really willing to take the risk?" I begged.

"Stay here. I'm going to alert the other Generals. We'll see if there have been any disturbances at the border."

I nodded, handing him his shirt.

"I saw them passing some ruin... a tower with a crescent moon-shaped window."

Laryk pulled me in, kissing my forehead before storming out of the room.

I sat on the bed, still shaken from the dream. My mind was stuck on my friends. I pulled myself into a ball and tried to steady my breath as I awaited Laryk's return.

I couldn't tell how much time passed before the door creaked open. I shot out of bed as Laryk rounded the corner.

"There have been no disturbances at the border."

"But I saw them," I said, furrowing my brow. "Are we sure? What if they slipped past somehow?" I crossed my arms.

"The entire border has been crawling with Base Guards since the last attack. For miles and miles. They would have been noticed," he said calmly, stepping in my direction.

"But the ruin, I saw it so clearly," I said, shaking my head. None of this made sense.

"Crescent Tower is too far south. It wouldn't make sense for them to be there," he assured me. "But we still have troops stationed in that area along the border." He took my wrist in his hand and pulled me against him.

"I don't know..." I murmured. I couldn't shake the feeling that something terrible was going to happen.

"Perhaps it was a memory. Not from tonight," he whispered, pulling me back into bed.

It was possible. My dream about the river was clearly someone's memory. I exhaled deeply. Laryk was right. If there were no disturbances at the border, then we were safe. For now.

I tried my best to convince myself, but the dark presence in my mind remained.

My eyes closed once again, and I forced myself back to sleep.

CHAPTER 47

CONSCIOUSNESS DRIFTED OVER ME, and I reached out, my heart sinking as my hand grasped at the emptiness where Laryk should have been. I was alone. Glimmers of light peeked in from behind the drapes. How long had I been asleep?

My feet found the floor and I stretched, the blanket slipping down my arms. I yanked it tighter around myself and marched across the room, flinging open the curtains with a flourish. Late morning sun flooded in, momentarily blinding me.

As I collected my garments from the floor, all I could think about was how they got there. The memory of Laryk's stormy entrance into the courtyard played on repeat in my mind. Reflecting on the memory now, knowing he'd been riddled with jealousy, pleased me more than it should have. Shivers ran up my spine as my imagination became a bit too realistic.

I began to dress, wondering how long I had until this Esprithe damned ball began.

As I approached the door, hushed murmurs echoed from the other side. Pressing my ear against the rugged wood, I waited to hear them pass. The last thing I needed was to be caught sneaking out of the General's quarters.

I closed my eyes, focusing on the voices from outside. Both were female, and one sounded familiar... I just couldn't put my finger on it.

"Poor girl. Hasn't she realized that he just craves a conquest?" I heard one of them whisper. Blood Clot. Anger stormed through my gut and I felt my fingers curl into clenched fists.

In my periphery, a dark shadow flew across the corner of the room and my head shot to the left, freezing the breath in my chest.

But nothing was there.

I let my face fall into my hands. Was I going crazy? Were my emotions driving me to this place of paranoia—one that could prove to be the deadliest of distractions? Or was it the unanswered questions... The ones that played in the back of my mind more often than I cared to admit?

I ran my hand through my unkempt hair and steadied myself.

Laryk had been clear with me about his feelings toward monogamy. I wasn't an idiot to think we would ever be... something more, but he had called me important. And different. And said those beautiful words that were seared permanently into my brain.

I spun, pressing my back into the wooden door. My emotions had nearly destroyed me over the last few days. There was no point in letting myself wander into impossible fantasies. Even if this was fleeting, even if it was more to me than it was to him... Perhaps I could accept that.

Taking a deep breath, I replayed the words over and over again in my mind, trying to convince myself of their truth.

But my insides ached at the idea. I couldn't even lie to myself anymore.

I was falling, tumbling, spiraling for this man, and that feeling was terrifying. Hope was terrifying.

I never used to let myself do it.

My head leaned back against the door as I steadied myself. I'd be the one by his side at the ball tonight, however poor the timing may be. A part of that made me feel better, but I wasn't sure if it should have.

My fingers edged the door open, and I crept down the hall, quietly rushing towards the initiate's quarters.

A change of clothes was undoubtedly necessary.

As I neared my room, my pace slowed. The door was ajar. *Esprithe sake.* Had I really not closed it properly last night? A wave of annoyance rushed through me as I replayed the drunken steps I'd taken to the courtyard.

My decision-making skills had clearly been at their best since leaving Luminaria.

I shook my head, bounding forward and slamming the door open the rest of the way before jumping back, lowering myself into a defensive position. Someone was in my room.

"Are you going to attack me?" I heard the bubbly voice crack before bursting out in full laughter. My heart swelled, and I ran to find a head of perfectly primed curls sitting on the bed opposite mine.

"Osta?" I breathed, pulling her into a hug. I hadn't seen my best friend in weeks.

"Are you surprised?" She sang as I released her. Her hair bounced in spring-laden ringlets as she hopped around the room. "I was hoping to surprise you last night, but you were nowhere to be found," she said, cocking her head and narrowing those aquamarine eyes.

"Care to divulge what bed you found yourself in?"

I felt my face flush and looked down, escaping her excited gaze. "Wait. How are you even here?" I asked, eyes shooting back up. I plopped down on the bed, crossing my arms, "Did you come here with the Soleil family?" I asked, a desperate attempt to distract her.

"Yes, well… Lord Soleil was summoned to Emeraal after the attack. Lady Soleil and I will be staying here while the Lord leaves with the troops to Stormshire tomorrow," she said, pursing her lips. My heart felt heavy. The thought of Osta anywhere near the West made me want to vomit.

"Wait. Do you know what's going on?" I looked at the door, making sure it was closed.

"Well, they told me we were facing a threat we didn't know much about, but that I would be perfectly safe. So, I assumed it couldn't be that big of a deal." She shrugged.

"They told you it was safe? Osta, it's dangerous for you to be here. I know it's not Stormshire, but it's close enough."

"Fia, you think everything is dangerous." Osta's exasperation was palpable, "The Lord assured me himself. No harm will come my way."

"I was under the impression he didn't affiliate much with the Guard."

"Not normally, no. But they figured his focus could be of use around the border." She shrugged her shoulders, finally calming enough to sit next to me.

"What is his focus?" I asked, assuming it would be true to the Soleil family line, and therefore something involving fire.

"It's an interesting one. I'm not sure I understand how it works, exactly, but he can pick up traces of essence and discern where they originate from. I guess you could say he's like a bloodhound for magical signatures. I think they are hoping he can–"

"Figure out how the enemies move. Maybe even discover if they've been places we aren't aware of," I stated, eyes focused on the wall straight ahead. "That could be very helpful. I'm surprised they haven't used him before."

"They have a few times, I believe, but there seems to be some kind of political issue between him and the Guard. If I was going to wager a guess, I'd assume it's because of his brother. They're estranged, you know," she said, leaning onto her hand.

My mind shifted to Baelor. He was so awful. I could only imagine what his father was like back in the day.

"I guess it makes sense. So, you travel with them wherever they go? Why would Lady Soleil follow him this far West?" I gulped. I never imagined Osta would find herself in an active warzone.

Osta scrunched her nose. "I'm actually not sure why she needs to be here. But if Lady Soleil goes, I go. That's the agreement." A bright smile returned to her lips. "And she's incredible, honestly. I couldn't imagine having a better boss. She loves every design I show her." Osta bit her lip, but the smile still spilled over. She was radiating pure joy despite being in perhaps one of the most dangerous parts of the Isle.

I didn't want to ruin her excitement by divulging all the details. She was here now. There was nothing I could do.

"You deserve the world, as I've told you before." I sighed, glancing toward the balcony. At least I'd successfully distracted her.

"So, now it's your turn. Where exactly were you all night?" Her head snapped towards me, eyes ablaze with curiosity.

Guess not.

I felt my stomach twist. If she had caught me first thing this morning, I would have melted into a puddle and spilled all of the illicit details, but now? Blood Clot had certainly cast a dark shadow over my evening, despite how much I tried to shove what she said from my mind.

"Well, erm–" I started, scrambling to find the words.

"You were with the General, weren't you?" She squealed, hitting my arm and bouncing up and down on the bed.

I shrugged but said nothing.

She screamed.

"I knew it!" She clapped. "I need to hear everything. I knew from the very beginning—at the ball when he was undressing you with his eyes." She shook her head, an all-too-satisfied smirk forming at her lips.

"Well, I need to start by telling you what happened on the

journey here." I turned towards her and hoisted my leg onto the bed.

I spent the next hour filling her in on every detail. From discovering my dream walking abilities, to Blood Clot's words outside Laryk's door just a few hours before.

"She's just jealous. She probably hoped you could hear her! Why else would she have that particular conversation right outside the General's chamber? She had to have known you were in there," Osta said, sighing with irritation and rolling her eyes. "I mean, it's obvious, is it not?" she asked.

"I kind of figured no one knew I spent the night in his bed…" I trailed off.

"You're sure no one saw you follow him to his room? Were you being sneaky about it?"

My face flushed.

"I mean, I don't think we were being super noticeable." I bit my lip, recalling how I had slammed the bottle down and stormed off after him in the middle of a very crowded courtyard.

"Well, I guess… there's a small possibility that someone *could* have seen..." I swallowed the lump forming in my throat.

"See? Exactly. And gossip like that travels so fast in places like this. I mean, what else is there to do?" She stood, beginning to pace.

"You said you're attending the ball with him tonight?" she asked, that familiar elevated octave taking over her voice.

I nodded, eyeing her movements with suspicion.

"And he sent gowns for you to pick from?" Her eyebrows peaked as she stood on the tips of her toes, fingers twisting in anticipation.

A sigh escaped my lips before breaking into an exasperated smile. "It's that chest." I pointed across the room. "Do your worst."

Osta immediately unbuckled the clasps and started digging through, throwing all hues of fabric across the room in a frenzy.

CHAPTER 48

After two hours of Osta forcing me to try on every gown in the chest, she left to go tend to Lady Soleil.

It wasn't long before I was retrieved from my room, the attendants ushering me to chambers located at the peak of one of the towers.

The circular space was cast in green, the emerald, stained glass windows creating jewel-like patterns on the floor. Great balcony doors were propped open on either side of the room, giving a spectacular view of the city below and snow-capped mountains in the distance.

An overflowing clawfoot tub sat in the middle of the floor, flower petals dancing across the surface. Steam was rising from the warmed water, and the crisp air moving through the room carried the scent of teakwood and vanilla.

I almost jumped out of my skin when the attendant silently stepped behind me, trying to lift my blouse.

"Uh-um I appreciate your help, but I will undress myself..." I stuttered, stepping away from her reach. I neared the edge of the tub and quickly slipped out of my garments.

I sunk beneath the surface of the water, out of the cold and away from the strangers' curious stares. I'm sure they were wondering who I was to be receiving such treatment. I was wondering the same thing.

Once I had bathed, the ladies worked on my hair. I had to admit the combs felt wonderful gliding over my scalp and down the expanse of my back.

A fire roared somewhere out of sight, and from it, they retrieved a metal tray with rods glowing red from the flames. I glanced at them curiously as the women slipped on protective gloves, taking sections of my hair and weaving them around the rods until they flowed in smooth, perfect curls. The sides were effortlessly swept back and clasped with an elaborate emerald hairpin. Fitting for the setting and what I presumed to be another gift from the General.

"Have you been missing sleep dear? You have quite the dark circles under your eyes. I have a pigment that would cover this. Shall I use it?" She was already looking for it amongst the other compacts and bottles.

I let out a snort, imagining how odd I would look if I suddenly lost the shadows that had plagued me my entire life. "Thank you, but I'll be fine without."

This didn't stop her from adding a rosy hue to my cheekbones and painting my lips a shade of deep scarlet.

"Alright, have a look and see what you think," she instructed, and I finally allowed myself to look in the mirror.

While this was probably the closest to royalty I'd ever felt, I did notice the darkness around my eyes was more prominent than normal. My fingers reached up to touch my skin. My opal irises stood out in stark contrast.

Maybe the restlessness of the last few days mixed with the long travel had affected me more than I thought.

A part of me still felt out of place. Perhaps I always would. But the other half of me felt…really fucking pretty. Even more so because Laryk had arranged all of this himself.

CHAPTER 49

I TOOK in the cavernous view of the ballroom below. The walls were much like the rest of the fortress, carved out of gray stone and lined with emerald stained glass.

Moonlight filtered in from above. Candles and mounted torches illuminated the space, casting a golden shimmer over the massive room. Aossí twirled to the sounds of live harps and flutes playing haunting melodies.

The bodies moved in unison, performing a dance that must have been tradition for the people of Emeraal. I looked around, trying to find a familiar face in the crowd, but I was still too far above.

I moved to take my first step onto the marbled stairs, lifting the lengths of my dress so as not to trip. I had felt the weight of the gown as soon as Osta had tossed it in my direction back in our shared room–luxurious but *heavy*.

Black fabric cascaded down my frame, weaving around my arms in delicate patterns before descending into waves of black lace that created a train in my wake. My shoulders were left bare as the neckline's star-dusted edges dipped into a perfect *v* across my chest.

I reached down, adjusting my dress. I had hidden two of Ma's breathing vials under my waistband, and they shifted as I moved.

I gripped the railing hard as I lowered myself down the stairs. Eyes turned in my direction, and nerves began prickling the back of my neck.

Laryk was nowhere to be found.

As I reached the bottom stairs, my heart was fluttering wildly in my chest. There were so many Aossí looking at me now, parting to create space. Their eyes were a mixture of wildness and curiosity.

"Fia, it's perfect!" I whipped around to find Osta a few paces behind me, wearing a deep green, silk gown that mirrored the haunting beauty of Emeraal. My heartbeat softened as I made my way over to her. The eyes that bore into me before had returned to their socializing.

She took my hands in hers. "I know it's not *my* design, but it's stunning nonetheless," she whispered, spinning me around. "The General has great taste."

"I'd rather you not mention that to him. His ego couldn't possibly get any bigger." I grinned, finally noticing the couple standing behind her.

I cleared my throat, motioning for Osta to make introductions.

Her eyes went wide. "Oh, forgive my bad manners!" She shot around, dragging my arm with her. "Fia, meet Lord and Lady Soleil."

"Fia Riftborne, we've heard so much about you from Osta. It's lovely to finally meet you," Lady Soleil said with a grace that seemed foreign to me.

"It's a pleasure to meet you both, truly. Osta has told me how wonderful it is to work for you." I smiled politely, attempting a curtsey.

"We will have to catch up later in the evening, after dinner perhaps," Lady Soleil said. "Right now, I'd better find our seats. Osta, darling, would you accompany me? I'd like to introduce you to a friend of mine."

"Of course! I'll see you later, Fia." She smiled brightly at me. Lady Soleil shot a glance toward her husband that I couldn't quite read before she and Osta sauntered off into the crowd of bodies beyond.

My gaze wandered up to meet Lord Soleil's. His attention moved to my left hand, where my Riftborne branding sprawled out beyond the sleeve of my gown. The Lord paused, raising an eyebrow slightly before something flickered across his eyes.

"Pleasure to meet you, Fia. Forgive me. It's a lovely dress you have there." He shook his head as if returning from a trance, smiling before moving to pass me. Before he got too far, I felt his hand on my arm.

He leaned in, whispering, "it's great to have you on our side." And soon enough, he was disappearing into the bodies as well. I looked at my marking and tugged the fabric down around my wrist.

Alone again, I swiped a shimmery cocktail from the refreshment table and looked around.

Still no sign of Laryk. I sighed, turning towards the outskirts of the party. I sipped the drink, and flowery bubbles spread across my tongue.

Narissa's words found their way back into my mind as I watched the couples dancing gracefully ahead. Had he changed his mind? I shifted in my seat and looked down at my dress nervously. Suddenly, the bodice felt too tight... the skirt verging on ostentatious.

An uneasiness crept over me as I downed the rest of my drink. I set the glass on the table and slowly pushed it away.

"Shall I get you another?" I heard a whisper as Laryk's lips brushed against my ear.

A calming haze rushed through me, enveloping me in a delicious heat.

The spark turned into a full blaze as I locked eyes with him. Any previous worry I had burned to ashes. His hair was free tonight, cascading down his shoulders in mesmerizing waves of copper—the way I loved it most. He wore a dress suit, tailored to perfection, in all shades and textures of black. Golden accents sparkled atop the velvet that stretched over his broad frame. The wickedest smile formed on his lips as he looked me up and down.

He approached me slowly, narrowing his eyes. "If you keep looking at me like that, I'll abandon this dinner altogether and take you to bed." His voice was low, predatory. The embers within me lit once again, and I bit back a smile. It was nearly intoxicating to be around him in this state.

And in an instant, he was pulling me against him. "You know how I love you in black," he whispered, tugging at my body through the dress.

A distant fragment of my mind considered the eyes that were undoubtedly watching, but this raging wildfire of a moment we found ourselves in was slowly incinerating my ability to care.

I longed for his mouth on me. I inhaled deeply, trying to absorb every single fiber of his being. The dizzying aroma of vetiver and burnt amber filled my nose. The man himself was the living embodiment of ecstasy.

"Dance with me," he murmured.

It wasn't a request.

Before I knew it, he was pulling me into the sea of bodies moving methodically through the room.

He laced his fingers through mine, wrapping his other arm possessively around my waist. Our bodies met in a fiery collision as he pulled me against him.

And then we were moving, spinning, twirling. My mind couldn't keep up. All I could do was stare into his eyes and continue to lose myself. I wanted to live in this searing moment forever.

The song came to an end, and reality began to creep back in from my peripherals. A sinking feeling devoured my heart as he pulled away, my body cold in the places we had touched. Like coming down from an incredible high, the sound of the Aossí around us broke through my trance, and just like that, the wild blaze smoldered out, and reality snapped into focus.

"Let's find our seats, Fia." Laryk pulled me through the crowd, our fingers still intertwined. I wondered if we were going to be sitting together, given our considerable difference in rank.

He led me to the longest table along the edge, only a few paces over from the raised dais where the King and Queen would be seated.

He arched an eyebrow before pulling out a chair and gesturing for me to sit down. I obliged, glancing down the length of the table. There was no one I recognized.

"I'll return to you shortly. There's something I have to take care of." He planted a kiss on my forehead before sauntering off to the other side of the ballroom. My eyes followed him, wondering what exactly he was leaving to do. Just as I was about to look away, I saw a glimpse of blood-red hair. Anger pulsed through me as I saw him grab Narissa's arm and lower his face to hers.

My control snapped like a frayed rope, and I stood, pushing my chair back as I turned and paced toward the two of them. I did my best to calm my expression, but my emotions were at an all-time high. Out of the corner of my eye, a black shape emerged, and my attention flew left, my heart stopping in my chest.

Relief washed over me once I realized it was the elaborate costume of a woman I had never seen before.

She was taller than me. With one of the most beautiful faces I had ever laid eyes upon. Her hair was clipped short. It wasn't a style you saw often in Luminaria. And there was something about her skin... it was too perfect. Ethereal, haunting.

She wore a taxidermy raven on her shoulder and was dressed completely in drapes of black. My eyes scrunched, taking in the oddness of her attire. She made eye contact with me and tilted her chin to the side, narrowing her eyebrows. There was darkness surrounding her eyes… shadows. Like mine. *Who was she?*

She took a step in my direction, but a slice of copper hair slid into my peripherals, and I refocused myself. I would have to find her later. Right now, I had a Blood Clot to deal with. I straightened my dress before continuing on my way.

Poison ran through me as I took in just how close Narissa was to Laryk. I was tired of feeling her hateful glances at every encounter. We had yet to even *speak* to one another. This was ending. Tonight.

As I approached the two of them, I overheard the tail end of Laryk's harsh whispers. "I told you to accompany the troops to Stormshire. You being here is in direct defiance of my orders."

She spotted me, and her eyes turned cold, a cruel smirk forming on her lips.

"Fia, I told you I'd be back. Please give us a moment," Laryk said, facing me.

"I thought it would be a good time to finally introduce myself. It's Narissa, right?" I plastered on a smile. "It's a wonder we haven't spoken until now. It seems we have a lot of the same interests."

I couldn't tell if Laryk wanted to laugh or reprimand me, but the tension was thick and riddled with static. I calmed the familiar shiver that ran down my spine.

I didn't need the translucent web to annihilate this bitch, I was going to do it with words.

"You speak of *my* direct defiance, but your pet is still standing here. Did you not just tell her to leave?" Narissa scowled.

"Ah, is this the infamous *best behavior* you were telling me about?" I asked, directing my question towards Laryk. "She sure seems the champion of camaraderie."

Laryk's jaw ticked as he turned to face Narissa. "If you plan to keep your place as a lieutenant in my Faction, I suggest you stand down now."

Anger flickered in Narissa's eyes as she glared at Laryk, nostrils flaring. "So, you expect me to leave for Stormshire tonight?" she hissed.

"First thing in the morning. Until then, return to your chambers. I can't allow your personal grievances to paint my faction in a bad light, especially at a time like this."

"*I'm* painting the faction in a bad light?" Rage echoed in her laughter, "You're the one fucking a Riftborne. How do you think that looks?" She paused, "How do you think that makes *me* feel? You know what they did to me. To my family."

"Ahh, there it is. Glad to know you have such bigotry heading your faction, *Laryk*. That's certainly a great look." I crossed my arms, nodding toward Narissa. I was going to let her bury herself.

As his first name rolled off my tongue, her eyes lit up and she finally turned toward me. "That's General Ashford to you, whore. All of you are the same," she spat, moving her face close to mine. I smiled back at her, unmoving.

Laryk grabbed her arm and shoved her away from me. "Narissa. Go. Now. Before you really piss me off," he growled. "I'll have you shipped off to another base and demoted if you say another fucking word."

Narissa's eyes were still burning with anger, but I saw a flash of sadness wash over them. She looked back and forth between the two of us and paused, opening her mouth only to close it. She turned on her heel and bounded off toward the stairs. I could practically feel the heat coming off of her as she strode past.

"Fia. I told you to stay at the table," Laryk said, placing a hand on my back and guiding me through the crowd once again.

"You know I'm not the best at following orders." I shrugged, a smile still plastered on my face.

Laryk sighed. I could hear his eyes roll as we neared the table.

"She's usually not that vicious," he stated, pulling my chair out.

"I told you she thinks you're together," I said, sitting down. "And I know you've probably done things to lead her to that conclusion." I felt a pang of nausea hit me. Is that what he was doing to me too? Could I be sure he hadn't, at one point, told her she was important, that she was the key to winning this?

Laryk turned his full attention on me, narrowing his eyes. His hand moved to my thigh, sliding up the slit in my skirt. "You know we're not," he murmured, leaning over to nip at my ear. His breath left my face flushed. I shifted in my seat as his hand traveled further up my leg, his eyes piercing into mine.

And then the trumpets started, announcing the arrival of the King and Queen. He dropped his head, pulling away his hand as we both turned our attention to the doors in the back of the hall.

I watched their familiar, imposing silhouettes glide across the room, making their way to their thrones. They were surrounded by their personal security—guardsmen in emerald uniforms. I dipped into a bow with the rest of the room, only rising once they had stepped onto the dais.

The King turned to face his subjects, lifting his hands in a triumphant gesture. "Be seated." His voice boomed through the space.

"We now face perhaps the greatest threat that our kingdom has ever seen," the King said, lowering his head. He paced across the dais.

"Aossí of all kinds have given their lives to protect the Isle against an enemy that is imperceptible, unrelenting, and savage in their quest to destroy our home. But we will not let them win. We will fight to the very end for Sídhe. We will not succumb to the darkness." He lifted his chalice high in the air, and the room all joined him, pressing their drinks towards the cathedral ceiling.

The sound of a wooden door creaking open pierced the cheers. Then silence.

A chill ran through the room, followed by a subtle breeze. And one by one, the candles were snuffed out. Only the filtered, green moonlight remained. Everyone was still, eyes darting around the space.

One of the Royal Guards accompanying the King and Queen stepped forward, placing his hands on them, and with a wave of energy, their forms disappeared from view.

My breath caught in my chest.

They were here.

They were not going to Stormshire.

The Wraiths were coming here the whole time.

That's why I saw them passing the crescent tower.

My pulse quickened, and for a moment, I felt like I might faint. But I couldn't. The time had come. This was the war, and I was right in the middle of it.

Laryk grabbed my arm, gripping it tightly as the energy shifted. A snap sent our eyes flying to the back corner. I could hear the breaths of every soul near me.

Shadows pummeled through the room, shifting and expanding, shrouding it in complete and utter darkness.

A mind-shattering scream echoed through the halls, and a familiar metallic smell filled the space around us.

Blood.

CHAPTER 50

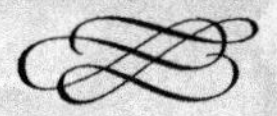

My fears were brought to life as the inky swirls swarmed the hall. Darkness erupted in bursts around them. Intentionally, strategically… as if they were controlling it, passing the void back and forth between them.

The darkness seeped from the shadows, black tendrils reaching out to meld with other shades of nothingness, enveloping the entire room in a cloak of night.

The lessons had taught us that the Wraiths and the darkness were one in the same. But if my eyes were to be believed, the Wraiths were their own entity. The darkness was just a symptom of their presence… it was following them.

I looked to Laryk in a panic. His eyes were tracking the room at an impossible speed. He pulled out the dagger he kept against his hip and dropped to his knees, yanking my skirts towards him and ripping through the fabric with his blade in quick slices. The dress fell just below my knees.

I could run.

I could fight.

"Fia, can you sense them?" He spoke in a rushed tone, tearing off his jacket.

I tried to quiet the overwhelming fear in my mind enough to draw out the tendrils of my focus. When they didn't immediately begin their ascent, I yanked them up by sheer will, casting them around us.

Hundreds of glowing orbs shot through the darkness. In the chaos it was hard to differentiate between Wraith and Aossí.

The minds all looked the same.

Behind us, officers ordered civilians towards the barracks. Their shouts were cut short as the Wraiths got close enough to rob them of their breath, leaving their words trailing into the void.

I looked around frantically, searching for Osta.

But I couldn't find her.

We stood our ground as Aossí rushed past us, desperate for safety within the fortress walls.

A sliver of bronzed hair caught the moonlight, and I saw a figure in an emerald dress following the civilians to safety.

The deepest part of me relaxed, knowing Osta was safe, but every other nerve ending was on fire.

"There's too much going on in here right now. I can't tell anyone apart," I whispered. My head was pounding trying to keep the nerves at bay. The wind picked up around us as hisses erupted from above. The sound of daggers whipping through the air echoed, followed by the metallic clang of swords being unsheathed.

"Wraiths will be targeting the arcanite on the northern lawn. We need to get there." Laryk was gone, replaced by General Ashford. Something flickered in his eyes, something I had never seen before. *Fear.*

I ripped one of the vials from my dress and pressed it into his hand. "If you get surrounded, drink this."

"What—?" His forehead wrinkled.

"Ma created it, but there's no time to explain. Just trust me," I pleaded, my hand closing around his for a beat longer. I didn't want to let go.

He took one last glance in my direction before sprinting toward the door.

I took off after him. Laryk threw the giant doors open, and we ran into the cold winter night as silence slammed into us. It was brighter now, with the moon and stars illuminating the sky. Stillness drenched the courtyard, a stark contrast to the chaos and death just steps away.

"This way!" he shouted before turning left and bolting across the cobbled path. We ran in unison as darkness descended before us. Muscles clenched as I braced myself, channeling forth the tendrils once again, readying them for battle.

As soon as we breached the shadows, I shot the web forth, searching for a mind to latch onto. Orbs glowed all around us, darting from one side to the other with maddening speed. I followed one with all of my concentration, losing it every time it changed direction.

If I couldn't center my focus on the mind, I couldn't command it. I couldn't destroy it. The familiar feeling of uselessness crept back into my body, but I shook it off. I didn't have time for such feelings.

"Fia!" I heard Laryk shout, and I searched for his mind in the choas, finding it immediately. I sprinted in his direction just as his hand shot out, firing his dagger toward an inky shape. A guttural hiss erupted through the darkness, and Laryk reached for me. "Fia, where are you?" I was right in front of him. I could see him. Could he not see me?

"Laryk–" I began to scream, but the air was knocked out of me.

In an instant, I was thrown back, sailing violently before slamming down into the wet earth below.

I landed on my shoulder and heard it crack. A cry escaped me and pain shot through my entire body, but I shoved it from my mind.

I had to find Laryk.

The wind picked up, and my feet lifted off the ground against my will. Suddenly, a form was spinning around me violently, creating the vortex I knew would soon rid the space of air.

I reached down, quickly grabbing the vial from my waistband, and popped off the top, downing it as fast as I could.

Calm your breathing.

The air began to thin around me, and my eyes closed, reaching out with the web. I could see the mind racing around me like an insect. I just had to concentrate.

I had to latch on.

Fia, make the damn connection.

The air was gone now. It was only a matter of time before the potion wore off.

Hurry. I unsheathed my dagger, focusing on every single fiber of the web, feeling them like they were an extension of my own body. I waited for the right moment.

Come on.

Seconds flew by, turning into minutes as I watched the orb circle me. My ears were ringing from how hard I fought to track the Wraith. I was going to implode.

Suddenly, an explosion erupted behind us, and the Wraith slowed, just for a split second.

It was all I needed.

I threw the dagger.

And I hit something solid.

A gurgled hiss broke the silence around me, and I fell to the ground.

I climbed up, my feet racing forward through the pain. The valley at the base of the hill came into view.

Hundreds of Base Guards surrounded the giant spire of arcanite, creating a shield of bodies. Walls of fire erupted around the guards and a shimmering dome, what seemed to be a shield, encapsulated the point of the arcanite from above. I watched in terror as Wraiths flew toward the giant stone, only to dive back into the shadows. Something tugged at my heart. I had to get down there. I had to help.

Find Laryk.

I extended my web once again and began sprinting down the hill. The orbs lit up around me from the shadows. I veered left, digging my dagger into the mind of a Wraith as it flew back from the flames. I may not have had the full capability of my focus, but at least I could do something.

I dodged the minds that flew in my direction, escaping their attempted vortexes and attacking when I could.

As a Wraith lunged, I dove to the ground, rolling backwards into a crouch. It flew too close to the dome above, becoming disoriented for a split second.

Running as fast as I could, I jumped into the air and slammed my dagger down hard into the shadowy mass, hearing another hiss escape the Wraith as it flew back into the outskirts of the lawn.

As I landed, I caught a glimpse of copper hair to my left.

Laryk.

He was fighting for his life, rolling, dodging, and striking with expertise and precision, but the Wraiths were closing in.

I raced toward him, joining him in battle. We fought side by side as the air around us thinned.

I wasn't going down.

Not tonight.

My dagger connected with another shadow, sending it shooting off into the darkness.

Everything paused.

The inky forms blasted into the sky in unison, forming a net of blackness above the dome. The officer began sending off fireballs toward the mass, blowing holes right through it. And suddenly, the Wraiths flew into the distance, off behind the fortress and into the night.

Everyone looked around in shock, wondering if it was over. If we had really won. I fell to the ground, catching my breath.

I felt Laryk beside me.

"When did you get there?" he gasped.

"Right before they started the vortex. You couldn't see me?" I wheezed, coughing from the smoke that surrounded the lawn.

"I couldn't see anything." He narrowed his eyes and looked at me. "You could see me?" he asked, confusion lacing his voice.

"Not well, but yes, a little," I responded.

"You mean, you could see my mind?" he questioned, reaching out for me.

"Well, I wasn't looking for it. I could see you. Just as you are right now. I mean, it was dark with all of the shadows, but I saw you fighting. It's why I ran over here," I said as he pulled me up. His brow furrowed before softening.

"Is it over?" I asked, looking at the devastation that had erupted through the valley.

Without answering, he grabbed my waist, pulling me toward him. In an instant, his mouth was on me, desperate, longing. Despite the pain still radiating from my shoulder, my hands flew into his hair as I savored the feeling of his body against mine once again.

I never wanted to let go.

His teeth caressed the swell of my lip—a silent request to invade. Our tongues clashed, my head tilting back with the force of it. He was devouring me, taking over all of my senses until once again, it was only us that existed. Need coursed through us, connecting our wills, and I thought this moment might last forever. I was begging it to last forever.

A scream broke through our walls, and the fantasy crumbled around us.

We tore apart, eyes scanning the lawn once again. Everyone was on alert, trying to figure out where the sound had come from.

Another scream tore through the night, and all of our heads

shot left, to the fortress just as huge, double doors flew open and civilians began spilling out onto the lawn, running for their lives. A smog of shadows followed in their wake, enveloping the area in darkness. I caught a sliver of emerald in the mass of bodies and my heart stopped. Osta.

It was strategic. The Wraiths were using them as shields.

Fuck.

I stole one last glance at Laryk before taking off toward the commotion. By the look on his face, I knew that he couldn't see me.

"Fia!" I heard him shout from behind, but there was no time.

Just as I reached the borders of the shadows, a group of Wraiths circled Osta and the Soleils.

Osta let out a blood-curdling scream.

Fury shot through my entire body as I felt myself falling into a place I hadn't been in a long time. A place of no control. A place where sheer force erupted from me and took down anything in its path.

I couldn't stop it.

A scream escaped from my chest and the shadows around the lawn came pummeling towards me at once, gathering at my feet and surrounding my entire being. My arms shot out to each side, palms open as the inky swells dove into my hands like a river. The weight of the darkness was so intense, my body dropped, and I was on my knees, shaking as it filtered into me. It surged through every vein, every pathway. I could see it, swirling in the corners of my view.

Soon enough, the darkness around me was gone, absorbed into my own body.

My legs trembled as I tried to hold it in, my mind screaming for a release. I didn't know what was happening. How I was doing this. My grip on the energy inside was beginning to lessen, and I felt the structures of my mind snapping. It was like a caged beast trying to break out through my skin.

Clutching my head in my hands, I held back for as long as I could, allowing every ounce of my focus to expand, to try and overcome this foreign darkness. My mind was searing with pain, and I could feel the seams being ripped apart inside me, tearing holes in my mental sovereignty.

Silence erupted around me. And everything went black.

I was in a void.

My hair lifted off my shoulders, crackling with static.

The darkness had infected my blood and bones. In this instant between reality and the void, something wicked within me purred, as if an alignment had been made. A deal I had no part in.

I wasn't in a void.

I was the void.

An intoxicating rush flew across my body, dying to be unleashed.

I let it out.

Shadows erupted from my fingertips, roaring through the valley, taking down everything in their wake.

My shadows.

I was the void.

My hair whipped around me as darkness overcame the land.

Wait.

An echo of something whispered in my mind.

I was doing something. I was saving someone. My thoughts reeled, trying to remember. And then my vision locked with a pair of familiar aquamarine eyes.

Osta. I was saving Osta.

She stared back at me, concern drowning her features as she kneeled with the Soleils. The wind still whipped. My arms dropped down to my side, and I gasped for air, falling to my knees.

The entire lawn was still.

Every eye was on me.

What just happened?

My body went limp, and I stumbled forward, earth slamming into my broken shoulder as I hit the ground. A searing torrent of pain shot through me. But it couldn't hold a candle to the confusion that gripped every fiber of every thought.

I clawed at the ground, forcing myself up enough to see the destruction around me. Laryk's stared at me from across the lawn. His eyes were wide with something. Horror.

Laryk?

Memories came flooding back.

My heart skipped at the sight of him.

I needed him. I needed him to help me.

My hand hit the ground again, grabbing the dirt and pulling myself forward as shadows crept up in my peripheral vision. I tried to scream, but my lungs were shredded.

Laryk took a step forward, then hesitated. I wanted to scream for help. Why was he just standing there?

Dark energy surrounded me, slithering across the grass like smoke, lacing up my arms, caressing my face, and tinging my vision with an iron hue.

"Fia! No!" Osta screamed in the distance. I tried to tear my vision to her. To see her, even if for one last time. My best friend. The most important person in my life.

But I was frozen solid.

My eyes locked on my lover across the lawn. Fear ripped through me as my body lifted from the ground, the feeling of shadowy tendrils enveloping my limbs.

Someone do something!

I wanted to scream, to writhe, to fight. But my body betrayed me.

Please.

It was just a single thought, a single request that permeated my mind. One that I so rarely employed. My heart slammed into my chest, and time slowed as I waited.

And waited.

But no one came. No one moved.

A glimpse of copper hair reflecting the moonlight was the sight I clung to as everything disappeared. My body soared through the night, brushing past trees and whipping over the expanse of the West.

Crescent Tower gleamed in the distance.

My eyes blurred, either from tears or from exhaustion.

I had never felt such heaviness. Such emptiness.

Everything went black.

CHAPTER 51

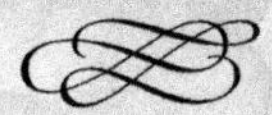

"WHY ARE WE BRINGING HER?" A female voice hissed through the night. Wind whipped past my face, throwing my hair into violent swirls. My consciousness was in and out, drenched in a thick haze and my body remained limp as though an invisible weight clung to my bones.

"You saw what she did." The man's voice was deep, commanding. I could understand them, but the captors had strange accents that seemed foreign to me. Their words were sharper, more guttural and clipped.

"But she's one of them," the woman urged, irritation breaking through her words.

"Clearly, she is not," he responded coldly, "Her soul is bound to the dusk."

"That's impossible."

And my vision went black again.

~

"WE CAN'T LET her see the route. What if she escapes?"

The voice stirred my mind, which was swirling with fog. I held onto consciousness by a thin rope.

"That's why we're counting on Rethlyn to keep her out until we reach Ravenfell," a woman said. "If Rethlyn fails, I'm slitting her throat myself." I heard the clank of a dagger echo through the night.

"No one touches her until Aether gives the go ahead," a man said flatly.

Suddenly, gravity shifted, and I felt arms lifting me.

"Who wants her?" the female asked, a mocking tone to her voice.

"She'll ride with me," a deep-voiced male said. He seemed like the leader, the one they called Aether. Suddenly, I was being carried. I did my best to keep my body limp.

Large hands grabbed my waist and hoisted me onto what felt like a saddle. A strap was wrapped around my shoulders and chest as I felt my back slide against a rigid torso. My consciousness began slipping once again.

"She's strapped in. Let's go. Vexa, you lead us off. We should make it to Ravenfell just before dawn." I felt the chest behind me rumble with the words, and in an instant, we were being propelled forward. Strong hooves hit the ground, racing across rocky terrain.

Just as my vision went black again, I felt my stomach twist as the beast jumped, leaving the ground behind us as we launched into flight.

All of it felt like a dream.

~

THE WIND WHIPPED through my hair as consciousness returned. A shock ran through my body as I realized we were flying. I bit back a scream and forced my body to still, to stay limp against the chest of the man behind me.

My eyes opened slowly through my lashes. We were soaring up above the clouds.

How was this possible?

We hit a strong gust of wind, and I let my head slump further, giving me a better view of whatever creature we were riding.

Giant black wings stretched out a length of at least double my height. They were lined with velvety fur but webbed like a bat. I peeked through my other eye, finding the back of a horse's mane. But if this was a horse, it was much larger than the ones in Luminaria.

My eyes became heavy again and I urged myself to stay awake, fighting remnants of the unnatural unconsciousness that was being forced upon me by the one they called Rethlyn.

"Prepare for landing," I heard the woman's voice shout, and suddenly, we were nosediving. My hair shot forward violently before flying back across my face. A scream built in my throat, but I swallowed it down.

As we tore through the clouds, dark towers appeared in the distance, looming over what looked like a dimly lit city.

Ravenfell, they had called it.

The architecture seemed like something out of a nightmare. Black and sharp, with bladed detailing. The skyline was made up of daggers. Horrifying statues sat on landings throughout the spires.

Fear shot through me as my consciousness finally came back in full swing.

I had to do something.

I had to escape.

My muscles went rigid as I slowly coaxed the tendrils from my spine. They began weaving their way up, spilling out over my skull, and I gently pushed them out, searching for a mind to command.

I felt the body behind me shift, and my head snapped around to face him. But all I could make out in the darkness were two glowing, golden eyes.

My heart lurched.

I recognized them.

"Rethlyn, she's awake! Put her back under! Now!" the man shouted.

And in an instant, my vision faded to black once more.

CHAPTER 52

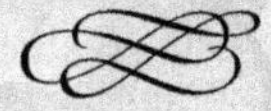

UTTER DARKNESS CREPT in around me, invading my mind like a storm in the night. My body was weightless, floating in the void, untethered to reality.

Thick fog loomed over every thought as I drifted through the nothingness. Everything felt numb, save for the tiny prickles dotting my spine. Familiarity broke through the trance as I recognized the peculiar feeling.

The tendrils that I'd come to know danced, delicately lacing themselves around my mind, pulsing with warmth—an embrace that now brought comfort.

They grew and grew and grew, overwhelming my world, freeing themselves from the shell of my skin and extending into the darkness, flickering like candles in the night.

They reached and reached and reached, searching for something. For anything.

What were we looking for again?

My thoughts still felt drenched, heavy, swirling.

In the distance, a shimmering orb came into view, and my tendrils flittered towards it like a moth to a flame.

Then I remembered.

We were looking for a mind.

The ball of light in the distance was glittered with translucent fibers, shifting between pastel shades of pink, blue and violet. Then colors that didn't exist, colors I had only ever seen within my own mind... within my own web.

As my tendrils approached the entity, a sense of something not so foreign began to trickle into my thoughts.

Like I had been here before. Seen this before. Been this before.

Nothing made sense, yet everything felt exactly as it should.

My webbing surrounded the orb, gently snaking... searching... learning... adapting.

Violent light surged through me as contact was made.

Fiandrial.

The name echoed through the expanse, and in my head, and through my limbs.

Fiandrial? That name...

We've been waiting for you to find us.

We've called out to you from the darkness, but you weren't ready to see us yet.

What?

It's still too soon.

There are things you must do.

But the path has been set.

The choice has been made.

White-hot light took over my vision as a torrent surged through the tendrils, loosening the bond.

What was happening?

Who was the mind?

I couldn't help feeling like I had heard it before...

But not in this lifetime.

When the time is right, you will find us again. Wake.

~

My mind pulsed with searing pain as my eyes shot open and darted around, not recognizing the room in which I found myself.

My heart began to race.

Where was I?

I was in a bed, my body enveloped by white sheets and thick throws in varying shades of gray. What I thought might have been sunlight trickled in from a window on the wall to my right, but I couldn't make anything out at this vantage point. The rays were muted, as if it were raining, but I didn't hear the drops outside.

The walls were made from shimmering black stone, uneven and rigid. I noticed a table at the end of the bed with what seemed to be a pile of dark fabrics.

Exhaustion was still heavy in my limbs, weighing my body down and forcing my eyes to close once again... Maybe some more sleep wouldn't be so bad....

Wake up. You're in danger!

My mind was screaming at me.

I winced, attempting a sitting position. I pushed myself up, bracing for the pain that should have radiated from my shoulder.

But that pain never came.

I inspected the bones I knew had broken only to find that there was nothing out of place.

Find a way out of here.

My feet flew to the barred windows, searching for any give.

Unsurprisingly, there was none.

We were at a dizzying height, almost touching the clouds. Charcoal mountain tops loomed in the distance. There was no green... no color, just varying shades of desaturation.

This couldn't be happening.

I walked to the door, knowing it would be locked, but I tried anyway. My heartbeat quickened as the handle remained stiffly in place.

Think.

I needed a plan. And fast. Crawling back into bed, I tried to calm my breathing. My thoughts were a whirlwind. I shifted uncomfortably, feeling layers of lace and tulle twisted around my thighs. I was still wearing the tattered dress from the ball.

Was that only last night? Memories from my last moments in Emeraal came racing back.

How far was I from home?

Fear flooded my body as I recalled the long journey here. The beasts, the voices, the towers.

I was in one of those towers.

No. No. No.

I was stuck, potentially with no way back. In the grasps of the enemy who had been killing us by the hundreds without a second thought. My hands began to tremble as the reality sank in.

How could anyone rescue me here?

Why had Laryk not raced after me? He had just stared with a dumbfounded look on his face. And Osta's scream right before I blacked out...

I couldn't bring myself to imagine what Osta was going through right now. I was sure she thought I was dead.

Perhaps death would have been better.

Tears welled in my eyes. Why did they bring me here? And even stranger, why were they keeping me alive?

Don't work yourself up.

There was no time to panic. There was no time to let my mind spiral through the possibilities. Whatever the reason was, I wasn't going to cooperate. I'd die fighting.

My mind was so cloudy, it was hard to stay focused. I shifted my thoughts to the voices that brought me here. What they said. Where I was.

They had called it Ravenfell.

While I didn't get a look at them, I knew now their shadows were just a mirage, a defense to hide the truth of their physical forms. Forms that didn't seem so different from us.

Forms that spoke the same tongue.

I leaned back, trying to clear my thoughts. If I wanted to survive, I had to find a way out of here. It would only be a matter of time before they decided to kill me…

Or worse…

Don't go there.

Once I managed to calm my breathing, my thoughts settled on the only thing that made sense. My eyes slammed shut, calling forth the tendrils, urging them out of their hiding place. I was met with resistance. My mind swirled. Refocusing, I goaded them up my spine, feeling relieved when they finally made their way to my skull.

My connection to them felt different…

Weaker.

I took a deep breath, casting them out, sending them to the ether. Perhaps there was a mind we could take. They fluttered along the walls, to the door, through the cracks below…

An orb appeared mere paces beyond the room.

A mind.

It glowed with a warmer hue than the ones I was used to, but it would work all the same. It pulsed within my reach, calm and unassuming.

A perfect target.

The tendrils slithered toward it, ready to strike, but as soon as they reached the glowing orb, they were zapped, rejected, sent soaring back into the depths of my spine, terrified.

What the fuck?

A commotion came from behind the door, and seconds later it was swinging open.

"Don't try any of those mind games on me, Princess. It's not going to work."

A gasp flew from my lips as the large figure stepped through the doorway; his presence rang throughout the entire room. Suddenly, I felt incredibly small.

Raven-colored hair brushed his shoulders. Onyx designs traveled across portions of his pale skin. They looked foreign and strange. He was dressed head to toe in black leathered armor with detailing like I'd never seen before.

His face was square and sharp, boasting features that could cut diamonds. Pointed ears peered out of his dark locks, lined with silver metal piercings. There was another bar at his eyebrow. His expression was dark and impossible to read. His irises glowed like golden embers.

But around them…

Oh Esprithe.

Memories of the ball surged back into my mind. Of the woman I had seen… The one who'd shared my perpetual shadows.

Just like the man who stood before me.

A silent scream erupted within me, but no sound came. Words that wanted to tumble out died on the tip of my tongue.

My jaw opened. Then closed.

The man let out a chuckle and shook his head. But there was an edge to his laughter. A bite I couldn't quite place.

Anger surged through me, and finally, words came. Just not the ones I wanted.

"Why did you take me?" I asked, trying to keep my voice strong, but it came out more like a petulant child.

I winced.

"Why did we *save* you?" he corrected. I recognized his deep baritone from the journey here. He was the captor sitting behind me on the flying beasts. Aether.

Save me? You've got to be fucking kidding.

"You'd be dead if we hadn't brought you to Umbrathia." He crossed his arms. His voice was unemotional, cold.

"You kidnapped me. You didn't save me. I was taken against my will–"

"You're the one who revealed yourself. We did you a favor," he snapped, cutting me off.

"Revealed myself? Do you know how crazy you sound?"

"Spin it how you want. We don't leave our own behind. There aren't enough Umbra left as it is."

"*Umbra?* What are you talking about?" I was getting frustrated. My head began to pound once again.

"You're a shadow wielder. They would have killed you in a second after you exposed yourself."

Silent confusion enveloped me.

Our eyes stayed locked in a stalemate. His stare was so intense; it reminded me of someone else.

Laryk... My heart felt like it would weigh me down. We had wasted so much time. If I had known it would be so short... Mist threatened to blur my vision, but I fought it back with a newfound ferocity.

"Liar," I finally seethed.

His eyes narrowed, but a glimmer of something shot across his endless golden irises. It happened in an instant, gone just as soon as it arrived.

"Believe what you want, Princess. I don't have time for this. I have a realm to save from those monsters you seem so fond of."

If he calls me Princess one more time, I'm going to explode.

He turned for the door, pausing for a moment before walking out. "Apologies. We don't have any gowns for you to wear. But there's a change of clothes if you'd like." He motioned towards the pile of fabric.

Wait, what did he say?

"That's fucking rich. You come into our land and kill indiscriminately, but we're the monsters?" Anger surged through me.

He stopped dead in his tracks, slowly turning back to face me with a new crease between his brows. I could nearly see the heat emanating off his skin as his eyes sparked with silent rage.

"I've been fighting for the freedom of Umbrathia since I crashed into its rocky depths a lifetime ago. The ones you align yourself with have been draining this world, taking everything from us. People are starving. Children are dying. Warmth has all but disappeared. Soon, there will be nothing left. They'll do to us exactly what they did to Riftdremar." His gaze drifted down, lingering on the marking sprawled across my left hand. Those golden eyes burned into a liquid bronze.

"They branded you?" His voice was hoarse, tinged with something dark.

I could almost feel my Riftborne mark searing further into my skin. Fears from my past began to trickle into my mind, the ones that used to plague my entire existence, keeping me chained to the shadows of life. The ones I had grown out of. The ones that were based on misbelief…

I shoved them to the furthest reaches of my mind. I would never return to that place.

That weakness.

A mixture of rage and uncertainty poisoned my blood, numbing my veins. It wasn't true. It couldn't be. There was no way I could trust a single word out of his mouth. These were tricks—lies—meant to disarm me in some way.

How many of us had he murdered? I thought of Gentry and Val. The air being forced from their lungs, their bodies twisting and contorting as they fought for life. For survival. The closed caskets that their parents buried.

No.

"I won't fall for your manipulations," I hissed through clenched teeth.

The room went deadly silent as my heart pounded in my chest. For what seemed like an eternity, our eyes stayed locked in a death grip.

Suddenly, the air sparked with energy, and Aether shot towards me, wrapping his hands around the bar of the bed frame. Fear raced over my skin as his knuckles turned white. Those golden, terrifying eyes flickered again, anger brewing in their gilded depths.

He didn't come any closer, but the space between us seemed to thin, like the air was being siphoned. My eyes were trapped in this moment, forced to sear into the ones of the man before me. My hate mingled with something far more terrifying in the depths of my core, something that felt like a betrayal. Something that felt like it would be my undoing.

Time stilled as energy crept along the surface of my skin, prickling my hairs, dancing across my shoulders. Worming itself into my mind. It was the wind, the vastness of the sky, the whisper of a thousand stars. It was the sting of rain, the bite of a blade, the caress of silk. It was a warmth–an overwhelming sun, blazing through time and space, burning through the walls of this stifling room, straight into my soul. It was like something snapped, breaking the universe in two.

Our weighted breaths were the only sounds that permeated the silence.

I had to break free, to sever this connection before it consumed me whole. A pain seared through me as I tore my eyes from his and gasped for breath, curling my fingers into the ashen sheets. He stumbled a few feet back, balancing himself on the wall behind him, spinning around so that his face was obscured.

What the fuck was that?

"You've been lied to." His words ignited something deep in my core, urging my rage to a boil. Violent pulses echoed from within me, sending my mind into the darkest of places.

I couldn't handle it anymore. The feelings were too much. Too confusing. Too powerful. I was going to explode. I summoned the web, desperately trying once again to reach his mind. But this time, I was going for the kill.

As swiftly as I pushed it towards him, it was returned to me. The blowback was so intense that I felt the searing pain radiate through my mind.

"You'll have to be quicker than that," he spat before trudging out and slamming the door behind him.

I wanted to scream.

I stood up, pacing the room. Irritation was heating every vein in my body, and I had no intention of quelling it. What was the worst I could do? They would end up killing me anyway.

Better now than later.

I'd cause absolute pandemonium. I'd scream so loud that the entirety of this cursed realm heard my cries. I'd drag myself out of here with missing limbs if I had to.

I reached down, feeling for the dagger I kept secured to my thigh. My mind seeped with a delicious flavor of rage as my hand found the hilt and tore it from the strap.

My powers didn't matter.

I'd slit his throat.

Either he was going to die, or I was going to fight until he dragged the life from my very bones.

My feet hit the floor with a newfound purpose and started towards the door when a glimpse of white hair stopped me in my tracks.

It was a mirror... Me.

But something was off.

I tilted my head to the side, inspecting it, slowly moving closer. My hair was still in ringlets from the ball. The shadows surrounding my eyes did appear darker, but still, that wasn't it.

I crawled onto the bed, placing my face directly opposite the glass. And stared. My skin was the same ivory hue. I moved my face closer.

My heart stopped.

The opal eyes I had always known. The ones that glowed with white light anytime I used my focus. My one defining trait that had never changed–never faltered.

Those were gone.

Replaced by something haunting.

Something sinister.

It was as if ink had been dropped into my eyes.

My hand shot over my mouth as I backed up, and my gaze

darted across the room. I felt my pulse begin to race. I had seen this before. In Mercer's classroom.

The way he had poured the ink into the water, the twists and turns, the blackness spreading out, taking over, colonizing the clear liquid within.

It swirled in the corners of my eyes, past the opalescent irises. Like a battle for control.

And then the realization flooded me...

The darkness around my eyes... growing deeper since being in the West... The shadows I'd seen since arriving to Emeraal...

Wraiths could only use their abilities when close to their homeland. This was the first time I'd ventured outside Luminaria. The first time I'd ever neared the tear between worlds.

The void, the shadows, the lawn slammed into my mind, memories tearing through walls I had built to protect myself.

He had called me a shadow wielder.

Shadow wielder.

My heart froze. Whispers of a name echoed in the back of my mind.

One I had heard in a dream.

Fiandrial.

RIFTBORNE

HISTORICAL RECORD

The Esprithe, Second Edition

In the realm of creation, where the cosmos dance in eternal embrace, there existed six Esprithe, beings of divine essence, each imbued with unique powers and revered by mortals throughout the realms.

In the beginning, there was Sibyl, the Esprithe of Foresight. She gazed into the infinite expanse of time, seeing the threads of destiny woven into the tapestry of existence. With her sight beyond sight, she guided the paths of mortals, offering glimpses of what was to come, and thus, she became revered as the harbinger of fate.

Mortals therefore named the first phase of the year, Sibyl.

Next came Conleth, the Esprithe of Wisdom. From the depths of the cosmos, he gathered knowledge, wisdom, and understanding. With a mind vast as the universe itself, he illuminated the minds of mortals, teaching them the ways of the world and the secrets of the universe, earning adoration as the sage of enlightenment.

Mortals therefore named the second phase of the year, Conleth.

Niamh emerged as the Esprithe of Dreams, drifting through the ethereal realms where reality and imagination intertwine. She whispered to mortals, weaving visions of wonder and enchantment, guiding them through the labyrinth of dreams, and thus, she was revered as the patron of reverie.

Mortals therefore named the third phase of the year, Niamh.

Ainthe, the Esprithe of Memories, arose next, holding within him the echoes of the past. He collected the fragments of time, preserving the memories of ages long gone. With a gentle touch, he reminded mortals of their history, their heritage, and their legacy, earning reverence as the keeper of forgotten knowledge.

Mortals therefore named the fourth phase of the year, Ainthe.

Eibhlín, the Esprithe of Judgement, descended from the heavens with scales in hand. She weighed the deeds of mortals, discerning truth from falsehood, justice from injustice, therefore becoming hailed as the guardian of righteousness.

Mortals therefore named the fifth phase of the year, Eibhlín.

Last to emerge was Fírinne, the Esprithe of Truth, cloaked in the mantle of absolute verity, piercing through lies and deceit. He illuminated the path of righteousness, and thus, he was revered as the embodiment of absolution itself.

Mortals therefore named the sixth phase of the year, Fírinne.

As the ages passed, the Esprithe witnessed the ebb and flow of mortality's journey. They observed the rise and fall of empires, the clash of civilizations, and the scars left by countless wars and conflicts. With each passing moment, the burden of their divine duty weighed heavier upon their shoulders.

Despite their efforts to guide and enlighten, the Esprithe watched in sorrow as Mortals veered further from the path of balance and harmony. Their teachings were twisted, their words manipulated, and their guidance ignored by those consumed by greed, power, and ambition.

The once steadfast faith of mortals began to wane, replaced by doubt and skepticism. Whispers of disbelief echoed through the mortal realms, and the bonds that once united Mortals and Esprithe began to fray.

ACKNOWLEDGMENTS

First and foremost, a massive shoutout to our friends and family who, bless their hearts, listened to us ramble on about made-up worlds and questionable character choices for far too long. You've read more terrible drafts than one could possibly fathom, and we owe you all a drink (or twelve).

To our boyfriends: You've survived our obsession with fictional elven men and bizarre plot twists with admirable patience. We promise to stop talking about focuses and wraiths for at least a week after this book comes out.

Our D&D crew deserves a high five (or a tankard of ale) for inspiring countless world-building ideas. You've unknowingly helped create a fantasy realm filled with whimsy, magic, and way too many nights ending in a tavern. Thanks for the adventures.

To our alpha and beta readers: You are the real MVPs. Thank you for wading through our messy first drafts and providing invaluable feedback. Hearing your thoughts really inspired us to push through to the end, making us feel like we really created something special and worth finishing.

Last but certainly not least, a huge thank you to Jules, our editor extraordinaire. You've managed to turn our chaotic mess of words into something resembling a novel. We're eternally grateful for your patience, guidance, and ability to understand our incoherent mind-spirals so eloquently.

ABOUT THE AUTHORS

Bree Grenwich and Parker Lennox are two platonic soulmates who have been nearly inseparable since meeting at 19. Their shared love of fantasy, badass heroines, and steamy romances fueled their dream of co-authoring a novel, which they've finally achieved with their debut, *Riftborne*. When they're not conjuring worlds filled with female empowerment and swoon-worthy relationships, they're binge-watching reality TV or obsessing over the last Dungeons and Dragons session.

Bree enjoys spending time with her boyfriend, who she claims is *indeed* a man written by a woman. A true Pisces, Bree finds solace in weekends by the sea or lake, engrossed in a book with music drowning out the world. She also holds a fascination with the paranormal and all things witchy, a love that undeniably creeps into her writing.

Parker, on the other hand, splits her time between the Southern US and the beautiful wine-country of Bordeaux, France, where she visits her boyfriend (living proof that romance novels can mirror reality!). An artist at heart, Parker expresses her creativity through graphic design, photography, and delectable culinary adventures, always with a sourdough starter bubbling away in the background.

Together, they weave addictive Romantasy novels for the New Adult audience.

www.grenwichlennox.com
Parker's IG: @ParkerLennoxAuthor
Bree's IG: @BreeGrenwichAuthor

Printed in Great Britain
by Amazon

55476738R00243